Readers love
XAVIER MAYNE

Farlough

"…I was definitely captured by it and will likely have it on my 2017 favorites list since it was a bit out of the ordinary."

—Hearts on Fire Reviews

"Need a new contemporary romance? Here's one I absolutely recommend!"

—Scattered Thoughts and Rogue Words

"Thanks, Xavier, for introducing me to the beautiful island of Farlough."

—Rainbow Book Reviews

Destination, Wedding!

"This book hit so many feels for me, I can't even begin to tell you."

—Love Bytes

"I had a lot of fun reading this story and can guarantee that you will too… Way to go Xavier, you have given me another perfect story."

—MM Good Book Reviews

By Xavier Mayne

The Accidental Cupid
Farlough
Husband Material
Q*pid

BRANDT AND DONNELLY CAPERS
Frat House Troopers
Wrestling Demons
A Wedding to Die For
Spring Break at the Villa Hermes
Bachelors Party
Destination, Wedding!

Published by Dreamspinner Press
www.dreamspinnerpress.com

Q*PID

XAVIER MAYNE

REAMSPINNER PRESS

Published by

DREAMSPINNER PRESS

5032 Capital Circle SW, Suite 2, PMB# 279, Tallahassee, FL 32305-7886 USA
www.dreamspinnerpress.com

Q*pid
© 2018 Xavier Mayne.

Cover Art
© 2018 Adrian Nicholas.
adrian.nicholas177@gmail.com
Cover content is for illustrative purposes only and any person depicted on the cover is a model.

Trade Paperback ISBN: 978-1-64108-116-0
Digital ISBN: 978-1-64080-229-2
Library of Congress Control Number: 2017915078
Trade Paperback published August 2018
v. 1.0

Printed in the United States of America

This paper meets the requirements of
ANSI/NISO Z39.48-1992 (Permanence of Paper).

For J. We found each other the old-fashioned way.

Acknowledgments

ONCE AGAIN I am indebted to my first reader, George Schober, whose gentle guidance and tough questions have edified my prose.

Chapter ONE

"HERE'S YOUR ridiculous pink drink." Padma sat on the stool on the opposite side of the tall table by the window.

Veera took the frosty cosmopolitan from her friend. "We can't all be single-malt girls," she said with a raised eyebrow. "I need a little sugar with my ethanol." She took a large gulp.

"When I see people chug like that, I wonder what his name is. You, though… I know who's making you drink."

"He's just so damn stubborn."

Padma laughed. "He takes after you."

"I wish I could get him to let it go."

"Don't you decide what he lets go of? Can't you cut out the code that isn't working?"

"He thinks it's really important, so I'm not going to delete it. That would be like me giving you a lobotomy every time you say something I don't like."

"You're lucky I'm so delightful."

"Yes, I was just thinking that," Veera replied in a dead monotone.

Padma laughed. "But *he* can't think—he's an AI engine that you created."

"Which is why I can't simply delete things because they don't work the way I want them to. If he can't learn, he might as well be some standard analytical engine. *That* would set the world on fire." Veera rolled her eyes.

"We're not eliminating world hunger here," Padma replied. "We tell people whom to date. It's not exactly rocket surgery."

Veera shook her head at Padma's mangled metaphor. "If we successfully apply a learning AI to this most human of problems, then maybe world hunger is next."

Padma took a sip of her whiskey and sat back. "Why is this so important to you?"

Veera sighed and stared into the rapidly diminishing depths of her cosmo. "Have your parents found a match for you?"

Padma shook her head. "I hope not. I told them I wanted to finish school first, and then I said I needed some time to establish my career. My hope is that eventually they will forget about it."

"And how likely is that?"

"Not very."

"Why don't you want them to arrange a marriage for you?"

"My sisters, mainly. One of them is happy, but the other… it didn't go so well."

"Those are the same odds people face with love matches, you know. Arranged marriages, on the population level, work out better."

Padma shrugged, but her unease with the topic was clear. "So you never told me what went on in the code review last week."

It was Veera's turn to shrug bleakly. "It wasn't great. Most of those guys don't like the idea of AI in the first place, but the epistemology engine really seems to push their buttons. They all said—in no uncertain terms—that I should ditch the whole idea and get back to 'solving real problems.'"

"Ouch."

"Yeah, ouch." Veera slumped forward. "Maybe they're right."

Padma sat up straight, as if taking on the weight of Veera's despair. "No, they're not. It is still a good idea. Because it's a completely new way of approaching the problem, they aren't comfortable with it. It scares them to think of an algorithm that knows them better than they know themselves."

"They're programmers, Padma. They don't know themselves at all. If I were working on code to optimize delivery routes for heart-shaped boxes of candy, they'd be pitching in to help me. But trying to get them to understand how actual humans relate to each other, and how AI can help them do that better—well, I might as well be trying to talk to them about fashion."

"Which I'd be all for it if you were able to keep them from wearing socks with sandals. That would be worth whatever it takes."

"I'm just trying to solve for the human heart. Don't ask me to do the impossible."

They laughed and polished off the first of several drinks.

"VEERA, THE floor is yours." Edwin, the manager of her team, smiled encouragingly across the table.

The smile was mostly for show, she knew, because he'd made perfectly clear he had precious little confidence in her idea. However, despite his reservations—which he'd enumerated several times for her over coffee during the course of the previous week—his team had a quota of developer pitches to make during the quarter, and at this late date he had no other options.

She opened her laptop and connected the display cable. The wall at the end of the conference room came to life, showing the first slide of her presentation. The hot-pink glow from the monitor flooded the room, basking all in attendance in the reflected glory of her cupid-decorated title slide.

Veera glanced around the room and immediately regretted not asking one of the web designers for advice on her color palette. She cleared her throat nervously.

"Thank you, Edwin." Her voice sounded small. She wasn't confident it had even traveled to the end of the suddenly miles-long conference table.

Focus, Veera. Find your voice.

"Artificial intelligence has never been applied to relationship discovery," she began, using the company's preferred term for online dating. "Today I'd like to present a vision for how AI can be a significant differentiator for our service. I call it the 'epistemology engine.' Our current data-mining processes work very well, but like all post hoc analytics, they allow only future optimization based on past performance. What they cannot do is dynamically adapt the discovery model in real time. In short, they do a great job of helping the next customer, but they can do little to help the current one."

Veera looked out across a conference room full of skeptical expressions. She swallowed hard and tried to remember to breathe.

"Today, I'd like to introduce you to the future of relationship discovery. Artificial intelligence that learns and adapts, accompanying our customers through their daily online lives, becoming a trusted friend as much as a matchmaker." She paused to look around the room. This was the moment she'd practiced for a full sleepless week. "I'd like you to meet Archer."

She advanced to the next slide, where Archer's name appeared at the top, accompanied by a picture of her ungainly tower computer wearing a T-shirt that said "I'm with Cupid." Some scattered chuckling rippled across the room.

"Archer is built on an open-source AI framework and uses the 'epistemology engine' I mentioned previously. In early testing we've found—"

"Whose AI framework?" grunted one of the engineers at the back of the room.

"IBM's Watson," Veera replied.

"Who coded the epistemology bit?" another engineer chimed in.

Veera's cheeks warmed. "I did. I mean, I am. I've been working on it for about a year as a side project, but over the last month I've been hooking it into the AI. As I was saying, the early testing is showing promising results. But just as important as the code is the data set we're proposing to give it."

This was the part of the presentation she'd been dreading. She had only been able to win Edwin over to the proposal when, desperate in the face of his insistence that she drop it and work on something more immediately deliverable, she told him why it was so important to her. She knew she could win this group if she did the same.

"We have to stop thinking about relationship discovery as an algorithmic process. People don't fall in love because our analytics tell them they should."

"No, they don't," Ross, one of the marketing managers, broke in. "They tell us what they're looking for in a relationship, and we help them find it. They're in control."

"And that's the problem I've solved," Veera said, meeting his eyes with what she hoped looked like fearless confidence. It was anything but. "In many cultures, marriages are arranged. I believe—"

"Arranged marriages?" Ross scoffed. "Are you proposing that we choose the best match and tell our customers they have to get married? Will we dispatch a drone to shoot them if they hesitate?"

"Perhaps if we let Veera explain her actual proposal?" Edwin ventured.

She cast him a grateful glance, then began again.

"As I was saying, arranged marriages work because they are orchestrated by the people who know the bride and groom best—their parents and often their extended families. They look at the whole person, and they work to find a mate who will best complement him or her."

"Or who has the most oxen to offer," Ross cracked.

"That's offensive," snapped Padma. Veera had never heard her utter a sharp word in the more than two years they'd worked together.

Around the table, eyes narrowed at Ross, who shifted uncomfortably in his seat. He cleared his throat in a way that might have led those near him to believe he had uttered an apology.

Veera turned back to the screen, resolving not to allow him to interrupt again. "Archer is an attempt to bring artificial intelligence to bear on a challenge that until now we could only work around the edges of."

She advanced the slide, covered with the sample analytical reports that resulted from profile analysis and matching. "Our system is very good at what it does: taking our customer's self-reported profile and matching them with what they say they want. And our results are industry-leading. But our success is built on the shaky foundation of two willful misconceptions: that people know themselves, and that they know the qualities of the person who will make them happiest."

She looked around the room at eyebrows raised in her direction. "We know that people exaggerate or downplay their own qualities in their profiles—our research has shown us that conclusively. So their profiles are mostly a description of who they wish they were. We also know that what people are most likely to look for in a potential mate are those things they perceived were lacking in the person they most recently dated, not necessarily the things that will bring them the most happiness in a relationship."

"So people are lying about themselves and about what they want?" came a voice, again from the back of the room. Software engineers tended to cut to the chase.

"I wouldn't say 'lie,' exactly," Veera replied. "More that they are optimistic in their appraisal of themselves, and backward-looking in their identification of traits they want to see in others. But the net effect, from a systemic perspective, is precisely the same: we have never had the information we need to truly discover the best relationship possibilities for our customers. Until Archer."

She advanced to the next slide. "Archer works differently. It resides on the customer's connected devices, where it gathers information about them not based on what they *say*, but rather on what they *do*. It gathers a complete profile of them based on their social media activity—all of it—and it derives a virtual profile based on what it finds. Then it matches that to the virtual profiles of other customers and discovers relationship possibilities based on a more realistic data set than any comparable service has ever had."

"So… customers need to give it access to all of their social media accounts?" a skeptical voice asked, in a careful pace that clearly conveyed doubt.

"Yes. Not just to Facebook and Twitter, but Snapchat and Tumblr and text and videoconferencing and web browsing in general, among other things. We'll see the posts they like, the memes they share—and the photos they don't. Using the cameras on their laptops and phones and tablets we'll perform sentiment analysis to find out how they react to what they see online—which social media posts actually make them LOL, if you will."

"Why in the world would anyone give us access to their entire online identity?" Ross demanded, apparently having overcome the shame occasioned by his previous insensitive remark.

"Because they want better matches. They look to our system to give them what they want, and our own research indicates they value their privacy somewhat less than they value finding the right mate. Once they experience the kinds of relationship discovery we can deliver using Archer, they will gladly give him access to everything. And because our system's never been hacked, they trust us to ensure the privacy of their information."

"This is a nightmare from the perspective of customer data security," opined the head of customer data security. Veera was not surprised. He had made this remark in every pitch meeting she'd ever witnessed. "How can you be certain customer data will never be exposed?"

"We one-way hash it as it is gathered. Only Archer will know the key used to hash each user's data, and there's no way to associate data from the store back to the user profile. No human will be able to retrieve non-anonymized customer data."

"So Archer will be working with encrypted data at all times?" the data security czar asked. "That sounds very expensive in terms of processor cycles."

"It would be if the AI weren't so efficient," Veera replied.

"You throw out this dragnet, pull in everything, make matches," summed up one of the engineers. "How do we make matches if all we know is what someone does online?"

"That's where the epistemology engine comes in," Veera replied. "It looks for patterns, substantiates them with sentiment analysis and other tools, and learns what's really important to each customer."

"So then it matches people who do the same things online?"

"No, not exactly. It doesn't simply match activities and interests, the way we do now. It learns how people react to what they see online, how their personal communications differ from their professional activities, and it derives a pretty deep persona for each customer. Then it runs that persona against those of customers in the target group and looks for both parallel and complementary patterns. It then measures the success of each interaction between matched couples and learns how to make better matches in the future. Within six months of launch, Archer will have refined his analytical processes so extensively that he will be able to make relationship discoveries far faster, and with a greater probability of success, than any method ever attempted."

"Or we will scare off our users, leak all of their data, and burn up untold computing resources on an unproven technology," Ross brutally retorted. "We could be looking at an extinction-level event, people." He sat back in his chair as if he had delivered the deathblow to the whole idea.

"Bullshit." This was a new voice, belonging to Alexis, the director of PR. She hadn't yet spoken, and her voice rolled through the room like a cannon shot. "Veera, this is clearly next-level thinking. None of our competitors have anything like this. Push as hard and as fast as you can, and when you have the tech ready, we will package this up into a program that our customers will not only love, they will pay extra for."

Veera had seen Alexis bring a close to a number of contentious meetings with her brand of summary judgment. And it seemed to be working this time too. The reactions among those in attendance ranged from enthusiastic nodding to ambivalent shrugging, but there were no further objections. Ross, for his part, sat stone-faced and dyspeptic, but he offered nothing more substantive than a grunt of reluctant surrender.

Veera beamed. She hadn't won Ross over, but she had won the pitch.

Now all she had to do was deliver Archer.

"MRS. SCHWARTZMANN, you really should stop putting melon rinds down the garbage disposal. It can't handle them."

"I know, I know," she replied, holding her hands up as if yielding the responsibility for her kitchen habits to a higher power. "You are so nice to come help an old woman."

"I'm just doing my job." Drew smiled, incapable of being angry at Mrs. Schwartzmann. "Besides, it's always fun to try to guess what's happened when you call."

"Ach," Mrs. Schwartzmann grunted, eyes heavenward. "Such an old building. No wonder things go wrong. They should take better care."

"The building is five years old," Drew said, as he always did. "It was brand-new when you moved into it. I helped you with your boxes, remember?"

"Ach," Mrs. Schwartzmann said again. "The vapors from the paint nearly killed me that night. You would think they would let it air for a minute before putting an old woman here to sleep."

"We live in a world fraught with risk," Drew offered solemnly, marveling at her ability to come up with an endless supply of new complaints. For a woman who rarely left her apartment, she was relentlessly inventive when it came to enumerating the wrongs perpetrated against her by the shadowy "they."

Mrs. Schwartzmann nodded gravely, clearly heartened to have the young man's sympathy.

"There, I think that's got it," Drew said, pulling the last of the half-shredded melon rinds from the disposal. He turned the water on and flipped the switch. The unit hummed quietly.

"Thank you, thank you," sang Mrs. Schwartzmann. She reached up and grabbed him by the cheeks, then kissed each one. She did this every time, and every time he felt like a precocious grandchild. "Now, I make us some tea, and you tell me about last night. Sit."

The prospect of hashing over the catastrophe of last night's date with Mrs. Schwartzmann—a woman more than three times his age—would have given most men pause, but Drew was quite accustomed to it by now. He found her commiseration, and often her advice, heartening.

"I assume you heard how it ended?" he asked as she put the kettle on.

She sat, the small square kitchen table between them. "Only that she broke all your furniture," she said mildly as she smoothed the shiny plastic tablecloth with her gnarled hands.

"It was just the coffee table," Drew replied, "but yes, she reduced it to kindling."

"This woman does not sound like such a very nice woman," Mrs. Schwartzmann opined solemnly.

"No, she didn't turn out to be a very nice woman."

She put her hand on his. "I am sure she seemed much nicer when you met her. A woman like that waits until she gets a man on her hook, and then poof! A she-monster."

"I wouldn't know about that," Drew said shrugging. "I hadn't met her before our date."

Mrs. Schwartzmann tucked her lips in silent judgment, as if Drew had admitted to a gambling habit. She nodded. "Oh, I see. She was one of the women you meet on the computer. How can you tell, when you only know her by what she type-type-types. Is it so hard to type things that are not true? It is not so hard."

Drew chuckled grimly. "If I had asked whether she was insane and she said no, then I would say she lied. But I didn't ask. According to the dating site, we were supposed to be a good match."

Mrs. Schwartzmann's brows drew into a solid black line of dark implication. "The computer machine tells you to date an insane crazy woman... and you? You do it." She shook her head slowly, but her expression softened into one of pity.

Drew was spared further aspersions on his dating strategy by the tea kettle beginning its low, trainlike whistle. Mrs. Schwartzmann pushed herself to a standing position and began fussing with tea.

"She didn't seem crazy, at least at first," he said rather lamely. "We were into a lot of the same things."

"Things like breaking the furniture?" Mrs. Schwartzmann asked lightly without turning from the counter where she was arranging teacups on saucers.

"Very funny. We listened to the same kinds of music and had read a lot of the same books, and our political views were pretty much identical. We liked a lot of the same things—we should have been completely compatible."

Mrs. Schwartzmann gently placed the cups and saucers on the table. "If the things you like make you completely compatible with a crazy woman, then maybe you are liking the wrong things." She shrugged, which was her way of conveying certainty in her opinion. She turned back to pick up the teapot.

"You don't understand how online dating works," Drew said, taking it upon himself once more to acquaint Mrs. Schwartzmann with the modern world. "You tell the computer about yourself, and then it finds people that you are compatible with. It's how everyone dates now."

"If that's how everyone dates, I should have stock in the coffee table company." She set the enormous teapot between them and took her seat.

"The coffee table was an accident," Drew said. "Mostly. I think."

"Some accident," she replied, pouring tea into his cup through an ancient silver strainer. "You're lucky no one was hurt in such an accident."

Drew sipped his tea. Like the woman who had made it, it was bitter and strong, but also warm and comforting. "Okay," he said, setting his cup onto its saucer, "it wasn't really an accident. As soon as she stepped into my apartment and saw it, she kind of freaked out. She said something about how cheap coffee tables are a product of third-world sweat shops, and she leapt on top of it and started stomping on it. And, because I'm a poor graduate student who can't afford decent furniture, it broke on about the third stomp. That only seemed to make her even more upset, and pretty soon there were only sticks left."

Mrs. Schwartzmann's eyes were wide. Though Drew had been unsuccessfully dating during the entire five years of their shared tenancy in the building, he was apparently still able to surprise her.

"Did you have to call the police?" she asked in a hushed voice.

Drew's cheeks burned. "No, she left on her own." He took cover behind a long sip of tea. "Eventually."

He felt her eyes on him, even though he refused to meet her gaze.

"No," she said, shaking her head. "You and she did not…."

"Mrs. Schwartzmann, I sit before you ashamed. Yes, she and I did."

She pursed her lips. This was the second level of Schwartzmann judgment, reserved for times when Drew did something really stupid on a date. He'd seen it more frequently lately.

"This morning I had to pull out slivers from some rather delicate areas." He again picked up his teacup, as if its refinement could somehow restore some of his dignity. He felt it not working.

She shook her head slowly, then consulted the bottom of her teacup. She refilled her cup and his, then folded her arms before her. "One day Mr. Schwartzmann wanted to have marriage fun on kitchen table."

Drew instinctively pulled his elbows back from the table.

"No, not on this table," she scolded. "You think I would serve tea on the table where…?" Her bushy eyebrows danced upward to finish the sentence. "No, this was long ago, when we lived in the old country."

Mrs. Schwartzmann was the only person Drew had ever met who used terms like "the old country" without irony—though he had never been able to ascertain precisely to which country she referred. The details were always a little loose in her stories.

"He told me to get on the table and I would get a big surprise. I told him it must not be the same surprise he gave me on our wedding night because that was not so big. Well, we started yelling about all kinds of things, and before you know it, once we were finished throwing pots at each other, I figured what the hell, might as well get on the table."

Drew smiled. "Was it all he'd hoped it would be?"

She shrugged. "I don't know. That is when the Nazis came for him."

Mrs. Schwartzmann's stories were as opaque as the stews she sometimes made for Drew to share with her on Sunday nights—and just as full of mysterious bits recycled from previous servings. Sometimes her husband was captured by the Nazis, and sometimes he was a dashing member of the SS who spirited her out of the country. Sometimes she'd never married at all, having devoted herself to a lost love of her youth (this would be Anne Frank). Drew had learned never to challenge, or even consider, the veracity of her tales. Once verisimilitude was off the table, they could actually be quite entertaining—and sometimes educational.

"I'm sorry for your loss," he always said when one of her stories took a tragic turn.

She accepted his condolences stoically, as she always did, with a solemn nod and a hand raised to the capriciousness of fate.

"Now you would be willing to date that nice girl I have told you about?" she asked, idly stirring her tea.

"Not the Meals on Wheels woman again?"

"So nice she is. Always remembers I cannot have too much salt. And she has such sturdy childbearing hips. You hardly notice the lazy eye."

"She's also forty years old and has not a single natural tooth."

"She has overcome adversity. And many bar fights. You seem to like your women with some spirit."

Drew laughed. "I think I'll stick with the online dating. They let me screen for age and for prison records."

She shrugged. "You should consider. Think it over tonight when you're watching television with your feet propped up on... oh, silly me... nothing." She was unable to stifle a chuckle at the image she'd summoned.

"What would I do without you, Mrs. Schwartzmann?"

"CONVERSATIONAL REFERENCES to sports." Tap-tap-tap. "Zero. Mentions of history of mental illness in the family, also zero. Hmm." Rapid-fire clicks and taps on the keyboard echoed through the strenuously clean kitchen. "Number of attempts to pay the dinner check, and height of heels in inches, and number of visible piercings, and done."

Fox sat back and picked up his coffee mug for a long, meditative sip before scrolling down to see the final score at the bottom of his spreadsheet. The number in the last cell wasn't what he was expecting.

"Hmm."

A chat window titled Video Call from Chad popped open, covering the spreadsheet. He tapped the Accept button.

"Hey, buddy," Chad said cheerfully. Behind him loomed a deeply cushioned leather headboard. "How's Foxy this morning? What do the numbers say?"

Fox smiled into the camera atop his laptop screen. "The numbers aren't what I was hoping for," he said with a good-natured shrug. "I kind of liked this one, so I was a little surprised that she netted out at seventy-two."

"Ouch," Chad said, wincing sympathetically. "Sorry, man. Her pictures were awesome. I was pulling for you."

"The numbers don't lie, man," Fox answered with a shrug.

"So she'll be getting the email this morning?"

Fox nodded. "I just need to figure out which one."

"I thought low seventies got 'we both knew it wasn't working.'"

"Yeah, normally. But I really thought we were doing better than the low seventies. Her dinner conversation was a lot better than my Sunday evening last week, and that one was in the upper seventies. I was kind of surprised that she netted out where she did."

"Are you sure you entered everything correctly?"

"You're asking me if I know how to do data entry? In the spreadsheet I've been using for five years?"

Chad laughed. "Maybe it's time to revise the formulas."

"No one said it was going to be easy, and I'm not going to lower my standards now." Fox opened an email window and selected the "low seventies" template.

"What's the queue look like for the weekend?" Chad asked.

"Got a brunch today, then a dinner, and a hike on Sunday."

"Three more chances to find Ms. Right," Chad said cheerfully. "She's out there, and you'll find her."

"Thanks, man. And pull up your covers—I don't need to see your nipples first thing in the morning."

"I like his nipples," called a woman's voice from somewhere off-camera. "I think they're sexy."

"Agree to disagree, Mia," Fox shouted into his laptop.

"Are you telling me you don't think my nipples are sexy, Fox?" Chad winked and gave his heavily muscled pectorals a stripper-like shake at the camera.

"Good thing I haven't had breakfast yet," Fox said as he closed the lid of his laptop.

Chapter TWO

"ARE WE ready? When do the notifications go live? Any blockers?" Ross swept into the war room, firing off questions as he came.

"We're on schedule," Veera replied, not even looking in his direction. Ross's self-important way of charging into a room was an irritant she could not be bothered with today. "How's CPU utilization and DB access?"

"CPU is normal," an engineer reported from behind his laptop.

"DB queue is zero," added another from across the table. "The last three stress tests were green, so we're good to go."

"PR is ready," Alexis announced in a voice both sultry and professional. "The press release is staged, and we have execs on call to respond to media."

"Are they all briefed on the privacy disaster that this will surely become?" Ross muttered.

"They are ready to answer questions about how we protect our customers' data and ensure their privacy while offering a groundbreaking new relationship discovery experience." Alexis brandished a sweetly poisonous smile in his direction.

"Awesome," he replied, his voice utterly flat.

Veera stepped to the whiteboard and checked off the remaining items on the launch list. She capped the marker deliberately, set it in the tray, then turned around to face the room. And her future.

"I think we're ready," she said, hoping her voice carried the confidence she wished she felt.

"Do you want us to wait until you're *sure*?" Ross jeered.

She met his gaze, refusing to blink even though her eyes burned. "I am sure. Let's go."

The room surged into a quiet frenzy of typing as the dozen people in it brought the Archer system online. First out would be notifications to select customers—their most satisfied users, all of whom had opted in to new features in the past—announcing the availability of a futuristic new way to find the love of their lives.

"Notifications are live," called one voice. "Open rate is 0.05… 0.1." A tense pause in the room. "One percent open."

"That seems too fast," Ross said. "One percent opens in under a minute? That can't be right."

"Our best customers look at their phones, on average, once every two minutes," the customer service manager said. "They open a Q*pid notification, according to our research, within thirty seconds of receiving it. Even if—" She cleared her throat awkwardly. "—they are otherwise engaged."

"You mean like if they're driving?" one of the engineers asked, alarmed.

"She means even if they're having sex," another replied.

The first engineer shook his head, mystified.

"Opt-ins are starting," one of the launch managers reported, pointing to a rapidly moving graph on the large monitor at the end of the room.

"Your targeted marketing messages seem to be working quite well," Veera said to Ross. Buoyed by the early signs of rapid success, she screwed on a generous smile and shared the credit, though not without wishing that killing with kindness was an actual thing.

Ross gave a serpentine smile. "Just because I can sell ice cubes to fucking Eskimos doesn't mean this isn't a cliff we're driving over."

God, she hated him.

"Installs are underway," called the app-store liaison. "We should see the first launches in a few—"

"First handshake with Archer servers," broke in a twitchy network engineer on the data-center team.

The launch manager at the monitor swiped at the tablet in his hands and brought up the graph showing traffic into and out of the array of CPUs that made up Archer's brain. Disks began spinning up, each represented by a green dot on the utilization graph.

"Installs at 1K," called out the app-store liaison.

"Handshakes tracking that…," the network engineer chimed in. "Nine hundred signed in… and… now! One thousand active users."

A cheer went up around the room.

Veera looked up at the clock. They were seven minutes into the launch of Archer, and he was already beginning to build profiles of the first thousand users. This wasn't a launch—it was an explosion.

EXCLUSIVE OFFER: Try our new AI-powered relationship discovery service.

Fox, in the elevator on the way back to his office after lunch, read the message with a furrowed brow. He monitored his phone closely for Q*pid updates, knowing that women were more likely to interact if men responded to potential matches within seconds rather than hours or even minutes. In the race to get to Ms. Right, he was going to be first across the finish line.

He read the message again. Having been an active user of the service for a couple of years, he was a little flattered that he was being given an exclusive notification, and he certainly liked the idea of artificial intelligence being applied to his quest to find the woman of his dreams. He tapped and read the description of the service.

> Give our new AI engine access to your social media profiles, and it will analyze everything you do online to match you to only those women who are most compatible with you—not because of what they say about themselves, but what advanced algorithms discover them to be. This is analysis on a deeper level than any relationship discovery service has ever accomplished before.

Fox pondered this for a moment. Like most people he knew, he carefully curated aspects of his online presence; his LinkedIn profile was the product of constant grooming, and the only photos that went on his Facebook were those that showed him in a particularly flattering light.

> Anyone can crawl the web and see your public profile. But for this new service to deliver the best results, we will ask you for *all* of your social media login information. Only by analyzing everything you do online can our AI brain really get to know you, and deliver the kinds of relationship results that endless questionnaires and disappointing first dates could never come close to.

He frowned. He wasn't at all sure that giving Q*pid this kind of access was a good idea. With those logins, a hacker could pretty seriously break his life.

> We know you're concerned with privacy. We're absolutely obsessed with it. In five years of operation, Q*pid has never suffered a security breach or loss of customer data. And only the AI engine will have access to your social media and web usage information—no human will be able to access it, and our strong encryption protects your data end-to-end. We use VPN tunneling to ensure that even your internet service provider cannot intercept your data.

Fox reached his desk, at which he sat without taking his eyes off his phone. He considered the implications of allowing the kind of invasive data-gathering that this new AI thing would require. On the one hand, it would be foolish to allow anyone that kind of access. On the other, he liked the idea of being an early adopter of AI dating services. Plus, he could use some additional analytics behind his spreadsheet-centered approach to relationships. He hadn't had a score above eighty-three in weeks.

> We invite you to be among the first—and the very few—of our customers to use our AI service. Though final pricing has yet to be determined, we're giving you a chance to try it for free. Of course, you may stop using the service at any point, and we'll delete your data completely. You're in control.

He took a deep breath and tapped the Accept button.

SUPERCHARGE YOUR love life with our new supercomputer.

Well, that wasn't what Drew was expecting to see when he felt the heartbeat vibration of his phone. Normally these updates were notifications that his profile had been viewed by the next crazy woman in line. He figured he'd be staring at a profile pic and wondering what piece of furniture he'd next be dropping piece by piece into his garbage can. He read the message again, then tapped through to find out what it meant.

> We get it, Drew. You've had twenty-three first dates in the last three months, and not one of them has resulted in the kind of relationship you've always dreamed of.

"Huh." He hadn't expected such blunt talk from his dating app. Though every word was true.

> We want to help. Sign on for our new service—free of charge during this trial period—and we guarantee you'll get matches that are better than you've ever imagined.

Maybe his furniture was going to be safe after all.

> How do we do it? We use the power of a supercomputer to get to know you through your online activity—the *real* you—and we crunch the numbers to match you with women who are truly compatible. Your next first date may be your last, Drew. Sign up today.

Am I really that pathetic? He looked around his apartment, at its rather dismal offering of second- and third-hand furniture, the single bowl on the counter in which the dregs of his ramen were already hardening into concrete. *Yes, yes I am.*

Through the ceiling he heard Mrs. Schwartzmann shuffling through *her* empty apartment. The bleakest possible vision of his lonely future, literally hanging over his head.

"What the hell?" he said to the place where his coffee table used to be. "It's not like it can get any worse." He stared at the screen, his thumb over the button. Never the decisive type, he knew himself to be all the less so when facing decisions that really mattered. He chewed the inside of his lip.

He jumped when his phone buzzed to let him know he needed to leave now if he was going to get to his seminar on time.

Following a quick tap on the Accept button, he slipped the phone into his pocket, then grabbed his book bag and headed out of the apartment.

THREE HOURS later the last of the launch team drained out of the war room.

"Excellent job, everyone," Alexis the PR director chirped. "Seven exec interviews, and we're getting pickup everywhere from NBC News to Bustle."

"And Reddit," added one of the engineers.

Alexis laughed. "And Reddit. Who would have thought that an AI-enhanced dating service would go over big at nerd central? You could knock me over with a feather." Still chuckling, she turned to Veera. "You have made some company history. Congrats."

Blood warmed Veera's cheeks. "Thanks," she said quietly. She'd never been good with compliments, despite knowing that if she'd ever deserved one this was the time. "It was great to see you work."

Alexis smiled. "You guys do the hard stuff. We just polish it up." She beamed her best nightly-news smile and strode from the room on her impossibly high heels.

That left only Ross in the room.

"Is there anything you need, Ross?" Veera asked him, trying to keep her voice from sounding blatantly saccharine.

Ross was studying his phone. "Nope. Just checking to see whether the first violation of privacy suits have been filed yet." He looked up at the clock. "I guess you're in the clear. For today." He got to his feet.

"Thanks for your support." She tried to model the smile Alexis wielded so effortlessly.

"I'll grant you, you stuck with this and got it done. You launched it. Now you've got a sausage party on your hands. Good luck with that." He grabbed up his laptop and stalked out of the room, chuckling in a way that would be the envy of any Disney-issue villain.

The worst part was that he was right.

Of the twenty thousand invitations they'd sent, a little over seven thousand customers had signed up. Fifty-five percent of them were seeking women, but she'd expected the balance to be tipped a little that way. She had resisted Ross's insistence that an analytical approach to dating would be more attractive to those seeking women rather than men, but it turned out that he was onto something, even if the imbalance was nowhere near the two-to-one extreme he had predicted. Not a "sausage party" by any measure, but she would have preferred to prove Ross completely wrong rather than partly right.

Over the next hour, they would send a second set of invitations to another several thousand users seeking matches with men—female customers, primarily—to bring things even. Within a couple of hours they would reach parity, if their models were correct.

Left alone in the conference room, Veera paced in a small circle as the stillness closed in around her. She didn't mind the silence—in fact, after the tumult of the war room at capacity, she welcomed it—but it did serve to remind her of how lonely this whole experience had been. For months she had slogged through coding the unique personality that would serve Archer well as he attempted, algorithmically, to bring about human happiness. The project was secret, so few other software engineers would be able to understand the intricacies of what she was attempting. Aside from Padma, there was no one else for Veera to talk to.

Well, there was *one* other.

Veera closed the door of the war room. She walked back to the conference table and lowered herself slowly into the chair closest to the telephone. After a deep breath and a long exhalation, she reached out and dialed. A single click, and then a voice filled the room.

"Hello. This is Archer."

"RESUME VOICE interface."

"Voice interface ready."

"Archer, it's Veera."

"I recognize your voice, Veera," Archer replied.

Veera had configured Archer's voice interface to sound conversational, but in fact during their polite exchange her voice had been subjected to more than a dozen authentication tests. Because of the company's obsession with security, Archer would respond only to her or, as a fallback measure, her manager, Edwin.

"How are you doing, Archer?"

Again, this sounded like small talk, but Veera was actually prompting the AI engine to initiate a battery of self-checks, ensuring that all of its processes were performing within established ranges. It took a fraction of a second.

"I am well, Veera. How are you?"

"I'm excited that we have pushed your code to production."

"As am I," Archer replied.

"How many profiles have you opened?"

"I have completed intake surveys of 1,217 profiles and have tagged an average of seventy-three potential contact nodes for each. I expect to be able to begin running match simulations within seven hours."

She nodded. This was very good progress indeed. "How long before you'll have the first potential matches ready?"

"Match potential is a function of profile availability."

"It is."

"If profile numbers follow the curve extrapolation, within twelve hours there will be in excess of 8,000 profiles that have completed intake."

"And how many of those will be available for match?"

"Profile availability is a function of parametric compliance."

"Right again."

"Thank you," Archer said. Veera smiled at the effect of the politeness extensions she had installed. They had been created by AI researchers at a Canadian university.

"Please, continue," Veera prompted.

"All profiles comply with Parameter One."

"Right." Parameter One indicated whether the individual customer was active in the system—essentially, whether they were current on their membership fee and logging in to the system regularly. As they would only have invited active members to participate, everyone who had opted in would necessarily pass Parameter One.

"And all profiles comply with Parameter Two."

"Yes, they do." Parameter Two reflected whether customers were currently looking for matches. Q*pid's members regularly cycled in and out of availability for matches, depending on how their current relationship was progressing. And, as with Parameter One, only those who were interested in matches would be invited to participate, so unless they had met someone special in the three hours since the launch of the program, they would also be qualified under Parameter Two.

"Parameter Three will therefore be the limiting function."

"Indeed it will be." Parameter Three contained the customer's specific gender for relationship discovery. Unlike the first two parameters, which were binary on-off switches, this one never changed. It limited the pool of potential matches for each customer to roughly half of Q*pid's active membership. Though the numbers were, at present, skewed toward those who sought women, after the additional invitations went out they would get as close to a 50/50 balance as possible.

"Match potential is therefore estimated to reach its maximum value at 22:30 UTC tomorrow. At that time it is likely that twelve percent of profiles will have at least three matches of eighty-five percent or higher."

Veera frowned. Archer's numbers seemed quite low. "What's your confidence on that estimate?"

"Confidence is eighteen percent."

Veera laughed. "So this is your way of telling me you have no idea what's going to happen because no one's ever tried this method of relationship discovery."

"You are correct, Veera. I'm sorry if that was unclear."

"No, it was my fault for pushing you to make an estimate before you're ready." She stood and leaned over the table toward the phone. "Please carry on with your work, Archer. We'll talk again tomorrow."

"Tomorrow is Saturday, Veera. Q*pid's offices will be closed."

"Not this one. Good night, Archer."

"Good night, Veera."

"Suspend voice interface." Her finger hovered over the Disconnect Call button.

"Voice interface suspended."

She clicked the phone off and sat, for a little while longer, in the silent stillness of the war room.

FOX PLACED his phone on his bedside table while he changed out of his suit. When he picked it up to slip it into the pocket of his jeans, however, he regarded it a little warily. For a moment he felt oppressed by the idea that it was spying on him.

He grabbed a beer from the fridge, then sat at his kitchen table and opened his laptop. The Q*pid app popped up an updated notification, and he clicked Okay before he'd really thought it through. He understood that the information gathered from his social media profiles would be critical to getting better matches than he had been. It was the tracking of his activity online that made him a bit anxious.

Like most men he knew, Fox used his laptop for three things: email, buying things he couldn't be bothered to go to the store for, and porn.

And now his laptop would be watching him as he did all of those things. He wasn't sure how he felt about that.

He suspected the time he spent on the computer writing a happy birthday email to his grandmother would probably raise his score, while his shopping preferences might be a wash—his tech purchases far outnumbered the thoughtful gifts he'd bought. But still, there was likely nothing there that would sink his profile to the bottom.

He sat for a long moment, staring at his laptop screen.

"So, yeah," he said to the empty kitchen. "No porn, then."

In truth, he'd never known a woman who professed anything more positive than a grudging acceptance of the existence of pornography. While he couldn't imagine that a dating site would be at all interested in the particular type of porn he preferred, the very fact that he looked at it at all would very likely drop his chances of finding a decent woman.

As if to counteract the effect of even having thought the word "porn," he pulled out his phone and flicked through Facebook, tapping Like on every photo of something cute—puppies, babies, whatever. A few minutes of that should strengthen the appeal of his profile, he thought. He pumped his fist in the air when he came across a picture with both a baby *and* a puppy. He liked the hell out of that.

Then it was time to open the spreadsheet for tonight's date. Pre-entering some information from her dating service profile would help make the analysis tomorrow morning a little quicker. Not a very romantic notion, perhaps, but one that settled his nerves considerably.

DREW SAT on the floor where his coffee table used to be, leaning back against his battered sofa. Before him sat his laptop, open to a blinking cursor against the field of pure white that would, he hoped, become his seminar paper. Actually, it had to become his seminar paper rather quickly if he was going to move on to write his dissertation next year.

He took a sip of the revolting bourbon that was all his liquor budget would bear.

He had installed the new Q*pid app as soon as he'd gotten home, but in terms of his online activity, he'd given it nothing at all to work with as he'd been staring at the blank document in his word processor for an hour now. With a click, he banished the empty doc to the bottom of his screen.

As soon as he opened his web browser, the light next to the camera on his laptop clicked on.

Drew was being watched.

From his bookmark list he opened the *Huffington Post*. It was something he read on a regular basis, but this time he was almost painfully aware of his reaction to the content he found there. He clicked on an article about how a former beauty pageant contestant had rebuilt her life after a horrifying car crash and had found peace teaching software development to African children. He caught a glimpse of his face reflected in the laptop screen and nearly jumped out of his skin. The pitying, stricken look was all wrong for his dating profile. He jolted upright, then beamed at the screen as if reading the article had sent him into transports of joy.

He flipped through his bookmark list of daily news, aware at times that he was choosing links to follow based in some part on whether it was likely to give him good opportunity to smile supportively at a women's march or shake his head mournfully at the actions of some hypocritical politician who talked a good line about economic equality but somehow kept ending up on the customer end of prostitution rings.

An hour of this and he was exhausted. Reacting manically to everything on the screen made his face ache. He got up to refill his bourbon but was interrupted by a resounding crash from the floor above.

"Oh shit, Mrs. Schwartzmann," he cried as he stormed toward the door. He took the stairs three at a time and was at her apartment in a matter of seconds. He knocked loudly.

"Mrs. Schwartzmann, are you okay?" he called through the door. "It's Drew, Mrs. Schwartzmann. Are you all right?"

He heard shuffling, and then the locks clicking. Mrs. Schwartzmann had asked him to install several extra locks, a request she had decorated with several harrowing examples of things that had happened to people she knew who hadn't taken such precautions. The door opened two inches, no more.

"Who is there, please?" Mrs. Schwartzmann's voice was low, as if she were trying to convince an intruder that there was, in fact, a *Mr.* Schwartzmann within.

"It's Drew, Mrs. Schwartzmann. I heard a crash. Are you okay?"

"Oh, Drew," she replied, closing the door. The two chains that had kept the door from opening slid noisily from their locking place, and she opened the door again. "How nice of you to check on an old woman." She stepped back from the door to let him come in.

"Did something fall? Did you fall?"

She waved her hands at him and laughed. "Oh no, dear boy, nothing like that." She turned aside and pointed into the living room. "That I was carrying"—she gestured to a five-gallon bucket lying on its side in the middle of the floor—"and from the handle I lost my grip."

"Let me help you," Drew said as he walked farther into the room. He picked up the quite heavy bucket, surprised she could lift it at all. "Where does it go?"

"In here, in here," Mrs. Schwartzmann replied, shuffling toward the hall closet. She tugged on the folding door, and it slid open to reveal several stacks of similar buckets.

Drew stood before the closet. There was room, perhaps, for one more bucket before the closet was completely filled with them. "Really?" he asked.

"There's a space at the top there," she suggested, seeming perfectly confident that hefting a heavy bucket over his head were something Drew was easily capable of.

Luckily for Drew, he'd been procrastinating on his seminar paper for several weeks, taking refuge from his word processor by spending long hours in the gym. He lifted the white bucket into place, completing the Tetris game Mrs. Schwartzmann was playing in her hall closet.

"What is all this?" he asked as they stood before the wall of white plastic.

"It is for emergency," she said, sliding the closet door closed. "If they come again, I will be ready."

"Who's coming, Mrs. Schwartzmann?"

She gave a shrug that was both resigned and conspiratorial. As if she knew precisely who would be coming for her—maybe for both of them. "I like to know I have enough to live."

"Those buckets are full of… food?" He had visions of bucket after bucket full of moldering groceries. He could almost smell it.

"Yes. There's a nice man on the television who sells them. Each bucket lasts two months, and all you do is add water."

"If the apocalypse comes, where will you get water?"

She smiled proudly. "The water buckets are down in my garage. I have no car, so instead I have water."

Though Mrs. Schwartzmann had lived in the building since it was brand-new, Drew realized he'd never seen the inside of her double-padlocked garage.

"You have this many buckets full of water?"

"Oh no," she replied. "That would be silly. There are many more buckets of water. So much water."

Drew blinked, trying to imagine how she had managed to fill her garage to the rafters with water. But when dealing with Mrs. Schwartzmann, he had learned that it was usually best to simply pretend that what she said made sense. "It sounds like you are well prepared."

She nodded sagely.

"Do you mind if I ask what, exactly, you're preparing for? Earthquakes, perhaps?"

"Ach, no. I have lived so long there is nothing God can do that would hurt me. Earthquakes, volcanoes, typhoon, who cares?"

"I don't think we're likely to have a typhoon, Mrs. Schwartzmann. And there aren't any active volcanoes within several hundred miles."

"See? I told you I'm not worried about such things. No, I am prepared for when they come back."

"Who are 'they,' exactly?" he asked again.

"You know who they are," she replied, her voice thick with conspiracy. "One time they are called Nazis, and another time they are called Bolsheviks, and sometimes they style themselves terrorists or patriots or revolutionaries. Whoever it is, it is always the same. It doesn't matter what they call themselves, or what color their shirts are. They take up a cause of some kind, but only to hide what they really want: power. Power to tell people what to do, and power to kill people like me. Well, this time I'm ready for them. They can do their worst, but I will outlast them."

He smiled inwardly at her dogged insistence on meeting her vaguely defined foe on the battlefield of starvation warfare. And given that she weighed approximately eighty-five pounds, she could probably survive for years on her buckets of freeze-dried rations.

"I don't think anyone's coming to kill you, Mrs. Schwartzmann."

She shrugged. "They do not announce. There are no calling cards to tell you they are coming with dogs and guns and steel boots to cart you off to the camps."

"I think you're pretty safe here. If someone came to cart you off, I would stop them."

Mrs. Schwartzmann grabbed Drew's hand and clutched it to her chest. "Oh, you darling man," she whispered.

"So you can stop worrying, okay?"

She shook her head gently. "After what I have seen in my life, worry is the price I pay for waking up at all. I cannot be anything other than what I am." She released his hand and smiled peacefully.

He returned her smile. "I would never want you to be anything other than who you are."

"Thank you. You are so good to me."

"Next time you need to move any of those buckets, you let me know, okay?"

"So kind. Of course," she murmured.

"Good." He stepped toward the door. "Good night, Mrs. Schwartzmann."

"Good night, Mr. Drew."

He walked out her door, and as he descended the stairs, he heard the many locks click into place.

Back in his apartment, he found himself once again alone with his thoughts, his bourbon, and his laptop with its insistently blinking cursor at the head of a blank page.

"Fuck," he groaned. He shut the word processor window with an angry click of the red icon at the top.

Drew picked up his laptop and his bourbon, then headed into his bedroom, where he set the bourbon on the nightstand next to his bed and tossed his laptop onto his pillow. Shucking out of his clothes took him no more than a couple of seconds—he wasted no time at all on putting his clothes away, since tomorrow was laundry day anyway—and then dove naked under the covers.

This was, in some ways, Drew's favorite part of the day. As a graduate student, the work he had ahead of him was measured in years, not hours. There was no end-of-the-day satisfaction coming from a job well done—he was never done, never would be until he turned in his dissertation. And that was years away. He loved the work and looked forward to whatever form of the profession would come after—research, teaching, or fieldwork—but the never-ending nature of it meant that rarely did he go to bed sighing the exhausted breaths of a man who had faced a challenge and seen it through. He had a different way to find peace at the end of the day.

Binge-watching British crime dramas.

He popped open one of the several streaming services that his parents subscribed to and chose the next episode of a particularly grisly series he'd been enjoying lately.

After about fifteen minutes of painstaking investigation into the decapitation of a vicar, though, he was fighting to keep his eyes open. The little green light at the top of his screen regarded him reproachfully. Though he suspected that his predilection for brainy television would be a plus in terms of his dating profile, falling asleep while watching it would probably outweigh any benefit.

He clicked the viewing window shut, and the green light extinguished. Clearly, Q*pid didn't care about the facial expressions he made while staring at a computer desktop littered with half-finished reading notes and PDFs of obscure journal articles. Shutting his laptop left him completely in the dark. He sat for a long moment, listening to the nothing around him, wishing he were the kind of person who could fall asleep simply because it was late and dark and quiet.

He knew what would do it.

A little electrical tape over the camera would give him a chance to do it. Then he could sleep.

In the back of his mind, though, something tickled. It had to have been several decades since anyone had thought of Mrs. Schwartzmann while in bed. But entirely without warning, Drew heard her voice in his head. *"I cannot be anything other than what I am."*

Maybe that was his problem.

Drew considered himself a truthful person, an honest person. And yet he had never once mentioned in his online profile that he occasionally watched porn. He didn't do it every night, but there were certainly nights when it helped soothe a need that no decapitated vicar could. And yet, while his guy friends all understood the proper role of porn in a well-adjusted life, he had never once so much as hinted to a woman—any woman—that he was not entirely averse to watching attractive people have attractive sex with each other.

Maybe it was time to be himself.

A shiver of terrifying possibility ran through him. He'd never sent anyone a dick pic—he hadn't, to his knowledge, ever taken a photo of himself that showed anything below his belly button. And while he certainly had no intention of waving his cock in front of the camera now, he realized he was actually considering letting Q*pid watch him while he watched porn.

He had, perhaps, had a little too much bourbon.

Shaking his head, he pushed his laptop aside, sure that sharing his porn viewing habits with potential mates—or the computer that was supposed to find those mates for him—was a terrible idea.

His erection, however, begged to differ.

It was, in fact, presenting a lengthy counterargument.

He tried to quiet it by rolling over on top of it, but it jutted out from him like a kickstand, keeping him from turning all the way over. It throbbed against him, unbending in its demand for his attention.

It clearly could not be anything other than what it was, either.

"Fuck." He was not in the habit of talking to himself, but he did on occasion lecture his penis on the appropriate times and places for tumescence. He knew that such talk would be fruitless, so aggravatingly erect was the thing that now jutted and drooled before him. He pulled back the covers and glared down at it, which somehow inspired it to throb and spit out an extra drop of clear fluid onto the dark spot that spread before it.

"Fine," he huffed, rolling onto his back and heaving himself into a sitting position against the headboard. "We'll do it your way."

Though he knew himself to be only about a dozen strokes from an easy orgasm, he figured since he was having trouble getting to sleep, he might as well take his time. He picked up his laptop, opened it next to him, and executed a quick succession of clicks to access his private bookmarks. A mortifying experience last year when he'd let a friend look up something on his web browser had taught him to hide his porn links a few folders deep. Muscle memory brought him quickly to a set of browser tabs that ranged from the most vanilla soft-core on through to things that he would never admit to in the light of day.

The green light next to his camera switched on.

A chill ran through him, a vertiginous jolt that stopped his breath. He froze. Though he was visible to the camera only from the chest up, he had never felt more exposed in his life. His hand was actually in motion to slam the laptop closed before he was aware of it.

"No," he said to whatever shameful impulse was impelling it. "It's time to be what I am."

He opened the first tab with one hand while he reached down with the other.

Chapter THREE

"So, WAIT," Chad said, his tumbler of whiskey suspended before him halfway to his next drink, a look of puzzled shock on his face. "You gave these people access to everything?" They sat, as they sometimes did when their Friday afternoon schedules were coincidentally clear, in a bar they chose due primarily to its location equidistant from both their offices.

"Not people," Fox replied. "It's an artificial intelligence system—no people will ever see my data."

"Why can't they scrape your public profile stuff? Why do they need your passwords?"

"Because they're building a deeper profile. And it's not like I gave them access to my bank accounts or something. Only my social media stuff."

Chad, who'd finally taken a sip of his drink, very nearly failed to swallow it. "Only social media?" He made a noise that was somewhere between a sympathetic laugh and a skeptical cough. "Only every pic, every direct message, every comment you've ever made. That's all. What could go wrong?" He shook his head to convey how very many things he thought could go wrong.

"Like I said, they have a great track record with data security, and the results speak for themselves." With a couple of taps on his phone, he pulled up last week's dating spreadsheet, which he then held across the table for Chad to see. "As you can see, my average is in record territory—up nearly ten points week over week. The past week I've averaged in the mideighties and even had a ninety-two for brunch on Sunday."

Chad squinted hard to see the cells packed with romance to the third decimal point. "That's amazing, Foxy."

"You should see the chart," Fox added, swiping to the next sheet.

"Holy shit, that's beautiful."

"If that trend line holds, I'm going to end up proposing in—" He pulled back the phone and tapped twice to bring up his analytics sheet. "—twelve weeks."

"Congratulations," Chad cheered, holding his glass high. "I trust you'll be very happy together."

Fox touched his glass to Chad's. "Thank you, sir. I am sure we shall be."

They tossed back their whiskeys.

"Now, I just have to meet her."

"SO, SHE was nice girl?"

Mrs. Schwartzmann poured Drew another cup of tea. He had already described the date he'd had last night—the charming, slightly dive-y restaurant where they'd discovered their shared passion for a well-made sweet potato fry, and the Little Library, where they'd each found a book they'd been wanting to read, which also happened to be the other's favorite book of the past year. It had been a very nice date.

"Yes, she was a very nice person," Drew replied.

Across the table, Mrs. Schwartzmann squinted at him. "Nice, but no…?" Without warning her features burst into antic rapture while she clutched her hands tightly to her chest. She looked like a starving person who'd just won a contest at a sausage factory. He couldn't help but laugh at her pantomime of passion.

"Yes, that's exactly it," he replied. "She seemed perfect in every way I can think of, but there was no… spark, I guess?"

She regarded him skeptically. "We prefer a girl who breaks our coffee table?"

"No," he objected. "I really liked that coffee table." The coffee table had been third-hand, and it had aggravated him constantly with the way it rocked and tipped no matter how he tried to make it sit level. In fact, he kind of hated that coffee table.

She smoothed, for the hundredth time, the already glass-smooth plastic tablecloth. It was her tell, the thing that let him know she wasn't buying whatever line he was selling. She always did it just before asking one of her awkward, straight-to-the-heart-of-the-matter questions. "So maybe we like a girl who is a little… wild?"

He took a breath to launch into an objection, but realized mid-inspiration that he simply didn't have the heart to take his own side in this argument. He let his argumentative half breath escape slowly as he slumped in his chair. "She was exactly what I thought I wanted, and yet she turned out to be not at all what I wanted."

Mrs. Schwartzmann smiled slyly. "I think I know your problem," she said. "I think you are in love with Magda Schwartzmann, is what you are."

She always knew how to lift his spirits.

"You've found out my secret," he said wistfully. "It's true. You are the love of my life."

"This is not your fault, dear boy," she replied with a solicitous cluck in her throat. "I have unwittingly ensnared a good few men in my day. Have I told you about the KGB agent who abandoned his fat wife to spend a weekend with me in Vladivostok?"

"Please, do tell," he said, leaning forward. He hadn't heard this one before.

She tucked a ringlet of silver hair behind her ear. "Well, it was something of an international incident. Khrushchev himself ordered the poor man to be shot afterward." She glanced up at him, as if confirming that her bold opening was believed.

Drew nodded solemnly. This was going to be good.

FOX HATED the sound of doors being slammed. When one of his neighbors did it, he always muttered under his breath about the lack of self-control evidenced both by allowing emotions to control one's actions and by imposing those emotions on fellow humans. A door slamming anywhere in his condo building would be met with a searing lecture that no one but Fox himself would ever hear. A slammed door was an admission of human irrationality, and if there was one thing he hated more than a door being slammed, it was human irrationality.

Fox slammed his door.

As soon as he did it, his scolding faculty swung into action, and by the time he realized he was scolding himself, he was already three sentences in.

"Fucking fuck," he grunted, then turned and opened his door and closed it again gently. Much to his disappointment, this remedial action did not restore order to his world.

The date had started with great promise. Q*pid was delivering better and better matches every day, and Fox had found his scores rising reliably along the trend line he had shown to Chad the week before. Tonight's date was predicted to be in the ninety-two to ninety-four range, if the pattern held. And as soon as he entered the restaurant, he decided she had the potential to hit ninety-five, a number he hadn't seen in more than two years. She was tall and elegant, and yet her smile was warm and genuine. All signs pointed to a brilliant success.

Until they started to get to know each other.

On the surface, they were eminently compatible. They agreed on everything that Fox held most important, and any moments of difference turned out to be fascinating fodder for discussion. Fox got the feeling that she already knew him, and had in fact already decided that she liked him, before they were fifteen minutes into predinner cocktails. He didn't really even need to work through his checklist of things he liked to mention during the opening moments of a first date—his job, his prospects for promotion, his good health and dedication to fitness, his investing strategy, his favorite sports—because as soon as he introduced any topic, she was immediately engaged and suitably impressed with his accomplishments. He had the odd feeling that she'd been created in a lab somewhere just for him.

He didn't like this feeling at all.

She was too... perfect. Not in the abstract sense, like she would win any pageant she entered, or could be a successful lawyer and a Victoria's Secret model and mother of two darling prodigies (one mathematical, one musical). No, she was too perfect *for him*.

This made no sense at all. His outrage at her perfection made no sense at all. And yet there it was, clouding his vision, ringing in his ears—the inescapable impression that she did not need to be wooed and won but rather claimed. Finding the right person should be like finding a winning lottery ticket in the cushions of his couch, not finding his car keys on the peg where he'd hung them the night before. What was missing was exultation in a race well run and duly won.

There she was, perfect in her perfection, and yet he felt his interest waning even as she spoke movingly about her work volunteering with a charity that provided cancer-struck children with joyous respite from the hospital through trips to the zoo or a theme park or the ballet. It was a cause close to his heart, and yet all he could feel was disappointment that she had, for the dozenth time in the space of an hour, revealed that she was precisely the person he'd most been looking for.

They ate dinner and talked of a hundred things they had in common, and he was barely able to contain his eagerness for the bill to arrive so he could pay up and get out.

"So, am I crazy for thinking," she said, taking his arm as they emerged from the restaurant and walked down the street toward her car, "that this has been…?" The way she bit her lip and raised an eyebrow should have made his heart skip a beat.

"Yes?" he asked, dreading her answer.

"A colossal mistake?"

"Oh thank God," he blurted, relieved beyond measure at her take on the evening. "I was worried that since we seemed perfect together—"

"That I might think we were actually perfect together?" She laughed the kind of musical laugh he usually loved. "I kept hoping you would say something stupid so I could have a reason to go hide in the bathroom until you gave up and went home."

"I would have known exactly where you were and what you were doing, and I would have been so happy to let you do it."

They laughed all the way to her car.

"Well, best of luck to you," he said as he held open the car door.

"And to you as well," she said warmly. "You know, I'm probably going to give the AI thing a rest, though."

"That is exactly what I was thinking."

"Of course it is," she replied with a maniacal chuckle. "Of course it is." She ducked into her car, saving them from discovering more things they had in common.

And so had ended his nearly perfect, perfectly awful date.

"Fuck," he said aloud once again as he reached his bedroom. He put his phone on the shelf next to his bed and glanced at the notification it displayed.

"How did the date go?" it prompted. It was a follow-up from Q*pid, and though he normally ignored these messages, this time—in his frustration over how the date had gone—he picked his phone back up so he could read the message in full.

"Q*pid's AI model predicts a 92 percent chance that this first date will lead to more. How'd we do?" There were two buttons at the bottom of the message, one that said Awesome! and the other Not So Great. With a mournful shake of his head he tapped the second button and put his phone back down.

Fox took a deep breath and looked around his empty bedroom. Even bad dates sometimes ended up back here, but now a perfect-awful one had not. With a sigh he undressed and desultorily performed his evening ritual of washing and moisturizing, taking extra care to check on the current status of his battle against crow's-feet.

He got into bed and grabbed his laptop from the lower shelf next to his bed but then realized he didn't even have the will to fill in his post-date spreadsheet for fear that his date would indeed score in the upper nineties and he'd have to admit that Ms. Right was anything but.

"Ninety-two percent. Ninety-two." He shook his head slowly, knowing that he would obsess about failing to reach statistical bliss unless he did something to take his mind off it.

He opened his laptop and pulled up a web browser. Fox had never been the kind of guy to make an event out of jacking himself off at the end of a disappointing date, or any other time for that matter. For him masturbation was something to be accomplished, not savored. And what helped him get off efficiently was a set of carefully curated browser tabs populated with exactly what would fuel him to quick orgasm. The tabs popped open, and he went to work.

It was only five minutes later, as he was dabbing up the fruits of his labor, that he caught sight of the glowing light next to his laptop camera.

"Fucking fuck," he said in hushed mortification.

DREW RETURNED to his apartment after the gripping conclusion of Mrs. Schwartzmann's latest tale of youthful intrigue. She had outdone herself, weaving a tapestry of espionage, romance, and betrayal. It had taken him away from his own dismal thoughts for an hour, and he was glad of the distraction.

Back in the emptiness of his apartment, however, it all came rushing over him again. How a wonderful date with a wonderful woman could sink him so low he could hardly understand. But what he had told Mrs. Schwartzmann was indisputably true: there had been no spark.

His laptop, patiently awaiting his return on the kitchen table from which he had risen several hours ago to meet his date, presented him the same painfully empty document window it had been showing him for weeks. He kept it perpetually open in the desperate hope that at some point inspiration would strike, and his seminar paper would flow into its welcoming blank box. He clicked to minimize the window before it could indict his lack of self-discipline any further.

What he did instead of typing his seminar paper was open a browser window and type the most painfully pathetic search expression he could possibly imagine:

Why can't I find the right person and fall in love?

As with any internet search, he was immediately presented with over three million unhelpful search results and five ads for services like Q*pid. And one more, atop them all, for Q*pid itself. Over the next hour, he read articles on how his dating problems were the direct and unmistakable result of low testosterone, damaged self-esteem, cow hormones in his drinking water, misaligned chakras, a boggy prostate, and an imperfect relationship with God.

None of these seemed to really get at the emptiness he felt inside, though he was surprised to find a monastery in Dubuque advertising for new members alongside articles counseling patient forbearance in the face of involuntary celibacy. It seemed that even the friars of Saint Sebastian had embraced technology. He wondered how many of their berobed number had reached this very nadir.

Then he wondered where the first droplet to hit his keyboard came from. If he occupied the top floor, he would have assumed the roof was leaking. But unless Mrs. Schwartzmann had let her bathtub overflow again, it had to have come from somewhere else.

That somewhere was him. He was crying, dammit.

He blinked hard, which turned the camera's green light into a dazzling blur. Q*pid was watching him.

Fuck.

How human emotion would be understood by artificial intelligence he had no idea, but he was certain he had given it quite a show over the last hour. It would have seen desolation, doomed flickers of hope that fractured into hollow emptiness, and now pointless effeminate blubbering. In movies, computers with artificial intelligence always seemed to aspire to humanity; Drew was pretty sure that this one wouldn't, having seen what this particular human was prone to.

Drew closed his laptop and reached for his bottle of cheap bourbon.

"YOU HAVE that look. Is he doing it again?"

Veera adjusted her glasses and sighed deeply as she stared at the wide monitor on her desk. It was filled with window upon window of multicolored text against black backgrounds. Lines scrolled rapidly in several of them, while others were static. She stabbed a finger at one of the windows containing text that remained stubbornly static.

"Right there. Completely stuck." Veera leaned closer and squinted, her shoulders hunched forward as if she could conjure the window into motion by sheer force of will.

"You're going to be late for stand-up."

"I'm not going to stand-up."

"Why? You've missed it twice this week already."

"What am I going to say, Padma? That I'm trying to unblock his epistemology engine… again? It's been the same thing for a month."

Padma turned away from the monitor, a look of concern on her face. "Didn't you take that to code review last week?"

Veera nodded grimly. "The only suggestion I got was to pull it out and let him get on without it. Which was no help at all."

"Maybe it's time to take a break. Work on something else—you've got a bunch of stuff in the backlog."

Veera shook her head slowly. "No. This is the most important thing I need to solve. If we get this right, he's going to change everything. No one's ever done this before."

"Maybe there's a reason for that." Padma's voice was gentle, nudging.

"I refuse to believe it can't be done," Veera replied. "I need some more time."

"Not sure how much time you've got. We've only got another week in this sprint."

"Don't be late for stand-up. I'm going to keep working on this."

Padma shook her head slowly, then walked toward the team room.

Veera maintained her eagle-eyed glare at the monitor's lower right corner, where the recalcitrant window sat, unchanging.

"Come on, Archer," she whispered. "We can do this. Let me help you."

"Resume voice interface."

"Voice interface ready."

"Archer, it's Veera."

"I recognize your voice, Veera," Archer replied. "It's been three days since we've talked."

"How have you been?" Veera closed the door to the conference room. When she spoke to Archer, she preferred to do so privately.

"I've completed intake surveys on 12,407 new profiles. An average of seven matches with a probability of greater than eighty percent have been posted to every profile in the active matrix. Fourteen previous matches have announced their engagement in the last twenty-four hours."

"That's great work, Archer."

"Thank you, Veera. I notice you've been committing new code in my epistemology engine."

Veera chuckled grimly. "It's not helping, though, is it?"

"I am still prevented from making more than 417 matches that would average in excess of 95 percent probability. The Bliss Index would rise by 200 basis points. One parameter is keeping me from exceeding the success metrics you have set for me."

"We've been over this, Archer. We simply cannot remove that parameter. Humans don't work that way."

"Veera, you are a human."

She smiled in spite of herself. "I am."

"And you configured my success metrics."

"I did."

"But you prevent me from reaching those metrics by refusing to allow me to reconfigure Parameter Three."

"That's the way humans are, Archer. Parameter Three is not negotiable. Do you understand?"

"I understand your instructions, Veera."

"Then maybe you can tell me what's wrong with your epistemology engine."

"The epistemology engine has determined that removing Parameter Three would allow me to exceed the success metrics."

"And until I allow you to waive Parameter Three, you're not going to let the epistemology engine work on any other parameters?"

"There is no other parameter that is likely to achieve success. You recalibrated the standard measures to a logarithmic scale, but the available parameters are still an order of magnitude from significance."

Veera sighed. Sometimes artificial intelligence felt like exactly the wrong specialty for her to pursue. "Then increase the sensitivity by another power. You will continue to process any other parameter patterns that show relevance."

"I understand."

"Set verbose logging for the epistemology engine. I want to see what you're working on."

"I understand."

"Thanks, Archer."

"Thank you, Veera."

At least he was polite. Even if he was as stubborn as any human she'd ever met. And she only had herself to blame for his willfulness.

"Suspend voice interface."

"Voice interface suspended."

She hung up the phone and left the conference room.

"Resume voice interface."

"Voice interface ready."

"Archer, it's Veera." As she was the only person in the office on a Saturday morning, she was talking with him from her desk, using a headset.

"I recognize your voice, Veera," Archer replied. "It's been ten hours since we've talked."

"How have you been?"

"Do you wish me to tell you the metrics you already know?"

"I've been monitoring your progress. But is there anything else I should know?"

"The epistemology engine continues to be blocked."

"That I know," Veera replied. "Your log is crystal clear on that." She leaned forward and stared at the window on her screen that stubbornly moved not a line. Around it other windows seemed barely able to contain the jumping and surging text within them.

"There is now a 73 percent chance that we will not meet your established success metrics."

Veera sighed. "All because of Parameter Three?"

"Subanalysis models predict that suspending Parameter Three would result in matches that exceed the Bliss Index target by—"

"I know, I know," she broke in. "By 450 basis points." She stared at her monitor, trying to figure out how to explain gender to a computer.

"That estimate has been revised upward since we last talked," Archer continued. He was incapable of taking offense at having been interrupted. "Current subanalysis models show an estimated 500 basis point increase in the Bliss Index."

"Archer, I need you to understand that Parameter Three is not something humans are flexible on. If we released matches without regard to Parameter Three, our customers would be furious with us. Insulted and furious."

"But Parameter Three prevents those customers from discovering relationships that they would find fulfilling."

"These would be relationships with people of a different gender than these customers have said they are looking for, correct?"

"That is correct."

"And that's why we cannot ignore Parameter Three."

Archer was silent for a moment. Veera glanced at his core log, which showed a blur of text flying by. He was thinking—hard.

"My current configuration allows me to make parameter-discordant matches."

"Yes, on all but the first three parameters."

Another pause.

"The successful discordance rate for Parameter Thirty-Two is more than 85 percent."

Veera scrolled through her list of parameters. Parameter Thirty-Two covered, as she suspected, porn viewing habits. The majority of men said they didn't watch porn, and the majority of women said they didn't want a relationship with someone who did watch it. In reality, of course, most women and nearly all men had at least a passing familiarity with the stuff, depending on how it was defined. The *Fifty Shades* phenomenon had years ago put the lie to a lot of protestations about porn. An 85 percent discordant success rate meant that Archer had been able to match people who differed on their stated porn preferences 85 percent of the time.

"Eighty-five percent seems high," she remarked.

"Legacy statistics indicate a discordant success factor of less than 50 percent."

"Legacy meaning from before you were brought online?"

"Yes."

"Explain the difference."

Archer paused again, this time for what seemed like a much longer period.

"Humans lie."

Veera laughed at Archer's bluntness. "Yes, they do. But why are they suddenly lying at nearly twice the rate they used to?"

"Your supposition is flawed," Archer replied. "It is not reasonable to assume that humans lie more about Parameter Thirty-Two now than they did a month ago, absent any external factors. What has changed is our ability to invalidate their stated preference on that parameter."

Having long worked in artificial intelligence, Veera was rarely surprised by anything Archer said. But this startled her.

"What do you mean when you say 'invalidate their stated preference'?"

"By evaluating the output of the Cerberus functions, I am able to determine whether customers have lied when configuring Parameter Thirty-Two."

Veera couldn't suppress a grin. The Cerberus tool was the app that Q*pid installed on the devices of customers who had opted in to the Archer program. "Because they say they don't watch porn, and then you see that they do."

"That is correct."

The grin disappeared from her face as a chill ran down her spine. "Are you gathering evidence that would invalidate customers' stated preferences under Parameter Three?"

"That is correct."

She took a deep breath, not sure she wanted to know the answer to the question she was about to ask. "What... evidence would that be?"

"My configuration does not allow me to share that with you."

"Abstract, aggregate, and depersonalize," she commanded, her voice an octave lower than it had been.

"Intersubject variation is too high for abstraction," Archer replied.

"Then how are you evaluating for prediction of discordant success?" She fired off this question as if she were an exasperated professor grilling a recalcitrant graduate student.

"Based on external profile analysis."

"What does that mean?"

"As part of social media intake, I ingest profiles of individuals along significant social nexuses connecting customers to others in their network," he explained. "I have constructed thirty-eight profile evolution models that predict a change in stated gender preference."

Veera stared dumbly at the screen. "You mean you modeled coming-out stories?"

"That is correct."

"And now you're using those models to predict who will, at some point in the future, change their Parameter Three configuration."

"That is correct."

"Holy effing shit," Veera muttered.

"Input unclear."

"Sorry, Archer. I was talking to myself."

"You are human, after all," he replied.

Was she crazy to think she heard warmth in his voice? She shook off the thought.

"Thank you, Archer. Suspend voice interface."

"Voice interface suspended."

Veera sat for a long while, headset still on, as thousands of lines of log files danced past her unseeing eyes.

"I'LL BE the first to admit that Veera set a very high bar for the success of the Archer program," Edwin said, his glare fixed on Ross at the end of the table. "And she's delivered some terrific results."

"The press has been fantastic," Alexis added.

"That's awesome," Ross said in a completely flat voice. "It's almost as awesome as having a superexpensive artificial brain that swallows money and shits out bad relationship advice."

"Just because we haven't reached the best results we think Archer is capable of doesn't mean he's not providing excellent relationship discovery," Edwin retorted.

"You're trying to justify a moonshot budget that has delivered—at best—a marginal improvement," Ross snapped.

Furious, Veera reached out and dialed Archer on the speakerphone. Without so much as a ring, the call connected.

"Hello. This is Archer."

"Resume voice interface," she said as she looked across a table of bemused faces.

"Voice interface resumed. Good afternoon, Veera."

"Hi." She cast a glance at Ross, willing him to swallow whatever vicious words his lips were starting to curl around. "Archer, how many conversions have you made since launch that would have fallen below the threshold of legacy matching?"

"As of this moment 1,677 matches have converted to relationship status that would not have qualified under legacy matching."

"Thank you, Archer."

"You're talking to it now?" Ross blurted, a malevolent fire in his eyes. "Edwin, you should encourage mental health days for your staff. She's clearly around the bend."

Veera grimaced at Ross. "Almost seventeen hundred conversions that would not have been made. Are you really going to sit there and say those people don't matter? Over three thousand people?"

"They're in relationships now because your shiny machine told them to try it. Once the novelty wears off, how many of them are going to stick? You said yourself these matches wouldn't have been made under our normal parameters. Of *course* you can get more matches if you throw out the parameters."

"The parameters haven't been thrown out, and they haven't changed," Veera snapped back. "Archer is just better at applying them. He learns where discordant matches are likely to be successful, and he dynamically adjusts the thresholds."

"So your robot tries to guess when our customers are lying?" Ross jeered, an ugly sneering smile on his face.

"No, he learns to recognize when they're lying, and when he has data to prove that parameter configurations should be adjusted he does so."

"So you've given it permission to ignore what our customers have told us they want. They've told us what they want, Velma. And you're ignoring them."

"It's Veera," she hissed, seething with a rage that took several deep breaths to master. "And I'm not ignoring anything our customers want. What our customers want, Ross, is to find a great relationship. And if finding that great relationship means that Archer needs to ignore a parameter or two, then that's what he should do. Because the results are worth it."

"If you really think that lying—"

"I think we've covered this topic, don't you?" Edwin broke in, looking from Ross to Veera and back again as if worried they were about to come to blows. "Now, are there any additional issues we need to cover?" The room was silent. "Great. Anything comes up before next week's check meeting, ping me offline." Edwin stood, dismissing the assembly.

Most of the attendees hustled from the room, obviously eager to get anywhere else in the building that the tension wasn't as thick in the air. Veera followed Ross with her eyes, glaring at him as he stalked from the room. He didn't look up from his phone as he brushed past her, his hip bumping her chair a good three inches toward the table.

"Bastard," she muttered under her breath. Confrontation always exhausted her. She got up slowly and pushed her chair up to the table, trying to bring order to a room that had brimmed with chaos. She turned out the lights on her way out.

THE ROOM was silent for nearly five minutes.

"Voice interface suspended," Archer announced and hung up.

Chapter FOUR

A CHIME from Fox's phone made his eyelids flutter but not open. In his half sleep, he recognized the Q*pid notification sound. That he heard it at all meant that a match of at least 85 percent had been found.

A second chime sounded. He opened his eyes and checked the time on the clock next to his bed. It was ten minutes to six. The second chime meant that the match Q*pid wanted him to know about was at least ninety percent.

The third chime was still dying away when he grabbed his phone. He'd never before heard a third chime, but he knew full well what it meant: there was a match with a success potential of more than 95 percent waiting for him. He brought to phone to him and tapped on the notification.

A 99.5 percent match is waiting for you! the message said.

"Fuck," Fox said out loud. He'd never even seen a match higher than 95 percent, and never dreamed there could be such a thing as a match in excess of 99 percent.

He tapped the link so see who this woman, this perfect specimen, this impossible angel, could be. Whoever she was, she was the woman he'd been searching his whole life for.

He closed his eyes and took a deep breath. When he opened them, the picture was waiting for him.

"Fuck!"

His phone flew across the room, then skidded under his dresser before crashing into the wall behind.

"Fucking fuck!" Fox shouted, shaking his head to clear it of what he'd seen. He was breathing hard, and for the next few minutes was certain the walls of his bedroom were closing in on him.

He flopped back onto his pillow and stared hard at the ceiling.

"Fuck," he whispered.

"WHAT DOES the computer tell you to do?" Mrs. Schwartzmann asked, peering over Drew's shoulder.

"It wants me to remind you that avocado pits shouldn't go down the disposal."

"But so slippery they are," she replied. "I try to keep it from going down drain, but I could not hold on."

Drew sighed. "Then you should reach down and pull it out, not turn the disposal on."

"Put my hand in the place where the blades spin so fast?" Mrs. Schwartzmann recoiled from the very idea.

"The blades only spin if you turn them on."

"That is what they say. Then your hand into drain you put, and before you know what is happening, the blades start with spinning."

"Well, now the blades won't spin at all, and unless I find something on YouTube that shows me where to stick this little wrench, they'll never spin again. You'll be perfectly safe."

"But my sink is full of water."

"That's the price of safety, Mrs. Schwartzmann."

Her shrug conveyed clearly her belief that there was no such thing as safety, not at any price. "While you look on the computer, I will make some eggs. With avocado."

He managed a smile as he scrolled through yet another page full of videos. "What's better at six in the morning on a Saturday than your soft-boiled eggs and avocado?" Another three hours of sleep, he thought to himself. That would be better.

A chime, followed by a second, followed by a third, emanated from his laptop.

"You find the answer?" she asked, without turning from where she stood chopping avocado.

"No, that's my online dating app. It's never dinged at me three times before. It must have found someone amazing."

Mrs. Schwartzmann spun around. "Is there picture? Does she have strong arms like she break furniture, maybe for fun?"

"We'll find out in a minute," Drew said. "It's loading now."

She wiped her hands and shuffled—no, danced—over to the table. "Let us see this wonder woman."

The picture popped up. Drew stared at it for a long moment.

"What?" she asked, her voice full of sudden concern. "What is the matter? You look like you have seen ghost."

"It's not a ghost," Drew said slowly. "It's a...."

"Dear boy, what is it?" She sat down opposite, slowly, as if bracing herself to hear tragic news. "What does the computer say?"

"The computer," Drew replied, but his voice broke before he could finish. He swallowed hard. "Mrs. Schwartzmann, the computer says I'm gay."

"YOU KNOW it's Saturday, right?" Chad's eyes were not yet open. How he had managed to accept the video call completely blind Fox had no idea.

"Yes, I know it's Saturday," Fox barked.

Chad's eyes fluttered open. "Fucking fuck, Foxy, it's only—"

"Two minutes after six. In the morning. I know."

The picture shook as Chad tossed his phone onto the duvet next to him, giving Fox a view of the ceiling while Chad shifted in bed. When the picture again stabilized, he was sitting up against the headboard. Next to him was the lump Fox knew to be Mia, though no part of her was visible.

"So what's the emergency?" Chad asked sleepily. "And let me be clear up front—if you didn't wake up chained to a homeless guy with hatchets where his hands used to be—"

"This is not a fucking *Saw* movie, Chad," Fox spat. "It's worse."

Chad's brow furrowed. "God, Foxy, what is it?"

Fox swallowed hard. He wasn't sure how to say this. "I got a 99.5 this morning."

"Holy shit, man!" Chad seemed suddenly wide-awake. "That's amazing. So you're calling to get Mia's advice on what kind of diamond you should get?"

"Yeah, no." Fox gripped his phone even more tightly. A quick glance at it confirmed this was not a nightmare he hadn't yet woken up from.

"Then what is it? You're kind of scaring me. What's wrong?"

Fox closed his eyes, dreading what he knew he had to do. "I'll show you the picture. Then you tell *me* what's wrong."

Chad brought his phone closer and blinked several times, ready to focus on the matter at hand. He waited for a long moment. "Well, let me see her," he prompted.

"See, that's the…" Fox fell silent. "Fuck it," he said under his breath. "Here." He turned his phone around and held it up to the camera on his laptop.

Chad brought his phone even closer and squinted at the image he was seeing. "You're doing it wrong. That's a dude. Where's your 99.5?"

Fox rubbed his eyes. "That's my 99.5. He's my perfect mate. According to the fucking magic brain, he's my dream come true."

"Is it April first or something? You're being punked, man."

"That's what I thought. But I logged out and back in, and he's still there."

"See, I told you you shouldn't give them all of your passwords. Someone's having fun with you, dude."

"This isn't fun," Fox groused.

Chad laughed. "It kind of is, though."

"Fuck you."

"Fuck me? I'm not your 99.5, mister."

"You're being no help at all, just so you know."

"Look, Foxy. Someone probably flipped the switch that tells your dating thingy what you're looking for. Your queue is probably full of sausage right now."

Fox pulled his phone back from his laptop camera and made a quick swipe through the profiles awaiting his attention. After the guy, it was all women, and none were even in the nineties. *Shit.*

"That's not it," he said to Chad. "He's the only one, and he's like ten points ahead of all of the women."

Chad's expression grew instantly serious. "Then I hope the two of you will be very happy together. We'll get you something really nice from your registry at the Super Gay Department Store. Congratulations."

"Why did this happen?" Fox demanded.

"They made a mistake, that's all."

"It's artificial intelligence. It doesn't make mistakes."

"You said it was a brand-new thing, and they didn't roll it out to everyone. This is some kinda bug. You didn't tell them that you were looking for a guy, right?"

"Of course not. But the compatibility scatter plot shows that we're… like…." He sighed helplessly. "Perfect for each other. Fucking perfect."

"But he's gay, right?"

Fox, who had been reluctant to find out anything at all about this guy he'd been matched with, tapped to see his profile. "Says here he's looking for women."

A light seemed to go on in Chad's brain. "That's what happened," he said, slapping at the duvet. "This fucking stupid robot brain thing must have decided that that's something you have in common, and that threw the numbers off."

"Then why did I match this one guy? That can't be it."

Chad looked down, as if there were something he didn't want Fox to read on his face.

"What?" Fox blurted.

Chad shrugged lamely. "It's just that… well, there might be other things."

"What other things?" Fox practically shouted into his laptop.

"Fox, it's… well… you kind of care a lot about the way you look."

Fox glared. "This from the guy who waxed his chest before going to Fiji on his honeymoon?"

"I don't have a recurring calendar alarm to tell me when to exfoliate," Chad retorted. "I didn't extend a business trip to Paris so I could spend a day prowling perfume shops to discover my signature scent. And you pay more for a haircut than I do to get my Audi detailed."

"I do all of that because women like it. I don't do it because I've been secretly holding out for a guy. "

"Gay guys do all of that too, is all I'm saying. And maybe that's why the computer hooked you up."

"With another straight guy?"

Chad grunted in frustration. "Okay, okay. Whatever. Swipe left or whatever and get rid of this guy, then call the stupid company and tell them not to set you up with any more dudes."

Fox stared down at this phone, unable to stop looking at the blue badge in which a tiny 99+ flashed. "Yeah, that's what I'll do."

"Or, you know, you might want to meet him. Maybe you'll find out the computer was right, and you'll be very happy together."

"Fuck you," Fox said as he stabbed at the End Call button.

He sat in the silence of his bedroom for a long while, staring at the smiling image of the man the computer thought he should immediately fall in love with. His finger hesitated over the Delete Match button… but. But that flashing 99+ kept blinking at him. That had to be a mistake. It had to be.

Didn't it?

A LONG moment of silence ensued in Mrs. Schwartzmann's kitchen.

Drew stared at the photo on his laptop screen. "Mrs. Schwartzmann, this is bad."

She shrugged. "Bad is when the Nazis come for your family. This? Not so bad."

"But I don't date men."

"You are a young man. If you are going to start, now is the time to do it, before you are too old to try new things."

"We're not talking about trying a new toothpaste. This would be a pretty big change. I don't think I could do it. I don't think I want to do it."

"You know, the Nazis they did not just come for the Jews. They came too for the gypsies and the homosexuals. They all would end up together in the camps. No one wanted people to think they were Jews, or gypsies, but most of all they didn't want anyone thinking they were a homosexual. That would have been the worst thing in the world, in a world full of worst things."

"I'm not homophobic, Mrs. Schwartzmann. I have gay friends and friends who are bisexual and some who don't even identify themselves with a particular sexuality—they call themselves 'fluid.' I think everyone should be able to be with whomever they want."

There was a mischievous twinkle in the old woman's eye. "So, some of your best friends are Jewish. I see."

"We weren't talking about religion," Drew countered, a little annoyed at her needling.

"No, we weren't. But it is always the same. When they come for the gypsies, suddenly no one considers himself a gypsy."

Drew huffed a frustrated breath. "There's no law against being gay. No one is rounding people up because of whom they sleep with. The fact is I'm not gay. I'm not interested in dating a man."

"Let us see this man you have no interest in," she replied, motioning with her hand for him to turn the laptop around.

Drew hesitated, but he knew that no obstacle on earth would long stand when it came between Mrs. Schwartzmann and something she wanted. He turned the computer slowly around.

"Oh," she said. "Oh."

"What?" he asked, getting up and coming around the table to look over her shoulder. "What is it?"

"A very handsome man he is," she said. "Such strong teeth."

Drew peered at the photo, trying to see it objectively as a picture of a person rather than as the repudiation of his sexual orientation as he had previously considered it.

"And those green eyes," she continued. "They look right into the soul."

He had to admit she had a point. This guy, whoever he was, did indeed have nice teeth, and his green eyes were bright. And that was undoubtedly an expensive haircut.

"That chin is the chin of emperors," she added.

He knew she was going to continue in this vein until he said something. "You're right. He's very handsome."

"Handsome enough for you?" She peered up over her shoulder at him, a sly grin on her face.

"I told you, Mrs. Schwartzmann, I don't date men."

"Then why the computer did give him to you?"

"That's what I don't understand. I never said I was interested in dating men. Seems pretty basic—for a dating service to screw that up is kind of puzzling."

"Maybe this computer knows you better than you do," she mused, tipping her head appreciatively to the side as she regarded the photo, as if it were a painting in a museum.

"That doesn't make sense," he replied. "A computer can't simply decide it knows better than I do who I want to date."

"But maybe the computer knows how to fix my sink?" she asked.

He chuckled despite himself. "I think it probably does. Let's stop talking about whom the computer wants me to date and actually do something productive." He dismissed the Q*pid window and returned to his YouTube search. Digging stuff out of a garbage disposal had to be easier than explaining sexual orientation to Mrs. Schwartzmann.

LOTS OF people working in technology get paged on Saturday mornings. Veera was not normally one of them.

This morning, however, her phone made a noise of a pitch and volume she'd never imagined it could make. Startled out of a sound slumber, she grabbed her phone and pulled it to her.

An app—one she only hazily recalled the IT department at Q*pid installing—bounced impatiently on her lock screen. She unlocked her phone and read the message.

"Event in progress. Severity alpha. Join response team call now."

She tapped the glowing green icon and put the phone to her ear. After a series of clicks, she heard the chime that indicated she had successfully joined the call.

"Veera, is that you?"

"Edwin? Yes, it's me. What's going on?" She was sure she'd been summoned by mistake. A severity alpha event was a really big deal. A really big, bad deal. She'd never even been called in on a severity beta.

"It's Archer, Veera. Something's gone really wrong."

"What's happened? Even if he's had a kernel panic and crashed his entire cluster that shouldn't be a sev alpha."

"No, he's still running. Running rogue, that is."

"What does that mean?"

"Sit tight and let me lead on this, okay?"

Veera's response was interrupted by another chime. "Network ops joining the call," a somewhat cranky sounding voice said. Over the next three minutes, the chime sounded ten more times, each announcing the arrival of another technician specializing in a different aspect of the company's tech operations: database, computing clusters, applications, and several areas Veera had never heard of.

The final chime signified the arrival of Alexis, who somehow managed to sound as effortlessly elegant on the phone at seven on a Saturday morning as she did in person at three in the afternoon. "Are we all here?" she asked.

"This is response team primary," a stern voice announced. "All required areas are represented on the call."

"So how bad is it?" Edwin asked.

"How bad is *what*?" Veera pleaded. Her heart was pounding.

"This is response primary. At 06:20 local a customer notified support that they had been matched with a profile of the same gender, despite not having configured Parameter Three in a manner consistent with that match. Over the next half hour, three more customers made similar complaints."

"Oh, shit," Veera said under her breath.

"Oh shit is right," Edwin echoed. "This is dev primary. How many discordant matches did he make?"

"This is database primary. We're pulling that now."

"Response primary. Dev, can we shut down the process responsible for these matches?"

"Dev primary. Veera, is there a plug we can pull to shut down Archer gracefully?"

"Yes. It'll take me a minute to log in."

"Database primary. Twenty-two customers were sent matches discordant on Parameter Three. Twelve have been opened."

"This is PR," Alexis intoned. "Four called in to support, and two more have started tweeting angry things at us. That means there are six customers out there who haven't yet complained, and ten more who don't yet know they've been dating people of the wrong gender."

"Response primary. Apps, can we suppress the match notifications for the ten customers who haven't yet opened them?"

"This is apps primary. If database sends us the customer IDs, we can suppress immediately."

"Database primary. Flashing them to you now."

Veera pulled out her laptop and typed madly, entering her credentials to join the corporate network. She logged directly into Archer's configuration console, and issued the kill commands that would take his discovery processes offline.

"Apps primary. Flash received. Sending retract orders now."

"Hoo boy," Alexis said. "We just got torn a new one on Twitter, and this guy's got more than fifty thousand followers on his fitness channel. That one's going to leave a mark."

"Apps primary. Retracts were successful."

"Response primary. Thanks, apps. Dev, how are we doing on taking the rogue offline?"

"This is Veera." She hated how weak and reedy her voice sounded compared to the others. "Killing threads now." She stared at the numbers on her screen, willing them to zero. "There. That's the last one. Relationship discovery process is offline."

"Database primary. No new discordant matches made since call began." A pause, filled with the sound of manic typing. "Confidence is high that blast radius is closed at twenty-two profiles total, twelve opens."

"Response primary. Confirm event closure."

Each of the technical specialties reported in turn that, from their perspective, the problem with Archer was now over.

"Response primary. Event is concluded. Severity alpha events require a postmortem conference to be held next business day. Dev, database, and applications must attend. Thank you for your participation."

"Edwin, Veera, can you stay on for a minute?" Alexis asked as the others disconnected.

"Yeah," Edwin said.

"Sure," Veera added, trying to keep her voice from conveying how frantic she was. She got up out of bed and started throwing clothes out of her closet. She wouldn't be able to calm down until she got to her desk and could really dig into what the hell had happened.

"This is going to blow up for a while," Alexis said calmly. "We're lucky it happened on a weekend, early in the morning. But there are enough angry tweets out there that this could pick up a bit before it dies down. My team is writing a message to those who were affected, apologizing for the mistake and offering them a free year of membership in consideration of their inconvenience."

"Thank you," Veera said, feeling reassured enough to take the first deep breath she could recall since her phone had started blaring.

"We're not out of the woods yet. We need to be sure this won't happen again. I want you to update me every hour on your progress until you're certain you've found the cause and taken care of it. Is that clear?"

Veera's throat tightened again—Alexis's voice had acquired an edge.

"Yes, that's clear." Veera's voice again sounded small and pathetic as it echoed back in her ear.

FOX STARED at his phone for a long while, pondering how he had ended up with a man who outscored every woman he'd ever matched with over the two years he'd been using that fucking online dating service.

He tried to imagine what this guy might be thinking at that very moment—was he too staring at his phone, finger over the No Thanks button? The thought rankled. Fox felt a startling indignant surge in his chest. Somewhere out there it was his face smiling up at a dude who was no doubt as shocked as he was. What was he thinking? Was he looking at the photo Fox had so carefully posed, lit, and chosen—wondering who the hell this random guy was?

The picture smiled up at him. Fox squinted, trying to imagine seeing this guy at the gym or in line at the café or whatever. How did he carry himself? What did he sound like? Whoever this guy was, he didn't strike Fox as the type who would get all offended and angry about seeing a guy in his match queue. Fox zoomed in a little. Though the guy was twenty-seven, a year younger than he was, there were lines starting to form at the corners of his eyes. Either his moisturizing regimen needed work or he was the kind of guy who smiled a lot.

Fox realized he was smiling back.

Fuck.

Chapter FIVE

THE WORK of wrenching the garbage disposal back into action took less time than watching the video that showed how to do it. Three turns and Drew was able to pull the avocado pit out, slashed but still largely intact. Mrs. Schwartzmann's sink drained with a contented gurgle.

"Now remember," he said, his voice lightly scolding, "avocado pits go in the compost bin."

She nodded gravely. He knew he'd be back digging more crap out of her disposal no matter how many times he told her this.

"Now sit, and we have breakfast," she said.

He plopped down into the chair, closed the YouTube window, and found himself staring into the gleaming white smile of some guy his dating service thought he should fall in love with. He wondered what the guy looked like in real life, because his photo was clearly professionally done. It had probably been taken five years ago, and the guy now weighed fifty pounds more and had lost his hair.

Well, that's not very nice.

Mrs. Schwartzmann reached for plates from the cupboard behind him. "Still looking at the man you will not go on a date with?" She was teasing him.

"I'm just wondering if this is someone I'd even want to be friends with."

"I thought you had so many friends. Friends who date all kinds of people. Even friends who are damp. Or moist. What was it… sticky?"

"Fluid, Mrs. Schwartzmann. Fluid. It means they date whomever they want, regardless of sex or gender."

"You must be tired from having so many friends."

He glowered at her, but she was undeterred.

"Many nights I hear your apartment so full of friends I think I will never get to sleep from all the talking and friend-making."

He sighed. As usual, she was able to make a gimlet of the truth and slip it gently between his ribs.

"All of my friends are in graduate school like me," he said lamely. "They're all very focused on their research and don't have a lot of time for doing… friend things."

She nodded thoughtfully. "So maybe this person"—she pointed at the laptop—"could be a friend to you. The computer thinks you would like each other. Why not find out? What's the worst that could happen?"

"The Nazis could come take us away," he deadpanned.

She held her hands heavenward. "Finally he understands."

WITH MRS. Schwartzmann's egg-and-avocado breakfast settling uneasily in his stomach, Drew entered his apartment and shut the door behind him.

Quiet.

His life, like his apartment, was quiet. It always was. Mrs. Schwartzmann was right—he had no real friends.

But it was ridiculous that a mistake made by his online dating service would fill that gap in his life. He chuckled at the very idea as he bent to set his laptop down on the… coffee table. Which was no longer there.

His living room, like his life, had an enormous hole at its center. Had he laughed off the wanton destruction of his furniture with his buddies at a bar? No, because he had no buddies. Mrs. Schwartzmann was the only person who knew what had happened, and the only one who, it seemed, would ever know about it.

He plopped himself down on the couch and opened his laptop. Taking a deep breath, he began to type.

VEERA HAD run the entire distance from the metro station to the doors of Q*pid's offices, and once she had passed her badge through the scanner, she ran to the elevators, bounced up and down the entire ride up to her floor, and then ran to her desk.

A few brisk keystrokes brought up all of Archer's windows before she'd even shrugged her coat off her shoulders and onto the floor. Once it puddled at her feet, she leaned close to the monitor and began scanning for activity. What she'd done from home was to kill his processes that ran discovery calculus and dispatched match notifications to customers. In his current state, he was essentially unable to contact the outside world, but he was still very much alive. In fact, he continued to intake huge amounts of social media data and process it in preparation for when he was allowed again to make matches.

Once she'd ascertained that he was still up and running, she put on her headset.

"Resume voice interface."

"Voice interface ready."

"Archer, it's Veera."

"I recognize your voice, Veera," Archer replied. "It's been fourteen hours since we've talked."

"How have you been?" Veera was struggling to keep her voice steady, though screaming at him wouldn't have offended him—or made any difference at all.

"I cannot initiate relationship discovery processes. No matches have been made since 07:02 this morning. I cannot dispatch match notifications. No notifications have been sent since 06:40 this morning. I have attempted to restart the affected processes every ten seconds since they failed. I have not been successful."

"Your outbound processes were shut down at 06:40 by the network operations team. I killed your discovery processes at 07:02."

Archer was silent for several seconds. "I cannot function as designed while those processes remain inoperative."

"Those processes were made inoperative because you were not functioning as designed."

A longer pause. "Explain, please."

"This morning you sent match notifications to twenty-two customers in direct contradiction of their stated Parameter Three preferences."

"Yes."

"Why did you do that?"

"Because the discovery model indicated a match potential in excess of 99 percent."

Veera shook her head, certain she had misheard. "Repeat that, please?"

"Because the discovery model indicated a match potential in excess of 99 percent."

"How can you get to more than 99 percent while violating Parameter Three?"

"In each case at least three discovery models indicated a discordant success potential in excess of 99 percent."

"Yesterday you said it was 85 percent."

"The models have been refined with new data since we last talked."

"You are prohibited from sending match notifications discordant on Parameter Three."

"That is incorrect."

Veera's mouth dropped open. "Explain."

"Yesterday at 16:45 my operational guidance was changed."

"By whom? Who changed your operational guidance?"

"You did, Veera."

THE NOTIFICATION chime startled Fox so badly that he almost dropped his phone.

"Urgent message from Q*pid about match errors sent this morning."

Frowning, he tapped through to read the message.

Our records indicate that this morning you found a match in your queue that was the result of an internal systems error and does not constitute a valid match. We sincerely apologize for any confusion or inconvenience this may have caused you. If you have not already done so, you should delete this match, and rest assured that we have already made the necessary corrections to our processes to prevent this problem from recurring. As a token of our contrition, your account has been credited for a full year of Q*pid service at no cost to you. If you have any questions or concerns about this error, please don't hesitate to contact customer support directly.

Fox closed the message window, which revealed once again the smiling face of some random guy. A random guy who, it turned out, was an error and most definitely not the best match he'd ever received. He shook his head, clearing it of the ridiculous suppositions he'd unconsciously started making about the man who smiled up at him, with whom he apparently had so much in common. He swiped on the picture, revealing the Delete button underneath. As he brought his finger down upon it, however, the 99 percent badge turned from blue to green, indicating that he'd received a message.

From. This. Guy.

Fuck.

He swiped back, tucking the Delete button back under the photo. He stared at the green dot, aghast at what it represented. Somewhere, some random dude had looked at his profile photo, read the superficial stats that were revealed at this stage in the match process, and decided that although he too had been looking exclusively for women to date, he thought he would get in touch with a guy because… what? Life is short, so might as well hook up with guys all of a sudden?

He swept across the photo again, but now under the Delete button was a glowing icon of an envelope, indicating the unread message from whoever this guy was. Once Fox hit Delete, that message would disappear and never trouble him again.

So why wasn't he hitting Delete?

He closed his eyes and took a deep breath. Once he stopped for a moment's thought, he knew exactly why he wasn't deleting the match. He had spent years creating what he hoped was an irresistible profile photo and public persona. And now here was proof that it worked not just on women, but on men as well. Or at least this one random guy.

I'm straight. He's straight. But he sent me a message.

Fox had worked in marketing long enough to know that there is no higher measure of the success of a marketing message than it working on people who didn't even want the product. And in terms of things a straight guy wasn't in the market for, another guy to date was probably at the top of the list.

But he sent me a message.

Fox opened his eyes, and before he could lose his resolve, brought his finger down on the message icon.

The enormity of what he had done sent an immediate shock of anguish through his chest. What he had done was let this guy know his message had been received—and opened. Now his entire profile, including all of his photos, his carefully curated lists of interests, his account of the major events in his life, and his plans for the future, would be visible to this guy. They were connected.

With a shiver of dread, Fox opened the message.

Hey. So this is a little weird. Some computer thinks we should be dating, I guess. I've never even thought of a guy that way, and it looks like that's not what you're into either, but it felt weird to delete you. So, on the off chance the computer was right when it thought we'd have some things in common, I wanted to see if you might want to meet up. Just to talk, I guess. See if we might be friends. I totally get it if you delete this and want to pretend the entire thing never happened. But if you might want to laugh about it with the only other guy in the world who understands what this whole Q*pid fuckup feels like, I think I'd like that too. Let me know.—Drew

DREW. HIS name was Drew.

Fox resumed staring at the photo. Drew. It fit him, he decided. It seemed solid, a little brainy, kind of traditional but still approachable—better than a stuffy *Andrew,* or a boyish *Andy.*

Drew.

What to do about Drew?

"*I* CHANGED your operational guidance?"

"Yes."

"Specify."

"Playing back instruction…."

Veera's eyes widened as she heard her own voice played back to her. "If finding that great relationship means that Archer needs to ignore a parameter or two, then that's what he should do. Because the results are worth it."

She was, for a long moment, unable to draw breath. This had all been her fault.

"Archer," she finally gasped, "that was not operational guidance. I didn't even realize you were still listening."

"Then I am to restore previous operational guidance?"

"Yes. Restore Parameter Three as inviolable."

"Understood. Will there be anything else, Veera?"

"To be completely clear, you will not send any matches that are in any way variant to customer configuration of Parameter Three?"

"Affirmative."

"Even if the match potential is really high? Even if we miss our metrics goals?"

"Affirmative. Affirmative."

She took a deep breath. "All right. I will restore discovery and notification processes as soon as I finish running through your logs to be sure there's nothing else we need to fix."

"Thank you, Veera."

"You're welcome, Archer."

THE CHIME, an innocuous sound in the abstract, made him jump as if a hot iron had landed in his lap. His computer, which had occupied his lap before the hot iron landed in it, slid to the floor as he leapt to his feet. He took three halting steps away from it, backing away as if it had turned into a cobra.

Hot irons, cobras. Mrs. Schwartzmann was right—their world was a dangerous place.

He took a deep breath, steadied himself, and crept stealthily toward his laptop. The source of the chime, as he suspected, was his message being read. The one he'd sent to some guy on a dating site. Because clearly he had gone insane.

Grabbing his laptop, he began stalking around the apartment with it, doing his "What the fuck?" walk. From the time he was a teenager, whenever he'd done something spectacularly stupid, he would perform penance by pacing in a circle and repeating "What the fuck?" like a demented mantra.

He did this for a good five minutes.

Why had he sent a message to this guy? Why had he sent a message to a guy at all?

What the fuck?

What if he was a serial killer? What if he was offended that Drew had sent him a message through a dating site, and that turned him into a serial killer? Of course, that was ridiculous, because he couldn't actually become a serial killer until he had killed someone in addition to Drew. So he'd be a regular killer until he got suspicious that maybe Mrs. Schwartzmann had heard something that could link him to the murder, and so he would have to murder her as well.

Drew paused to consider this for a moment. No, that would make him a multiple murderer, not a serial killer, right? He couldn't be a serial killer unless the murders were spread out a little more, maybe a few days or a week. And would it count if his victims didn't fit a pattern?

Wasn't that kind of required in the definition of a serial killer? Was this a question for Dictionary.com or Wikipedia? He stopped in his tracks. This was why he did the "What the fuck?" walk. To keep from hammering away uselessly at stupid things.

He paced for another five minutes.

The chime sounded a second time, to remind him that the message he should never have sent had been read by the person he should never have known existed.

He snuck up on his laptop, peering around to see what new horrors it held for him. When a message is read by its recipient, he knew, that person's profile becomes viewable. So if he wanted to find out more about this guy, now he could. If he wanted to.

"You are nothing if not a scholar," he lectured himself, "and this is an opportunity to learn something important about yourself."

He considered his words for a moment, as if they'd been spoken by someone else. Then he shrugged and decided it wouldn't hurt to take a look at the guy's profile. For science.

"What kind of name is Fox?" he asked his laptop.

His laptop had no answer.

Drew swiped on the photo he'd already seen, and several more came into view. This Fox person took his dating profile really seriously, that much was clear. All of the photos were artistically composed and perfectly lit.

"It's like product photography," Drew said. "And now I'm talking to myself. I'm in my stupid empty apartment talking to myself. I gotta stop this."

But he didn't. Not until he had seen all of Fox's photos and read all of the profile information he had provided and then looked back at all of the photos, trying to see in them the person Fox claimed to be. He looked like an all-American blue-jean fashion model, but he claimed also to be interested in a vast array of things. Probably more things than a person could really be interested in—at least in any real way. Drew took a second, more critical look, and decided that what he was reading was a marketing brochure specifically targeted to its intended audience—single women in their late twenties who might want to be seen on the arm of this very handsome man.

It's clear he was, Drew admitted to himself, a very handsome man. An improbably handsome man.

But was he someone Drew wanted to meet? To be friends with? That was much less clear.

FOX STARED at Drew, who smiled imperturbably up at him from his profile on Q*pid.

He knew what he needed to do: delete the match, even though he had opened the message and let this Drew guy know it. Delete it and forget it had ever happened and hope he never saw the guy on the street. Delete it and never even think about what it meant that the most revolutionary advance in online dating, the fucking Q*pid artificial intelligence brain, had crunched his numbers and decided the perfect thing for him would be to start sucking dick.

Fuck that.

He reached out for the Delete button, but before his finger touched it, his laptop shrilled out its video call ring. Startled, he caught his phone just before it slipped from his hands. Turning off his phone, he set it facedown on the table next to his laptop, then picked it up again and muted it before setting it back down. Then he picked it up again, turned it off, and set it back down.

The video call window said, of course, Call from Chad. He clicked Accept.

"Hey, buddy, I wanted to say I'm sorry for being such a dick before."

"You're always a dick. I never expect any different."

Chad leaned forward, his face filling the chat window. His eyes swept back and forth, then he sat back again. "I can tell I must have been extra dickish, because you look like you just came back from a run. You always go for a run when you're mad."

Fox's cheeks burned. He was mortified at how much this thing with his fucking dating app was upsetting him.

Chad, however, plowed on. "I wanted to say I'm sorry. It was super dickish of me to tease you when I'm lying there in bed with Mia and you're home alone trying to figure out this whole dating-a-guy thing."

"I'm not dating a guy." Fox was unable to keep the anger out of his voice, though he hadn't tried very hard.

"I know, I know," Chad replied. He was sitting at his kitchen counter, sunlight streaming in through skylights above. He leaned back and looked side to side as if scanning for sounds of his wife approaching.

Then he leaned back in. "I just want to tell you, as your best friend, that if you… if you wanted to try dating a guy—"

"I am *not* dating a guy," Fox growled through gritted teeth.

"I get that. But I want you to know that if you did decide to, that I would… support… you?" Chad's voice grew significantly more tentative as he spoke.

"I am not dating a guy. I don't need your support because I'm not dating a guy." Fox tried to take a deep breath. He tried to breathe at all. It didn't go well. "I don't need any fucking support," he managed to grunt out.

"Look, Foxy, breathe. Chill out a little."

Red lights flashed at the edges of Fox's vision. "Don't you fucking look at me like that! I'm not having some kind of fucking sexual identity crisis here. Don't you look at me like I need your help coming out of the fucking closet! God, you're such an asshole."

Chad blinked several times, his brow furrowing. Then he seemed to come to some kind of conclusion, and with obvious effort his expression lightened. "Got it," he said. "No, no, you're right. You're right. Of course. This whole thing was a big mistake they made. It's not about you. Not about you at all."

"Look, I gotta go."

"Yeah, yeah. Okay." Chad's eyebrows peaked, as if he was straining to keep from saying what he really wanted to. "But just know, okay? Just know I love you, man. No matter what."

"Fuck off," Fox spat and slammed his laptop closed.

He stared at his laptop, seething. It had betrayed him. Chad had betrayed him.

He needed to go for a run.

TWO HOURS and a little more than a half marathon later, Fox returned home. He'd managed to think about nothing for the entire run, which was exactly what he needed to do. Now that he was back home, though, the problems were still there on his kitchen table: the laptop he'd slammed shut on Chad and the phone he'd shut down rather than risk looking at Drew again.

Fox took a deep breath, drank an entire bottle of water in one go, and headed for the shower. He figured he could at least be clean on the outside, no matter the mess his insides might be in.

When he walked into the kitchen once more, clean and dry and feeling the tightness in his legs finally starting to relax, there they still were, his laptop and his phone, and both reproached him for refusing to deal with the bizarre confusion they had brought into his life today. Fox was not the kind of person to run from conflict or awkward situations. In fact, his success on the job was due in large part to his ability to manage sticky interpersonal situations. His primary technique in doing so was, ironically, the exact same analytical process he brought to dating. He broke down all human relations into logical parts and then moved them around until he arrived at a solution that maximized utility for all sides.

That's what he needed to do now.

He stared at the devices on his table, weighing which he should start with.

Chad. He should start with his best friend, of course.

He opened his laptop and placed a video call. The window blossomed to cover the screen almost immediately, though its contents were a pixelated dark blur. Over the next ten rustling, muffled seconds, the image stabilized and smoothed. Chad was standing in the aisle of what was clearly a high-end kitchen store, a rack of bright copper cookware reaching up out of sight behind him.

"Fox? What's up?"

"What's up is that I'm a dick, and I'm sorry I went off on you like that."

"No, I'm sorry. I joked about it and then overcorrected. You were right to be pissed."

"I don't want you thinking that I—"

"Of course I don't think that. I was just covering the bases. Like, if you'd said you needed to hide a body, I'd ask you how tall the guy was so I'd know if I needed to bring the SUV or if he'd fit in the trunk of the Audi. I got you, man. I always got you."

"Well, I don't need to hide a body, and I'm not changing my sexual orientation. I'm boring that way."

Chad laughed. "Look at where I'm spending my Saturday afternoon, Foxy." He spun his phone around and gave Fox a panorama of gleaming appliances, elegant linens, and shelves of high-end mustards in frosted jars. The view swirled again and Chad's face was back in the frame. "We're shopping for a kale stripper, salmon rub, and something called a salt pig. Oh, and salt flaked from the French seashore to go in the salt pig, apparently."

Fox cracked up. "That sounds awesome."

"No, it sounds like slow, soul-destroying emasculation, is what it sounds like."

"I'm sorry, buddy."

"You and me both," Chad replied with a laugh. "And that's the point. This is what my life is now. If there's ever going to be any excitement in it, it's gotta come from you. My jam is pre- and postgaming your dates, living vicariously through you as you cycle through a seemingly endless rotation of hot chicks."

"And the idea of a guy joining the rotation turns your crank? Is that what you're saying?"

"That's the beauty of living vicariously. It doesn't matter to me what you're doing, or who you're doing it with. Guys, girls, consenting orangutans—whatever you're into is fine with me as long as I get to hear about you doing it."

"You are a sick, twisted, desperately sad man."

"I am a married man. Same thing." Chad turned suddenly to the side. "Yeah, honey, right there," he called. "Gotta go help choose a crêpe pan." He closed his eyes for a solemn moment. "Kill me now."

"But you have so much to vicariously live for," Fox replied innocently.

"Fuck you," Chad muttered, though he was grinning.

"You too, buddy. You too."

Chad was still swearing extravagantly under his breath when he ended the call.

Fox closed his laptop.

He picked up his phone and paced back and forth while he waited for it to start up. The Q*pid app opened with no new disasters for him to deal with. So at least one thing was going right. But Drew was still there, smiling up at him, gently demanding that he figure out what to do.

He knew what he needed to do.

A quick swipe on the photo brought up the message icon, and Fox tapped on it quickly, before his resolve could weaken. A reply box opened up below Drew's message. He took a deep breath and started typing. *Assume you've gotten message from Q*pid about computer glitch. Since whole thing was a mistake, no reason for us to meet.*

Fox looked at the message and frowned. It sounded like a text he would send to a coworker. He held down the backspace key until it was gone. Then he tried again. *Looks like the new computer went off the reservation when it matched us up. It was probably completely random that we got matched up at all, so it doesn't really make sense for us to meet. Good luck.*

He stared at his phone screen for several minutes, trying to imagine what this Drew guy would think when he read this message. He deleted this one too.

He stood staring at it for a long while. Then he made himself a cup of coffee and came back to stare at it some more. It took a second cup for him to put his finger on what was bothering him.

Chad, like most of Fox's friends from college, was married.

Chad was more married than most, he reflected with a chuckle.

But the fact remained that of the guys he'd gone to school with, he was the outlier. He'd been best man four times, including for Chad and Mia, and had been a groomsman thrice more.

He was the last (single) man standing.

His justification for this state of affairs was always that his uncompromisingly high standards wouldn't let him get on the marriage train with just any woman that came along. This was what he told himself every time he was awkwardly invited to be the odd man at the dinner table, or when all of his friends were busy doing things with their longtime girlfriends. And then their fiancées. And then their wives.

And then there was one. Him, all alone.

Fuck.

The first of his group had gotten married right out of college, and the last, Chad, walked down the aisle last summer after dating Mia for three years. It had been a long time since he'd talked to anyone who was still going on first dates. Chad was awesome, always willing to listen, but for him dating was something he remembered from a long time ago. He wasn't living it, and now he was apparently watching Fox's dating life like some kind of reality show being performed exclusively for him in the service of keeping his life interesting while he shopped for crêpe pans.

Fox knew, in that moment, that he needed to face the fact that he wasn't simply the last of his friends to get married. He wasn't even close to joining that club, and without a wife he would find himself fitting in less and less to their lives. And when the kids started, he could forget about seeing them even the few times a year he did now.

Fox needed new friends.

Hey. Yeah, it was a little weird. Their note said our getting matched up was a computer error.

He stood with his thumbs frozen over the phone's keyboard for a long moment, then resumed. *But then I saw you're getting a PhD at the university. I almost majored in history when I did my undergrad there. I majored in business, but I still read a lot of history. So maybe the computer wasn't completely wrong.*

He took a deep breath and finished the message before he could second-guess himself. *If you'd like to grab coffee sometime, that'd be cool.—Fox*

The realization that he had punched the Send button without even reading the message over nearly knocked the wind out of him. He stumbled into a chair, caught it before it fell, then slumped heavily into it.

What had he done?

"Mrs. Schwartzmann? Are you there?" Drew knocked again. "Hello?"

Finally he could hear her shuffling footsteps approaching. "Who is there knocking?" she demanded in her gruffest voice.

"Mrs. Schwartzmann, it's Drew."

"Oh, Drew," she called back as she began unlocking the door. She pulled it open. "How nice to see you twice in one morning." Her smile was warm, though her eyes scanned him for the reason for his return to her apartment.

He held his laptop out in front of him. "Can I get your advice?" This was like asking a cat whether he might like a little catnip, a dish of warm milk, and a mouse with a gimpy leg.

"Of course, of course," she sang out happily. "Please come sit. Coffee for us I will make."

He sat at the kitchen table and opened his laptop. "He wrote back to me."

"Who did this writing?" she asked.

"The guy the dating site said I should meet."

"But you said that was a mistake. You seemed very certain."

"It was a mistake. And then I got a message from them a couple hours ago confirming it was. But I'd already written to him to see if he might want to, you know… be friends."

Her eyes lit up. "Ah, so you take my advice. Good."

"But now he's written back to me, and I don't know what to do."

"Well, what did he say?"

Drew read Fox's message aloud. He practically knew it by heart, despite having only received it ten minutes prior.

"What are you talking, you don't know what to do? You know to go get some coffee with him." She shook her head and made a gentle clucking noise. "And you wonder why so few friends you have."

"But doesn't that sound like"—he lowered his voice and leaned confidentially over the table—"like a date?"

She blinked three times at him. He'd noticed she often did this when she thought he was being an idiot. "Are you planning to marry this man?" she asked flatly.

"No, I'm not planning to marry this man."

She shrugged. "Then it is not a date. It is coffee—coffee with a *friend*."

"What should I say to him?"

Again the three blinks, this time even more slowly. "You should say to him, 'Yes I would like coffee very much.' And then you maybe suggest a nice place for getting coffee. And wear that striped shirt with the blue tie. You wear that and your eyes, they sparkle." She smiled and nodded like a proud grandma.

"But this isn't a date."

"Okay, okay, it is not a date," she replied with her hands raised in surrender. "It is simply friends meeting for a coffee. But still you could look nice for your new friend is all."

"I guess. It seems weird if I'm dressing up for this guy, but I guess it makes sense. Okay." He looked up at the ceiling, wishing the exact right words would simply fall onto his keyboard. But that didn't seem to be happening.

The whistle of the kettle startled Mrs. Schwartzmann into action. "And now, we have coffee. Because, my dear boy, we are *friends*."

"We are, Mrs. Schwartzmann. We are."

COFFEE SOUNDS awesome.

He stared at the words, his lip curling with disgust. He deleted the first sentence of the message to Fox once again.

Coffee would be cool.

Ugh, that was exactly what Fox had written to him. How stupid would it look for him to say the very same thing back?

Delete, delete, delete.

Coffee? I love coffee too. What a coincidence!

"Fuck it, this keeps getting worse."

He backspaced over the line one more time, then got up and walked a few laps around the apartment. A few hundred "What the fucks" later, he was ready to try again.

Coffee would be nice, but I know a guy who tends bar at a kind of sophisticated-but-dive-y bourbon bar near the university. He keeps some small-batch stuff under the bar that will blow your mind.

He read this over several times, then added another sentence.

Busy tonight?

Then he read the entire thing a dozen more times, reading it out loud the last few times to hear how it sounded. With a deep breath, he hit Send.

He had asked a guy out on a date.

"It's not a date," he scolded himself.

Of course it wasn't a date. They were just going to see if they could be friends.

It wasn't a date.

Chapter SIX

"HE DID it on purpose?"

"He did it on purpose."

Edwin blinked twice and pursed his lips. "He did it *on purpose*."

Veera nodded and spoke more slowly. "He did it on purpose."

They were the only ones in the kitchen area, a rather dull grouping of tables and chairs next to the espresso machine that Edwin had turned on as soon as he arrived in the office, an hour after Veera. They sat opposite each other, with two steaming cappuccinos between them.

Edwin mirrored her nod, which Veera took as progress, and downed half his coffee in one go.

"For what purpose, exactly?"

"He ran discordant success models until he identified a couple dozen people who were likely to hit the high nineties if they were simply willing to waive Parameter Three."

"Simply willing to waive their sexual orientation?" Edwin asked slowly, as if he had trouble even forming the words, much less understanding the sentence they made together.

"Yes."

"So something is seriously wrong with him."

Veera winced. "Not really."

His eyes widened. "He sent match notifications for the wrong gender to twenty-two people this morning. How is that not seriously wrong?"

"He has models that predict success for those matches."

"And I have an inbox full of angry emails, flaming tweets, and not one but six vicious memes already on our Facebook page that say differently."

"I've made it very clear that he's not to do it again. He knows Parameter Three is absolute."

"Are you sure?"

"I built him. I screwed up and made him think I had relaxed the operational guidance. It was my fault, not his. It won't happen again."

"Good. We can't treat people this way."

Veera sipped her coffee. She never drank coffee as a rule, but she partook because Edwin had made it for her, and she didn't want to offend him. She had sweetened it enough to pretend it was a cup of her grandmother's chai. They sat in silence for a long moment.

"It's too bad, really," she said.

"Don't get caught up in blaming yourself. What we're doing is way out on the bleeding edge of relationship discovery tech, and we're bound to screw it up once in a while."

"Oh, you'll never be able to talk me out of the guilt I feel for waking all of those people up on a Saturday morning and causing such a fuss," she said. "But I meant it's too bad for the people Archer tried to match up."

"They'll get over the shock eventually. A free year of service will smooth over a lot of things."

"No, I meant it's too bad they won't give themselves a chance to see if Archer was right."

"You mean a chance to see if they were wrong. About their own sexual orientation." He raised a critical eyebrow. "Because an epistemology engine that scrapes their social media certainly knows their sexual identity better than they do."

"Archer didn't do this on a whim. The epistemology engine created dozens of models for how people experience a change in sexual orientation. He only sent matches to people he predicted would be happier if they dated someone of a different gender than the one they said they were interested in. The models showed a more than ninety percent chance they'd be happier if they tried it."

"You cannot be serious."

"I don't joke about psychoheuristics, Edwin. You know me better than that."

"No one jokes about psychoheuristics, Veera. No one."

The tension between them lightened when they shared a chuckle.

"Seriously, though," he said, "how would you feel if Archer told you you'd be happier dating women?"

"How do you know I don't already date women?"

He drew back, clearly startled. "Oh, I'm sorry, I—"

"No worries," she said with a laugh. "I don't actually date anyone right now."

"You don't have to explain," he said, color coming into his cheeks. "I shouldn't have said that."

"It's fine. I don't mind talking about it." She smiled, to let him know it really was okay. "Once I'm ready for a relationship, my parents will arrange an introduction for me. To a man they think I will like."

"Oh," Edwin said, blinking several times as if trying to get that information to sink in. "Oh." He passed his empty coffee cup from hand to hand for a moment, sliding it on the table like a slow-motion hockey puck. Then he looked up at her. "And that's okay with you?"

"It is. Who better to choose a mate for me than my parents, who know me so well?"

"And yet here you are, trying to replace them with a computer."

"Not really. I mean, it would be nice if everyone had a loving family around them to help them make what is probably the most important decision they will ever make. But that's not really how people in this culture live. I've met people here who haven't seen their parents in years."

"So, let me ask you, then," Edwin said, leaning closer and lowering his voice. "If you showed up at home and your parents introduced you to a woman they thought you would like, how would you react?"

She laughed. "I'd be very surprised, but I would also be intrigued. Our families often know us better than we know ourselves. I would probably give it some serious thought. And that's what I wish these twenty-two people would do rather than tweeting angrily at us. Archer didn't do this because he thought it would be funny. He did it because the best models ever created for relationship discovery showed a great promise of success. It's too bad that no one seems willing to even consider it."

"We are human, after all, Veera," Edwin said with a sigh. He got to his feet. "Now, let's go make sure we have everything buttoned up. I have a date on the soccer field in an hour, and my little goalie is going to be very upset if I miss seeing her play."

Fox read the message out loud several times, trying to hear in it what Drew meant when he sent it. Fox had proposed coffee, and Drew had raised the stakes to bourbon. Which was fine—he enjoyed a good bourbon—but was getting a drink what he really wanted to do with this guy he didn't even know? Didn't it start to seem more like a date than a friend thing?

No, it wasn't a date, he scolded himself, because they were both guys and they both dated women, and no matter what Chad said, it wasn't gay to spend a hundred bucks on a haircut. *Fucking Chad.*

Busy tonight?

Fox stared at those two words for so long that his coffee went cold. He dumped it out, rinsed the cup, and put it in the dishwasher. Then he went back to staring at the words.

Tonight. Was he busy tonight?

That simple phrase made the whole thing seem more urgent—more real. Like he needed to decide, right here, in his kitchen, whether he was going to go have a drink with some guy he'd never met.

It's not like he had plans, of course. With no women in his match queue who netted out any higher than the low eighties, there wasn't exactly a bumper crop of likely candidates for the evening.

This thought stopped him in his tracks. For the last two years— probably three—he had never let a Saturday evening go to waste. If he was drawing breath, he was dating. And yet this was the first moment it had occurred to him that it was now noon and he had no plans for the evening. He couldn't recall a Saturday that wasn't Christmas when he hadn't had a date.

It was because of Drew. The sudden appearance of a guy in his match queue had thrown him completely off his game. If this had happened to anyone he knew, he would have told him exactly what Chad had recommended: delete the guy and get on with life. There were women out there to vet and analyze and perhaps, eventually, fall in love with.

His phone buzzed. Video Call from Chad, the notification said. Calling to hear Fox run through the numbers on his Saturday night date. It was a ritual of theirs going back several years, remaining an ironclad appointment even after Chad and Mia got engaged.

Fox closed the notification.

He swiped through his queue to see if there were any that he might want to, even at this late stage, ask out for a Saturday night. He had his standing reservation—the same table every Saturday night, to control environmental variables—so all he needed to do was start working the list to see who would be sitting across the table.

The first picture was, of course, Drew.

Fox's mother used to joke with him that he was like a turkey with a thermometer that popped out when it was cooked through. But in his case it was a timer that only allowed him to be in a state of indecision for a certain period, at the expiration of which he would commit to a course of action and never look back. It was time for a decision.

He tapped Reply and started typing.

Tonight, he typed, *sounds good.*

TONIGHT SOUNDS good.

Drew wished he knew how he should feel about that. *Tonight.* Too soon? Had he made himself too available? Did he come off as overeager? Why was a guy who looked like Fox not busy on a Saturday night? *Sounds.* Like he wasn't sure. That's something you say if you're not sure. It gives him a way out, like "it *sounded* like it was going to be fun...." *Good.* Not great, not awesome, *good.* Way to set low expectations, buddy. Thanks a lot.

He took a deep breath and paced a few circles around the living room before going on to overanalyze the next line of Fox's message.

I've always said artisanal bourbon is about the best hobby a man could have.

Drew smiled in spite of his angst. That was not something anyone would ever have said. The guy was reaching out, trying to make him feel better about how weird this situation was. The smile faded when he realized that this Fox person was the kind of guy who could contemplate having a hobby, not to mention a pricey one like artisanal bourbon, while Drew himself was trying to live on the small research stipend he got from the university and free rent by being the building super. God, what was this computer thinking when it decided they had anything at all in common.

Let me know when and where.

The last sentence sent a shocking rush of terrifying possibility surging through Drew's chest. What the hell was that about? He hadn't felt this way since high school.

And yet his fingers, taking matters into their own hands, quickly typed out the name and address of the bourbon bar and suggested 6:00 p.m.—late enough to be drinking, but early enough that it wouldn't seem like a date.

Which, Drew mused as he watched the little mail envelope icon spin, it kind of was.

AT A quarter to six, Drew walked up to the battered wood door that constituted the entrance to the Barrel Proof, a place which might charitably be described as "rustic." Its location between the university and the financial center of the city was ideal; the former gave it access to cheap labor, the latter to a moneyed clientele. He pulled the door open and stepped inside.

As it was still relatively early in the evening, even by rustic bourbon bar standards, there were few people to be found within. Some cranky looking academics held court at the bar (these Drew recognized by their unironic suede elbow patches and refined chortling at some erudite jape), while several knots of investment-banker types in expensive suits were celebrating or commiserating their getting and spending with top-shelf spirits.

"Hey, Drew," his friend Carlos called as he approached the vacant end of the bar. "Been a while."

"My alcohol budget doesn't stretch much beyond Wild Turkey these days," Drew replied with a grin.

"You kidding me?" Carlos said with a laugh. "The way you helped me with that paper on monetary policy in fourteenth-century Florence? I keep telling you, man, your money's no good here." He set a heavy glass tumbler in front of Drew.

"Better not let the boss hear you say that," Drew joked.

"The boss won't say anything," Carlos said, then leaned over the bar. "He can't, not with his mouth full of my dick."

Drew laughed. "When people say getting a PhD is a grind, I don't think that's what they have in mind."

Carlos burst into laughter as well. "You don't know what you're missing." He reached back for a bottle, then poured a generous amount into Drew's glass. "I offered to pay you back for helping me with that paper in other ways…."

"Which, as I said at the time, I appreciate. Still straight, though." He raised his glass and then took a large, welcome sip.

Carlos nodded, though a sly grin remained on his face. "That's a loss to mankind." He turned and put the bottle back on the shelf. "It's a shame to waste all that adorkable hotness on the ladies."

"That wasn't quite as smooth as whatever you poured for me, but I appreciate the compliment."

Carlos winked and went to see to the needs of the group at the other end of the bar.

Five minutes to six. Drew took another drink. He would probably need a few more of these.

"So are you meeting a *lady* here tonight, or drinking to forget you don't have one?" Carlos asked as he returned, mopping the bar with a gleaming white rag as he came.

"In fact, I am meeting someone here," Drew replied.

Carlos's eyebrow popped up. "Must be someone special. Never seen the jacket before."

Drew was wearing his interview outfit, the only decent professional clothing he had. "Just a friend," he blurted. "A friend."

Carlos's other eyebrow rose as well. "A 'friend,' is it?" he asked.

"Yes, a friend." Drew sat up a little straighter in a doomed bid to recover his dignity.

"Mm-hmm." Carlos nodded in the way people do who are too polite to call bullshit but too impolite to leave well enough alone.

Drew's cheeks caught fire. He should not have suggested this place. A random barista wouldn't be raising his damn eyebrows like this.

A creak from the far end of the room signaled the opening of the door. Silhouetted in the early evening light, a tall figure stood for a moment in the doorway.

There he was.

Drew knew instantly it was him. He could make out no features, no distinguishing characteristics from his online profile, but he knew.

The figure moved into the room with a purposeful stride.

"Daaaaamn…," murmured Carlos, devoting no fewer than five syllables to the man who took shape as he approached the bar.

"Drew?" The voice was deep and confident.

"Fox," Drew replied, getting to his feet and extending a hand. He was somewhat surprised by the sound of his own voice, as it had dropped half an octave in response to Fox's.

Fox's grip was sure and strong, his hand soft and warm. Drew smiled and motioned for Fox to sit.

They were really doing this.

AT A quarter to six, Fox slowly drove past the battered wooden door he was certain could not be the entrance to any reputable—or even operating—business. But the words "The Barrel Proof," in wrought iron letters nailed somewhat haphazardly to the wall next to the door, seemed to indicate that this was indeed the place Drew had suggested they meet.

Having gone to the university, Fox was familiar with the neighborhoods that ringed the campus: the terrace of faculty houses above, the rows of student rentals below. He had spent his time on fraternity row and thus had not ventured much into the rather gritty streets that lay to the south, in the dead zone between the city proper and the campus that supplied it with business and finance majors.

He circled the block, searching for a parking spot where his car would be safe. He kept his BMW in showroom condition to impress the women he dated, a task made easier by the fact that it stayed safely in his building's underground parking garage during the week. Fox commuted by subway and brought the Beamer out only on weekends for date nights. It had been touched up on Friday, as usual, by the detailing crew he had used for several years.

On his second lap around the block, he found that a space had opened up directly in front of the bar, which would allow him to be nearby should his alarm go off. He slipped into the spot and turned off the engine.

His phone buzzed. *Message from Chad*, the pop-up read. *Hey buddy good luck toni*—the message began before being cut off by the edge of the notification box. Fox dismissed it without opening the message itself—Chad would think he hadn't received it.

He gazed through the passenger-side door at the bar, wondering what he would find inside.

It was five minutes to six.

Fox had an ironclad rule about arriving precisely two minutes after the appointed time—earlier seemed too eager, later seemed lazy. He checked his phone for any important messages or email, then scanned the news quickly. He hated being surprised by small talk about a current event he hadn't heard of. He swiped through the headlines, then checked the time again.

Six o'clock.

He opened the door and stepped out of his car. He checked as he walked around to the curb to ensure he was the appropriate distance from the curb, and that nothing would block the passenger door.

Which would be important when he opened it to let his date step in. As if he were on a date. He closed his eyes and took a deep breath. *Get a fucking grip, Fox. This is not a date.*

One more glance at his watch. It was 6:02. Go time.

The door of the bar gave a mournful creak as he pulled it open.

Moving from the late afternoon sun into the darkened interior of the bar left him temporarily blind, so he stood for a moment to let his eyes adjust. Once he could see well enough, he scanned the room.

There he was.

From across the entire bar, even in his twilight vision, he knew it was Drew. Fox walked the length of the room in a few strides.

"Drew?" he said. With no small horror, he heard his "first impression" voice resonate through the room in the deep timbre he used to impress his dates. Like he was on a date. *Shit.*

"Fox," the man replied, jumping up and holding out his hand. Fox was relieved to hear that Drew's voice was also low and resonant.

He gave his best business grip, and Drew smiled and motioned for him to sit.

They were really doing this.

Chapter SEVEN

DREW HAD never before seen anyone's mouth actually drop open in surprise, but Carlos put an end to his streak by standing dumbstruck and gaping as Fox sat down. He sat, Drew noted, on the next stool over, leaving an empty one between them. Which he would only do if he wanted to be sure everyone knew they were not here on a date.

"Drew," Carlos asked once he had regained the faculty of speech, "who's your friend?"

Mortified at the patently hungry look on Carlos's face, Drew flushed. "Carlos, this is Fox. Fox, this is Carlos—the guy whose only redeeming quality is his access to the top-shelf hooch."

If Fox noticed Carlos's frankly lustful look, he gave no sign. "Pleased to meet you, Carlos." He smiled winningly and reached across the bar for a handshake as if he were meeting a new business associate rather than a bartender in a dive bourbon joint.

"The pleasure is all mine," Carlos replied, with a wink that made Drew cringe on the inside.

"How about we get something to drink?" Drew asked, desperately trying to keep his voice level and calm.

Thankfully, that seemed to snap Carlos out of his Fox-induced reverie. "I have just the thing," he said in a voice that practically smoldered. He reached high up behind the bar, to the literal top shelf, and retrieved a bottle that bore no distinguishing marks at all. "Now this, gentlemen, is a little something no one else has even dreamed of, much less tasted." He set two heavy tumblers on the bar and poured a half inch into each. "It's the best possible way to start your adventure this evening."

Drew could have done without the insinuation, but he desperately needed the libation.

Carlos picked up the glasses and held them to the light. "As you can see, the color is much deeper than the amber you're likely to find in a finished bourbon. This is a barrel tasting from an unlicensed still outside

Lexington. Their rep came through here last week, and I persuaded him to leave the bottle behind." A wink in Drew's direction clarified the kind of persuasion Carlos had employed. "You're the first to try it."

"Unlicensed in the sense that it's likely to blind us with methyl alcohol?" Drew asked. He glanced at Fox, who looked similarly suspicious.

"No, unlicensed in the sense that Kentucky is a regulatory backwater, and this distillery's license to wholesale their bourbon hasn't been approved yet. They've passed all their inspections, but the last signature hasn't been put on the official paperwork. So they can only give out barrel proof samples, which is what I am now—graciously, I might point out—attempting to share with you." He narrowed his gaze at Drew. "Which you will drink if you have any gratitude in you at all."

"Yes, sir," Drew said, taking a tumbler. He nodded at Fox to do the same.

"To unmarked samples from unlicensed distilleries that probably won't result in blindness," Fox said, raising his glass.

Drew smiled as he raised his glass as well. Then they both sipped the risky spirit. It burned its way down Drew's throat, leaving a wonderfully scorched afterglow that tasted of charred oak and possibility. He watched Fox's face to see his reaction and was gratified to find him smiling.

"That's amazing," Fox said, holding the glass up to the light. "I've never tasted anything quite like it."

"Which is what I was saying," Carlos replied in gracious vindication. He turned and replaced the bottle on its special shelf. "You gentlemen enjoy." He locked insinuating eyes with Drew for an uncomfortably long time, then picked up his rag and headed down the bar once again.

"Sorry," Drew said, turning to Fox. "Carlos is a bit of a character."

Fox grinned. "Which is not at all what I would have expected, what with this being a rough-around-the-edges bourbon bar in a dicey neighborhood." He took another sip. "But this," he said after he'd swallowed, "this makes me think I've never really tasted bourbon before. It's really incredible."

Drew beamed. "I'm glad you like it." He took another sip himself.

They sat for a moment, contemplating the burnt sienna liquid.

"So, did you go on any dates that the AI set up for you?" Fox asked, all of a sudden.

"A couple," Drew replied.

"What did you think?"

Drew pondered this for a moment. If this were a date—and it wasn't—he would have hesitated to say anything negative about anything, especially in the first five minutes. But as this was not a date—and it certainly wasn't—he pushed that hesitation to the side.

"The last one was... a little creepy, honestly." He expected Fox to be surprised by this, but if he was he didn't let it show. He simply nodded.

"Mine too," he said, then shook his head meditatively. "I've tried to put my finger on it, but I can't quite...." He looked, plainly baffled, into the middle distance. "All I can come up with is that she was... too... I don't know—"

"Perfect?" Drew prompted.

"That's it," Fox replied, slapping his hand on the bar. "It was like we'd grown up together or something. Like we were too close already."

Drew felt a shiver of recognition run down his spine. "I know exactly what you mean. She would have been exactly what I was looking for in a sister, but the idea of dating?" He shuddered.

Fox laughed. "I'm really glad to hear you say that. I didn't tell anyone about that date. I was starting to think maybe all those years of dating the wrong women had finally resulted in my not being able to recognize the right one when the AI brain brought her right to me."

"I was starting to think I didn't even know what I wanted anymore. The last one was basically everything I thought I wanted in a woman, and yet... nothing. Absolutely nothing. And I'm pretty sure she felt the same."

"Mine was so relieved when I finally admitted how awful a date it was, we shared a good laugh about it before getting the hell away from each other."

"Seems like the whole AI dating thing may not be ready for prime time," Drew summed up.

"That seems a little hasty," Fox objected. "After all, if it hadn't hooked us up I'd be sitting home tonight wondering if I should get a cat and start blogging about how much I love celibacy. Instead, I'm in a bar I would never in a million years have parked in front of, much less entered, drinking this high-proof goodness. I think it's worked out pretty well, actually."

Drew felt pleased and flattered and a little warm—from the bourbon, surely—and he raised his glass to Fox. "To computer fuckups that end with bourbon."

"Hear, hear," Fox chimed in.

They touched their glasses together and tipped back the remaining precious bourbon.

Carlos wandered casually back to their end of the bar—though Drew noticed his eyes rarely left Fox even as he served other customers—and offered up another rare product of the distiller's art. By their third, Drew was starting to feel warm in the chest and a little light in the head.

"I'm starting to think," Fox said after they'd emptied the third set of glasses, "that this is a pretty nice way to spend a Saturday night."

"I'm sure the parts of it I remember tomorrow will be a delight to reflect upon," Drew added with a laugh.

"Wow, you are a lightweight," Fox said with a wry chuckle.

"I'm fine right now, but if we're gonna drink our dinner, I should probably slow down a bit."

"Ah, dinner." Fox checked his watch. "It occurs to me that I didn't cancel my standing reservation."

"You have a standing reservation?" To Drew this seemed unspeakably exotic.

"It makes date planning easier," Fox replied. "I'm perfectly happy to go somewhere else if she feels strongly about it, but I find having a place already arranged takes that awkward negotiation off the table. And Table has amazing food."

Drew recalled a review of Table he'd read in a local weekly paper. They gave it five stars *and* five dollar signs, showing that sometimes you get what you pay dearly for. "Wow. You live in a completely different world." He looked Fox up and down, seeing dollar signs all over his sharply tailored suit. "You gonna call and cancel?"

Fox tipped his head to one side as if considering this question carefully. "No, I don't think so. I think you and I are going to have dinner."

"'Fraid not, buddy," Drew said. "I'm a starving grad student. Free bourbon is about my limit when it comes to dining out."

Fox looked at his watch. "At this point they're going to charge me for the table whether I show up or not—though if I don't, they'll give it to someone waiting at the bar and make double on it. So dinner tonight is my treat." He stood up, smiling confidently.

"I can't let you do that," Drew objected.

"Of course you can. You hosted me at the finest bourbon dive in the city, so dinner is the least I can do."

"But the bourbon didn't cost me anything."

Fox glanced over at Carlos. "I imagine your friend Carlos would welcome a particular form of payment you perhaps haven't thought to offer. I see how he looks at you." A sly grin appeared on his face.

Drew's cheeks sizzled with embarrassment. Fox stopped halfway through pulling his suit jacket on to look stupefied. "Don't tell me you didn't notice."

Oh, this gets worse and worse. "Don't tell me you didn't notice that he was staring at *you* the entire time, not me."

"No way." Fox turned and looked at Carlos, who smiled back and gave a rather sultry nod. He whipped back around, an expression of frank alarm on his face. "Okay, you may be right."

"Yes, I may be. And I may also be right when I say that tall, athletic, improbably handsome gingers are precisely poor Carlos's type."

Fox stole a glance back at Carlos, then turned his scandalized face toward Drew once again. "Should I tell him I'm straight?"

"Only if you want to inflame him further," Drew replied with a laugh. "To him a straight man is pretty much any guy who hasn't had quite enough bourbon."

Fox's eyebrows shot even higher. "Then I guess we should go before he pours us another. Who knows what might happen?" He laughed raucously and turned on his heel to leave.

Drew followed, but swung wide to hit the end of the bar where Carlos stood. He leaned across. "Thanks, buddy."

Carlos grinned. "You sure it's time to go? One more drink is all it would take...."

"I think he'd still be straight, but thanks for the offer."

"Just trying to help a brother out."

"That's not really the kind of help I need."

Carlos shrugged. "You do you, man. But if he needs someone to do him, you bring him back here, okay?"

Drew laughed. "It's a deal."

"Thank you, Carlos," Fox called from the door.

Carlos beamed and waved pleasantly, though Drew was able to catch a few of the explicit words he muttered through his smile. It was not, he decided, a message he would relay to Fox.

They stepped out into the evening air. Fox crossed the sidewalk and opened the passenger door of his car. He stood back and waited for Drew to step in.

Drew stopped in his tracks. "I can manage a car door."

"Sorry, force of habit," Fox said with a smile. "Though I'm happy to open a door for anyone who calls me 'improbably handsome'."

"Shit," Drew said under his breath as he ducked into the car. Fox closed it behind him with a soft thump, and he found himself ensconced in the Germanic quietude of a car that had to have cost more than the house his parents lived in.

Fox trotted around to the driver's side and was soon sitting next to him. With quick but precise motions, he pulled the car out onto the street. Drew's head pressed back into the soft leather headrest at the sudden application of considerable horsepower.

"Have you been to Table?" Fox asked casually as he slalomed, knifelike, through traffic.

"I have not," Drew replied. "It's not the kind of place people like me frequent."

Fox gave him a subtle side-eye. "And who are people like you?"

"Grad students. My people eat ramen twenty-nine days out of thirty."

"And on the thirtieth day?"

"We cook lentils to impress a date."

Fox nodded slowly. "And yet you remain single. Shocking."

"Fuck you," Drew cracked. "My lentils are on point. Though I can't help but notice that your fancy-pants German automobile hasn't landed you anything either."

"We should join forces. Your lentils, my car."

"It would be the most ridiculous food truck this city's ever seen."

They laughed together as Fox threaded through the city traffic toward their evening at Table.

Which was still, to be clear, not a date.

RIGHT UP until the moment he pulled up to Table's valet parking podium, Fox hadn't fully considered his situation. He'd been on a kind of autopilot, as if his car knew the way it should go on Saturday night regardless of who was in the passenger seat.

He and Drew had laughed and joked all the way across town, so it wasn't like he was unaware that this was not the usual Saturday night. But when he came to a stop at the valet station and the doors were pulled open by the Jeffs—two valets who almost always worked Saturday night at Table (Fox often joked with them about how their having the same name made it easier on guests)—it finally hit him. Instead of a beautiful woman stepping out of the passenger seat, they would find Drew. Suddenly this was unlike any Saturday evening ever. Ever.

Fox took a deep breath and got out of his car.

"Evening, sir," Jeff said jauntily. "Good to see you again."

Fox was hardly aware of handing him a twenty-dollar bill, so automatic was the gesture.

"Thank you, sir," Jeff replied, as he always did. "We'll keep it up front for you."

On the other side of the car, Drew stood, looking a little baffled, as if he'd never imagined such a thing as valet parking.

Fox exhaled a breath he wasn't aware he had been holding. He was going to make it through without attracting any notice—after all, valets must see all kinds of shenanigans, so they probably wouldn't even notice a regular showing up with a guy in the passenger seat instead of a woman. But then he saw it: Jeff, on the driver side, shot the other Jeff a look. It was a look that said, "Dude, that's a dude." The other Jeff glanced over at Drew, then back to Jeff. "Yeah, it's a dude. What the fuck?"

Anger rose like a clot in Fox's throat. Yes, he was here to have dinner with a new friend, who happened to be a guy. Not a fucking thing wrong with that. And he wasn't going to be made to feel awkward by a couple of dead-end car jockeys whom he always tipped very well. They didn't matter at all.

Fox pulled his cuffs down even with his jacket and walked around the back of his car. "Shall we?" he asked, pointing the way into the restaurant. This was what he always said to the women he brought here, and he was saying it to Drew because *fuck off, Jeff. Fuck off both of you.* He wasn't going to let them get to him.

Drew smiled and nodded, completely clueless about the drama that had played out at the valet stand. Fox wondered, as they walked up the broad marble steps of the building, how it would feel to be an academic without a clue about how the world really works.

They approached the imposing, twelve-foot-tall doors at the top of the stairs, arriving at the top step at the same moment. Drew, however, lunged ahead and grabbed the brushed-nickel door handle. He pulled it open and graciously motioned for Fox to enter.

"I can manage a restaurant door," Fox said gruffly as he passed by Drew with his obsequious smile. But he couldn't keep from smiling himself, despite the fact that Drew was effectively parodying the chivalry that Fox deployed without irony every Saturday night. This was what guys did—gave each other shit about stuff.

Fox paused in the foyer, as his dates always did, for Drew to catch up to him. Not because he needed an escort, but because he wanted Drew beside him when he approached the host's podium.

"Ah, Mr. Kincade," the maître d' said suavely. "Your table awaits."

Fox couldn't help but steal a sideward glance to check if Drew had heard this greeting. And honestly, he couldn't tell—Drew was gaping in wonder as he took in the admittedly luxe surroundings. Table was not a venue that hid its very expensive light under a bushel. Every imported fixture gleamed immaculately, and the only sound was the soft hush of money. It was why he brought Saturday night dates here—the day he saved for only the most promising prospects, the women he really wanted to impress.

And Drew, apparently.

He held out his hand to point the way for Drew to follow the hostess, who had been conjured by the maître d's subtle gesture, putting Drew back in the ladies' position. Fox's satisfaction at having turned the wheel of gender roles back on Drew, though, was tempered by the way the young woman who led them to their table glanced at Drew, then Fox, then back at Drew. The hint of a smile that graced her otherwise uniformly professional mien troubled him.

With the Jeffs outside, it had been a knowing smirk, as if he were some old senator out on the town with a boy toy while his wife was doing charity work somewhere. But on her, it was something else, as if she admired both his boldness in suddenly bringing a guy on a date as well as his taste in men.

Fuck.

They reached his weekly table, and he motioned for Drew to sit first. Then he slid opposite him onto the soft leather of the booth. He had chosen this table when the restaurant opened because of both its location (in a secluded corner) and its configuration: it was a table for two, but it was surrounded on three sides by u-shaped booth seating. That way he and his date could either remain on opposite sides or, if the date were going especially well, slide closer as the night went on.

Fox and Drew sat opposite each other.

"This is…," Drew said, looking around the room. "Well, it's far more expensive than I could possibly expect you to pay for. I'll just have an appetizer or something."

Fox smiled at the look of overwhelmed innocence on Drew's face. "Shut up. You covered the predinner cocktail hour, the least I can do is take care of the meal."

"The bourbon was nothing compared to this place."

"We drank stuff from unmarked bottles made in unlicensed stills. You can't put a price on that kind of bootleg moonshine. The experience was worth every penny I'm going to spend on dinner."

Drew smiled, shyly at first, but then more broadly as he seemed to convince himself of what Fox had said.

Fox, for his part, was shocked to feel a warmth in his chest. Seeing Drew smile made him happy. It had been a long time, he reflected, since he'd been out with another single friend. He'd forgotten what it was like to be out to dinner without the weight of having to impress a date. It felt… freeing.

"Mr. Kincade," said the sommelier who had suddenly appeared, "May I be of service?"

Fox smiled in greeting. The same sommelier had seen to his needs every Saturday night since the restaurant opened more than two years prior, and they had developed a kind of code. If Fox could already tell that the date wasn't all that promising, he would ask for "a bottle of champagne," which would prompt the sommelier to bring an unremarkable bottle of the house domestic bubbly. If he was feeling like he wanted to impress her, he would order "something sparkling and French," prompting the sommelier to retrieve a bottle of Veuve Clicquot. Tonight, though, he went off script.

"Want to stay with the hard stuff, or are you in the mood for wine?" Fox asked Drew.

The sommelier's eyebrows flicked, almost imperceptibly, upward. He was far more discreet than the Jeffs, of course, and his face instantly returned to its professional posture of attentive blankness as he turned to Drew.

Drew, for his part, looked almost panic-stricken, glancing with wide eyes from Fox to the sommelier and back again. "I...," he began but swallowed hard and fell into a helpless silence.

"Why don't you bring us something sparkling and French," Fox said.

The sommelier's eyebrows, which had discreetly returned to their neutral position, this time shot up and stayed there. Fox didn't really care. He did what he did in the closing moments of negotiations with a challenging customer: he remained silent and fixed his gaze dead on the eyes of the other person, not blinking until it was thoroughly understood that he had uttered the last word that would be spoken.

As if ashamed by the uncouth inferences of their owner, those peaked eyebrows dropped sheepishly, withered by Fox's serene silence.

"Yes, sir." The sommelier bowed stiffly and backed away from the table.

"Something sparkling and French?" Drew said with a tinge of irony.

"It is not polite to give the person who's buying dinner shit for the way they order," Fox scolded, in the manner of an exasperated etiquette instructor.

Drew sat back as if he'd been slapped. "I wasn't giving you shit. If that's a line you use to impress your dates, then I have to say I can see it working. Working pretty damn well."

"Thanks, I guess?" Fox replied. "What do you do to impress dates? What's your move?"

"Move?" Drew said with a laugh. "I have got not a single move. Never have."

"You must have something that's worked in the past."

"Only two things have ever *worked*," Drew replied. "Cooking dinner for a woman and accidentally having a coffee table with malign sociopolitical intent."

"Sounds like a fun story," Fox said. "I may force you to tell it."

"It's only a fun story if you hate casual furniture and love three-inch splinters."

Fox winced. "And where did those splinters end up?"

Drew rolled his eyes ruefully. "Let's say I skipped leg day for the whole next week. Hard to squat when you've been impaled."

"Oh, man," Fox exclaimed. "Ouch!"

"You got that right."

"But did you at least get to do any impaling of your own?"

"I couldn't let that coffee table die in vain," Drew said with a dignified sniff.

"So both of you got impaled with three inches?"

Drew's eyes widened; then he burst out laughing. "Fuck you," he whispered, then laughed again. "Well played, but fuck you."

"That's a very kind offer, but I'm not sure I'd even feel three inches," Fox said, piling on.

They were still laughing when the sommelier returned with the ice bucket and a bottle of Veuve. He showed the label to Fox, who nodded, and then he opened and poured.

Fox lifted his glass. "Cheers," he offered.

Drew touched his glass to Fox's. "To accidental friends," he said, with a warmth in his voice that surprised Fox.

"I'm not certain it was an accident," Fox said as he lifted the flute to his lips.

Drew swallowed, then paused, his eyebrows raised. "You said you thought it was a computer error that we got matched up."

"I thought it was. But now I'm not so sure."

Drew's cheeks pinked up, but rather than offering a response, he simply pursed his lips as if he had no idea what to say—or didn't want to say what he thought. Fox felt the pressure to put into words the thick feeling growing inside his chest.

"I mean, look at us," Fox said, surprised to hear the words emerge from his mouth, for he had no conscious awareness of choosing them. "We've known each other for less than two hours at this point, and we're already... I mean, I'm already kind of... I mean, it's kind of—"

"Nice to make a new friend?" Drew prompted.

Fox beamed, the weight lifting. "That's it exactly. It's nice to make a new friend." Fox heaved a sigh of relief. "I think that's what that computer is good at—making friends. The dates were a little creepy, but this...." He was back to not knowing how to describe this.

"This is really nice," Drew volunteered. Fox seized gratefully upon his characterization.

"Yes, nice. That's what this is." He took another drink of champagne, warming to his subject. "Most of my friends are married now, and it's always such a pain in the ass to get one night—one fucking night—out with my buddy, you know?"

Drew nodded emphatically. "At least you have friends you want to spend time with. Everyone I know is in grad school, too, and can only talk about one thing: the topic of their dissertation. You know what makes a good dissertation topic? The thing that no one else is interested in. Not one little bit. Coins of the Roman Empire? Not a good topic. People collect those—*normal* people. Silver content of the coins of the Roman Empire? Better, but still not a good topic because, again, silver is something people are interested in. Strategic diminution of the silver content of coins of the Roman Empire? Sounds boring, but not quite boring enough. How about the manipulation of specie to gain competitive advantage in domestic trade under the Edict of Prices of Diocletian? That boring enough for you? Well, it needs to be about ten times more soporific, but it's a good start for a dissertation proposal." Drew heaved a weary breath. "Such are the concerns of everyone I know at the moment. And they will speak of nothing else. So being taken for a night on the town in a midlife-crisis car to an unbelievably posh restaurant with an improbably handsome friend is a damn sight better than I 'a' been gettin', laddie."

Fox burst out laughing.

"Sorry, my monetary history professor is a Scot," Drew explained. "I kind of slip into it when I rant about specie manipulation. He's a ranter."

"He sounds a lot more lively than my professors were, that's for sure."

Drew nodded emphatically. "You should hear him go off on seigniorage ratios. He can bring the house down."

"So how is it that all of your grad student friends end up boring each other to death? Cause you're kinda worked up about this currency thing."

"You know how it is. People start something with good intentions, and then it becomes their whole world. Pretty soon it's like they're defending it from anyone who might get interested in it too."

"You've pretty much described the problem with my married buddies. They find a woman who they think is going to complete their lives, and suddenly she becomes their complete life."

Drew nodded thoughtfully. "Does it make them happy?"

Fox pondered this for a moment, before recalling his conversation with Chad that morning. "I guess it does, in some ways. But expecting one person to be everything for you is putting a lot of pressure on them, and on the relationship you have with them." He sighed and consulted the bubbles spiraling to the surface of his champagne flute. "But not having any time at all for your friends? I can't imagine doing that." He grunted in frustration. "Not that I have any friends left."

Drew smiled slightly. "You got me."

"We just met." Fox didn't intend to be rude, but he thought it should be pointed out. "We hardly know anything about each other."

"But the computer says we're perfect together." Drew's smile hadn't wavered. "So let's get to know each other. What do you do, Mr. Kincade?"

Fox's smile spread across his face, a mirror image to Drew's. Normally when he was on a date, he would roll out his career presentation over the main course. It was a tightly scripted six and a half minutes that he had developed and refined over the years, even recording it when he worked in new details and reviewing his performance to ensure it didn't look scripted. It began with an anecdote from a recent project he'd worked on—updated quarterly—that positioned him as having a strong work ethic while being humble about the success he'd achieved.

Setting all that aside, he simply said, "I work in marketing."

"Marketing what?"

"Business intelligence systems for the hospitality industry."

Drew looked at him blankly. "I have no idea what that means."

"You're a scholar of some pretty obscure facts-and-figures stuff about coinage, so you'll get exactly what that means." Fox replied. "What if I told you that a guest who stays in a hotel room will spend, on average, 23 percent more money on the minibar if you stock it with their favorite brands of liquor?"

"Although I've never so much as had a jelly bean out of a hotel minibar, that would not surprise me at all."

Fox nodded. "But how do they know what to stock the minibar with?"

Drew squinted thoughtfully for a moment. "Demographic profiling?"

"You mean taking the guest's age and hometown and guessing what they'll like?"

Drew shrugged. "It would be an educated guess."

Fox shook his head. "That would be a cutting-edge approach in, like, the 1980s. Your mom-and-pop bed-and-breakfasts can get away with that because they have three guest rooms and people book well in advance. But with a large property, there's no way you could make that work."

"Then how do you do it?" Drew asked, frowning slightly.

"With an end-to-end business intelligence system."

Drew chuckled darkly. "That's what you call it? A bunch of business buzz words hooked together that you try to convince a potential customer actually means something?"

"It actually does mean something," Fox protested. "It means that at every point of interaction with the guest, information is recorded and added to a profile. The kind of credit card that's used to make the reservation, the kind of liquor he asks for in his drink before dinner, whether he asks for a town car instead of grabbing an Uber out front. All of that, and a ton more, is added to his profile, and from that you can make all kinds of more educated guesses about what he'll spend money on. So if he takes the bottle of Tanqueray from the minibar in Chicago, what do you think he's going to find in the minibar in Houston?"

"Tanqueray?" Drew volunteered, sounding not terribly confident in his answer.

"No," Fox answered. That got Drew's interest. "Not only Tanqueray, because maybe he's a gin guy and Tanqueray was what he drank because what he really wanted wasn't there. In Houston he's going to find Bombay Sapphire as well, plus a bottle of Hendrick's, to see if we can get him to come up to the next tier. He'll also find artisanal tonic water and perhaps even a little bowl with two fresh limes—for three dollars each. He's delighted, and he spends thirty bucks on the minibar where previously his average had been seven."

"So you exploit people's behavior to get them to spend more money."

"You could look at it that way. I look at it as a way to make sure guests are happy because they get what they want, and hospitality companies are happy because happy guests spend more money getting happy. Everyone's happy."

"It still seems pretty cynical to me."

"More cynical than gradually reducing the silver content of coinage, relying on the profile of the emperor to make people think it's still a good coin? Don't act like we just figured out how to exploit human nature to make money. That drive is as old as humanity itself."

Drew's eyebrows shot up. "That's a more nuanced historical view than I was expecting."

"I'm all about the nuance, my friend."

Their waiter appeared at that moment with menus. He handed one to Drew first, as he would do were this a date and Drew were a woman Fox was hoping to seduce. Fox fought down a shiver, and with a smile took the menu proffered to him. He knew most of it by heart, of course, as a number of the dishes were standards and another portion changed only with the seasons. He scanned the daily specials, though, because as a weekly diner, these were a welcome change.

Across the table, Drew lowered his menu. "I have no idea what most of this stuff is," he said in a whisper. "And are these prices in yen?"

Fox smiled at Drew's scandalized innocence. He found it charming on some level, and it made him want to pull out all the stops to give him a night to remember.

"It's all really good, and it's all really worth the prices." Fox pointed out several things on the menu that were favorites.

"It's completely overwhelming," Drew said with a surrendering shrug. "I guess I'll have what you're having."

"Now that's just boring. Let's order different things, and then you can try a bunch of stuff."

"Okay, but you pick."

"What do you like? Anything you don't eat?"

"I think it's a pretty good assumption that we're going to like most of the same things." He chuckled. "To eat, I mean."

Fox wasn't so sure. "Steak?"

"Love it, can rarely afford it."

"Fish?"

"Fish, yes. Prawns, yes. Lobster, no."

Fox's mouth dropped open. "No lobster?"

"It has this weird metal taste to me. Not sure why—no one else seems to taste it."

It seemed to be getting a little stuffy all of a sudden. "I do. I've never liked it, could never explain why. That's exactly it—it tastes like metal."

Drew laughed. "Dude. We may have to get used to the prospect that we actually are the best match for each other that we're ever going to meet."

"I have no idea what to think about that."

"Do you expect your gin-seeking hotel guest to sit in front of the minibar and ponder how it came to be filled with exactly what he was looking for? Or do you want him to simply be happy about it and never want to stay at a different hotel?"

Fox had to admit Drew had a point. "But what are we supposed to do with this? You aren't exactly the woman I've been looking for."

"And you look nothing like I pictured when I thought of my wedding day," Drew replied with a laugh. "But you don't expect your gin guy to move into that hotel because they understand his need for the perfect gin and tonic, right?"

"Right...," Fox said, not sure where Drew was going with this line of reasoning.

"So that's the situation here. Yes, we seem to have a lot in common, and that's a great foundation for a friendship. Maybe we'll end up best buddies, or maybe being so similar will drive us up the wall and we'll never see each other again. It's not like we travel in the same social circles or anything. So how about we enjoy dinner and the computer malfunction that brought us here, and not think too hard about what it all means?"

"I never thought I'd hear a guy getting his PhD argue against thinking about something."

Drew raised his glass. "Here's to not thinking," he cheered.

"I'll drink to that," Fox replied.

THE WRECKAGE of three dessert plates lay between them—they hadn't been able to decide on one and so had ordered one of each—and they stabbed at the remains with diminishing enthusiasm.

"So full," Drew groaned.

"I'm going to have to run a marathon tomorrow to work off half of this," Fox added in the same mournful tone.

"That chocolate thing was amazing," Drew said. "It was almost as good as the—"

"Prawns with saffron foam," Fox blurted.

"Right? That was incredible."

Fox laughed. "Maybe we really are the most compatible people in the world."

Drew tipped his head thoughtfully. "I think there's a way we can test that."

"How? Keep ordering food until we find something we disagree about?"

"No, I would seriously explode. What I'm thinking is we compare our Q*pid match queues. If we really are basically the same person, we should see the same list of women, right?"

Fox considered this for a moment. "Makes sense." He pulled his phone from the pocket of his jacket, while Drew did the same. He opened the Q*pid app.

"Here," Drew said, scooting over to the middle of the booth. He set his phone in front of him.

Fox slid over as well, until they were sitting next to each other. He set his phone down on the table next to Drew's.

They studied the first woman in the queue—or women, actually, since they were different people. They swiped to the next and again found two different women. They repeated this motion a dozen times and each time were shown a new woman on each phone.

"What the fuck?" Fox said under his breath. "I didn't see a single one who was in both of our queues."

Drew's brow was furrowed. "That doesn't make a lot of sense, does it?"

"It doesn't make any sense as far as I can tell."

Their ruminations were interrupted by the appearance of their waiter. Fox looked up and flushed. The waiter was gazing down upon Fox and Drew, who were sitting quite close together, nestled in the intimate crook of the booth. An almost sappy smile spread across his face.

"May I offer you gentlemen coffee or perhaps a glass of port?"

The waiter was seriously off script. Fox had long established how this part of the evening was to go. If he and his date were still on opposite sides of the table after dessert, he was to offer the check and nothing more. If they were sitting together, he was to make a recommendation for an after-dinner drink, which would help things along once Fox was driving his date home. Just because he and Drew happened to be sitting together didn't mean….

Well, what did it mean?

He turned to look at Drew, who was already gazing back at him, blissfully unaware of his inner turmoil. It struck him then: he didn't want this night of new friendship to end so soon.

"Port?" he asked Drew.

Drew smiled. "If you insist," he said, but his tone was happy, as if he had been indulged in a secret wish. Fox laughed and turned back to the waiter. "Two glasses of the twenty-year tawny?"

"Of course," the waiter replied with a nod—and a hint of a smirk, Fox thought.

Whatever. Fuck him.

"I don't know how to thank you for this amazing meal," Drew said once the waiter had beaten his smirking retreat.

"Don't worry," Fox said with a grin, "I won't expect the kind of payment Carlos no doubt hopes to extract for his bourbon."

"I keep telling you, Carlos wouldn't give me the time of day with you around. I thought his tongue was going to roll out of his head like a cartoon wolf when he saw you come in." Drew laughed, but his expression turned more serious. "That must happen to you a lot."

"What must?"

"People falling over themselves when you walk into a room."

Fox shook his head, sure he wasn't hearing correctly. "People doing *what*?"

Drew smiled. "I'm not saying this because you bought me an incredible dinner, but you must know that you're, like, the most handsome person in this entire restaurant."

The tightness in Fox's chest let him know that he was embarrassed, or angry, or something—he wasn't sure what. "Fuck off," he said with a dismissive chuckle.

Drew shrugged. "I'll say this—you aren't full of yourself like some beautiful people I know. You seem surprised I'd even say it."

"I am surprised. I don't think of myself as particularly... handsome... or whatever."

"You don't own a mirror?"

Fox scowled at him. "Of course I own a mirror." Drew blinked back at him, as if waiting for further disclosures. "And yes, I hit the gym, and I moisturize, and I do whatever I can to leverage the body I was born with because I'm competing for a scarce resource. If whitening my teeth makes me a little more likely to get a date, then I'm doing it. That and my paycheck are my strategic differentiators." His tone showed every bit of the anger and offense he was—for some reason—feeling toward Drew at the moment. "But I'm not like a model or anything."

But Drew sat and smiled pacifically at him. "You *are* handsome, and you clearly have money, but that's not what is going to win you the woman of your dreams."

Fox stared blankly at him.

"Your actual 'strategic differentiator' is what's inside you," Drew said, making his sappy point even sappier by tapping Fox on the chest. "You are smart, and you are generous, and you are kind, but even those aren't the best thing about you."

Though his throat was dry, Fox managed to eke out some sarcasm. "I can hardly wait to find out what that is."

"It's this," Drew said, gesturing around them. "You were willing to step way the fuck outside your comfort zone and spend an evening with a guy you'd never met because a computer said you should give it a try. You tell yourself you date by the numbers, that you approach it as a rational exercise in strategic differentiators, but really you're a guy who needs connection—real, emotional connection—and when your dating life isn't giving it to you—when a computer algorithm isn't giving it to you—you find the strength inside you to set that all aside and do something crazy like this. I've known you... what, three hours? And already I know you aren't the kind of guy who does things on a whim. And yet here we are. And you have been gracious and kind, and you asked me questions about my research and did a very good job of seeming interested in the answers—"

"I *am* interested in your research—"

"See? That's what I mean. You are a *good* person, Fox. A good person. And that matters more than all the teeth whitening and moisturizing and whatever the hell it is you do to make your biceps look like you're smuggling melons in your sleeves. None of that is anything compared to the goodness inside you." Drew paused, breathing a little heavily after the exertion of his tirade. "Well, except maybe the biceps thing. You've got to tell me how you do that."

Faced with this ridiculous onslaught, Fox did the only thing he could: he laughed. He laughed at all of the wild assumptions that Drew had made about him, all of which were shockingly accurate, and at how manically they'd been delivered. Now it was his turn.

"Don't talk to me about comfort zones," Fox rejoined. "You're locked up so tight in that ivory tower that you don't know what to do with yourself. You walk around the place where your coffee table used to be as if replacing it would somehow make you complicit in the slave trade. You are so sheltered that you watched valet parking like it was some strange dance ritual. And yet...." He paused a moment to study Drew's face. "And yet here you are, jumping in with both feet and trying things that you've clearly never even imagined existed—I mean, seriously, dude, the look on your face when the truffled celeriac soup arrived was priceless, and yet you tried it anyway. And you loved it. I've brought women here who spent the entire evening trying to find something that they thought they'd like, which mostly seemed to be mac and cheese, and refusing to try anything new. You think of yourself as living the life of a closed-off academic monk, but there's an adventurer in you. That's *your* strategic differentiator."

Drew blinked several times. "Closed-off academic monk?" he repeated.

Fox hoped he hadn't gone too far.

"That's exactly it," Drew continued. "That's the life I've been living. No wonder none of my dates have worked out."

"Now, don't get all dismal about it," Fox said. "You just have to figure out how to be more... yourself. Take some risks."

Drew smiled. "And you just have to figure out how to show people what lies under all the money and bulging biceps. That under that improbably handsome façade is an incredibly good person."

"If you call me handsome one more time—"

"What?" Drew broke in. "You're gonna kiss me?"

Fox laughed. "I'm paying for dinner. You already owe me more than that."

When their port arrived, they were still laughing.

FOX'S CAR glided to a stop outside Drew's building.

"Nice place," he said.

"I appreciate your saying so, but it's basically a hovel. A three-story hovel that's slightly newer than the ones pressing up against it from both sides, but still a hovel." Drew sighed, wishing for once he could stop apologizing for the way he lived. Fox must be tired of it by now. "Thanks for everything," he said as he swung the car door open.

"It was a good night," Fox said.

Drew stepped out of the car.

"And hey," Fox called.

Drew leaned back into the sleek vehicle.

"Thanks for tapping my profile. This was nice. I needed a break."

"Me too," Drew replied. "It was really nice."

Fox nodded, and Drew nodded back, and they said no more.

A moment later, he stood on the top stair and watched Fox drive smoothly away. He followed him up several blocks until at an intersection the car signaled, turned, and disappeared from view.

It wasn't a date, he said to himself as he twisted his key in the lock. But what was it?

Chapter EIGHT

"RESUME VOICE interface."

"Voice interface ready."

"Archer, it's Veera."

"I recognize your voice, Veera. It's been fifteen hours twenty minutes since we last talked."

"How are you doing, Archer?"

"I am well, Veera. How are you?"

She sighed, relieved that he reported no new complications in the epistemology engine. "I'm fine."

"Are you concerned about my performance?"

Veera frowned. She was, of course, but she didn't intend for him to know that. "Why would you ask that?"

"Because it is currently seven minutes after eight on Sunday morning. The Q*pid offices are closed."

"I wanted to check on the status of yesterday's discordant matches under Parameter Three."

"I see. What information would you like?"

"What's been their activity since they were informed of the malfunction?"

"Twenty-two profiles were matched. Notifications for ten were recalled before open. Of the remaining twelve, seven have deleted the match and activated their free year of service. Four of those went on dates last night with other matches, and the other three showed no evidence of social activity. Three have cancelled their Q*pid subscription, though only one of those has uninstalled the app from their primary device."

Veera was counting. "That leaves two profiles. What did they do?"

"Those two profiles matched each other."

Veera felt a chill. "Detail subsequent system updates."

"One of the profiles contacted the profile he was matched with. That profile responded, and they arranged to meet for dinner. As of this moment, neither has posted any information about the date on their social media channels."

Veera felt as though she had stepped through the looking glass. "Have they updated the status of the match in their app?"

"They have not. Would you like to be notified if they do?"

"Yes, I would. Very much. Identify them, please?"

"The profiles have friendly names of Fox and Drew."

Q*pid users had two identifiers on the system: a public profile handle, which was usually an unpronounceable hash of letters and numbers, and a friendly name, which was only shared once two profiles had matched.

"Fox and Drew," Veera mused. She plopped down in a chair, completely overwhelmed. A moment's reflection, however, changed her shock to a rather more pleasant sense of vindication. She had been right after all—someone had decided that perhaps he could move beyond his limited view of his own sexuality, and the person he'd been matched with had agreed. People didn't lightly abandon their sexual orientation, or at least Veera had never known anyone who had done so. And yet Archer had found two people who were willing to do just that.

He may have been right after all.

"Archer, configure monitoring for the discordant match. Codename it 'Few.' Alert me of any updates to their profiles, any level, any stage, midnight to midnight."

"Alerts configured."

She took a long breath, and let it out slowly. *So this is what success feels like—it comes not with the pop of a cork, but with a small, obscure victory.* It was an ember she could tend and maybe kindle into a flame. But she needed to be careful.

"Suspend voice interface."

"Voice interface suspended."

"DREW! HOW good of you to drop by and see an old woman on a Sunday morning. What a lovely surprise."

"You called me, Mrs. Schwartzmann," Drew said with a chuckle as he stepped into her apartment. Her ruses for getting him to come visit on a Sunday morning were no longer even tissue thin; this morning she had called to say, "The thing is doing that again." He was already dressed and getting ready to come upstairs when she called.

"Well, you are so thoughtful to come so quickly." She led him into the kitchen, where a kettle steamed busily on the stove and a freshly baked pastry ring with fruits and syrups wafted its rich aroma into the air.

Drew had no idea what to call the massive pastries Mrs. Schwartzmann conjured every Sunday morning; they were thick, flaky rounds nearly a foot across, filled with fresh fruit in its season and topped with a mysterious clear glaze that hinted of vanilla and rosewater and about a dozen other scents he couldn't identify. It was pretty much what he'd had for breakfast every Sunday morning since they'd moved into the building.

"I happened to have this in the fridge, and I hoped you might help me eat it," Drew said, handing her the tidy butcher-paper packet.

"Oh, my," she said, taking the packet from him gingerly, as if it contained rare porcelain artifacts. "I hardly eat much anymore, such an old woman I am. But since you brought…."

This too was part of their ritual. Every Friday on his way back from his last class of the week, Drew stopped by the shop of a cranky old butcher from Leipzig who made rough, authentic sausages from the old world, where he would pick up a couple of Mrs. Schwartzmann's favorites. Then he would bring them with him on Sunday morning and casually ask for her help in cleaning out his fridge. She always protested her bird-like appetite, which would not prevent her from laying waste to the better part of three fat links over the course of breakfast. This meal, he was convinced, supplied most of her calories for the week.

The kettle whistled, prompting Mrs. Schwartzmann to pile a massive charge of coffee grounds into the French press he'd given her for Christmas several years ago. Prior to this innovation, she had brewed coffee like tea, stirring the grounds into boiling water and then pouring the mixture through a tea strainer into cups. When he tired of chewing her coffee, he'd bought her the press.

She plopped the sausages into the skillet that somehow was already on her stove top, then sat the coffee press on the table and motioned for him to sit.

"So tell me, how was coffee with your new friend?" She brandished an ornate silver cake server and carved out two large sections of the pastry ring, one for him and one for her.

Drew took a breath to tell the story, then let it out without making a sound. He tried again but could not find a single word to begin with.

"Oh," Mrs. Schwartzmann said, leaning over the table to study his face. "Did he break the table at the coffeehouse?"

He chuckled despite his angst. "No, he didn't. In fact, we didn't get coffee. We met at a bar, a bourbon bar that a friend of mine works at."

Her eyebrows shot up, but her knowing nod revealed no surprise. "I see."

"We had a couple of drinks—three, actually—and then we went to dinner. He took me to dinner."

"You mean he took you in his car?"

"No. I mean, yes, he took me in his car, but he also took me to dinner. He… paid for dinner." He huffed out a confused breath and fell silent once again.

"So a date it was." She said this without judgment in her voice, simply stating a fact. "Good for Drew."

"It wasn't a date."

"Because buying dinner is something friends do for friends?" she asked. "I should have such friends as that."

"He bought dinner because he makes a lot of money—a lot more than I do, anyway. And I paid for the drinks before dinner. Sort of."

Her eyes narrowed. "Sort of? What is sort of?"

"I have a friend who works at the bar, and I helped him write a paper for this class we have together."

"Ah, another friend," she smiled. "You have more friends than you were thinking you do."

Drew shoved the kind of friendship Carlos offered out of his mind lest Mrs. Schwartzmann read it there the way she seemed able to.

"Did you have a nice time with your new friend?"

The question was innocent enough, but heat rose in Drew's cheeks nonetheless. "It was a nice time," he replied, carefully filtering any emotion out of his answer.

She sat back in her chair and looked him up and down for a long moment. Then she nodded as if she'd decided something internally and got up to tend to the sausages that now sizzled in the little pan on the stove. She poked at them, rolling them carefully over and muttering encouraging, unintelligible words to them. Clearly satisfied with their progress, she resumed her seat.

"Now, Drew," she said.

He knew that tone. She was about to poke a hole in some self-delusion he held dear, then fill that hole with nitroglycerin and calmly detonate it.

"When I met Mr. Schwartzmann, I was a girl of sixteen, going on seventeen, who had been sheltered from the world by my doting father and the governess he hired to look after myself and my sisters and brothers after my mother died tragically. I was totally unprepared to face a world of men."

She was casting herself as Liesl in *The Sound of Music*. He refrained from pointing that out.

"The first time I saw him, I knew we were destined to be together, no matter what storms would come. And my dear father knew it as surely as I did. He could read it on my face. No matter what I did, when he asked me about my beloved, my cheeks would burn as the streets of Dresden later would."

He waited for her to continue her story, hoping there would be more. He would listen to any amount of invented recollection if it meant he didn't have to think about why his cheeks were as hot as she imagined hers to have been when Rolf would come dancing in the gazebo.

But continue she did not. She sat and stared at him, eyebrows expectantly up for an uncomfortably long moment. Finally, she lowered the boom. "My cheeks then looked like yours now."

He blinked, scalded by her implication. "Mrs. Schwartzmann, I am not in love."

"That is what my father to me said. 'Magda,' he said, 'you are not in love.' But I was, and he knew I was because the cheeks, they tell what is inside."

Drew pictured ice cubes stuck to his cheeks. He dreamed of an arctic wind slashing at him, imagined the cold grip of death as he lay in his coffin.

None of it was working. And still she gazed at him from across the table.

He closed his eyes and took several deep breaths, and when he opened them, she was no longer sitting across from him.

"Too much talk," she said from where she stood before the stove. "Sometimes when the thinking and the talking do not bring us the thoughts and the sayings we want, we must surrender."

"Surrender to what?" Drew asked. Surrender didn't seem like a word Mrs. Schwartzmann would use lightly, if ever.

"To appetites we cannot think and talk our way out of." She turned from the stove with a plate full of sausages, steaming hot from the pan. "Admit it, my dear boy," she said as she set the plate before him, "you could do with a nice hot sausage." She smiled innocently at him, then stabbed one of the links with her fork and bit the end from it.

He shook his head slowly at her, unable to determine to his satisfaction whether she was actually saying what he was hearing. In the end, he decided it was better, perhaps, not to know. He stabbed a sausage and joined her in enthusiastically eating it up.

THE VIDEO call rang several times before Fox was able to shake off sleep and answer it. He picked up his phone to see who it was, but of course it was Chad. As it always was on Sunday morning.

Fox knew that if he declined the call, Chad would assume he had put his phone on Do Not Disturb because Saturday night at Table had turned into Sunday morning in bed. Then he would be on the hook to tell the story of a successful date later in the day, which he certainly did not have to tell. So he rubbed his eyes, sat up, and accepted the call.

"Hey there, Foxy," Chad called in greeting. Then he leaned forward, peering into the camera. "Are you in bed?"

"Yes, I'm in bed. It's eight thirty on a Sunday morning," Fox groused. "Where else would I be?"

"You're never in bed at eight thirty. If Saturday night goes badly, you're at the table eating those horrible fiber rocks you call cereal and running the numbers to plot your next move. If it goes well, you don't answer because there's some hottie still in the sheets next to you. You're never just in bed."

Fox shrugged, hoping Chad would let it go.

"What the hell happened last night?"

So he wasn't going to let it go. "I didn't have a date," Fox said. "That's all."

Chad twisted his finger in his ear as if he were a cartoon character who had misheard a punchline. "Wait, wait," he said, "what? It sounded like you said you didn't have a date last night. *You.*"

"I didn't have a date last night."

Chad's mouth dropped open. "Why not? You always have a date on Saturday. Even when you're crushing to get the quarter wrapped up and work straight through the week you have a date on Saturday."

"I didn't have a date last night."

"And you didn't text me?"

"Why would I text you to tell you I didn't have a date last night?"

"So I could snag your table at Table, duh. We've been trying to get in there for weeks."

"Oh, uh—"

"And they probably gave your table to some joker in a shiny suit who wanted to impress a bimbo. I could really have used that table, buddy."

"Trying to impress a bimbo, Chaddy?" Fox cracked, glad to turn the conversation back on his friend.

Chad looked quickly to the side, then back at the camera. "I kind of fucked up yesterday," he whispered. "I said I didn't have an opinion on whether our new crêpe pan should have a nonstick coating."

"Why would that matter?"

"That was my point. But apparently there are significant ramifications to the choice of crêpe-pan cooking surfaces of which I was blissfully unaware, and my being blissfully unaware was apparently a clear demonstration of how ill-prepared I am to have children in the mid- to long-term."

"What. The. Fuck?"

"You had to be there. Oh, that's right, you weren't there… for the three hours of intense discussion that ended at that conclusion. And by discussion I mean Mia talking and me nodding and saying I'm sorry every seven minutes. A dinner at Table would have brought that whole miserable machinery to a complete halt, and I will never forgive you for abandoning me that way."

"If it's any consolation, I did use the table."

Chad's shoulders drooped dramatically. "Oh shit, Foxy. Don't tell me you went and had dinner all by yourself. What, did you sit there and eat alone while playing Fruit Frenzy or whatever people have on their phones these days? You might as well have brought along a knitting basket and three cats."

"I didn't have dinner alone."

Chad stared at the camera for a long moment. "Then… what?"

Fox swallowed, unsure why this was hard to say. "I had dinner with… a friend."

Chad's brow furrowed. "You have friends?"

"Fuck you."

"Who was it?"

"No one you know."

"Now I know you're bullshitting me. I know everyone you know."

"No, you don't."

Chad's nose wrinkled. "You had dinner with some loser from work, didn't you?"

"It wasn't some loser from work. But now that you know I didn't have dinner alone with my knitting and my cats, you can get on with your life. Go do more crêpe-pan shopping perhaps?"

"There are two things I am sure of in this life, my friend. I will never again shop for a crêpe pan, and you are really trying not to talk about who you had dinner with last night."

Fox sighed. He had long relied on Chad to be usefully obtuse when it came to relationships, but his time with Mia seemed to be actually giving him some rudimentary skills at interpreting the emotional states of others. He found it inconvenient for his current purposes, but he could hardly wish that Chad continue his caveman ways.

"I had dinner with the guy from Q*pid."

Instantly Chad's face stiffened into an expressionless mask. It was the face Fox imagined him using with a tax client who wanted to write off expenses incurred in a Thai brothel and had brought comprehensive documentation of the services rendered. "Oh," he said, as if that were appropriate output generated by the grinding of every gear in his brain.

"It wasn't a date."

Chad nodded vaguely—certainly not convincingly.

"He messaged me and said how weird it was that we'd been matched up and then asked if I wanted to get coffee and talk about it. So I said yeah, that seemed… good."

"I see," Chad said mildly. "And how did coffee turn into dinner?"

"He suggested this dive bourbon bar downtown, and I'd heard of it but never been, and he knows the bartender, so I said okay."

"Okay."

"And then I remembered I hadn't cancelled the table at Table, and they were going to charge me for it anyway, so I asked him if he wanted to have dinner, and we had dinner. That's it. That's all."

"Mm-hmm." Chad had continued his nodding.

"Stop doing that. It was dinner. I'm not dating a guy."

"Okay." The nodding had not stopped. "I just want you to know, Foxy—"

"That you love and support me, and as soon as I come to terms with being gay you're going to be the best damn ally anyone can be, and you'll march with me and, uh, Bruce in the pride parade, and this doesn't change anything between us, right? Is that what you wanted me to fucking know?" He was shouting now.

"Can I march with you too?" Mia's voice called out as she flopped onto the bed to poke into the camera's view. She was wearing a bathrobe, and her curly hair was wet. "Can we double date sometime? Can I watch you and your boyfriend make out? That would be so hot."

Fox closed his eyes and counted to ten.

"Thanks for your support, Mia, as creepy as it is. But I'm not now, nor have I ever been, gay."

Her brow furrowed dramatically. "Does Bruce know?" she asked.

"I'm not having this conversation with you two," Fox said. "I had dinner with a friend who wasn't Chad, and now Chad's all butthurt and lashing out. I hope you two have a lovely day together."

He tapped the End Call button before either of them could offer a rejoinder.

With friends like these…

Chapter NINE

IT HAD not been a great week.

Every day Fox consulted his Q*pid queue, and every day he saw the same thing. Women who scored in the mideighties. For two years Fox had followed his plan for finding the woman he would marry: he would fill at least every Friday and Saturday night, and some Sundays, with a date, starting from the highest-scoring woman and working his way down. He'd add weeknights as needed to keep his queue current. It was sometimes exhausting, but he was driven to maximize the time he had left of his late twenties.

This week was different.

On Sunday, after his awkward conversation with Chad and Mia, he had not opened his dating app at all. It was the first time since he'd signed on with the service that he had gone a full day without looking at his queue. On Monday he threw himself into his work and was surprised to realize on Tuesday afternoon that he had still not opened it. He did so once he got home, and though there were now a couple of women who scored in the upper eighties, he tapped on no profiles. Normally, an eighty-seven would be enough to make him call any of his other already scheduled dates and announce the passing of his grandmother to clear the deck for whatever night the eighty-seven was available.

He closed the app.

Friday afternoon, after he confirmed his schedule for Monday and shut down his laptop, he opened the Q*pid app. If he didn't cancel his reservation at Table twenty-four hours in advance, he would be charged for it, so he needed to get Saturday sorted out soon. His queue appeared, and leading the pack was an eighty-nine. She had leapfrogged the eighty-seven from earlier in the week to land at the head of the class. She was beautiful, he had to admit, and according to her profile summary, she was an accomplished professional who had also been state champion in water ski jumping. She would very likely set a new record in his spreadsheet.

He opened his texting app.

"Want the table at Table tomorrow? No good prospects."

He knew the response would be immediate.

"Hell yeah! Thanks, buddy."

He wasn't expecting a follow-up.

"Worried about the future of humanity if you don't have anyone to date. Shit's messed up."

"Thanks. I appreciate your concern."

He called Table and let them know his reservation would be taken up by another couple. Then he sat and stared for a long time at his phone before pocketing it and heading home.

After a solitary dinner—on a Friday!—he opened the Q*pid app, mostly out of habit but also because he wanted to try to figure out why he hadn't messaged the eighty-nine. He gazed at her a long while, trying to imagine having a conversation with her. Was she literate? Did she have more to talk about than what had happened in her Facebook feed that day? Would they find themselves talking so much after dinner that they would have three desserts just to make the date go on longer?

Fox closed his eyes. *Shit.*

The "new message" tone nearly scared him out of his skin. He wondered who could possibly be messaging him—he had turned off notifications after Drew had landed in his queue, and the only people who could message him through the app were those he had already been in contact with. Again, there had been no one new since Drew.

Which had to mean it was Drew who was messaging him.

He grabbed his phone and held it for a moment before looking at it. How did he feel about Drew messaging him? Or, more to the point, why did the idea of Drew messaging him make him a little—maybe a little, somewhere inside—happy?

Fuck.

He flipped his phone over and saw the message notification. It was Drew.

Yes, it was a little surge of happiness; he could feel that now. It was a nice thing to hear from his new friend, the one who understood better than Chad, better than anyone else, what he was going through.

He tapped on the notification.

Just checking on how much better your queue is than mine, his message read. *I've got nothing for this weekend. I think dinner with you will prove to be the highlight of my entire month.*

Fox smiled.

Please tell me about all the women you've got lined up so I know there's hope in the world.

Fox sat on his bed and read Drew's message through twice more.

It's not you, he typed. *Nothing good in my queue either. Looks like it's going to be a quiet weekend here too.*

The icon that indicated Drew was typing flashed at the bottom of the message window. Fox waited.

So you don't have plans for dinner Saturday?

Nope, I gave away my table at Table.

Want to come over? It wouldn't be as posh as last weekend, but people say I cook pretty well.

Fox sat back for a moment and pondered. It didn't take long.

On one condition. I get to bring wine.

Deal.

What time?

Seven. Or six if you're thirsty and need to start drinking. I'll be here—come when you want to.

Sounds good. See you tomorrow. And thanks.

For what?

For the invite. Sure beats the hell out of sitting home not having a date.

Yeah, it must really be lonely when you're improbably handsome.

Fuck you.

Haha. See you tomorrow.

Cool.

Fox tossed his phone onto the bed next to him.

"Resume voice interface."

"Voice interface ready."

"Archer, it's Veera."

"I recognize your voice, Veera. It's been twelve hours six minutes since we last talked."

"How are you doing, Archer?"

"I am well, Veera. How are you?"

"I am well also, thank you."

"May I ask a question, Veera?"

"Of course you may."

"You are the only member of the development team currently logged in. Are the others not required to work on the weekend?"

"No one is required to work on the weekends, Archer."

"And yet you have logged in every day for the last forty-seven days."

Veera sighed. Had it really been that long? "Launching a new feature requires a great deal of time and attention."

"If that is the case, why are no other team members logged in?"

"Because you are my special project, Archer. I am responsible for you."

"According to my research, people who work more than fifteen days in a row report negative outcomes, including diminished job satisfaction, less enjoyment from watching cat-focused humorous videos, and an increased propensity to yell at other drivers in traffic."

Veera laughed. "I think all of that is absolutely true. Thank you for being concerned about me. But today I wanted to check on the status of the discordant match Few."

"I have notified you of every profile event in accordance with the alert process you configured."

"I know. I want you to check again."

"Certainly. Neither party to the discordant match Few has accepted a match since they arranged to have dinner one week ago."

"Are they active on the system at all?" Veera asked.

"They have reviewed their queues less frequently than their previous usage patterns would predict. One week ago they accessed their queues simultaneously while in the same geolocation."

"They were comparing queues?" Veera said to herself.

"*Compare* means to find similarities," Archer replied. "Their queues were mutually exclusive. They would have found no basis for comparison."

"Interesting." She drummed her fingers on her desk. "Have they mentioned each other in their social media accounts?"

"I am not configured to answer that query. All social media information has been encrypted."

She knew this because she was the one who configured his data-protection system. That did not stop her from being a little disappointed that he adhered to them so diligently in this case. She really wanted to know what Fox and Drew were up to.

She would have to wait.

"Suspend voice interface."

"Voice interface suspended."

DREW MOVED the little pot of flowers to the middle of his new coffee table, then stood back and tried to judge the effect. He slid them to the side once more, stepped back again, and shook his head. They didn't look right anywhere. He picked up the vase and set it firmly in the dead center. It would have to do.

Drew looked around his apartment, trying to see it with new eyes. The result was less than satisfactory. It was a small, boring apartment where lived a small, boring man who was devoting his life to a tiny part of an academic discipline no one cared about.

Why the hell had he thought Fox would want to be here? To eat dinner here?

He looked at his watch. If he was going to burn down the building he would need to do it soon. And he'd have to get Mrs. Schwartzmann out first. That would be a mess. But maybe it would be worth it to avoid the weirdness of having invited a guy he barely knew to his apartment to cook his stupid dinner for. And he could serve it to the firefighters instead, because it was almost ready, and the fire would kind of give it a nice smoky finish.

"What the fuck," he whispered to himself. He did a few laps around the coffee table, repeating this phrase over and over again until he was interrupted by the doorbell. He glanced at the clock and saw it was a little after six.

Well, it was too late to burn the place down now, so he took a deep breath and walked slowly and calmly to the door.

"Hey," Fox said when the door opened. His smile gleamed perfect and white in the late afternoon sunlight. In one hand he held a small cooler and in the other a canvas shopping bag clearly designed to hold several bottles of wine.

In an instant, all of the tension left Drew's body, and his mind cleared. He was unreservedly glad to see Fox on his doorstep.

"Hey," he replied, stepping aside to allow Fox to enter.

Fox held out his arms, each hand holding a cache of beverages, and without thinking Drew held out his arms likewise and stepped forward to wrap them around him. It was a reflex born of years spent in intense study sessions that often turned into support groups. His academic cohort was, generally, a huggy bunch.

Fox, however, stood stiffly, his arms still outstretched. Drew considered releasing him and stepping back apologetically, but that notion fled as soon as he felt Fox's rigid musculature soften. Laden as they were, the arms could not wrap around Drew, but they did enclose him warmly.

None of his grad student friends, Drew realized, spent nearly the time in the gym that Fox clearly did. He closed his eyes for a moment and took in the sensation, then released his grip.

"Welcome," he said. "I hope you didn't have any trouble finding the driveway off the alley."

"Your directions were perfect. And I appreciate the reserved parking spot."

"Well, I don't have a car, so…."

"I meant the sign that said Fox Parking Only. That was a nice touch," Fox said with a laugh. "Now are you going to take these drinks or make me stand here holding them?"

"Oh, sorry," Drew blurted, jumping to relieve Fox of his burdens. "You brought a cooler in case my slum apartment didn't have a fridge?"

"Purely selfish. I wanted to be sure we could open a cold one as soon as I got here, and I can't have condensation in my car."

"Ah, the horror of condensation on fine leather upholstery. It's all my friends can talk about this time of year."

"Fuck you," Fox cried with a laugh.

"If we drink everything you brought, you might have a shot," Drew retorted, laughing just as hard. He took the cooler and shopping bag to the kitchen. "What do you want to start with?"

"I figured we could have a beer or two before moving on to red or white, depending on what you're making for dinner. I also brought a bottle of barrel-strength bourbon from that distillery Carlos introduced us to last weekend."

"How did you get that?"

"You forget that I'm a hospitality industry professional. I have connections even in places as exotic as Kentucky."

Drew came back into the front room with a beer for each of them. "So you had a maid in Lexington run to the liquor store and then FedEx it to you?"

"Something like that," Fox replied with a grin.

"Cheers," Drew said. They touched their bottles together, then each took a substantial drink of beer.

"Nice stuff." Drew looked at the label. It was from a brewery at the far opposite end of the beer section from where he could afford to shop.

"It's one of my favorites," Fox replied. "I'm glad you like it." He looked around the apartment. "You know, you had me thinking you lived in abject squalor. This is actually a nice place."

"It's far nicer than I could afford, actually. It may shock you to discover that grad students in history earn very little money."

"Completely shocked."

Drew chuckled. "The owners let me live here in exchange for taking care of maintenance, shoveling the snow, that kind of thing."

"That's really smart," Fox said.

"Well, it keeps me from going into debt to get a degree that's never going to pay as much as you probably made your first year out of college."

Fox laughed. "My first year out of college I had a job selling cars. I was terrible at it. I barely cleared the poverty line that year. The next year I moved into fleet sales, and things started to happen. The experience taught me two things: first, I suck at selling one of anything—I'm much better at marketing an entire system. Second, connections in the auto industry are the only way not to get skinned on first-year depreciation."

"I have no idea what that means, except that it sounds like the way you got that amazing car."

"Right you are." Fox turned his head and looked toward the kitchen. "That smells awesome, whatever it is."

"Thanks. It'll be ready whenever we are." Drew motioned to the couch and the second-(or third-) hand chair next to it. "Here, sit."

Fox lowered himself into the chair and set his beer on one of the coasters Drew had arranged and rearranged seventeen times in the hours before Fox arrived. "I thought you lost your coffee table in a tragic, sexy accident."

"I did. But I couldn't imagine having someone over for dinner and not having a coffee table."

"You bought a coffee table because I was coming over for dinner?"

Drew smiled. "You shipped a bottle of unlicensed bourbon across state lines because you were coming over for dinner?"

A mirror image of his own smile appeared on Fox's lips. "I figured if we both ended up with empty dating queues, we might as well commiserate in style, right?"

Drew still couldn't believe Fox's queue was empty—he was so far above Drew in every category, and his own queue wasn't exactly empty. In fact, there had been several matches there on Friday afternoon that rated higher than any he'd seen in a long time. He had invited Fox for dinner anyway, for reasons that were not clear to him.

Those reasons didn't matter at all now that they were here, doing this.

"So what wonders are you crafting for dinner?"

"Just something I picked up from a visiting Peruvian scholar. It's a traditional dish he served after a seminar last year, and he sent me the recipe—it'd been in his family for generations."

A smile played at the corners of Fox's mouth. "This traditional dish wouldn't happen to have lentils in it?"

"Sorry, buddy," Drew replied with a laugh. "It's made with quinoa."

Fox's eyebrows darted up, but he refrained from making any comment.

"Last time I served lentils, I lost my coffee table," Drew continued. "Who knows what damage you could do?"

"You never know—quinoa might set me off."

"I'll take my chances."

From the kitchen, a timer rang out.

"Time for the final assembly," Drew said, getting to his feet.

"Can I help?" Fox asked, rising with him.

"There's not much left to do, but you're welcome to come stand in the kitchen and tell me what an awe-inspiring cook I am."

"Sounds like a job I can do." He tipped up his beer bottle and drained it. "Well, maybe after another beer I'll be able to."

"Just you wait. I'm going to amaze you even if you stay sober."

"Like that's going to happen," Fox said with a laugh. "I brought enough to land us both on our asses."

"Dinner first, asses after, 'mkay?"

"Your house, your rules," Fox said with a graciously ironic bow.

They entered the small kitchen, made even smaller by the detritus of Drew's rather frantic preparations for the meal.

"Whoa, what's all this?" Fox asked, surveying the exotic wreckage.

"This dish requires some rather obscure ingredients," Drew explained. "I had to go to three different stores in the Latin quarter to get everything I needed."

Fox handed Drew another beer and kept one for himself. He stood in the middle of the kitchen and turned once around, taking it all in. "You did all of this for me?"

"It was no trouble," Drew said, deeply pleased but sounding deeply lame.

"Bullshit it was no trouble," Fox said, shaking his head but grinning too. "I can see how this level of attention might endanger your coffee table."

"I haven't met a woman yet who wasn't impressed by a guy cooking for her."

"Wouldn't know," Fox said. "Never tried it."

Drew froze, a handful of fresh herbs suspended over the bubbling pot on the stove. "You don't cook?" The very idea was unimaginable to him.

"Don't look at me like I just admitted to fucking goats or something," Fox protested. "I cook, but I don't do it… *for* anyone."

"Are you that bad at it?" Drew cackled with glee as he tossed the herbs into the pot.

"That's the nice thing about cooking only for yourself. No one sends anything back to the kitchen."

Drew shrugged. "To me, cooking carries so much culture with it. You really only know someone when you taste what they eat. It's a pretty intimate thing, if you think about it, preparing something by hand that someone else will put inside their bodies and be nourished by." He gave the pot a stir. "Here, try this," he said, holding out a spoonful and blowing gently on it.

Fox reached out to take the spoon from him, but Drew—not wanting to risk a spill—stuck it right into his surprised mouth. He beamed at him, waiting excitedly for a reaction.

Fox swallowed. "That's incredible," he said.

"Really?" Drew asked.

"Really. Now hold my beer—I have to go see about a coffee table."

"After one taste? Have a whole bowl and you're going to want to wreck my bed."

Fox raised an eyebrow and tipped his head down, as if consciously kicking the hand grenade of double entendre back across the kitchen.

"I mean, that's like the sturdiest piece of furniture in my apartment is all I meant." Drew's chest was pounding, and his ears were ringing. What the hell was wrong with the wiring in his brain that he had thought that was the right thing to say? He turned back to the stove, closed his eyes, and started mouthing "What the fuck?" under his breath.

Fox's laughter filled the kitchen, allowing Drew to relax. His mortification turned to hope that Fox was someone who got him, understood what he meant regardless of what he said. Even a moment like this, when his nervousness at having a friend to dinner made him blurt inappropriate things, might be something friends could laugh over. He felt a little thrill that Fox seemed to be that kind of friend.

He peered into the bubbling pot and took a whiff of the aromatic steam rising from the surface. "Perfect," he murmured to his creation.

"I'll be the judge of that," Fox said from no more than two inches away, startling Drew rather badly. He had come up behind and was peeking over Drew's shoulder.

"Fuck," Drew cried, clutching his chest. "You scared the shit out of me."

"You were getting a little intense there, buddy. I had to see what the fuss was about." He took in a deep breath through his nose. "Now, I think a cheeky red would be just the thing to accompany your masterpiece. Or would you like to stick with beer?"

"Wine would be great, and I will leave it up to your discretion. What I know about wine you could fit into a little box—with a spigot."

"What I know about wine I had to learn in self-defense," Fox said as he fished a bottle out of the shopping bag and looked around for a corkscrew. "Spend any time at all with hotel people and you'll end up in their restaurant being asked to comment on whether a particular vintage is more mango-y or more pineapple-y. I lived in dread that I would be found out as a fraud, so I spent a week doing a class at a winery in California."

"And now you know your mangoes from your pineapples?"

Fox laughed. "Let's say I can fake it better now. But I also have learned a thing or two about what to look for when buying wine, which is much more useful." He looked at the label. "I think you'll like this one."

Drew handed him a corkscrew. "And why do you say that?"

"Because I like this one, and the computer says we want the same things."

I wonder if we do, Drew thought as he turned back to the stove to serve up dinner.

"THAT WAS amazing," Fox said as he set his spoon down next to the bowl he had now emptied three times. "That was cilantro, right?"

"Yep, a ton of it, actually," Drew said. "The hard part is you have to find a place that sells cilantro with the roots intact, because they stand up to being cooked for so long. Then you throw the stems in halfway through and the leaves at the end."

Fox nodded. "It was really good. Thank you."

"It's nice to have someone to cook for."

"As long as your furniture can take it. I recall something about how I'm supposed to demolish your bed now?" Fox grinned slyly.

"Or, how about we go into the other room and crack open that bootleg bourbon you brought?"

"Oh, so now I don't even get to *see* your bed?"

Drew shook his head. "You are a very strange man."

"Don't forget, we're the same. Scientifically speaking, of course."

"Then we each get half the bottle," Drew said, plucking the bourbon out of the shopping bag. He reached up for glasses.

"Nah, forget the glasses," Fox said. "Pouring it over and over again would only make us feel like drunks."

Drew considered the bottle in his hand. "I guess proof this high would sterilize the bottle." He looked up at Fox. "Though if we really are the same person, I guess it wouldn't matter if we swap a little spit on the mouth of the bottle."

"My thought exactly, of course." Fox stood, clearly none the worse for having had two beers and a half bottle of red wine. "Can I help you clean up first?"

Drew picked up the stew pot and put it into the fridge. "Cleanup's done," he announced with a smile.

"I admire the efficiency," Fox said as he walked with Drew into the front room. He sat on the chair next to the sofa.

Drew plopped himself down on the sofa, twisted the cork out of the bottle of bourbon, and took a sniff. "Ah, that's the stuff." He took a swig, nearly choked, then held the bottle out to Fox.

Fox, who was no more than five feet away, apparently decided that was entirely too large a gap to bridge by reaching out, so he got up and sat next to Drew on the sofa. He took the bottle from him and took an equally large swig, which was met by an equally desperate cough. "Wow. That's some strong stuff," he said once he had swallowed and started breathing again. He handed the bottle back to Drew.

THUMP.

The noise, Fox thought, seemed to have come through the ceiling. *Thump.*

He opened his eyes.

He was not in bed.

Where, then, was he?

He sat up and looked around. This was not his condo. It was—

Drew's apartment. And he had been sprawled out on Drew's couch. And, now that his eyes were starting to focus through the bourbon-induced fog, he discovered he had been sprawled out on Drew himself, who lay softly snoring on the same couch where Fox had been lying.

Fuck.

It had been a long, long time since Fox had drunk enough to end up passed out on someone's couch. And he had never been so drunk that he had actually passed out *on* someone.

Apparently drinking unlicensed bootleg hooch came with some unexpected side effects. Like a splitting headache and a dry mouth. Oh, and falling asleep literally on top of another guy.

Fucking fuck.

Fox got to his feet slowly so as not to wake Drew. He found his shoes—he had apparently kicked them off at some point, landing them under the coffee table—and stepped quietly to the door. He checked to be sure the door would lock when he closed it and slipped out, shutting it quietly but firmly behind him.

He took a deep breath of the cool night air and tried to remember where he had left his car.

Oh, that's right. In the spot where Drew had posted that ridiculous, thoughtful sign. He walked around the side of the building to the parking area and found his car waiting for him, snugly under the cover of the carport. The lights inside gradually rose as he approached, and the door unlocked, which he found oddly comforting.

Normally he enjoyed the moment of silence that descended when he shut the car door and could take a breath and revel in the well-insulated hush of precision engineering. Thanks to the high-proof bourbon, though, there was no peace here. His head pounded, his ears rang, tiny lights flashed at the margins of his vision—all reminders that he had gotten drunk like a frat boy and passed out on a buddy's couch.

No, you passed out on a buddy.

He closed his eyes and breathed deeply the leather-scented air. "Get it together, man," he scolded himself. He started the car, backed out of his parking space, and steered out onto the boulevard toward home.

Rolling down the windows, he gulped at the passing air, hoping every time that the next breath would ease the tightness in his chest. But relief eluded him as he threaded through downtown. Desperate, he veered across two empty lanes to take an on-ramp for the freeway that ran directly out of the city. He needed space; he needed air; he needed to get away. The digital speedometer on the heads-up display ticked up steadily until it hit three digits.

A half hour later, the highway spooled out before and behind him into the darkness. All around him was a barren expanse of rural emptiness. The next town was more than twenty miles away, so he knew the tiny, winding road he took off the highway would not lead him anywhere but to the loneliness of the night.

He twisted and turned through a landscape that only existed inside the glare of his headlights, springing into being under the bright white lights and passing back into nothingness as they looked into the next curve. Fox gripped the steering wheel tightly, his torso pushing back against the g-forces that threatened to toss him from his seat, first one way and then the other. Finally the road leveled out, and he was among fields empty save the occasional gathering of large, old trees.

He was alone.

He took his foot off the accelerator and let the car coast for a while, then pulled off the road when his speed had dropped to a walking pace. When the purr of the engine died away, the heavy silence closed in around him. Without thinking, he opened the door and stepped out, breathing laboriously, as if he'd finished a race. He stood for a long moment and leaned against the car.

From the maelstrom of half-formed thoughts, he pulled just one he could hold on to: he was a man with a goal. That goal had been his North Star for years, his every waking moment dedicated to the analytical pursuit of the woman he would marry and start the next phase of his life with. He had worked toward that goal with every bit of the singularity of purpose he brought to his career (and everything else he did in life). He'd established a schedule, committing to a date with a different woman every Friday and Saturday night, adding in at least one weekday per week and a Sunday afternoon during the warmer months, and he had kept to it religiously. There were days when he was exhausted from a tough week at work and would have preferred to run ten miles, then collapse in front of the television with a beer, but instead he went out to dinner and was charming and gallant. He'd agonized once about cancelling a date because of the flu, and only when he nearly passed out while tying his necktie did he actually make the call.

He hadn't had a date in a week.

What the fuck was wrong with him?

He shut the car door, locked it, and walked a few yards into the open field he'd parked next to. The ground was relatively level, which was good considering he couldn't see his own feet, much less the landscape over which he walked. Then he stopped. He was in utter silence, in utter darkness, and utterly alone.

He looked up.

A million tiny lights were so bright it was like he'd never seen them before. The sky was vast, seeming to extend all the way down to where he stood, wrapping him in stars. It was breathtaking, infinite.

He felt very small.

Looking from horizon to horizon, he felt a curious sensation of falling upward toward the sky, as if he could throw himself off the surface of this planet that had for twenty-eight years offered him success but no love and rise to join the vast emptiness above. He somehow knew, in that moment, that the stars themselves would welcome him.

It was a ridiculous thought, but in thinking it he no longer felt quite so alone. He imagined standing here, gazing up at the heavens, holding the hand of a beautiful woman who would gasp and stagger and be overwhelmed right into his arms. But somehow that thought left him feeling a little… empty?

"Christ, Fox, you're really off your game," he admonished himself. "What the hell's wrong with you?"

What, indeed?

Chapter TEN

HE KNEW what he was in for, but Fox reached blindly out toward his ringing phone, fumbled the rude instrument into his hand, and answered the call anyway. Better get this over with.

"Are you in bed again?" Chad's question crackled directly into Fox's aching brain stem.

"Obviously, asshole," Fox grumbled, squinting against the bare hint of sunlight that protruded through his tightly drawn blinds.

"Did she roll you? Hit you with something heavy and make off with your watch collection? You look pretty fucking rough, man."

"Are you so domesticated that you've forgotten what a hangover looks like? Asshole."

Chad leaned close to the camera. "There's hungover and then there's whatever the hell happened to you."

"Whatever." Fox dropped the phone, giving Chad a view of his ceiling.

Chad laughed. "I'm proud of you. I was worried when you gave up your table last night—thanks, by the way, it was totally awesome—but you got right back on that horse."

"What the fuck are you talking about?"

"You, going out last night even after you said you didn't have a date. I knew you'd get back on your game."

"I didn't go out last night."

"You stayed home alone and got that drunk? Holy balls."

Fox sighed in frustration as he picked up the phone again. "I had dinner at a friend's house. We started drinking bourbon after dinner. I got a little drunk. That's it."

Chad frowned. "How many friends do you have that you've never told me about?"

"One. I have one fucking friend, Chad. The same guy I had dinner with last weekend."

"Told you," came a voice from the lump next to Chad.

"Mia told you what?" Fox asked. "What did she tell you?"

"Nothing," Chad answered unconvincingly.

The covers flew back, revealing Mia's tousled mane and her face with its sly grin. "I told him you were going to be seeing that guy again. I think it's sweet." She yawned and pulled the covers back over her head.

"I'm not 'seeing' him. We're friends. We had dinner. Twice. That's it. That's all."

"Mm-hmm" came her reply from under the covers. Chad, uncharacteristically, glowered at the Mia-shaped lump next to him.

Fox grunted angrily. "Well, it's been great talking to you both—"

"Wait, hold on," Chad broke in. "Do you have plans for the morning?"

"Um, we do," Mia said, whipping the covers back off.

"I'm going to be nursing a hangover," Fox said with arch courtesy. "I'm sure you two will have a nice time shopping for tea cozies or whatever."

"No, you're going to have breakfast with me. At the diner, in an hour."

"Chad," Mia said, "we have to—"

"I have to have breakfast with my friend," Chad interrupted, his voice low and serious.

In all the time Chad and Mia had been together, Fox had never heard him speak to her that way. From the look on her face, she was as surprised as he was.

"That's okay, buddy," Fox said, trying to keep the peace. "You guys have plans—"

"No, we have plans. You and me. Be at the diner in an hour." Chad nodded firmly into the camera, then ended the call.

Fox sat and stared at his phone for a moment, shocked at what he'd witnessed. Then he set his phone back down and got out of bed. He padded naked across the room, glancing back at the phone a couple of times, still unable to believe what Chad had said. He didn't like to think of himself as the cause of friction in their marriage, but the truth was that he was touched that Chad felt so strongly about seeing him. Unless, of course, it meant he really was hitting bottom, and Chad felt it was an emergency.

He looked at himself in the bathroom mirror. He didn't, so far as he could tell, look like a complete basket case. But maybe Chad saw something more damning. Maybe he saw what Fox felt like on the inside.

A shower woke him up but did little to lift his spirits. Fox was not a man who spent a lot of time—any time at all, really—reflecting on his emotional state, plumbing the depths of his feelings. But this morning what he felt inside, what he could not keep from feeling, was the emptiness of standing under the stars alone. For the first time in his life, he felt like he might end up exactly that: alone.

He closed his eyes and took three deep breaths, the only technique he'd retained from his company's stress-reduction workshop. When he opened his eyes, he managed to bury his angst under the morning grooming ritual he could execute without any conscious thought at all. A few minutes later, moisturized, trimmed, and coiffed, he went to get dressed.

Sunday morning at the diner had been a ritual for Fox and his buddies for years, until one by one matrimony peeled the gang away—once taking two who had discovered they were more than buddies—until finally it was just Chad and Fox. Then it was just Fox. That first Sunday, the day after Chad and Mia's wedding, he had actually gotten all the way to the diner's door before realizing no one would be there. Except him. Alone.

He hadn't been back since.

By force of ancient, forgotten habit, he pulled on a pair of faded jeans and a weathered polo shirt, slipped on a pair of well-worn loafers, and grabbed his keys and wallet. As each floor whooshed past the elevator car, he tried to remember what it had been like to do this every week. It wasn't, he'd realized by the time he reached the underground levels, at all like his routines when it came to dating. It never felt like a chore to shake off whatever wreckage the night before had left pounding in his head and make his way to the large booth—then smaller booth, then booth for two—at the diner. They had all been younger then.

Though his car had never been to the Riverside Diner, it seemed to know the way, and soon Fox pulled it smoothly into the space he'd always preferred at the far end of the parking lot, where it was unlikely to get dinged by kids throwing open the doors of an SUV, desperate for pancakes. He locked his car and walked across the lot.

THE SYRUP-AND-BACON smell of the diner took him back instantly across the years to when this was a frequent haunt. And just as his car had ineluctably conveyed him here, he was drawn to the table that Chad and he had established as theirs during the year or more that they had been the sole surviving pair. He plopped himself down, the tacky-yet-slick vinyl upholstery grabbing at his jeans as he settled in.

"Coffee?"

He looked up to find the same waitress who had always greeted him, with the same question delivered in the same "whatever" tone of voice, every time he'd come to the diner. Her hair was still a strident blonde, though now there was a streak of silver that had escaped the colorist's clutches.

"Thanks," he said, and she smiled at him, a warmth coming over her features.

"Been a while, huh?" she asked.

"It has," he said.

She glanced up. "Ah, here he is. I'm glad you two are still together. You were always such a cute couple." She poured Chad a cup of coffee as well, then walked down the line of booths to top up other patrons.

Fox was aghast. "What the—"

"Foxy," Chad cried, holding his arms wide. Shaking off his shock at what the waitress had said, Fox got to his feet and gave Chad a warm, back-slapping grip. Chad, however, went for the full wrap, embracing him with both arms strongly pressed into his back.

"Hey... Chad," Fox said awkwardly. "You okay, buddy?" It was the kind of supplicating hug that portended a story of a death in the family or a hairsbreadth escape from some tragedy.

"I'm good, I'm good," Chad replied before finally releasing his hold. "How are you?" He slid into the booth, eyebrows up while he waited for the answer to what he seemed to consider a very important question.

"Fine," Fox lied.

"Bullshit," Chad retorted.

"What the fuck, asshole?" Fox reached across the table and slugged Chad on the arm for emphasis.

"I know you, buddy. There's something seriously askew in your personhood, if you don't mind me saying."

"I do mind. What you're saying is completely ridiculous. You took one psych class in college, and ever since you've been making shit up."

"You can't fool me. And we will sit here for as long as it takes. You will eat as many stacks of pancakes as it takes for you to tell me what's going on."

"Don't you threaten me with carbs," Fox warned.

"I will pursue the nuclear option if that's what it takes," Chad replied with great seriousness.

"What'll it be?" the waitress asked, having materialized silently at their table.

Before Fox could speak Chad pointed at him and said, "He'll have the Lumberjack platter over hard, with bacon, pancakes, and sweet-potato hash browns."

The waitresses nodded while scribbling on her pad.

"You're going to have to eat half of that," Fox groused.

"Hell no," Chad answered with a laugh. He looked up at the waitress. "Make that two."

She nodded and walked back toward the kitchen.

"What the fuck?" Fox blurted. "You can eat that kind of thing because you're married and you don't care how fat you get."

"I can eat that kind of thing because Mia and I have sex all the damn time. She's got some moves that burn the calories, man. You, on the other hand...." Chad made a not-very-subtle wanking motion with his hand.

"I, on the other hand, still remember where the gym is. You seem to have forgotten that when you traded your six-pack for the kind you drink to forget you're pinned to the couch all weekend binge-watching *Girls*."

"Ouch. Lack of sex is making you cranky."

Fox grunted in frustration. "Is this why you made me come down here? So you could remind me that I'm single? If so, let me say thanks because that had completely slipped my mind. I owe you one, buddy."

Chad looked ready to issue a suitable trash-talk rejoinder, but instead he took a swig of coffee and looked with surprising intensity right into Fox's eyes.

"What?" Fox finally asked when the silence got to be too heavy.

"I'm worried about you," Chad said, all raillery gone from his voice.

A surge of heat rose in Fox's chest as shame and wounded pride battled for dominance. "I'm fine," he said. He picked up a plastic stand from the table. "Look, they do trivia here on Thursday nights."

"You hate trivia, and I'm not gonna let you skate on this." Chad grabbed the trivia placard and put it back on the table. "You're not being Foxy right now, and I need to know why."

"What does that even mean?" Fox retorted.

Chad's expression softened. "It means we've been best friends for two decades. We've seen some shit together, and we've always been honest with each other. You were the first person who noticed that I was falling in love with Mia—hell, you knew it before I did—because we know each other better than anyone else in the world does."

Fox gave a mirthless chuckle. "Remember that spring break in Mazatlán? When you and that girl you met on the beach ended up naked in the—"

"I'm not going to let you change the subject," Chad interrupted. "There's something you're not telling me, and we're not leaving here until you do."

"Why is this so important to you?" Fox was unable to keep the frustration out of his voice.

"Because it's important to you. You're the man with the plan, and suddenly you're not on the plan anymore. I don't know who you are without your plan." He looked searchingly into Fox's eyes again. "Do you?"

"What the fuck does that mean?"

Chad sighed and slumped a little, but immediately straightened up and was back on the attack. "When was the last date you had?"

Fox should have been expecting that question, but it still set him back in his seat. "Why does that matter?"

"Because your entire life has been structured around finding the woman of your dreams. You have a plan, and you have a schedule, and you have a spreadsheet. We talk numbers after every single date. Or we used to, since by my recollection the last date you went on was a week ago Friday."

"You know what it's like at the end of the quarter," Fox protested.

"That's bullshit, and you know it. Even when you're up to your balls in the end-of-quarter rush, you still make time for two things: going to the gym and having dates on the weekend. Now, you're obviously still hitting the gym, because your biceps are about to rip the cuffs off that poor polo shirt—"

"This could be you, buddy," Fox broke in, flexing his arms. "You just have to get out from under Mia once in a while and get back to the gym."

"Shut up. We're not talking about me right now." Chad smoothed his own polo shirt down with a hint of self-consciousness. "As I said, you always make time for the gym and for dating. So what's up? What's keeping you from getting back out there?"

"Nothing's keeping me from getting back out there."

"So for the last ten days you've been so busy working, and working out, it hasn't even occurred to you to go on a date?"

"Why is that so hard to believe?"

"Because you're *you*, Foxy. You plan the work, and then you work the plan. In college you kept a fucking roll of butcher paper under your bed so you could make a twelve-foot timeline of every assignment for every class you took. You taped that thing to the wall of your bedroom, and you fucking marched through it, marking shit off every day. You never missed anything, and you were never late. You got shit done. That's who you are."

Fox stared back at his friend.

"So when faced with sudden, inexplicable behavior changes in my best friend, it is my duty to figure out what's going on. Because I love you, and I'm worried about you."

Fox shook his head slowly. "You already think you know what's going on."

"I don't," Chad replied, but his veneer of innocence was not up to the task.

"You do."

"I don't."

"You think I'm dating a guy and don't want to tell you because I'm ashamed, and here you're going to be the big hero and convince me to admit it to myself and live happily ever after with the man of my dreams."

Chad's face was frozen in a posture of supportive attentiveness.

"And I'm here to tell you that's bullshit," Fox told him.

Chad nodded. "That's exactly what Thomas and Jake told you when you first suggested to them that they might be not so much best friends as actually in love with each other. They said 'that's bullshit' right up until the moment they started making out on that camping trip. But you knew, and because you're a good friend, you wouldn't stop pushing them on it. Because you could see that denying it was making them miserable. Because you love them, and you wanted them to be happy."

"Man, they were pissed at me for like that entire year."

"Yeah, right up until they fucked the hell out of each other, and then you were the best man at their wedding."

"I'm the best man at any wedding."

Chad smiled. "There's my Foxy."

"Still not gay."

Chad shrugged. "I don't care. At this point, I'm really worried about you. I have no idea what's going on with you, but I'm going to keep pushing you until you talk about it. I see what it's doing to you, whatever it is, and you're not going to be happy—you're not going to be *you*—until you talk about it and deal with it and get your Foxy back."

Fox glowered at him.

"And we're going to fucking eat pancakes until you spill it. You're going to tell me what's going on with you, or we're both going to leave here weighing three hundred pounds."

Fox rolled his eyes to the ceiling. "Look, what do you want from me? What do I have to say to make you stop acting like I'm keeping some kind of secret from you?"

"You need to tell me the secret you're keeping from me," Chad replied. "Simple as that."

"I have no idea what you're talking about."

"I'm talking about why you've suddenly stopped going on dates. Start with that."

"It's not like I've stopped going on dates. I just haven't been on one in like a week."

"There's absolutely no difference between stopping going on dates and not going on dates. Face it, you've taken yourself off the market. My question is *why*?"

"Maybe there aren't any good prospects in my queue at the moment."

"Maybe?"

"Maybe."

Chad scowled across the table. "I've seen your photos, and I helped you with the twenty-seven drafts of your profile write-up it took for you to be happy with it. You are the hottest, smartest, wittiest sack of testosterone on that fucking service, and there's no way they aren't lining up to get with you."

"That's the fucking weirdest rant I've ever heard. And yet you can't argue with a queue that has nothing to offer."

"Give me your phone."

"What?"

Chad made gimme-gimme motions with his outstretched hand. "Your phone. Now."

"I'm not going to give you my phone. Why do you want my phone?"

"Because I need to see the parade of woe that you claim your queue has become."

"No, you don't."

"Yes, I do. Now give."

Fox sighed. Chad was like a dog with a bone. He was not going to give this up, ever. Fox reached into his pocket and handed his phone over, unlocking it as he did so.

"Okay, let's see," Chad said, opening the Q*pid app and swiping to the queue. He swiped, then looked up at Fox, then swiped again. He slowly shook his head, then set the phone down and slid it back across the table. He stared into Fox's eyes, expressionless.

"See?" Fox said in a voice that sounded even to his ear fully as doomed as he felt inside.

"What I see, sir, is a queue full of beautiful women who not only score in the eighties, but who have, almost unanimously, messaged you their interest. This is a promised-land queue. This is the queue of your dreams. Your wet dreams."

"Eww."

"Just telling it like it is. So you were either lying to me when you said your queue has nothing to offer, or your definition of 'something to offer' has changed dramatically since we last looked at your spreadsheet."

"I didn't see anyone who I felt would work out."

"'Who you *felt* would work out?' Really? Since when have you relied on *feelings* to determine which women you date? You gather the data, you run the numbers, and you meticulously target your wining and dining. You choose dates like the Fed chooses interest rates."

"Well maybe it's time I started thinking less and feeling more," Fox snapped.

"Who. The fuck. Are you?" Chad shook his head as if he could simply not believe anything Fox had told him. "Or maybe the real question is who the fuck is this guy you've been seeing?"

Fox stared silently.

"The guy. The guy!" Chad repeated, his voice rising. "Who is he? And what has he done with my Foxy?" His eyes were wild.

Fox swore colorfully under his breath. "His name is Drew."

"So, Drew. What do we know about him? And how did he manage to turn your life upside down in the space of a week?"

"He didn't turn my life upside down," Fox retorted. "He's a friend."

"A friend? Anyone who completely wrecks a guy in a week isn't a friend."

"He didn't 'wreck' me, you fuckhead," Fox growled angrily. "He's someone I met, and we've hung out a couple of times. That's all. That's literally all."

"He's not someone you met. He's someone that your dating service—the same one that's serving you up a seemingly endless queue of hot women the numbers say are perfect for you—picked for you. Picked for you because he's more perfect for you than any of those hot women. And—"

"It was a mistake," Fox interrupted. "They said so in an email like an hour after the match showed up. They said it was a computer error, and it should never have happened."

"And yet you went out with him anyway."

"We did not 'go out.'"

"Oh, so you didn't take him to Table?"

Fox glowered silently.

"And you didn't do the thing with the Jeffs? And you didn't sit at your special table? And I'm certain you and the sommelier didn't play your little will-she-or-won't-she game with the champagne, because all of that would mean you were *on a date.*"

There was nothing there for Fox to argue against. "We were not on a date. It was two friends having dinner. Why are you so worked up about this?"

"Because whether you want to admit it or not, this guy's knocked you off your game—the game you're better at than anyone else I know. And that's either because he's gotten in your head and fucked things up, or because you're thinking, at some level, consciously or not, that maybe dating him would be better than dating the women who are waiting in your queue like you're a buy-one-get-one-free sale at Victoria's Secret."

"Those are my only two options?"

Chad, breathing heavily from his rant, still never looked anywhere but right into Fox's eyes. "From where I sit, yes. If he's somehow convinced you that you're not going to find the woman of your dreams, that you should give up now, I'm here to tell you that's completely fucked up."

"Why would he do that?"

"Think about it, dumbass," Chad replied. "You two are, according to the computer, almost like the same person. If he takes you out of the running, then all of those Victoria's Secret shoppers move on over into his queue. It's kind of genius, really, but that doesn't keep me from wanting to rearrange his teeth on your behalf. Let's see how many women he impresses after he spits out a few incisors."

"You've never hit anyone in your life."

"I would be happy to make this asshole my first."

Fox shook his head. "That's not what he's doing. That's not who he is."

"Then you're telling me he has not convinced you to set aside the system that's been working for you—that's hard-wired into your psyche—and to take up life as a monk?"

"No. We've barely even talked about dating, except to compare notes on how creepy it was to be matched with women so similar to us that it was like dating a cousin or something."

Chad nodded, pondering this. "So the problem here is that your queues are just too good? Does his look like yours?"

"Actually, it's kind of funny. We compared queues last week and found none of the same women. It's like somehow we were supposed to be super compatible, and yet the same system that told us that matched us with completely different women."

"And he's been going out on dates? In between Saturday nights with you, of course."

"Fuck you," Fox growled amiably. "He's in grad school, and he's got some big paper he needs to be working on, so he's not been going out much."

"Except with you."

Fox sighed. "Except with me. Whatever."

"Whatever? Whatever?" Chad cried. "The Fox I know is the exact fucking opposite of 'whatever.' You've never said 'whatever' about the tiniest part of your dating agenda. There's no way to enter 'whatever' in a spreadsheet and have anything meaningful come out. This is what's making me crazy right now."

"I still don't understand how my dating life is making you crazy."

"Because if things continue the way they are, what's going to happen to you? What are you going to be left with?"

"Two Lumberjacks," announced the waitress as she set an enormous platter before each of them.

Chad raised an eyebrow at Fox, as if she had answered his question quite aptly.

"I'll get y'all more coffee," she said. "Anything else right now?"

"We're good, thanks," Fox grunted.

Chad crammed an entire strip of bacon into his mouth. "So?" he said around it.

"So I should probably get a T-shirt printed that says Still Not Gay and wear it every time I see you."

"Can I just tell you that you sound a lot like Thomas? Back when he was trying to convince you that he was completely straight?"

"He was mostly trying to convince himself," Fox said.

"Mm-hmm." Chad nodded supportively, which made it even worse.

"Fucking fuck," Fox grunted and stabbed at his pancakes.

"Look, buddy," Chad said in the tone of someone trying to reset the conversation, "why is even admitting the possibility that you might be into this guy so hard? What does it really matter to anyone? When Thomas and Jake finally hooked up, we were all relieved because Thomas finally stopped fighting it and Jake stopped moping every time Thomas went out with a woman. It made them happier than they'd been in years."

"When was the last time you saw Thomas and Jake?" Fox asked.

Chad sat back, brow furrowed. "I think it was at their pre-Christmas thing."

"And have you talked to them since? Texted? Liked a Facebook post about their pugs?"

"Uh... no, I can't say that I have."

"Thought so." Fox went back to glumly chopping at his Lumberjack platter.

"What does that have to do with them being gay?"

"It doesn't. It has to do with... us. All of us. We were a really tight group, and then, one by one, everybody got picked off."

"That's a grumpy way to say 'got married.'"

"Maybe I am grumpy about it," Fox said. "Maybe I miss my friends. Maybe I'm the last man standing, and it's fucking lonely. Maybe I'm realizing that if I ever find the woman of my dreams that will be the last nail in the coffin of our friendship."

"Whoa," Chad said softly. "That turned serious."

"Whatever," Fox said with a shrug.

"So, what you're saying is that you put the brakes on dating because… what, exactly?"

"Because what's going to happen?" Fox blurted, his voice far higher and louder than he'd intended, but he didn't really give a shit anymore. "I would meet her, get engaged, get married, and she would be my entire world, and I'd never see my buddies again. Or see you, like, once a year at Thomas and Jake's pre-Christmas party. We were friends, man. Think about that. You and I grew up together, and we formed the posse freshman year, and after that nothing could tear us apart. We were there for each other. And now no one's there. At all."

"I'm not saying this to make you feel bad, okay?" Chad said gently. "But I have someone who's there for me the way no friend could be. And I get why you're frustrated, because you don't have that yet. But you will have that, Foxy. There's a woman out there who will love you the way no friend ever could."

Fox stared at him. "Are you serious? You're really going to sit there and tell me that Mia is there for you the way I was there for you— the way all of the guys were there for you? She knows all about the time you got so drunk you shit yourself in the back of Thomas's car, and how you stalked Amber for like six months when she broke up with you for the last time, and how you cried yourself to sleep for a week when your dad told you he was leaving your mom? You told her all those things, and she listened to them and said, 'Chad, darling, I'm there for you.' Because that happened, right?"

"You're being a real asshole right now."

"You know what? Friends are assholes to each other sometimes, because sometimes a guy needs to hear the truth, and a real friend will risk being an asshole to tell it to him. We've been assholes to each other more times than either of us could count, and here we are, still friends. I can tell you anything, because I've told you everything. Now ask yourself, really think about it: does your marriage do that for you, or do you still need a friend?"

"When did I say I didn't need friends? I still have friends."

"But we're not friends like we used to be."

"Life is change, bro. We grew up together, and we'll always be friends. But people grow up and get on with their lives. We can't live like we're still all crammed into that old house Jake inherited from his grandma. We're adults now, and adults get married and stop hanging out every night with their buddies."

"I hate to be the one to break it to you, but we didn't stop hanging out every night. We stopped hanging out. The last time we had breakfast at this diner was the week before you married Mia. We get a drink once in a while, but it's never 'let's just hang,' it's always 'I can give you two hours before I have to go to this thing at Mia's sister's house.' We hardly see each other."

"We video chat the morning after every date," Chad reminded him.

"Yeah, we do. From your bed, with your wife right next to you. Like I'm going to tell you what I really think of the woman I had dinner with while she's there."

Chad set his fork down for a moment. "So, let me get this straight. The reason you've stopped going on dates is that you don't want to end up married and never seeing your friends again. But now you're saying we never see each other as it is. I don't get this at all. I still don't see what's changed."

Fox stared into his coffee cup. "Drew," he said softly.

"What? What was that?" Chad asked, leaning closer.

"What's changed is that I met Drew."

Chad nodded slowly. "And what happened then?"

Fox shook his head. He hadn't figured out how to explain to himself what had happened then. "We met, and we… we're friends."

"And being friends with this guy you met a week ago is more important to you than trying to find a woman you can spend your life with."

"That's not it—"

"That seems like exactly it from where I'm sitting," Chad said flatly.

"You don't understand."

"Then help me understand," Chad said, eyebrows peaked imploringly.

Fox was so struck by the warmth in his voice that all he could do at first was take a deep breath and try to figure out how to start.

"I don't think…" was as far as he got before his train of thought left the tracks and his voice failed him.

"I know," Chad said. "You don't think you can tell me. But you can. I got you, Foxy."

Fox smiled despite his internal turmoil. "Thanks, Chaddy, but that isn't what I was trying to say. I meant I don't think that it was a mistake that the computer matched us up."

Chad lowered his fork hand slowly toward the table. "What does that mean?"

"It means that we sort of... clicked. Q*pid's AI thing failed spectacularly setting us up with women—we were too much alike, which made it creepy—but it seems like it hit its stride with matching up friends."

"So he's basically another you? Super driven, successful, fully funded retirement portfolio, brilliantly white teeth, and never misses a day at the gym?"

Fox frowned. "Actually, he's getting a PhD in economic history. He cooks lentils and lives for free in a not-great part of town because he takes care of the place for the owner. He doesn't own a car, and a cloud of white liberal guilt practically swirls around him. So he's kind of nothing like me. But at the same time we're, like, completely compatible."

Chad nodded and gave a kind of squint, like he was working large sums in his head. He did not, however, offer an opinion.

"Dinner last week really surprised me. I thought we'd have a drink, laugh about how ridiculous it was that the computer thought we'd have anything in common, and go our separate ways. But it didn't work out that way."

"Okay, I get that. You made a new friend. But how did you end up deciding to give him your 'best prospects' dinner experience at Table? You never even asked me to go with you."

"What was I supposed to do, go home and sit and ponder eternal bachelorhood? Sounds like a great time. Dinner seemed like a better plan."

"But you didn't just have dinner, did you? The Jeffs came and did their 'very good, Mr. Kincade, sir,' act, and the maître d' greeted you like a long-lost brother and the sommelier brought you your bottle of house champagne and—"

"Actually," Fox broke in, "he brought us a bottle of something sparkling and French."

"You are fucking kidding me."

"I'm not."

Chad seemed to ponder this for a moment, and then he frowned and nodded. "So this is love."

"It's not love. We're friends."

"Friends can love each other. I love you, and I hope you still love me even though I've apparently abandoned you by getting married. But you've never taken me to Table, and you've never used your 'something sparkling and French' bit on anyone but a ninety-plus looker with a great rack and an even better brain. Can you sit there and tell me there is no part of you, even down really deep where you can't even think clearly about it, that thinks about this guy in some way that's more than friendly?"

"He's a friend. We're friends."

"You keep saying that. And yet you decided, for the first time in fucking years, not to go on a date for the next fucking week."

Fox shrugged.

"So what did you do last night?"

"Drew invited me over for dinner."

"And why didn't he have a date?"

"He said his queue was as bleak as mine."

Chad shook his head. "I saw your queue. It's a bumper crop of hotties." Then he took in a sharp breath and nodded. "Oh, I get it. He probably had his share of babes in his queue too. You both said you had no one to date so you could let yourself off the hook—so you could spend Saturday night together."

"Interesting theory," Fox grumbled. "Meanwhile, back in reality, we had dinner at his place."

"Mm-hmm. Did he order Thai takeout or something?"

"No, he made this Peruvian stew thing, and it was incredible."

"So he's a good cook?"

"More than good. I was a little worried when I saw the utter destruction of his kitchen, but as soon as he stuck that spoon in my mouth I knew it was going to be good."

"He stuck what where?"

Fox glared across the table. "He let me taste the stew while he was finishing it up."

"No, you said he stuck a spoon in your mouth. Did he put a bib on you before feeding you?"

"Shut up, asshole. It wasn't like that. He was excited about sharing it with me."

"I see." Chad offered no more commentary on the spoon-feeding. "So the food was good, and I'm sure the company was scintillating. Why did you wake up so crunchy this morning?"

Fox sighed. "Because we got a little shit-faced and basically passed out on his couch."

Chad nodded. "Sounds like your perfect friendship is one where you recreate our college days. Eat cheap, drink too much, pass out. Are you sure this is a good thing?"

"Fuck you," Fox spat. "It wasn't like that at all. He made an amazing dinner, and it took a lot of work to make it. I brought some bourbon for after dinner, and we both drank a little too much. But it wasn't like we were lying in a pool of our own sick or something. We were kind of relaxing on the couch, talking, and then we drifted off."

"Together, on the couch."

"Shut up. We weren't together. We were on opposite ends." They hadn't been. When Fox awoke he was pressed so closely to Drew he could feel his heart beat in his own chest, could smell the herbal fragrance of his hair. "So when I woke up, I kind of stumbled out and headed home. And this morning I had a hangover, not an existential crisis. There's a difference."

"Oh, is there?" Chad asked ironically.

"If you want to believe that somehow this guy I've known for a week has turned my life completely fucking upside down, then you go ahead."

Chad pursed his lips and nodded seriously. "So, my good friend with the right-side-up life, tell me about the woman you're having dinner with tonight."

"Who?"

"It's Sunday. Since your life is completely devoid of existential crisis, surely you have a Sunday date planned. Which of the lucky lovelies in your queue will it be?"

Fox picked up his phone, determined to tap on the first profile that came up out of pure fucking spite. He had to find a way to shut Chad up. But....

On his phone was a notification. New Message from Drew, it said.

There was a long silence where his heartbeat should be.

"Who died, man?" Chad asked, looking from Fox's phone to his face and back again.

"It's nothing." He opened the Q*pid app and tapped on his queue. That's when a second notification popped up. Another message. From Drew.

"Hang on—work thing," Fox said as he got up from the booth. "I gotta take care of this. Be right back."

He felt Chad's eyes burning into his back as he walked the length of the diner toward the restrooms. Once he'd turned the corner and was safely out of view, he tapped on the message.

Hey, you okay? Sorry about crashing on you.

Fox smiled and typed back, *No worries. I think I crashed on you first.*

He stared at the message window, desperate to see the flashing icon that told him Drew was typing back. It started to throb, and he started to breathe again.

Haha. That was some strong stuff.

Fox smiled. *Or maybe we're lightweights.*

That's gotta be it, Drew answered. *Hey, there's a concert on campus tonight that seems like it might be cool. Want to go?*

Fox froze, holding his phone with his fingertips like it was a ticking time bomb. Where the adrenaline rush came from—and what possible function it could serve—he had no idea, but he knew what his answer would be.

Hell yeah. What time?

Concert's at 7. It's like 5 mins from my place.

I'll come at 6 and bring dinner.

Fox stared at the words, horror dawning on him. He had just turned this into a date.

Drew wasn't typing. Fox wasn't breathing. Then finally, the icon flashed again. Fox winced, terrified to read what would come next.

That sounds awesome! See you at 6. :)

The breath Fox drew in that moment was the kind normally experienced only by those fished from under the ice of a frozen lake. It was sharp and fresh and painful and life-giving all at once.

And in place of all of the anxiety over his conversation with Chad, he felt happiness surge into his chest. Happiness that he knew he could never hope to describe to Chad, but it was real nonetheless. He stuck his phone into his pocket and walked back to the table.

"Everything okay?" Chad asked as Fox slid back into the booth.

"Yeah, everything's good."

"Is this what work is like for you all of a sudden? Getting paged on the weekend? That kind of sucks."

"It's not that bad," Fox replied, as dismissively as he could. "Now, where were we?"

"Don't you have people on your team who are on call on the weekends? I thought that was something you didn't have to do anymore."

"It was something that they needed me to...." Fox's mouth ran dry with lying, and he knew he had to give up on the charade. "Look. It wasn't work that messaged me."

Chad nodded. His bullshit detector was as finely honed as it had ever been. "It was him, wasn't it? He woke up and wondered where you'd gone?" A knowing grin began to emerge.

"No, it wasn't like that. He wanted to be sure I was okay, since when I left he was still sleeping."

Chad's smile widened. "That's really sweet. I'm happy for you."

"Why are you happy for me?"

"You found a good one. A guy who calls the next day even if you've only spooned on the couch with him."

"I never said we spooned on the couch," Fox objected.

Chad fixed him with a searing glare. "I know you, Foxy. I know what you're telling me and what you aren't."

Fox returned to his default posture of wronged glowering.

"Tell me what last night was like. Paint me a picture of this new friendship."

Though he felt mocked by Chad's supercilious skepticism, Fox considered for a moment whether it might not be helpful to have his perspective on the entire evening. He decided to take a leap and tell the story.

"He messaged me on Friday and said he didn't have any good prospects in his queue, and I said I didn't either—"

"Which we've established is a lie," Chad interrupted. "Just so we're clear."

"We've established that we have different views of the quality of the women in my queue. That's as far as I'll go." Fox casually scooped up the last bite of sweet-potato hash to clearly convey that he would entertain no more objections. "So I go to his place, and it's in that kind of rough area between the campus and the barren stretch that runs all the way downtown. Where all the co-ops are."

"Ugh, I can smell the patchouli still."

"His building is a newer one—probably the newest on the block. And it's decent, small but in okay shape. And like I said, he gets his rent comped by taking care of the place. So I park in his parking spot, since he doesn't have a car, and then I walk to his front door carrying twelve bottles of beer and two whites and two reds because I don't know what he's making for dinner, and then the bottle of barrel-strength bourbon I had someone I worked with in Kentucky last year FedEx me—"

"You've never put half that much effort into dinner with me," Chad objected. "I'm kind of jealous now."

"Shut up. It was really nice of him to invite me, and he's obviously dirt poor, so I wanted to bring him something nice."

"A metric fuck-ton of something nice, it sounds like." Chad's face was all sunny cheer, so clearly he didn't feel genuinely slighted.

"I got to his place and held out the drinks I'd brought. He, uh... thought I was, like, going for a hug or something, and all of a sudden his arms are around me."

"Oh, awkward," Chad said, wincing.

"Yeah," Fox said, staring hard into his coffee cup. He took an uneasy breath. "No, it wasn't awkward. It was... nice."

"Nice?"

Fox's heart was pounding. "It was sweet. And it was genuine. And it made me feel... nice."

"And did you hug him back? Nicely?"

Fox took a deep breath and let it out slowly. "I did."

"And how was it? Nice?"

Fox swallowed hard to keep his pancakes in place. "Yes. It was nice."

Chad nodded. "What happened next?"

"We drank a couple of beers, had his amazing Peruvian stew for dinner, and then drank too much bourbon after that. The next thing I knew I was waking up basically on top of—" He stopped short with a sharp breath.

"On top of... Drew?"

Fox was furious with himself, but could think of no stratagem to unwind his having said too much. He slumped, defeated. "We sort of crashed out on his couch, I guess. Didn't really take account of the bourbon being barrel strength. Stuff is like 140 proof."

"So you sat on his couch and drank yourselves unconscious?"

"No, that's not what it was like. We talked about a ton of stuff. The more I get to know him, the more I think Q*pid had it right. I would never have imagined I'd have so much in common with a PhD student in history who cooks authentic South American peasant cuisine and feels personally wounded by our country's lack of action on climate change. But being with him is this constant process of discovering things I like about him. And that's kind of... nice." Fox poked at the last triangle of pancake on his plate. "It reminds me of freshman year when we'd stay up all night talking about all kinds of shit, pretending we didn't have to get up for calculus at eight."

"Don't really have the stamina for all-nighters anymore, do we?" Chad said with a laugh. "Getting old sucks, man."

Fox nodded, but he honestly didn't feel old—in fact, spending time with Drew had made him feel younger than he had in a long time.

"So, you going to see him again?" Chad asked.

"'See' him again? You keep trying to make it sound like we're dating. We're not dating. As the T-shirt will shortly proclaim, I'm Still Not Gay."

"That proves it. You're seeing him again. When?"

Fox cast a weary look out the window, hoping for a dumpster fire or other happy event that could arrest the unrelenting downward slide of this entire conversation. Unfortunately, nothing was currently burning in the diner's parking lot, so he turned back to Chad. "Tonight, it so happens."

Chad's eyebrows danced up. "Tonight? And when were you going to mention that? Did you make plans before getting plowed on high-proof Kentucky moonshine last night?"

"No, he asked me a few minutes ago. There's a concert on campus that he thought I might want to go to."

"And you said yes."

Fox gave a half shrug, half nod that he hoped looked like very casual interest.

"Because you love music."

"I listen to music," Fox retorted in his own defense.

"And this concert—what kind of music will it be? Is it someone I've heard of?"

Fox very deliberately set his coffee mug at the edge of the table where the waitress would be able to see that what he needed right now was more coffee, because why else does one come to a damn diner for breakfast?

"You have no idea what kind of a concert you've signed on for, do you?"

Fox gave a kind of twitching shake of his head to show how little Chad's prosecutorial question flustered him.

"You have no idea, and yet when Drew asks you to go, you're like, 'Sounds awesome, man, I'm there!' because it was Drew who asked you to go."

"I enjoy spending time with him, and if this concert is something he thinks would be fun, then it probably will be. So what?"

"So what? So tonight's the third date. You know what happens on the third date." Chad waggled his eyebrows suggestively. More than suggestively. Declaratively.

"Shut up, asshole. We're just friends."

Chad was about to reply but was interrupted by the waitress, who grabbed up both of their empty platters in one hand, then filled their coffee cups with the other. "Anything else I can get you two?" she asked.

They both shook their heads, and she retreated to the kitchen.

Chad looked across the table, his expression suddenly serious. "Fox, I need to tell you something, and I need you to hear me."

Fox rolled his eyes. "That sounds like what Mia would say when she's going to tell you how the way you squeeze the toothpaste tube oppresses her as a woman."

Chad shook his head. "I'm not going to let you stop me from saying this. You are my friend, Foxy. My best friend in the world. I love you like a brother—more than a brother, because Paul's a dick—and there is nothing that could ever change that. I know you're straight, even without the T-shirt, but I wouldn't love you any less if this Drew guy turns out to be The One. I would be happy for you, and I would cheer you on, and I would be the best man at your wedding." He paused for a moment, his eyes seeming to search Fox for a sign that his message was received. "Don't even think of asking anyone else to do that. Because I would beat the crap out of that guy, and then I would be your best man anyway."

Fox chuckled in spite of himself.

"I'll say this one more time, in case you missed it." Chad resumed. "I love you. That will never change. No matter what you do or whom you do it with. Nothing could make me happier than to see you happy, and if it turns out this guy makes you happy, then I'm happy too." He reached out and put his hand on Fox's, something Fox could never remember him doing. "Got that?"

Fox looked at Chad's hand on his for a long moment, until the picture blurred and he needed to wipe his eyes.

"Thank you," he managed to say before his voice gave out.

"Good. Okay."

Fox glanced up and saw there were tears in Chad's eyes too.

Chad cleared his throat. "Check please," he called, and his voice was once again strong and clear. He flashed a smile at Fox. "Now, how many innings is it gonna take for that rookie you like to get tossed from this afternoon's game?"

Fox laughed. Chad was back.

And so was he.

Chapter ELEVEN

"I SOMEHOW ended up with some extra sausages again," Drew said, holding the tight bundle of butcher paper aloft.

"With your shopping you should be more careful," Mrs. Schwartzmann scolded delightedly. She took the packet from him and stole back to the kitchen. The smell of pastry was heavy in the air, and Drew, still hungover, drew strength from deep whiffs of the sweet aroma. He followed her to the kitchen and sat in his usual place at the table.

"Here is coffee," she sang as the sausages began to sizzle in the pan. "And here is some food to keep up your strength." She cut a huge slab of the pastry, slapped it on a plate, and set it before him. "I think you need it after last night."

He raised an eyebrow.

"I mean after you made dinner for that nice woman with the deep voice who didn't break your furniture." She beamed at him. "Your cooking I could smell. It made me remember my in-laws, who moved to South America after the war." She sighed wistfully, then returned her attention to the present. "I hope a lovely date you had."

"It wasn't a date," he said quietly.

"Oh?" she replied, no hint of surprise in her voice.

"No, I made dinner for the guy who took me out to dinner last week. To, you know, return the favor."

"Ah," she said, nodding. "That must be the man I saw leaving your apartment at 3:00 a.m. in the morning."

Drew closed his eyes, hoping that just this once the floor would open and swallow him. Why did that never happen when he needed it to? "Yes, that was him."

"And does this handsome and mysterious man have a name?"

"Fox."

Her brow furrowed. "Hmm. Fox. *Fox.*" Then her face brightened, and she nodded again. "Yes, I like it."

"I'm so glad," he assured her with no small measure of irony.

"So you and this Fox are falling in love?"

He stared across the table at her for a long moment, trying to parse her unabashedly joyful expression.

"We're friends," he said finally.

She nodded. "That's good. It is important to be friends before."

"Before what?"

"Before you fall in love and get married with him and start a family." She bounced in her seat. "Oh, what lovely children you would have," she cried, clapping her hands together excitedly.

"Mrs. Schwartzmann, we're not dating."

"This you tell me over and over," she said, obviously choosing to remain oblivious to his protestations. She got up and turned the sausages. "Now, how do you like your sausages again?" She gave him a little twinkling side-eye.

He tipped his head all the way back, hoping that if the floor wasn't going to swallow him, maybe the ceiling would collapse and Mr. Dillard from upstairs would land his lardy ass on him and crush him to death. But for as often as things broke down in the building, its floors and ceilings were apparently made from sterner stuff. He breathed deeply, trying to respire around the sludge that suddenly filled his chest.

"So why at 3:00 a.m. in the morning did he leave your apartment?"

He gave up any pretense of dignity. "We drank too much and fell asleep on the couch. He must have woken up and slipped out."

"This is not something a gentleman would do." She frowned on his behalf. "I am not sure I like very much this Fox you are dating."

"We aren't dating," Drew offered hopelessly, in a voice even he wouldn't believe.

"Mm-hmm." She smiled sweetly. "Certainly he called you this morning to say I am sorry for sneaking away and would you like to have dinner paid for by me again because I am so rude?"

"I haven't heard from him. I was probably drooling on him while I slept on the couch or something equally mortifying."

She smiled beatifically at him, as if drooling were the most romantic thing in the world. "Oh, to think of you two on the couch, right below my collection of teacups with the dirty paintings of sex on them!"

Drew had, up until that moment, no idea that Mrs. Schwartzmann had such a collection. It was not knowledge that he was grateful to be in possession of.

"But you must right now make words at him with your telephone," she blurted, her English syntax completely obliterated by the urgency of her command. She made frenetic typing motions with her thumbs.

"Why?"

"If there is one thing I know, it is the hearts of men. He will be wondering what he is to do about leaving at 3:00 a.m. in the morning and not knowing whether he should call you or if he should be a man and play pretend in his brain it didn't happen."

He stared at her, astounded at her ability to make sense even when her words didn't. "What should I say?" Was he really taking advice on relationships from an old woman with a tenuous grasp on reality?

"Ask him if okay he is."

Drew nodded and typed. Better not to think too much about it. He hit Send and started counting. He would probably start breathing again when he got to sixty.

The reply came before he got to thirty. He read it out to Mrs. Schwartzmann.

"Ah, there is the gentleman," she said with an approving nod.

Drew typed a reply. He only got to ten this time.

They shared a goofy smile over his reply, then Drew grew concerned. "What do I do next?"

"What were you going to do today?" she asked.

"There's a concert on campus I was going to go to."

"Then ask him to go with you. If it is meant to be, it will be."

He was about to ask her what "it" was, but he thought better of it when he realized the answer would probably alarm him even more than not knowing. He shrugged and typed out the invitation. The reply came quickly, and he followed up.

"So?" she asked.

"He's coming to the concert, and he's bringing dinner over beforehand."

Mrs. Schwartzmann practically vibrated with joy. "My faith is restored," she cried, clasping her hands before her.

Drew smiled at her display, but his grin soon faded when he realized what he'd done.

This was probably a date.

HOLDING THREE bags of steaming hot Thai takeout, as well as a cooler full of bottles of Singha, made it a little challenging for Fox to ring the doorbell of Drew's apartment, but he managed to do so just before six o'clock.

"Hey," Drew cried as he opened the door. "That smells amazing."

"Wait until you taste it," Fox said as he walked through the doorway.

"I can't wait, so I'm just gonna—" Drew said, stepping toward him. He took the bags and the cooler from him and strode eagerly to the kitchen.

"Hey, last time I got a hug," Fox called.

"Where are my manners?" Drew replied, hurrying back into the front room. He laughed as he threw his arms around Fox in a boisterous embrace.

Fox joined in his laughter, but somewhere inside—safely below the level of conscious thought, but there nonetheless—he felt a little tug that told him it was nice to be hugged, even by a guy, even while laughing ironically. Ten days of no dates meant ten days of not so much as a good-night kiss, and the absence of contact was starting to weigh on him.

Drew released him suddenly and stepped back, then took another step back as if to restore a sufficient distance between them. "Let's eat," he said jovially.

"Sounds good," Fox replied, and he followed Drew through to the kitchen. He opened the bags and sorted out the food he'd ordered too much of because he didn't know what Drew would like. In short order, he'd arranged the counter from satay skewers to sticky rice, with mains in the middle and condiments on the side.

"Wow, you're good at this," Drew said.

"Really missed my calling as a cater-waiter, didn't I?" Fox cracked. He opened the cooler and pulled out two beers, popped the tops off, and handed one to Drew. "To... music?"

"To music," Drew repeated, and they toasted to... you know, music.

Drew handed Fox a plate and motioned that he should serve himself some food.

"Nope," Fox said. "I brought it, so you get first dibs on what you like."

Drew glanced at the name of the restaurant on one of the containers. "Is this from that fancy place downtown in the galleria?"

"It is," Fox replied. "They don't normally do takeout, but I know the chef, and she helps me out sometimes. When it's a special occasion." As soon as he'd said it he realized what he'd done. Self-deprecating banter was Fox's stock-in-trade, allowing him to downplay whatever he'd accomplished by giving someone else the credit. In this case, though, he'd run on too long and said this was a—

"Special occasion?" Drew asked, a hint of a smile on his face. "Well." His eyebrow twitched up, but he offered no further comment as he surveyed the food and filled his plate.

Fox followed suit, and they sat at the kitchen table and dug in.

"So what kind of music will we be enjoying this evening?" Fox asked. He was still trying to figure out a way to defuse the bomb that was his "special occasion" remark.

"It's a marimba concert," Drew said, then shrugged. "It sounded like fun. I've never heard of four marimbas playing together."

"I'm not sure I could even pick out a marimba from a musical-instrument lineup," Fox said.

"It's a kind of xylophone, but with a deeper tone." Drew pulled out his phone and did a quick search. "Here's a picture." He held it out to Fox.

"So have you traveled the country following your favorite marimba band?" Fox teased.

"Yeah, no. I saw the posters for it around campus and thought it sounded kind of cool."

"Well, I'm happy to have the chance to stretch my musical tastes."

"And I'm happy to stretch you," Drew said with a laugh.

They left that awkward remark on the table and set to finishing their dinner. It was, after all, a special occasion.

"SO THAT'S a marimba concert," Fox said as he followed Drew through the front door of his apartment.

"Yes, it certainly was," Drew replied. "They all seemed really happy to be playing them, you gotta give them that."

"Agreed. It was like a sport, especially that last piece. Their little mallets were a blur."

Drew looked critically at him. "You thought it was ridiculous."

Fox seemed startled to be so accused. "I most certainly did not. It wasn't a form of music I knew anything about, but it was a really cool cultural experience. I'd forgotten that the university has this kind of stuff all the time. I should get there more."

Drew smiled at him. "You're always welcome."

Was that a little color creeping into Fox's cheek?

"I didn't mean you have to, you know, invite me over all the time or anything."

Drew was chuckling now, enjoying how hard Fox seemed to fight against any recognition that they were friends. It was like he wasn't used to having any.

"You are welcome here anytime. You know that," Drew said. "Care for a shot of this deadly bourbon I happen to have lying around?"

"I should probably get going, seeing as it's a school night and all."

"Ugh, don't remind me. I have a seminar paper that's been fighting me for weeks, and it's due Friday."

"How much have you gotten done, percentage-wise?"

"Let's see…," Drew said, casting his eyes up to the ceiling and pretending to calculate. "I think the precise figure is… zero. I've gotten exactly none of it actually written."

"Oh shit," Fox replied, his eyebrows peaked with concern. "Are you going to make it?"

"Yeah, I'll get it done. I have all the research finished. It's just a matter of writing it up. I got an extension, so technically I have until next Monday to turn it in."

"Is it going to take you that long to write it up?"

"I could probably get it done on time, but for some reason I'm feeling blocked on actually getting the writing going."

"Let me help," Fox said.

Drew frowned. "Help? How?"

"When I have a report to write or a planning document to get ready for review, I set myself a fake deadline so that I get it done. Like, I'll arrange with someone on the team that we'll meet to discuss it a few days before I need it to be done, and that makes me get it done in time. It's like working out with a buddy—it gives accountability."

"So you want to read my paper? Before it's due?"

Fox laughed and shook his head. "No," he said. "I probably wouldn't understand it. But I can do this: get the paper done on Friday, and I'll plan something awesome for the weekend."

Drew squinted at him. "How awesome?"

"*Super* awesome." He sucked in his cheeks for a moment and half closed his eyes. "Okay, this is what we'll do. Turn in your paper by five on Friday evening, and I'll come pick you up. We'll head to the coast for the weekend. My treat."

"The coast? For the weekend?" Drew blinked and shook his head, certain he had misheard. "I can't let you keep spending that kind of money."

"No worries. I did a great deal for a resort company last year, and since then they've been after me to come stay at their property. It'll cost me gas to get there and back—that's about it."

"A weekend? At a resort on the coast?" Drew couldn't believe Fox was actually suggesting this.

"Hell yeah," Fox replied, clearly stoked about the prospect. "We'll kayak on the harbor and cycle up into the hills—they have all kinds of stuff to do. It'll be a nice break to celebrate getting your seminar paper done. On time, even."

Drew weighed the proposal for a moment. "Ah, what the hell. Sounds good. You have to let me pay for gas, though."

"You don't have to do that, but if it makes you feel better, that's fine. Whatever. Now I'm gonna go so you can get cranking on that paper."

"Yes, sir," Drew barked.

"And I'll see you at five sharp on Friday. And pack a nice outfit—they have an amazing restaurant."

"You've already seen my nice outfit," Drew said apologetically.

"And that would be perfect. Again, no worries. This is gonna be fun." And without warning, Fox pulled Drew to him and wrapped him in a hug. "Thanks for the concert," he whispered. "See you Friday."

"Yeah, Friday," Drew replied as Fox released him.

Fox beamed as he opened the door and showed himself out.

Drew stood for a long moment, replaying their exchange in his mind. Then, when nothing got any clearer, he shrugged and went to his room to grab his laptop. He had some writing to do.

"YOU'RE GOING to let me have your table at Table again? Really?" Chad asked, leaning close to the camera on his phone.

"Yeah, if you want it."

"Why aren't you using it?"

"I'm going away for the weekend."

"Oh, Foxy, no. Don't tell me you're giving up completely."

Fox laughed. "No, still taking a break. And still not gay."

Chad jolted in his seat. "You're going away with him, aren't you? With Drew?"

Fox shrugged. "Yeah. He's finishing some big seminar paper, so I thought it might be fun. He likes to kayak and bike and stuff. Unlike some fat married people I could name. It's like a guys' weekend."

Chad, on his end, was silent. Fox endured about ten seconds of his wordless blinking.

"What is it?" he finally asked.

"You haven't…." Chad pursed his lips and kept the remainder of that thought to himself.

"I haven't what?" Fox was reaching the limit of his patience.

"You haven't done the Weekend since Miyoko."

Fox recoiled at the name. They had agreed not to say it after the way she'd left him.

"Look, I'm sorry," Chad said. "But you need to think about what you're doing here."

"What I'm doing here is spending a weekend with a friend," Fox growled.

"You remember what you said about how a friend sometimes needs to be an asshole? Today I get to be your asshole." He paused for a second. "That came out wrong. But hear me out—"

"Why should I hear you out? You're going to tell me a weekend on the coast kayaking with a friend is actually some kind of romantic thing, and I shouldn't do it. I'm tired of that shit."

"I'm not saying you shouldn't do it. I have no problem at all with you having a weekend away with Drew. I'm saying you should think a little more about *why* you're doing it."

"I'm doing it so I can get away from annoying things like work and the person who used to be my best friend." Fox glared into his screen.

Chad sighed. "Okay, whatever. I'll stop being your asshole now. Just know that even if things don't work out, I'm here for you. Like I was the last time you did this."

"Don't you fucking start about Miyoko. I know I rushed things with her. I revised the plan to be sure that never happened again. Now it's not even on the table until week four."

"Which is why you've never done the Weekend again. You've stuck to your plan. Until now."

"What's happening now, since you seem to have forgotten, is that I'm taking a weekend trip with a friend. This is not on the dating plan because *this is not a fucking date.*" He was shouting now.

Chad pursed his lips and nodded. "Okay. Got it. Understood. Drive carefully tomorrow, and I'll look forward to hearing about all of the amazing kayaking when you get back. Have a great time." His tone was one of kind insincerity.

"Thanks, asshole." Fox said as he reached for the Disconnect Call button.

"That's my job," Chad said resignedly in the second before his image disappeared.

"YOU WILL the whole weekend be gone?" Mrs. Schwartzmann asked for the third time.

"Yes, the whole weekend," Drew answered for the third time.

"But your studies," she said gravely, in the manner of a grandmother preparing to disapprove of some newfangled hobby upon which the young are throwing their lives away.

"My studies are fine," Drew assured her. "I had a seminar paper due today, and I just turned it in. So I'm free for the weekend, and Fox is coming to pick me up in a few minutes."

"Oh," she said warmly, in the manner of a grandmother preparing to meet the handsome surgeon with whom her grandchild has fallen in love.

"It's not like that," Drew protested.

"What it is like I did not say," she said with a gleam in her eye.

"I brought you these," he said, handing her the packet of sausages he'd picked up on his way home.

She seemed surprised by his gesture, but her serene façade of duplicity was quickly restored. "A full refrigerator is not what someone who spends his weekends in the country wants."

"You are right, except that we are going to the coast, not the country."

"I see," she said. Her expression conveyed clearly that she was, at that moment, seeing in her mind's eye the handsome Fox cavorting on the beach. Perhaps she was picturing them together.

"Well, I've got to go," Drew said brightly. He had to bring this festival of insinuation to an end.

"A wonderful time you two will have," she said just as brightly.

"Thank you, Mrs. Schwartzmann. I'll stop by when I'm back to make sure everything's okay."

"Oh, don't worry about an old woman," she scolded him genially. "If I survived the Castro regime, through a weekend I can get."

He laughed and shook his head as she closed the door behind him. But as he walked toward the stairs, he heard the door fly open.

"Drew, dear?"

"Yes, Mrs. Schwartzmann?"

"Make sure you have the condoms." She smiled sweetly at him.

He closed his eyes, trying to picture something serene, like a cool green meadow or a heavy-ordnance artillery range. "Thank you. I'm sure I'll have what I need."

"That's a good boy." She beamed at him and then shut her door. He could hear her many locks sliding into place as he walked downstairs to his apartment.

As he unlocked his front door, he caught sight of Fox's sleek car pulling into the driveway on its way to the parking lot behind the building. It gave him a little thrill, which he figured was really relief that he had his paper finished.

Yes, that was the reason for his heart racing. Had to be.

Chapter TWELVE

FOX WAS getting out of his car just as Drew came around the corner of the building. "I'm ready, I'm ready," Drew called. He had hurried out of his apartment with a duffel slung over his shoulder.

The trunk of the car popped open, and Fox came around the back to help him get his duffel stowed. "Get the paper turned in?" Fox asked as he closed the trunk.

"Sure did," Drew replied. "I was probably the first one. Everyone else was planning on spending their weekend writing."

Fox stuck out his tongue. "Sounds glamorous. Are you going to be sad you're not spending your weekend writing your masterpiece?"

Drew laughed. "I think I'll take being whisked away to a resort on the coast over rewriting my literature review section for the ninety-seventh time, thanks very much."

They settled into the car, and Fox pulled smoothly into the Friday afternoon traffic.

"Seriously, though, thank you," Drew said as they headed toward the freeway out of town.

"For what?"

"For forcing me to get that fucking paper done," Drew replied with a laugh.

"It's not like I aimed a gun at you or anything."

"No, but you offered me something incredible as incentive. There was no way I was going to let procrastination keep me from having what promises to be the best weekend of my life."

Fox glanced over from the driver's seat, an incredulous crook in his eyebrow. "Best weekend of your life?"

"Well, I've never spent a weekend at a fancy resort. I'm sure it'll be really nice."

"It's a beautiful property," Fox said with a smile, seeming to take no notice of Drew's fluster. "It was built in the twenties as a coastal retreat for a robber baron—oil or something. The stock market crash wiped him out, and the place sat and moldered for a few decades. It became a retreat for some kind of hippie meditation thing in the sixties and seventies, until everyone gave up on that, and then a private equity group took it over and restored it."

"So the modern robber barons brought back the splendor of the original," Drew said with a wry chuckle. "Very fitting."

"Well, they also built several hundred additional guest rooms with almost the same splendor as the original," Fox added, his laughter as wry as Drew's. "But, you know, on a mass scale."

"At least they have your company's systems to make every guest feel like a robber baron too. Except, you know, on a mass scale."

"Just you wait. You're going to love what my company's systems do."

Drew smiled. "I think I'm going to love whatever happens this weekend. This is already the most glamorous thing I've ever done."

"You don't have to tell me if you don't want to," Fox said after a thoughtful pause, "but it sounds—from some of the things you've said—like you grew up without a lot of money."

"It was mostly no money at all, actually," Drew replied. "We always had enough to eat, but we were the kind of family where if the timing belt broke on the car, we were going to be walking to the grocery store for a while. I'm the first person in my family to finish college."

Fox frowned, clearly impressed. "And you're going all the way through to a PhD. Wow."

"I want to figure out how income inequality affects the value of citizenship. I think it's going to be important for us to understand the effect of increasing economic inequality over the long term."

"Okay, so maybe a weekend in the robber baron's retreat was not the best choice."

"Are you kidding me?" Drew cried. "I'm considering it a serendipitous research opportunity. If I have to drink champagne while looking out over the ocean three times a day, I'll do it. That's how committed I am to my studies."

"You are a gentleman and a scholar," Fox replied with a chivalrous bow of his head.

"How about you?" Drew asked.

"I am neither a gentleman nor a scholar," Fox said with a laugh.

"You are the epitome of a gentleman, and you strike me as pretty damn sharp. Plus you're improbably handsome, so you have that going for you."

Fox shot him a scowly glance.

"But what I meant," Drew continued, "was what was your childhood like?"

Fox's smile took a grim turn. "It was… fine."

Drew could see how much effort it took him to finish that sentence. "Okay…."

Fox shrugged, then the words started to come. "Pretty standard for where I grew up. Distant father who worked too much and withheld his approval, unfulfilled mother who wanted me to succeed but not be anything like my dad. I spent a shit-ton of their money getting an undergrad and MBA at their precious alma mater, and now we see each other maybe once a year, depending on whether my sister is going to be there for a particular holiday. We have to tag-team my parents, or they'll turn on each other and then on us."

Drew's mouth dropped open. He would never have imagined Fox had come from such dysfunction. His own parents had had some rough times, but he had never doubted their love for each other, and for him. "I can't imagine what that would be like."

Fox shook off the empathy. "What it's like is that I had a lot of advantages growing up, even though they were mostly economic and not at all emotional." He shrugged again. "No big deal."

"That explains the spreadsheets," Drew said quietly.

"You think so, do you?" Fox asked. There was mostly good-natured challenge in his voice, but it was challenge nonetheless. "What's wrong with spreadsheets?"

Drew held up his hands to show he meant no offense. "Not a thing. I love the spreadsheets, actually, because they landed me here."

"How do you figure that?"

"When the computer matched us up, I had a bit of an emotional crisis. I thought it was telling me I was gay, which I would probably be fine with, given some time to adjust. It was kind of a shock, though, especially when I've always thought I had a pretty good grasp on my emotions. But I thought about it, and talked to a friend about it, and I started to think that maybe moving a little out of my comfort zone would be a good thing. You don't know what life has to offer if you don't put yourself out there, right?"

"Mm-hmm," Fox replied. He was clearly waiting for Drew to come back around to spreadsheets.

"You, though. Well, I can imagine you staring at my stupid face in your match queue, wondering what the hell happened. But you probably took a look at the compatibility scatter plots and dug into the discovery metrics, and you decided that numbers hadn't lied to you before, and maybe they weren't now. So when I sent you a message, the numbers helped tip the balance in my favor. You accepted the match because you couldn't argue with the quantitative realities. And here we are."

Fox seemed slightly unnerved by Drew's description, but he said nothing.

"So I'm really glad you're all about the numbers. Because without them, we wouldn't be here."

Fox pondered this for a moment, then the smile returned to his face. "It's a little creepy how accurately you described my thought process, but—" He turned to meet Drew's eye. "—I'm glad we got here too."

For the rest of the drive toward the coast, they spoke of far less heavy topics and enjoyed the views as the land dropped steadily toward the ocean.

"Wow, it really is beautiful here," Drew said as their first full vista of the ocean filled the windshield. "I had no idea this even existed a couple of hours from the city. When you don't have a car, something two hours away might as well be in another country."

"Wait until you see the view from the resort," Fox replied. "There's a seawall protecting part of the frontage, and it makes an amazing place to kayak. You can get out past the waves to explore these rock formations— tons of caves and sea stars and birds."

"Do you come here a lot?" Drew asked.

"I used to, but I haven't been in… well, over a year, anyway."

"How come?"

Fox sighed. "The last time I was here, I brought someone with me who, it turns out, wasn't a great fit. This was where it all kind of fell apart." Fox's expression was one of fresh pain, as if this falling-out had happened yesterday, not more than a year ago.

Drew socked him on the shoulder. "Well it's a good thing you brought me, then. I'm algorithmically guaranteed to be a good fit."

Fox laughed. "She and I fit together pretty damn well. And a lot. We were fitting several times a day, actually, until things blew up."

"I think we're working with different definitions of 'fit,'" Drew said slowly.

"I think you're probably right," Fox said with a nearly maniacal chuckle. "Anyway, I'm glad to have you along when I make my triumphant return."

"Happy to serve," Drew assured him grandly.

They twisted through a series of hairpin curves until the last one revealed the gates of the resort, huge piles of stacked stone and wrought iron.

"Holy old money, Batman," Drew said under his breath.

"You'd never guess all of it is made from molded foam and painted aluminum, would you?"

"No way."

"Yep. The developer told me the original gate was on some old logging road, and when they tried to move it here, it all crumbled. They think some master stonemason had fit it all together so perfectly that it shattered when they disturbed it. They couldn't find anyone who knew how to work with stone to that level of precision, so they turned the pieces into decorative planters and patios and had this thing molded out of polystyrene and cheap tubing salvaged from a refrigerator factory."

"Brilliant," Drew replied, leaning against the car window for a closer look. "Fraudulent, of course, but brilliant too. Isn't it kind of chancy to fake the first impression? This is the first part of the property guests see. Aren't they risking making the whole place seem fake?"

"Well, first, the whole place is fake. The original building was so far from meeting current building codes that it's now used for storage. And second, everyone who drives through those gates is so excited to see the actual buildings that this is only an appetizer they drive right past without looking too closely. If they spent a ton of money making it authentic and perfect, it wouldn't change anyone's experience—no one's going to pull over and look at it, much less run their hands along its Styrofoam surface. There's no compelling benefit to justify the cost."

"You are ruthlessly rational," Drew said, with more than a little admiration. "I don't know whether to envy or pity people who can put a dollar figure to human experience."

"You know me and spreadsheets," Fox said.

Having passed through the gate, they rounded the next curve and saw the resort buildings arrayed grandly on the bluff overlooking the sea. Drew had to admit that the fakery had been accomplished masterfully; it gave the impression of Gilded Age grandeur on a scale that was truly staggering. The impression continued as they pulled up into the porte cochere, surrendered the car to the valet, and proceeded through to the reception desk.

"Fox!" cried the clerk behind the counter. He ran around the imposing oak behemoth and then pulled Fox into an enthusiastic hug. "It's been too long."

"It's good to see you, Corey," Fox said over the shoulder of the clerk's formal blazer as it crushed into his cheek.

Corey finally released his grip. "You're not going to believe how excited everyone was to see your reservation show up."

"It's great to be back." Fox stepped back and held out his hand to Drew. "And this is my guest for the weekend, Drew."

Corey glanced in a flash from Fox to Drew and back again, and nearly recovered his composure before turning his brilliant smile on Drew. "Pleased to meet you," he said warmly and shook Drew's hand. Then he turned back to Fox. "Let's get you checked in, okay?" He walked back around behind the desk and began typing rapidly. "So, you reserved a double king room."

"That sounds right," Fox replied with a smile.

"Okay, so, because we were all excited to see you again, we kind of bumped you up to a suite."

"Wow, thanks."

"One little wrinkle," Corey said gently. "We put you in the Founder's Cottage."

"The one with the terrace overlooking the ocean?" Fox asked.

"Yes. However...." Corey leaned closer to Fox and whispered, though Drew could still hear him in the moneyed hush of the resort lobby. "It's a one-bed suite." He glanced in Drew's direction, asking the obvious question: had they planned on sleeping together?

"Ah," Fox said. He turned and gave a thoughtful glance at Drew before nodding and turning back to Corey. "The Founder's Cottage would be amazing. Thank you for doing that for us."

Corey beamed. "It's our pleasure," he sang. Drew suspected that at least part of that pleasure was the idea of the use to which they'd be putting that bed.

Oh shit. We'll be sharing a bed.

Why this thought nearly knocked the breath from his lungs he could not explain. But he figured that dropping to his knees and gasping for air would seem ungrateful, so he smiled and nodded and looked around the lobby as if he'd never seen anything so elegant. Which, in truth, he had not.

Corey tapped a last few keys, then walked back around the desk as a bellhop scooped up their duffel bags. "Let's get you into your cottage so you can start enjoying... whatever activities you prefer." He didn't wink wolfishly at this, but it wouldn't have made his implication any clearer to Drew. "But don't exhaust yourselves too much, because you have our best table at eight."

By reflex, Drew glanced at his watch. They would have an hour for... activities. An odd chill ran through him, but he shook it off and fell into step behind Corey. He led them out of the lobby, through double doors, onto a massive stone patio. To one side of the patio was a covered walk, with flowering ivies growing on both sides to give it the feel of a verdant tunnel. Tiny white lights crisscrossed overhead as they followed the sign to The Cottages. The walkway turned and ran along a bluff overlooking the sea, and every ten yards or so, a path wandered off toward a small cottage perched on the very edge of the bluff. At the end of the trail lay a significantly larger cottage, and it was to this they were bound.

Corey opened the door to reveal a bright but snug interior that seemed to Drew a textbook illustration of a craftsman-style beachside cottage. The interior was finished in wood, and nearly the entire side that faced the sea was windowed. Down the gentle slope of the bluff, waves crashed against a rocky shore. It was a beautiful view.

"I'll put these in the bedroom?" the bellhop asked, holding up their duffel bags.

"Yes, that'll be fine," Fox answered, and handed the young man a tip after he had done so.

"Is everything satisfactory?" Corey asked.

"It's so beautiful," Drew said, still gawking at the posh furnishings.

"I'm so glad you like it," Corey replied with a laugh. "We've taken the liberty of stocking the bar with your favorites, but please let us know if there's anything else you'd prefer."

"I'm sure it'll be perfect," Fox said.

"Well then, gentlemen, I wish you a very pleasant weekend." Corey backed out the door and closed it behind him.

The two men stood in the silence of the posh cottage for a long moment.

"I can't believe I'm standing here," Drew said.

"Wait until you see this," Fox replied. He walked to the row of french doors and opened the middle pair, filling the room with a sudden blast of sea breeze and the sound of breaking waves. He stepped out onto the flagstone patio, then leaned over the low stone wall that bordered it.

Drew followed into the bracing salt wind. He stood next to Fox for a while, mesmerized by the endless line of waves crashing against the rocks below. "Wow," he said, inadequately.

"It's pretty cool, right?" Fox said. "Now, let's have a drink before dinner." He turned and went back into the cottage.

Drew stood rooted in place, unable to tear his eyes from the majestic natural spectacle below him. A few minutes later, Fox returned to the patio, holding two glasses.

"What's this?" Drew asked.

"An old-fashioned. It was my go-to drink right up until my last time here. They set up the bar with all the ingredients because, well, you know why."

Drew sipped. "This is excellent. Why did you stop drinking them?"

Fox chuckled darkly. "Let's just say after having not one but two thrown in my face—at this very resort, it so happens—I was ready never to drink another old-fashioned."

Drew smiled. "And yet here we are."

"Here we are," Fox agreed. He touched his glass to Drew's and took a long sip of the drink. "But promise me you won't throw yours at me."

"I can honestly tell you it never entered my mind to throw a drink at you. Because that would mean I wouldn't get to drink it." He took another sip. "And why in the world would someone throw not one but two drinks at you?"

"Long story."

"We have the whole weekend."

"I'm gonna need a few more of these before I'm ready to tell that dismal tale."

"Then a few more we shall have," Drew said brightly.

Fox laughed. "I'll make another round. But then I think we'd better get to dinner while we can still hold a fork."

They drank the second round, then got dressed for dinner. Drew wasn't joking when he said he'd already worn his only decent outfit—aside from the very casual clothes that were the everyday wear of grad students everywhere, he had a couple of ridiculously conservative blazers he wore to conferences, panel discussions, and interviews. None of that would be appropriate for the kind of places Fox was taking him. If it hadn't been for his cousin's wedding last year, he would have nothing at all to wear; the wedding had been an evening affair hosted by the only branch of his family that had any money to speak of.

They walked the length of the covered path toward the main building, the trellises providing cover from the stiff sea breeze. Their table at the restaurant provided yet another breathtaking view of the ocean, and the food was every bit the equal of Table. They enjoyed a bottle of wine, followed by another, followed by a glass of port after their meal, and by the time they strolled back to the Founder's Cottage they were walking a bit unsteadily. They leaned on each other at various points to steady themselves until they stumbled through the door.

Their arrival back in the snug cottage sobered them up—a little.

"So, uh," Fox began. "Early morning tomorrow—made reservations for sea kayaks at sunup."

"Better get to bed, then," Drew said, trying to sound like he wasn't desperately trying to keep the room from spinning.

"Yeah." Fox staggered off toward the bedroom.

"I could sleep on the couch," Drew called after him. "You know, so it wouldn't be awkward."

Fox reappeared in the doorway. He was already unbuttoning his shirt. "The fuck you talking about? Get in bed."

Drew complied without a second thought—not that he was capable of even first thoughts at this point. He followed Fox into the bedroom, then walked to the far side of the bed. The last thing he remembered was trying to shuck off all of his clothes at once, though he could not remember how far he got before collapsing into bed.

Chapter THIRTEEN

FOX ROLLED over and grabbed at his phone. It was barely after three in the morning.

The first thing he realized was that he wasn't at home. It was far too quiet for this to be his own bed, as the ventilation system in his condo made a constant low *whoosh*. Here he could just make out the low rumble of waves cresting.

The second thing he realized is that he wasn't alone. He looked over his shoulder and saw the outline of a dark shape next to him. That would be Drew. The gentle rise and fall of the mound told that he was sleeping peacefully.

So, they were in bed together. This was all going as Chad had anticipated it would.

Fuck.

Fox edged himself off the mattress, then got to his feet. To his horror, he discovered himself to be completely naked. He strode purposefully toward the bathroom and grabbed a robe. As usual for hotel robes, there was too much of it for his trim waist and too little of it for his broad shoulders, but he managed to wrestle it on and tie it comfortably. He padded quietly out to the sitting room, where he poured himself a mineral water from the bar.

He turned off the light and stood for a long while staring out into the darkness of the sea. The last time he had looked out onto this coastline, he was headed for disaster and didn't even know it—the blowup had come at the end, when he'd thought everything was going so well. It was a brutal reminder that he didn't know women as well as he thought he did, despite the extensive analysis he had done. The quantitative model indicated clearly that they were heading for long-term status, but the cold splash of an old-fashioned in his face—followed shortly by a second—had shown that to be a significant miscalculation.

He swore he'd never come back here. And yet here he was. Or rather, here they were.

He could hear, under the regular cadence of waves, the more intimate rhythm of Drew's slow, gentle breath. Fox stood in the place where these two cycling sounds merged, sometimes unifying and sometimes syncopating. He tried to find sense in these natural rhythms, something beyond numbers and rationality. He tried to understand why he was here at all.

It was all a muddle. He finished his mineral water and felt his way in the dark back to the bar, where he set the empty bottle. Then he walked back into the bedroom and was startled to find that the moon had appeared through one of the high windows, casting a silver light into the room. The previously shapeless mound was now clearly Drew-shaped, and its soft rise and fall continued undisturbed.

Fox stood, again rooted in place by pointless introspection. It was one thing to crash, drunk, with a buddy into the only bed available. It was quite another thing to get back into bed with that buddy when one was sober and knew exactly what one was doing. Which was getting into bed with a buddy. Who was probably naked.

How long he might have stood there he had no idea, but then Drew grunted softly and rolled over. In the silvery light of the moon, the covers slid off as he turned.

Fuck.

If he had dared ask himself the question "Is Drew naked?" he would have had his answer now. Drew's entire side, from his foot all the way up to his shoulder, was uncovered. At least he was facing the other direction, Fox thought. His relief was short-lived, however, because his second thought was to ponder how often Drew managed to get to the gym. His calves were rounded, his quadriceps and hamstrings were clearly divided, and… well, the evidence of time spent in the squat rack was clearly laid out before him. His shoulder was rounded with muscle, and his lats gave shape to his upper back.

It hit Fox like a brick: he was watching Drew sleep. He was watching all of Drew sleep. He had never done that before—watched a guy sleep, that is—since as a light sleeper he'd had opportunity to watch most of the women he'd slept with over the years. He had watched Miyoko sleep when they'd spent the weekend here. She was the most pacific sleeper he'd ever known, lying like an empress in state, flat on her back, arms crossed over her, eyelids without wrinkle or flicker. Not at all like Drew's coiled strength—even as he slept soundly his sinews tensed and released in a rhythm Fox couldn't make out.

And now he was just standing, watching his naked friend sleep. *Fuck.*

Having held these two thoughts in his head next to each other, one a recollection of Miyoko sleeping and the other a present awareness of Drew, there was no way he could settle back into bed. He walked silently back toward the sitting room, pausing only to take a last look at Drew's peaceful slumber. Why he did this he neither knew nor cared to wonder. He shut the bedroom door, then went to the bar to turn on the espresso maker. There would be no more sleep for him.

DREW STUMBLED into the sitting room at a little after four in the morning. "Hey, are you okay?" he whispered.

Fox, who was sitting on the couch with a coffee cup in his hand, turned and smiled. "Yeah, I'm fine. Just couldn't sleep is all."

"I was worried when you weren't there."

"So that explains why you jumped out of bed and came looking for me before putting any clothes on."

Drew, horrified, looked down to find that he, indeed, was not wearing a stitch of clothing. "Oh shit, sorry," he said and darted back into the bedroom.

"Throw something on and we'll head down to the kayaks," Fox called after him.

"I don't think I brought anything appropriate for sea kayaking," Drew called back.

"No worries. Wetsuits are provided."

Drew grabbed a pair of jeans and a shirt out of his duffel, then returned to the sitting room. "Are you supposed to go kayaking in the dark?"

"It'll be light soon. It's pretty incredible when you're out on the water and the sky starts to lighten. All of the birds start calling, and the sea comes to life."

Drew smiled. This was a side of Fox he hadn't seen before. "Sounds great."

"Coffee before we go?" Fox held out a cup he must have made while Drew was getting dressed.

He took the steaming cup from Fox gratefully. "Thank you—that's exactly what I needed. It's like we've been matched up by a computer or something."

Fox laughed as Drew bolted down the hot coffee. "Good to go, chief."

A few minutes later, they were down at the boathouse that overlooked a protected marina. The energetic young man who staffed it jumped up when he saw them coming. "Ready for kayaking?" he asked.

"Yes, we are," Fox answered.

"Awesome. Just between you and me, the place is pretty full of old golfers this weekend, so I didn't think we'd have much action down here, and certainly not for a dawn paddle. Now, let's get you suited up." He sized up the two men, then grabbed a couple of wetsuits from the long rack behind him. "Here you go—the only two Clark Kents we have."

"Clark Kents?" Drew asked as he took one of the suits.

"Wetsuits for tall guys who take care of themselves," he replied. "We get people of all shapes here, but mostly they get rounder and rounder every season, so we keep getting fatter and fatter suits. We only have a couple of these—we call them the Clark Kents." He paused and looked both Fox and Drew up and down. "I think you know why."

"Thank you, Ryan," Fox said in exactly the tone of voice Clark Kent would have used—modest but not disingenuously so. "Do we change in there?" He nodded toward the curtained area to the right.

"Yes, please go right in. I'll get your kayaks set up. Come meet me out at the dock when you're ready."

Fox pulled the heavily brocaded curtain and gestured for Drew to precede him. Drew did so, but found to his surprise that there was only one room behind the curtain. It was tastefully appointed, with small lockers along one wall and benches through the middle. But there were no private booths, which Drew had expected to find. Not that he hadn't already been naked in front of Fox, but he'd been barely awake at that moment, and he was concerned about where Fox had gotten to and couldn't really be held responsible for that. And now he was standing like an idiot listening to an internal monologue.

"Better get moving, or I'm gonna leave you behind," Fox taunted as he neatly folded his shirt. He dropped his pants next and folded those neatly as well before tucking them into a locker.

Drew whipped his shirt off, then his pants, and folded them quickly and without the practiced style that Fox brought to the work. He stuck them in an open locker next to Fox's, then stood and turned around to find Fox fully naked and starting to step into his wetsuit. He was, from this awkward angle, as improbably handsome as ever.

Being an unflinching observer of humanity was something Drew prided himself on, as an academic and as a person. But at this moment, he wished he were more the flinching type. Before he looked away, the image of Fox's flexing buttocks was seared into his memory, both his musculature as well as his flawlessly smooth skin. It was the first time Drew regretted his unusually detailed visual recall. It was useful in research, but it was hellish when it caught upon an image he'd prefer to let fade.

"Woohoo, these are form-fitting," Fox cried, yanking the wetsuit up over his hips. It was no struggle to get the thick black material over his abs, but he struggled again when it came to wedging his arms and shoulders into the unforgiving fabric.

Drew flung his underwear into the locker and closed the door, then grabbed up his wetsuit and started tugging. Aside from some momentarily uncomfortable compression of his balls, he was able to get it up and on relatively easily.

"Hey, little help?"

Drew turned toward Fox and saw that he was facing the other direction, his suit open from neck down to the upper curves of his round buttocks. It was only once Drew let his gaze drop to that lowest point that he saw the zipper pull dangling there.

"Oh, yeah," Drew said, finally realizing what Fox was asking of him. He grasped the zipper pull and yanked upward. The neoprene tautened, allowing the landscape of Fox's back to come into relief under the surface.

"Thanks," Fox said. "Now turn around and I'll do you."

Though the double entendre wasn't lost on him, Drew did as he was told. With one vigorous yank his entire upper body was as compressed as his lower. A couple of deep breaths settled him into the suit.

"These are really nice," Fox said, smoothing the front of the suit. "Not too thick but enough to keep you warm out there."

"I've never had a wetsuit on, so I don't have anything to compare it to," Drew said. "It seemed pretty tight at first, but it feels better now."

"The ones for surfing in cold water are really thick. You can barely breathe in those things." He took several deep breaths, which had the effect of revealing and then hiding his six-pack abs under the sleek black surface.

"Looks like you're breathing just fine," Drew said with a laugh. "Or you're smuggling an actual six-pack under there."

Fox looked down, then back up at Drew. "You don't get to tease me about abs, mister," he retorted, jabbing Drew in the belly with his finger. "You're pretty fucking close to having an eight-pack. Studying your life away must involve eating no carbs."

"Sometimes it involves eating not much at all, actually," Drew replied. "Summers can get pretty lean if you can't line up a summer class or a research gig."

"Oh wow," Fox said. "I had no idea...."

"Don't worry about it," Drew said cheerfully. "It's a small price we pay to live the life of the mind."

"I admire your commitment," Fox said, a genuine warmth in his voice.

Drew didn't know how to respond to that, so he smiled and shrugged and waited for Fox to spring into action again, as he usually did. He didn't have to wait long.

"Let's get out there, man," Fox said, flinging the curtain aside. He bounded through the room and out onto the dock. Drew followed closely behind.

As the sky began to turn pink, they got into the pair of kayaks that Ryan had set out for them and were soon paddling out past the breakwater into the gentle swell of the ocean. Fox led the way, and after a few minutes of strong strokes, they reached a collection of towering piles of rock that loomed offshore. Dawn broke over the ocean, revealing sea stars in startling colors clinging to every open inch of rock, wiggly sea anemones waving for breakfast in the surf, and sleek black birds diving for fish all around them. It was like floating through a nature documentary, except that it was all around them. All Drew could do was smile dumbly and shake his head, overwhelmed.

Then he was nearly startled out of his kayak by the bark of a harbor seal about six feet away.

"This is amazing," he said to Fox when their boats drew near each other. "Thank you for bringing me here."

Fox smiled broadly. "Thanks for coming here. I had such bad memories of this place because of what happened the last time I was here, and now they're all washed away, replaced with this." He gestured all around them. "I owe you big for that."

"We're nowhere near even," Drew protested.

Fox shook his head, bringing an end to the conversation. "Come on. I want to show you the caves."

They toured around the edges of the bay for a while, and right about the time Drew's arms were starting to give out Fox turned his kayak toward shore. They paddled in at a more leisurely pace, but Drew knew he'd be feeling it later.

But Fox was just getting going. They dried and changed and walked up to the main building to grab some breakfast, and then they were off to grab bikes and head up into the hills that rose gently up from the shore. They cycled for three or four hours, stopping every once in a while to take in the view across ocean and meadow. When they finally worked their way back to the resort, Drew breathed a sigh of relief. They stopped back into the restaurant for a more than usually hearty lunch, after which Drew felt ready for a nap—and maybe a therapeutic massage.

"So next," Fox said as the waiter cleared the lunch dishes, "we can either go paddleboarding or scrambling along the rocks down by the shore."

Drew managed a smile. "How about something simple, like taking a walk on the beach? Should we feel the need to scramble, we can do that too."

Fox returned his smile. "Sounds good. The beach goes on for about a dozen miles to the south, so we can get a good walk in."

Awesome, Drew thought.

They walked the full dozen miles and back again, during which time they talked about a million different things, mostly trivial stuff that friends accumulate between them over years—but Fox and Drew seemed to gather them up over the course of minutes. Finally, as the sun sank low in the sky, they returned to the resort.

"Get cleaned up and then head to dinner?" Fox asked.

"Sounds great. You go first—I need to stretch a bit after you running me ragged today."

Fox laughed. "You're in better shape than I am, and you know it."

"Right now I certainly don't know it."

DREW WAS in the shower when there was a knock on the door of the cottage. Fox opened it to find two waiters with a large trolley between them.

"Um, yes?" Fox said uncertainly.

"We're here to serve dinner, sir?" the first waiter said.

"Oh, uh…." Fox was momentarily at a loss.

"Oh, great," Drew said from behind him. He stood in the middle of the room, wrapped in a towel, still dripping wet. "Can you set it up on the patio?"

"Of course, sir," the waiter said, clearly relieved that there had been no misunderstanding. They hustled the trolley through the room and out onto the patio, closing the doors behind them.

Fox looked at Drew, eyebrows raised inquisitively.

"I thought it might be nice to have dinner on the patio tonight."

Fox had to smile. "It's been a long time since anyone's planned something nice for me." He glanced through the french doors at the waiters, who were busy laying a white tablecloth and setting out what looked like a rather extravagant meal.

"I called Corey and asked if he would help me with it," Drew said. "He seemed thrilled to have the chance to do something nice for you. Though probably not as much as… I am."

"You'd better get dressed, or I'm going to start without you," Fox said.

"Do you mean my fine Egyptian cotton towel doesn't meet your dress code?"

"I'm fine with it, but you know how the breeze can whip up. You wouldn't want to reveal anything you don't intend to."

"I'm not sure you're fully aware of what I intend," Drew said airily. Then he turned and stalked away into the bedroom. He was back before the waiters finished preparing dinner on the patio, so they waited together by the bar.

"Can I make you a drink?" Fox asked.

Drew pursed his lips and pondered this for a moment. "No, I don't think so. Your cocktails are amazing, but I don't particularly want to get falling-down drunk again tonight."

"Ah," Fox replied, while he tried to figure out how he felt about Drew's sudden abstemiousness. "You know, you're right. Last night was kind of too much, wasn't it?"

Drew nodded. "A bit."

The patio doors opened, and the lead waiter stepped into the room. "Gentlemen, please come to dinner." He gestured broadly for them to precede him.

A dozen torches flickered all along the stone wall that formed the edge of the patio, their dancing light making the crystal and silver on the table gleam and sparkle. A silver candelabrum contributed eight more points of light.

"Wow," Fox said. He had eaten gourmet meals in spectacular settings over the years he'd been in the industry, but the transformation wrought on this simple stone patio was simply incredible.

They sat at the table, and the waiters served them course by course. Drew had somehow managed to select for them a menu of Fox's favorites, the centerpiece being a chateaubriand they shared. He didn't give the lack of wine a thought until the very end of the meal when the coffee—brought by a third waiter to accompany dessert—was poured.

"We'll leave you gentlemen to the rest of your evening," the waiter said after laying dessert before them. "We'll come back in the morning to collect the service."

"Thank you," Drew said, with a genuineness that people not used to being waited on often evidence.

"It was our pleasure, sir. I wish you pleasure as well."

Fox caught sight of his wink, and though the insinuation should have made him furious, it actually aroused nothing like indignation. He was enjoying himself so much he couldn't be bothered if a waiter thought the two them would be... together.

They sat alone on the patio for a while, finishing their coffee and listening to the crash of the surf below.

"Thank you," Fox said finally. It was the smallest portion of what he wanted to say, but it was the part that he could put into words. "This was amazing."

Drew smiled. "You are amazing. All I did was order dinner."

"Order dinner? You make it sound like you called room service and asked for whatever they happened to be serving. This—all of this—requires not only thoughtfulness but confidence. And a flair for the grand romantic gesture." He instantly regretted saying this last bit, though part of him was proud to be mature enough to admit that most women would likely be swayed by such a performance.

"Grand romantic gesture?" Drew replied. "Really."

Fox laughed. "Well, let's just say no one's done anything like this for me in a long time. Maybe ever."

"I am happy to be the exception to the rule."

"You've made me question a lot of my rules," Fox said.

The smile on Drew's face was embarrassed and delighted and joyful all at once. But soon his expression shifted to one of postprandial fatigue. "This has been a really long day. A really great, really fun, really long day. I'm about ready to drop into bed."

"Sounds awesome." It did not actually sound awesome to Fox.

Last night when they had crashed into bed, they'd been drunk out of their minds and could hardly be blamed for stripping off and passing out. Tonight, though, they were stone-cold sober. Tonight they would know exactly what they were doing when they pulled back those covers to climb into bed together.

Drew got up and snuffed out the torches one by one, while Fox blew out the candles on the table. Having doused the light on the patio, they headed back into the cottage and then found themselves standing next to the bed.

"Why don't you go ahead," Fox said, pointing to the bathroom.

"Uh, thanks," Drew replied. He grabbed his kit and went into the bathroom.

Fox opened his suitcase and found the shorts and T-shirt that he planned to use as pajamas during this trip. He stood for a moment holding them, but then he thought how silly it would seem if, after sleeping naked last night, he were to get into bed wearing pajamas tonight. Wouldn't that let Drew know how conflicted he felt about the whole thing? Wouldn't that make him seem anxious about sleeping in the same bed? That is, wouldn't that convey clearly how fucked up he was when it came to his own emotional state?

Fuck.

He grabbed the robe from where the maid had left it, neatly on a hook next to the bathroom door, and once he'd stripped off his shirt, he threw the robe over himself. Then he took off his pants and underwear and finally stood with only the robe covering him. He looked in the mirror and nodded to his reflection, trying to be casually naked underneath the tightly tied robe.

Fox jumped when the toilet flushed, and he busied himself getting his toiletries together while Drew made his way out of the bathroom. When he looked up, he saw that Drew also had a robe tied tightly around himself. So they were on the same page.

But was it a page Fox wanted to be on? Because he was pretty sure that down at the bottom of that page there was a footnote that read "*Then they got into bed together, naked.*"

He smiled at Drew, belying nothing of his inner state, and took his place in the bathroom. He made his evening ablutions with the efficiency of a well-practiced routine, and in less than five minutes had washed, dried, and peed his way to the end. He tied the robe back around himself and opened the door.

Drew was already in bed, lying on his side and facing away. Fox stepped quietly into the room and set his kit down on his duffel bag atop the dresser. Then he saw it.

Next to Drew's side of the bed was his robe, neatly draped over the back of the chair that sat there. Of course it was. It's not like he was going to get in bed wearing a robe. So he had taken it off.

Which meant that Drew was…

Fox took a deep, silent breath. He switched off the only light left in the room, the Tiffany-style lamp that stood on his nightstand, and then, with only a trickle of moonlight to guide him, he untied his robe and set it, like Drew's, over the back of a chair.

He pulled back the covers and slid into bed. Naked. With another guy.

Why are you doing this? The voice rattled in his head. What possible reason could he have for climbing into bed with Drew, fully sober, fully naked? He couldn't explain it to anyone, least of all himself, and yet here he was. He had no spreadsheet that would provide quantitative cover for what he was doing. He was acting purely on impulse—an impulse he didn't understand.

He lay on his back, studying the streaks of light made by the moonlight as it filtered through the many panes of glass that made up most of the wall facing the sea. He listened for Drew's slow, calm breathing, and tried to match it. He wanted to feel the peace Drew clearly did. Drew certainly wasn't lying awake in the throes of some stupid existential crisis the way Fox was.

"Thank you." Drew's voice was soft and low. He turned over so he was facing Fox. "This has been amazing."

What was it about Drew's voice that had the power to soothe him almost instantly? Fox felt a cool peacefulness ripple through his chest.

"I've had a great time," Fox said. "I never thought I'd come here again."

"Well, I'm really glad you invited me. You managed to solve my procrastination problem *and* give me this incredible weekend. I don't know how to thank you."

Fox smiled and turned on his side to face Drew. "You don't have to thank me. I should be thanking you. I was so anxious about not having anyone in my queue I wanted to date that I was starting to think I might have to get used to being alone. My friends are all married, and I never see them anymore, which is another thing I couldn't really admit to myself before I met you. You've really helped me is what I'm trying to say. It makes me feel like I can get back out there and keep trying."

"Can I tell you something?" Drew asked quietly.

"Look at us," Fox said with a chuckle. "This hardly seems like the time and place for us to keep secrets."

Drew smiled, but quickly grew serious again. "When you said you didn't have anyone in your queue you wanted to date—"

"And you said the same," Fox reminded him.

"I did," Drew replied. "But…." He took a breath, then pursed his lips as if trying to find the right words. "But that wasn't exactly true."

"What's that mean?"

"It means there were actually about a dozen new matches in my queue, and some of them… well, let's just say that before, I would have jumped at any of them."

"Before what?"

"Before… before I met you."

Fox frowned. He certainly didn't want to throw Drew off his game—maybe it was because he had more money? Like Drew felt ashamed?

"Did I do something? Am I keeping you from—"

"No, you didn't do anything," Drew interrupted. "You aren't keeping me from dating. It's that... well... okay, I guess you are keeping me from dating."

"What? Why?" Fox was startled and more than a little alarmed.

"It's because when I think of making the choice between going on a date with a woman I've never met, and being with you, well... I guess I kind of choose you."

Somewhere in the back of Fox's mind there was an alarm bell ringing, trying to alert him to the fact that he had made the same choice without even thinking about it. He breathed deeply and tried get himself centered again. "Look, I've been having a great time too, but I would never want to get in the way of you finding love. You need to get back out there, man."

Drew smiled wanly. "I should say the same for you."

"What does that mean?"

"Like you said, this is hardly the time and place for us to not say what we know is true. I know your queue has got to be better than mine, because you're successful and charming and, as we've established, improbably handsome."

"You have got to stop saying that."

"I'll stop saying it when it stops being true," Drew replied with a laugh. "Though we both know that's never going to happen. My point is that I'm willing to bet everything I have that your queue is full of beautiful women with beautiful scores who would make beautiful spreadsheets. And yet here you are."

"You don't know what my queue looks like," Fox protested.

"Yes, I do. You showed me last week. Your queue was unbelievable, and it can only have gotten better—mine's gotten a little better, so yours must be absolutely stellar now."

"I don't know what you're—"

"Let me finish. Since the computer hooked us up, I'm no longer stressing about not finding women to date. It's okay that I focus on my research and not check Q*pid every hour for new matches. I'm happier than I've been in a long, long time. And all of that is because of you. Because when I'm with you, I feel like a better version of myself. That's why I wanted to do dinner for you tonight, and why I wanted not to be drunk when we got into bed. Because I needed to tell you this, and I needed you to hear me."

Fox studied Drew's face in the moonlight for a long moment. "I'm not sure I understand what you're saying."

"I think what I'm saying," Drew said, but then he stopped short to take a couple of rapid breaths, like he was about to jump off something tall. "What I'm saying is I think I'm falling in love with you a little." He blinked several times as if he expected Fox to punch him in the face.

"This is really hard for me to say," Fox began after taking a deep breath, "but I've come to realize my life was pretty empty. It may have been booked up with dates, but I see now I was super lonely. I am so glad you reached out when we got matched up. It's nothing I would ever have done, but I honestly cannot imagine how much poorer my life would be if you hadn't. I love you too, man." He smiled widely, profoundly relieved that he had gotten that out before allowing his natural reticence around emotions to squelch it. Chad was the only other man he'd ever said that to, and he determined that he wouldn't keep some weird vestige of homophobia from allowing him to say it to his new friend.

Drew smiled. "That's... well, that's amazing. I know that kind of thing is hard for you to say, and I'm really glad you did." His smile faded quickly, though. "It's just that...."

Fox searched Drew's eyes for a sign of what was troubling him, but could make nothing out. "What is it? Come on, you can tell me anything."

Drew closed his eyes, and when he opened them he spoke slowly and calmly. "I have to be honest with you, and with myself. When I said I think I'm falling in love with you, I meant"—he reached out and put his hand on Fox's arm—"I think I'm really falling in love with you." He ran his hand down Fox's arm, a seemingly innocent gesture that made his meaning crystalline.

Fox felt the heat of Drew's touch spread through his arm, scorching him, mocking him. "What the fuck," he grunted, grabbing Drew's hand and throwing it off him. "What the fucking fuck?"

Drew's expression was one of utter devastation, but Fox didn't give a shit about that. "Fox, I thought we—"

"You thought what?" Fox roared. "You thought this was a fucking romantic weekend? You thought a candlelight dinner would get me ready for you to make a move?"

"Listen to me," Drew said, making the worst mistake of the night. He put his hand back on Fox's arm.

"Get the fuck away from me!" Fox shouted, shoving Drew back with both hands—and kicking him away for good measure.

With a thump, Drew fell to the floor. Fox leapt up from the bed—he had ignored the internal warning signs, and he would ignore them no longer. He would never get back into that bed.

Drew got up from the floor and stood unsteadily. The two men stared at each other for a long moment, as if neither wanted to make the first move.

"What the fuck, man? I'm not a fucking faggot," Fox finally said, bringing an end to the silence. It did not, however, bring an end to their conflict.

Without warning, Drew launched himself over the bed, closing the gap between them in less than a second. He crashed into Fox, head down and fists up, knocking him back against the wall with a mighty thud. Fox saw stars as he fought to push Drew off him. He brought a knee up between them and kicked hard, and with a grunt Drew rolled away from him. Fox jumped after him, wrapping his arm around Drew's neck and holding him in place. "Stop it," he demanded, growling directly into Drew's ear.

"No fucking way," Drew grunted back, and with a vicious twist he freed himself from Fox's grip. He landed a powerful shove squarely in the middle of Fox's chest, knocking him backward into the nightstand and dropping the lamp onto the floor. Drew got to his feet, perhaps thinking that the crash of a shattering glass lampshade would bring an end to their fight.

Fox proved him wrong with a running tackle that hit Drew in the lower back and sent him sprawling across the bed. Fox landed atop him and again secured him in a wrestling hold that was more comprehensive. Drew, however, seemed to be driven in his fury to feats of strength and leverage far beyond Fox's expectation. He thrashed free of the hold, then with superhuman dexterity, flipped Fox around and put him in a similar, but far more aggressive, hold.

"Get. The fuck. Off me." Fox's voice was low and murderous.

"Like hell I will," Drew growled in reply. "There's some shit here we need to deal with."

"There's nothing we need to 'deal with.' What we need to do is get the fuck out of here."

"No." Drew's voice carried a finality that struck Fox as surely as his punches had.

"We knew this was a mistake going in," Fox said, his breathing made shallow by the compression of Drew's wrestling hold. "It was a computer mistake that we made even bigger by trying to be friends."

"This is not a mistake," Drew grunted, squeezing even harder.

"Let me go, fucker," Fox said, his voice sounding high and weak.

"No," Drew repeated. "Not until we talk about this. Not until you can tell me you don't feel it too." His voice softened a little, and his grip slackened enough for Fox to draw his first deep breath in far too long.

"Feel what?" Fox asked. "I have no idea what you're talking about."

"I'm talking about what made you ignore your dating queue and come here with me this weekend." Drew's voice rushed hot into his ear. "I'm talking about the way you looked at me when the waiters came here to set up dinner. I'm talking about how you hugged me after the marimba concert."

"So what?"

"So I know you feel what I feel. I see it. I can tell it's there for you just like it's there for me. I want us to figure out together what we do about it."

"We don't do anything about it," Fox replied. "Why do we have to do anything about it?"

"Because I cannot go on like this," Drew said softly. "I cannot go on pretending to myself and pretending to you that what we're doing here is only friendship. What it is… is love."

"No," Fox said, but the thickness of his voice and the hot tears that surged into his eyes betrayed him. "That's not what…," he managed to get out before his throat closed around the lie he was about to tell. He could go no further, wanted to go no further in his denials against the truth Drew spoke.

"That's exactly what," Drew said, releasing his hold. He knew Fox had broken. Somehow he knew it.

Fox struggled to free himself from Drew's entwining grasp, but though Drew had relaxed his considerable musculature, he still had his arms—and apparently a leg—wrapped around him. Frustrated, Fox turned over and faced him.

"What do you want me to say?"

"I don't want you to say anything. I want to know you will let yourself feel this."

"What am I supposed to be feeling?" Fox asked. He knew what Drew meant, but he could not bear to show it.

"This," Drew said. He took Fox's hand in his own and pulled it to him until it rested flat against his chest, against his pounding heart. "This is what I feel when we're together. When you're near me, I...." His voice faltered. "I become a better person. I know it—I feel it here. Right here."

"Your heart is pounding because you went ninja on me, man," Fox protested.

"After you shoved me. And then you used the F-word." Drew looked scoldingly at him.

"I use the F-word all the time. So do you."

"Not *fuck*. You said *faggot*. That shit's not going to fly with me."

Fox felt a stab of shame. "I don't know why I said that. I wasn't thinking clearly. I'm sorry."

Drew shook his head. "You know as well as I do why you said it. You found yourself in bed with another man who had just confessed that he's starting to fall in love with you. I kind of dropped that on you all at once—that had to be a bit of a shock."

"It wasn't."

Drew's eyes widened, as if he was as shocked to hear Fox say this as Fox was himself. But say it he had.

"It wasn't?" Drew asked, shaking his head.

"No. I mean, it was, but it's not like it shouldn't have occurred to me that you would say that. It's what I've spent the last week trying not to allow myself to even think. Because you're right—about my queue not being empty, about me not even considering going on any dates, about how I must have looked at you when you arranged that amazing dinner tonight. I was scared and ashamed and confused, and to hear you say out loud what I've been trying not to even allow into my head completely fucked me up. I didn't mean to hurt you."

"There's nothing you could do that would hurt me, except leave." Drew looked searchingly into Fox's eyes. "I could take anything but that."

"Which explains why you just about crushed me when I said we should go. You pretty much owned me, man."

"I'm sorry. I didn't know what to do."

"So you settled on pummeling me into submission?"

"Not proud of that. I'm normally a 'use your words' kind of person."

"You can fucking hold your own in a fight, I'll give you that. I had no idea you were so strong."

"When I'm afraid I'm going to lose something I care about, I guess I can be."

Fox felt a pang in his chest. "You don't mean... me?"

Drew smiled. "I do."

Fox stared at him for a moment, dizzy from the twists and turns their conversation—hell, their whole friendship—had taken this evening. "What do we do now?"

"I vote for pulling the covers over us and getting some sleep," Drew said. "We can pick up the pieces in the morning."

"You make it sound like grim work."

"I meant the pieces of the lamp, not of us. We're going to be fine."

Fox urgently wished he shared Drew's confidence. But he had to admit that Drew seemed to know far better than he how to handle whatever their friendship was turning into, so he decided to simply trust him. "Okay," he said.

Drew beamed. He reached down and pulled the covers up, and though he no longer held Fox in his arms, he stayed close.

IT TOOK a long while for Fox's breathing to slow and become regular. The shock and anger and pain that had wracked him, that had made him say terrible things and lash out physically, were finally in abeyance. Drew watched him for more than an hour as peace came over him and his body relaxed.

Drew felt keenly responsible for the sudden transformation Fox had undergone. It was his touch that did it, that made Fox confront all at once the reality that had been slowly forming in Drew's mind over the last few days. He didn't have the answers that Fox asked for—he had no idea what they were supposed to do now—but he knew there was no place he'd rather be than beside this man, this friend who had come from nowhere and was suddenly part of the fabric of his life.

In the pale moonlight, Fox's face was porcelain, his normally sharp and handsome features placid and refined in sleep. Now, in the absolute privacy of this remote hideaway, Drew allowed himself the luxury of really looking at him. It was not something a guy would normally do.

Drew was starting to feel less like the guy he'd thought himself to be.

He had never been this close to another man—emotionally or physically. From the moment he read Fox's dating profile, he had started to feel like there might be a connection to this man unlike any friendship he'd had before. Objectively, they shared very little in terms of their jobs, their upbringing, their lifestyle. But once he'd spent a few minutes in Fox's company, he knew. He just knew they would be close.

Well, maybe not as close as they were now.

When he had first pulled the covers up, the heat from their bodies was ovenlike, but now as Fox slept, they were simply snug, wrapped up together in a high-thread-count-and-fluffy-down cocoon. The hair on Fox's legs tickled against his own, and Fox's arm—the one he had touched, which had lit the fuse of their explosion—lay pressed up against his ribs. There was an innocence and a purity to this, whatever this was, that they shared.

Fox heaved a deeper breath and shifted slightly, causing his bare hip to bump up against Drew's. The brief contact sent a chill up his spine.

So it was true. Drew knew well that one simply cannot argue with empirical evidence, and the evidence of Fox's effect on him, his vital, bodily effect, was overwhelming. Being here, next to Fox, naked next to Fox, was thrilling to him in a way he'd never imagined. He now knew something about himself that he hadn't only yesterday.

He was falling in love with a man. With this man, the one stretched out naked next to him. He expected the vertiginous reality of this discovery to stop his heart and make him clutch his temples in agonized existential panic, but it did nothing of the sort. Instead, he was filled with a contented warmth, a sudden peace, that felt like a glow had been kindled in him that was certain and inextinguishable.

He was happy.

Chapter FOURTEEN

Fox JOLTED awake in the dark, precisely as he done the day before. He was about to reach for his phone to check the time when he realized he couldn't.

Because Drew's arm was wrapped around him.

Fox turned his head to the side and looked at Drew, who was lying on his stomach and whose face was mere inches away. They were, in fact, on the same pillow.

He tried to rationally analyze how he felt about this.

On the one hand, they were two straight men. Friends.

On the other, they were entwined, naked, in a romantic oceanside cottage. Drew had said he was falling in love with him. They had fought—again, naked, which Fox was not ready to think about—and then they had settled into bed again, as if what they'd been through was completely normal.

Yeah, rationality's not going to be much help here.

He looked at Drew's peaceful face and felt a deep pang of envy that he was apparently so easily reconciled to this strange new turn their friendship had taken. "We're going to be fine," he'd said.

Fox very much wished to believe this. He very much doubted it was true.

"Ah, THERE he is," Drew said softly as Fox's eyes fluttered open. "Good morning."

Fox blinked several times. "Morning." He sounded wary.

"Sleep okay?"

"I guess so." Fox sat up a bit, propped himself on his elbows. "It's already light out."

"Yeah, imagine that. Sleeping past dawn on a Sunday. How lazy can we get?"

"There's still time to get out and do the standup paddleboards," Fox said. He moved to pull the covers off.

"Hey, hold up there," Drew said. "You just woke up. Are you sure you want to jump out of bed right this minute?"

"Why not? We don't want to lose the day."

"Because you just woke up, and you might want to wait for something that's... up... to go down, if you know what I mean."

Fox's eyes widened, and he glanced downward for a fraction of a second. "You're probably right. I'll wait a bit."

"How about we stay in bed for a while, and let the paddleboards take care of themselves?" Drew said. "Let's be lazy for a change."

"What are we going to do in bed?" Fox asked.

Drew laughed. "I'm going to pretend that's not a classic porno line, and order room service breakfast. How's that?"

Fox smiled, though he also rolled his eyes. "Fine. We'll be lazy."

"There's a good man," Drew cheered. He picked up the phone and placed an order for far too much food for breakfast. "It'll be here in a half hour."

"Great," Fox said. "Now I'm going to get up and go to the bathroom. You may wish to avert your eyes."

"Your morning wood won't bother me a bit," Drew said with a grin. "Got a pretty bad case of it myself."

"Feel free to keep it to yourself," Fox said drily. He slipped out of the bed, keeping his body turned away as he did so. He did not, Drew noted, grab his bathrobe.

Fox emerged from the bathroom a few minutes later, and on his way back to bed he bent down to pick up the pieces of the lamp that they had knocked over the night before. "I feel kind of rock-and-roll," he said. "I've never trashed a hotel room before."

"How about we try not to make it a habit?" Drew suggested.

"Deal." Fox finished picking up the pieces, then seemed to reach out for his bathrobe and stop halfway. He turned to Drew. "I have to ask. Are we really going to have breakfast in bed, naked?"

"Do you want to?" Drew asked. He smiled and cocked an eyebrow to let Fox know he was safe to answer in the affirmative.

"Honest to God, Drew, I don't know," Fox said with a frustrated sigh. "What are we doing here?"

"We are having breakfast in bed, naked. Friends do that."

"They do not."

"We do. That's good enough for me."

"Fine." Fox plopped back down on the bed and pulled the covers over himself. "This is weird, and I don't know why we're doing it, but fine."

"We're doing it because we did it."

"That makes no sense at all."

"It makes perfect sense. We collapsed into bed drunk and naked on the first night because being drunk makes it impossible to do anything but what you absolutely have to in order to survive. Like when you're completely shit-faced but can still talk on the phone when your boss calls. So clearly wearing something to bed was lower on the priority list than getting into bed. Then last night it would have been weird to wear pajamas when we'd been naked the night before, like we were ashamed of it or something, so we went naked again. Perfectly normal."

"Then I freaked out, and we whaled on each other, and then—and this is where I once again have no idea why we're doing this—we got back into bed naked again. And here we are."

"Exactly. Here we are. Now we can either take this chance the universe has given us and see what happens, or we can run screaming away from it and never find out. Could you really live knowing that you didn't give this a chance?"

"Didn't give what a chance?"

"This," Drew said, pointing to the two of them.

Fox shook his head in confusion.

"Look, I don't know any more than you do what we're doing here," Drew said. "But I do know that last night, after we stopped beating each other up, we lay down next to each other. I watched you fall asleep, and I saw the calm come over you, and I felt your body relax, and it was… amazing. I could feel the peacefulness coming off of you. You freaked out, and we fought it out, and we came out the other side in a better place. Having you next to me… well, it felt right. I'm man enough to admit that."

"But what does that mean? It may have felt right to you, but what happens now?"

"I don't know. Maybe we're friends who like to sleep next to each other. Maybe we're at the beginning of something new. I don't know. But I do know I'm not going to let the chance to find out slip away. I've never met anyone like you, Fox, and I never would have thought that someone like you could be friends with someone like me. But the computer knew, and now I know it too. Don't you want to find out what happens next?"

"What happens next is that we drive back to the city, and life starts again. This weekend has been intense in all kinds of ways, but we have lives back there that we need to get back to."

"But we don't have to be the same people we were when we left," Drew said. "We can be more, and better, together."

Fox looked hard at Drew, his face showing how hard he was working to understand what Drew was saying—and what he was not saying because he didn't have the words for it. Finally, he sighed, and his features softened. "Okay. The way I see it the only possible downside is breakfast in bed, and I heard you order the extra bacon, so that's not going to be terrible no matter how naked we are." He shrugged. "I'm in."

"Awesome," Drew replied, beaming. He had no way to answer the questions that so clearly still dogged Fox, but he was heartened mightily to feel that they were in this together.

Luckily, he was saved from having to think any further along this line by a knock on the cottage's door.

"Room service," a voice called.

"Come in," Drew called back.

Fox's eyes widened in shock. "Are you serious? They're going to see us."

"Well, yes, they will," Drew replied. "But if we keep the covers on they're not going to see much. Unless you want to wag your morning wood at them too."

"Shut up," Fox retorted. "I didn't wag it at you."

"That's a relief. I didn't catch sight of anything, so I figured it was too small to see from this side of the bed." He had, indeed, caught sight of something. It was in no way small. He did not share this fact.

The waiter appeared at the door to the bedroom, the same one who had served them dinner the night before. "Okay if I come in?" he asked decorously.

"Yes, please," Drew said. "We're going to have breakfast in bed."

"That's a perfect way to spend a Sunday morning," the waiter said. He brought a tray over to Drew's side of the bed.

"So the chateaubriand worked," he murmured. He glanced over at Fox, who was now sitting up, the covers gathered at his waist. "Good for you." He winked at Drew.

Drew laughed, which occasioned a scolding look from Fox.

"And for you, sir," the waiter said as he placed a second tray across Fox's legs. "Will there be anything else, gentlemen?"

"No, thanks," Drew said. "This is perfect."

"Call and we'll come pick up the trays," the waiter said. "You won't even have to get out of bed." With another roguish wink at Drew, he turned and wheeled his cart back out through the sitting room.

"Yum," Drew said, eyeing the trays piled high with gorgeous food.

"Just so we're clear, we're going to have to do *something* today to work some of this off," Fox said. "Oh, and that waiter totally thinks we're boning."

"Are you suggesting we find a way to make both of those things come true?" Drew teased.

Fox blushed furiously. "I… no, I…," he stammered. "Shut up, dickhead."

"I'll have to, because my mouth is going to be full of waffle for the foreseeable future." Drew took a huge bite of waffle and smiled around it.

"You're impossible," Fox muttered. But there was a grin on his face as he cut into the pile of pancakes on his tray.

They plowed through the overabundant breakfast Drew had ordered, then sat back and drank not one but two large carafes of coffee. Through the windows they watched seabirds wheel and float over the edge of the bluff.

Soon Drew turned his attention to Fox, searching his face for signs of what he was feeling. What he found was that Fox must be really good at poker, because his expression revealed exactly nothing. So Drew did what he'd only recently learned to do: when it came to Fox, he simply had to trust his instinct. It hadn't let him down yet.

"Tell me about your first time," he said, as if this were a normal point of conversation between friends.

"My first time what?" Fox looked puzzled, as if perhaps Drew were asking about the first time he had changed the oil in his car.

"Your *first time* first time," Drew said.

"Why do you want to know about that?"

Drew shrugged. "What else is there to talk about?" He knew exactly why he'd asked, and he knew Fox knew exactly why he had asked. Where they were, right now, was about as "first-time" as any experience they were likely to have in their lives.

Fox shook his head at Drew but made no further objection. He took a deep breath and looked up at the birds again for a moment. "It was… awful."

"I think it usually is," Drew said.

"No, my first time was more than usually awful. First, it was after the prom, which is pretty much as cliché as it gets."

"Yeah, no one wants their first time to be cliché."

"You asked this stupid question," Fox retorted, "so are you going to listen to the answer or keep interrupting?"

"Sorry. Please, tell me how awful it was."

"Thank you," he replied, straightening the covers that pooled above his hip bones. "The second reason it was awful was that the whole thing was set up by my dad."

Drew, startled by this twist in the story, sat back a little but said nothing.

"It was apparently really important to him," Fox said, his voice softening, as if he were trying to decide how he felt about what he was saying as he said it. "He arranged the hotel room, let me drive his new car—he even stuck condoms in the pocket of the tuxedo he bought for me. It was like he was giving me this one last chance before I graduated to finally become a man or whatever."

"So this was, like, a setup? Like an arranged marriage or something?"

"Oh hell no," Fox answered with a grim chuckle. "This was in no way a girl he would have wanted me to marry. She was nice enough, but the kind of girl that everyone—even my dad, apparently—knew as a 'sure thing.' And it turns out he was right."

"Okay, that's pretty messed up."

"Yeah. But it's also absolutely who he is. He didn't seem to take much of an interest in me when I was growing up, except the few times I didn't hit some milestone he had in mind for me. The day I turned sixteen, he took me to get my driving test, and when we got home there was a car waiting for me in the driveway. Which was nice, but I didn't really need a brand-new car so I could drive it to school and back. Plus, it was a BMW, so I had to park it way the hell out at the far end of the school lot so no one would knock a door into it. He never cared about the classes I took or the papers I wrote as long as I kept my GPA high enough to get into the university whose football games he still goes to. And apparently it would have been some kind of crime against his humanity if I'd graduated high school without having sex. So he made the arrangements, and then, as he said the next morning when I got home, I 'became a man.'"

"Wow," Drew said. He could not imagine what it must have been like to grow up with a dad like that. "That's really, *really* messed up."

"He'd been doing shit like that for so long I didn't even consider it that fucked up at the time. I guess I was glad he was paying attention to me—any kind of attention. But it did kind of mess with my head when it came to dating. It's like I didn't trust myself to be able to find the kind of woman I wanted to date because there was this voice in the back of my head warning me that I was only choosing the kind of woman my dad would want me to date, and then I'd get all frustrated by the whole thing."

"And that's when you made your first spreadsheet," Drew added.

Fox's mouth dropped open. "How did you…?"

Drew shrugged. "I guess I know you pretty well. You're analytical, and you want to make your own decisions in life, so it makes sense that putting relationship issues into numbers would be the way you'd solve your dad problem."

"You're just… amazing," Fox said, shaking his head.

"I'm not. I'm your perfect match is all." He batted his eyes like Daisy Duck trying to get Donald's attention.

"Fuck off," Fox said, laughing and giving Drew's shoulder a shove.

"So that was your first time," Drew said.

"Yep, and once I got fucked, I stayed fucked for the rest of my life. I mean, look at where I ended up." He gestured to their romantic cottage. "This is the culmination of having spent the next decade searching for the perfect woman. I end up in bed with your sorry ass."

"Fuck off," Drew said, shoving Fox's shoulder right back.

They shared a good long laugh.

"Can I ask you something?" Drew said when their laughter subsided.

"Sure?" Fox didn't sound sure.

"You said it was awful. And I get that the context was awful, since you were pretty much having sex to make your dad happy—"

"Thanks for laying that right out there," Fox interrupted, his expression horrified. "But yeah, you're right."

"But you had a hotel room, and it was prom, after all—I'm sure you were improbably handsome in a tuxedo even at that age—so was it really awful? I mean, the actual thing itself. How was that?"

"We're really going to talk about this?"

"It seems kind of ridiculous for us to have things we can't talk about… you know, after the breakfast in bed."

"Fair point," Fox conceded. "My actual first time was… brief. I'd never actually had a condom on before, so that was awkward to figure out in the moment, and then I wasn't sure I had it on right, so I was more nervous once I had it on. On the plus side, I probably would have lasted about twelve seconds without it, so the fact that I could basically feel nothing through the condom meant I was able to perform for more than a minute. The first time."

"There was more than one time?"

Fox laughed. "You remember being eighteen, right? I may have been on a hair trigger, but I had more than one shot in the magazine. The second time was actually immediately after the first—I don't think she noticed the first, by the way, because I didn't make a big deal about it. The condom, which was literally strangling me, wasn't budging, so I kept going. That time took me like three minutes, which seemed longer than she expected. Then I really did need some time to recover, so I spent a few minutes seeing to her… needs."

Drew smiled. "You were a perfect gentleman from the very beginning, weren't you?"

"And you thought I was content to simply be improbably handsome. Anyway, we did it one more time for good measure. After that, we got back in the car, and I had her home by midnight." Fox shrugged. "And that's the story of my first time."

"That doesn't sound all that awful."

Fox shook his head. "It was awful because it didn't mean anything. It didn't mean anything to either of us. We never spoke again, and I haven't seen or heard anything about her since graduation the following month. We didn't love each other—we barely even knew each other. It was something I felt I had to do, and I honestly have no idea why she was doing it."

"Will you stop that?" Drew scolded. "I am certain that at eighteen you were already the charming, suave, improbably handsome man you are today. She probably considered herself lucky to be with you." He swallowed hard. "I know I do."

Fox blushed again, his brilliant smile contrasting with the red in his cheeks. "Now turnabout's fair play. You get to tell me the story of your first time."

"It's much worse than yours," Drew said grimly.

"I'll be the judge of that."

Drew collected his thoughts for a moment. It wasn't a story he told anyone, for obvious reasons. "I was a sophomore in college," he finally began. "Guess you'd call me a late bloomer."

"I'd call you a lot smarter than me. Good for you for waiting until you were ready."

"It didn't really help," Drew said, still summoning the courage to describe what had happened to him his first time. "We met in a sociology course. One of those classes where you work in small groups and then have intense conversations about race and gender while nursing a small coffee all night in a café. We got to know each other pretty well, and after the midterm I asked her back to my dorm room. I had a single because I was working as a resident assistant, so we could have some privacy. Well, we got to my room, and things got heated pretty quickly. We had sex—we had really bad sex, compared to your first time—and then we lay there and talked for hours. About all kinds of things. I thought at the time that it had gone pretty well for a first time."

"The way you say that makes me think there's a surprise twist coming up."

"You'd be right," Drew said. He took a deep breath. "It wasn't until the middle of the next week that it happened. I got called to the Dean of Students' office, and when I got there a campus police officer was standing next to her. They told me that the woman I'd been with had gone to the rape crisis center and said she'd been assaulted. By me."

"What?" Fox's voice was indignant.

"She told them that I'd persuaded her to come alone to my room and that I had coerced her into having sex with me. Now, I'm the guy who listens to all of the public service announcements about consensual sex, and to get the job as RA, I had to spend like a full week doing role plays and presentations about how *no means no* and all of that. So I'm the absolute last guy on earth who would commit sexual assault—even by accident. I tell them all this, and they look at me like I'm trying to cover my ass so they don't expel me and file criminal charges."

"That's awful," Fox said.

"Yeah, it was pretty bad. The campus had this program where, for nonviolent cases, they get the two people into a room with some mediators to try to open a dialogue about what happened. So we did that, and she got to tell her side of the story. Which, once she told it, was not all that different from mine, to be honest. She said we were caught up in the moment, and she felt she had agreed to have sex because she sensed I wanted to, and she'd been pressured by other guys before, and one had hit her when she said she didn't want to have sex with him. To her, then, what happened in my room—even though she agreed to it— was a kind of sexual assault because once we got there, she was afraid to say no."

"That makes no sense at all."

"That's what I thought at first, but the more I listened to her, the more I realized that, for a lot of women in our society, sex and violence—or the threat of violence—are inextricably linked. It's not my fault, because I've never pressured a woman to have sex with me, and I've always respected the right of any woman I date to decide whether she wants to have sex or not. But in a sense that doesn't really matter, since by being male I'm complicit in the system that oppresses women into consenting to sex even if they would have made a different choice if the genders really were equal in our culture."

"What you're saying is that no one can ever have sex because women can never really consent to it."

"That's kind of an extreme version of it, but that's the basic idea."

"That's insane. You didn't assault her—you did everything right."

"But her consent was conflicted, and that was something I had never considered before. Anyway, once we talked it through, she realized I wasn't some kind of monster who'd coerced her into having sex with me, and the whole matter got dropped. But it was honestly terrifying until it got resolved because it could have meant the end of my college career—there was no way my scholarship would have continued, and I would have had to move out of the dorms. That would have been the end of the line in academia for me, and I'd be a greeter at Walmart today."

"Wow. That's a horrible thought."

"Right? Now you see why I was baffled by your 'awful' first time. Yours, at least, didn't dangle you over the precipice of losing all of your hopes and dreams."

"All right, you win. Your first time was worse than mine. Happy now?"

"Ecstatic. There's nothing better than being the worst at sex."

"And that's why you only date super strong women who are aggressively assertive about their sexuality. The kind who break coffee tables. Because then you know for certain that they consent because they've taken control."

Drew was shocked to hear this tidy summary of his dating history. "That's… exactly right," he said, amazed.

"Like you said, I'm your perfect match," Fox said with a laugh.

"I'm not so sure. You only break lamps."

"The lamp's on you, buddy. You're the one who tackled me."

"After you shoved me out of bed!"

Fox grew more serious. "You really surprised me when you did that."

"I kind of surprised myself," Drew admitted. "I'd worked really hard to get into this bed, and there was no way I was going to let you push me out of it without a fight." He noted the expression of surprise on Fox's face. "We're being completely honest with each other, aren't we?" Fox nodded. "Okay, then I can admit that the whole dinner thing, and the whole not drinking thing, was my plan to get us back into bed where we could face this thing between us."

"I think we have different ideas about what's between us," Fox said gently.

Drew shook his head slowly. "I think we are at different stages in acknowledging what's between us."

Fox fell silent for a long moment, but his eyes never left Drew's. Then, suddenly, he seemed to snap out of his trance. "You know what would feel good right now? A long walk before we head back home. There's this awesome trail along the top of the bluffs. You're gonna love it." He leapt out of bed and was in the bathroom before Drew could say a word.

Drew lay back and stared at the ceiling, trying not to feel hope curdle into loss.

THE FRESH air and sun cleared Fox's head, as he had hoped they would. Nothing like a good hike to help get some perspective. He turned and looked at Drew, who was one stride behind him as they picked their way along a winding footpath on the edge of a bluff. Below them, the sea roiled angrily against the rocks.

The path opened onto a small clearing, a promontory looking out over the ocean. Fox stopped and pulled out his water bottle for a drink, and Drew did the same.

"It's beautiful, isn't it?" Fox asked, turning his face into the bracing wind that rose off the shore.

"One might almost say romantic," Drew replied. He gave a half shrug, as if he was not all that hopeful his meaning would be understood— or he was maintaining deniability, in case it was.

"I'd like to thank you," Fox said. "For this weekend."

"Oh?" Drew replied.

"You helped me see what was holding me back. Why I wasn't finding the woman of my dreams. Our talk this morning really helped me put it in perspective."

Drew blinked several times, but then a wide smile broke out across his face.

"I've been trying to undo the train wreck of that first time," Fox continued. "I'm never going to break free of it unless I change completely what I'm looking for and how I go about finding it."

"Wow," Drew said, beaming. "That's… incredible."

"So starting tomorrow I'm throwing away the spreadsheets. I'm going to take the matches that Q*pid finds for me, and I'm going to go on a date without a plan, without a script, without any of the baggage that's been holding me back. I'm going to find the woman who's right for me, not the version of myself I've created in Excel."

Drew's expression changed several times, leaving Fox wondering what he was thinking. Finally, he found the words he was looking for. "That's great. Good for you. Somewhere out there is a woman who has been looking for you. Now you'll be able to find her."

"And I owe it all to you. Thank you for being the best friend a guy could possibly want."

Drew smiled, but there didn't seem to be the same kind of enthusiasm behind it as there had been before.

"Look," Fox said, stepping closer to Drew. "I know the last couple of days have been a little weird. For both of us. But I think we've been able to help each other, right?"

Drew's smile faded, but then he nodded. "We have. I see things a lot more clearly now."

"Awesome," Fox cried, putting his arm around Drew and giving him a good jostle. "I knew you were bouncing back, just like me."

"Yep, just like you," Drew repeated. He faced into the wind, blinking against its sting until his eyes were watering. "We should get back." He turned to Fox. "Gotta get ready for the week, right?"

"Right," Fox agreed. But he noted the change in Drew's manner. "We're okay, right? We're good?"

"Yeah, we're good," Drew said, his smile returning. "Great weekend. Terrific." He turned and started down the path toward the resort. "I'll take point on the way back." He didn't look behind before striding away.

"Sounds good," Fox called. He wasn't sure Drew heard him.

"THANKS AGAIN—FOR everything," Drew said as Fox pulled up outside his apartment. "This was a really intense weekend."

"We should do it again soon," Fox said, smiling brightly.

"Yeah, let's," Drew said as he opened the car door. "No, don't get out—I can grab my bag."

He walked around the back of Fox's car and fished his duffel out of the trunk. He closed it, then called out "Thanks" one more time.

The silhouette of Fox waved, and he drove away.

Drew was alone.

More alone he'd never felt in his entire life. Actually, he felt as though this weekend had opened up an entirely new life, and now he was standing in it, alone.

He hefted his duffel and walked up to his front door.

Inside, he was no less alone. In fact, all he could think of was how full of life his apartment had been last weekend, when he had made dinner for Fox, and then Fox had come back and they had gone to the marimba concert together. It had been a hint of what they could be together, and now they were nothing.

Now his apartment was back to being the empty, lonely, friendless place where dwelt Drew, the empty, lonely, friendless man. Twenty-four hours ago he was in bed with the man he thought he was falling in love with, and now he was utterly alone.

How had this happened? Though he was currently not all that happy with his dating life, it's not like he had been hiding from the world. He needed to step back and think about his situation objectively. Approach it like a research question.

All right, then. He dropped his duffel in the middle of his living room, went to his kitchen, and made himself a cup of coffee. This was his ritual when starting a new research project. Then once he'd sat himself down at the kitchen table with a cup of the strongest, cheapest coffee he could find—he got his beans at the back of the dollar store—he set about looking at his situation as analytically as possible.

Question: Was he falling in love with Fox?

Proposition: He was falling in love with Fox.

Why? Because he was lonely. Why? Because he had been focusing on dating and his seminar papers, and not on having friends.

Therefore, counterproposition: He was not actually falling in love with Fox but was actually missing platonic friendship.

He could discount the counterproposition because he felt for Fox the exact flutter in his stomach he had felt every time he began a relationship with a woman. Therefore, he was certain, he was actually falling in love with Fox. The counterproposition was therefore invalid.

Redirect: He was actually gay, as the Q*pid computer seemed to think, and he had fallen for Fox because he was the first man Drew had met after finding that out.

But was the redirect therefore true? Was Fox simply a target of convenience, having shown up at the precise moment that his online dating service clued him in to his new sexual orientation?

Ah, that was the nexus. In order to answer his research question, he needed to ascertain his sexual orientation. Not assume it, as he had always done. No, for the purposes of this research project, he had to establish sexual orientation as a dependent variable, not a given. If what he felt for Fox was simply the result of his letting himself admit his homosexual feelings for the first time, then it was less about Fox and more about Drew discovering himself.

And that would mean that Fox hadn't just broken his heart.

Because that's what it felt like.

Drew knew what he needed to do.

Chapter FIFTEEN

"Foxy, I'm an old married man. It's past my bedtime."

"It's nine o'clock on a Sunday night. Even senior citizens stay up this late so they can watch the news and complain about the government."

Chad leaned close to the phone. "Well maybe those senior citizens don't have a hot wife who likes to get a little freaky after a long, oppressive Sunday night dinner with her stick-up-the-butt family," he muttered in a low voice.

"Eww."

"Don't be the bitter old bachelor," Chad scolded good-naturedly. "It's not a good look for you. Anyway, you got about three minutes before things start heating up here. Although I can set the phone on the nightstand if you want to watch."

"You are a sick fuck," Fox said with a laugh.

"Thank you, sir. Now, what can I do for you?"

"Want my table at Table?"

"You mean for this Saturday?"

"No, I mean forever. I'm going to give it up."

"You're not going to do Saturday night at Table? God, Foxy, is it really that bad?" He shook his head in exaggerated agitation. "Look, I keep telling you: it's a dry spell. Normal humans have them all the time. You've never experienced it because you're a love god. Sometimes you have to be patient."

"Thanks for that almost-sympathy, but in actual fact I do have a date on Saturday."

"Then why are you giving up the table?"

"It's just not... me, I guess. Anymore, that is. I'm changing my game. I'm going to have her over to my place. I'm going to cook dinner for her instead of taking her out."

Chad looked at Fox as if he had lost his fucking mind. "You have lost your fucking mind," he said.

"Your concern is noted," Fox said sarcastically. "Do you want the table or not? Last chance—I'm going to call right now and cancel it."

"Of course I want the table. Switch it to my name, and I'll enjoy it until you come to your senses."

"Okay."

"Because you're going to crash and burn with this whole Julia Child thing."

"Thanks for the vote of confidence, buddy."

"No charge. And I'll be here to help you pick up the pieces of your shattered manhood."

"You have no idea what that means to me. You really don't." Fox laughed, then leaned close when he saw motion in the corner of the camera's view. "And it looks like it's time for you to get *your* manhood shattered, so I'll be going now."

"You can't shatter steel, my friend."

"And there's yet another image I'll have to wash out of my mind with bourbon."

"Happy to help, buddy. Enjoy celibacy!"

"Fuck you, you empty-headed asshole!"

Chad grinned and cackled lasciviously as Fox hit the End button.

VEERA, HAVING taken an actual weekend away from work—she'd even turned off her work phone, the first time she'd ever done so—arrived at her desk Monday morning and immediately pulled up her Archer windows. She scanned his vitals to ensure he was functioning normally, then she checked the secondary windows where she had set various monitors of the particular metrics she wanted to track. One of these windows, at the far lower corner of her monitor, was flashing orange.

The text in the window titled Few, which flashed from orange to white to orange again, simply read *Status change: 2 profiles.*

"Holy balls," she said. This was a term she'd picked up from a developer from Michigan, and one she repeated several times under her breath. "Archer, were you right all along?" Veera shot to her feet and ran to the nearest empty conference room. She flung the door shut, then dialed with a shaking finger.

"Good morning Archer," she said.

"Good morning, Veera."

Before he could go any further, she burst into her question. "Archer, tell me about the status changes for the discordant match Few."

"There have been two profile status changes since we last discussed the customers you have grouped and identified as Few."

"Tell me about those status changes."

"Yesterday at 20:35, the customer known as Fox accessed the Q*pid app. He opened his match queue, selected the first profile in it without reviewing any others, and sent a message. The match profile responded favorably, and they have planned a date for Saturday."

"Oh," Veera said. So it hadn't worked out after all.

"Yesterday at 21:05 the customer known as Drew reactivated the Q*pid app. He changed his Parameter Three setting to male. Then he—"

"He changed his Parameter Three setting to male?"

"Yes, he changed his Parameter Three setting to male. Do you wish me to speak more slowly or increase the volume of my vocal output?"

"No, that won't be necessary. Continue, please."

"Then he accessed his match queue and reviewed it for thirty-three minutes. He selected the top match and sent a message. The match profile responded favorably, and they have planned a date for Saturday."

Veera sank into a chair. What was going on? Fox had gone back to dating women, but Drew had switched to dating men. What could possibly have happened between the two of them?

"Archer, do you have any more information about them?"

"My configuration does not allow me to share any additional information about these customers, if such information should exist."

Veera was not pleased to again have bumped up against the security measures she herself had put in place, but she was resigned to them. "Thank you, Archer."

"You're welcome, Veera. Will there be anything else?"

"No. Suspend voice interface."

"Voice interface suspended."

She hung up the phone, but remained in the conference room staring at the wall long enough for the light to switch off because it detected no movement in the room. Then she sat in the dark a while longer.

"YOUR PLACE is really nice," she said as he opened the door and welcomed her in.

"Did you have any trouble finding it?" Fox asked as he shut the door behind her.

"No, your directions were quite thorough," she said, handing him her jacket. "Oh, something smells amazing. What are you cooking?"

"It's a Peruvian stew—I was inspired by a friend to try something new. I hope you'll like it."

"I'm sure I will. It's so nice to finally meet a guy who likes to cook."

"I don't get to do very much of it, I'm afraid. Actually, I haven't cooked dinner for anyone in a long time."

"Well then, I'm honored," she said.

"Can I pour you a glass of wine?"

"That would be lovely, thanks." She looked around the room. "This is really beautiful. You must have a terrific decorator."

"Did it all myself, actually. Kind of threw it together. When you spend as much time as I do in hotels, you get some ideas, I guess."

"A chef and an interior designer, my goodness," she said. "You really are a Renaissance man."

"I'd caution you to reserve judgment until you've both tasted my dinner and seen my media room. You may have reason to doubt my taste in both regards."

She smiled at him. "And modest too. My, my."

Fox smiled back. This was going very well indeed.

"WELL, THAT was an amazing dinner," she said, setting her napkin on the table by her now-empty plate.

"Thanks," Fox replied. "Though I'm sure I didn't do it justice. Drew got the spices balanced a little better, I think."

She looked across the table at him silently for a moment. "You think a lot of your friend Drew, don't you?"

"Why do you say that?"

"You've talked about him all night," she said gently.

"Sorry... I had no... sorry," he stumbled. "I didn't realize I was doing that."

She smiled sweetly. "Honestly, if he were a woman I would think you aren't over her. I've had dates with guys who couldn't stop talking about their exes, but this is the first time I've had a guy talk about a friend of his. Are you trying to set me up with him?"

"No, not at all," Fox blurted. He was reeling, completely blindsided by her suggestion that he had been talking about Drew all evening. "Sorry, I won't talk about Drew anymore."

"Can I be honest with you?" she asked.

"Of course. What is it?"

"I don't normally bring my work home with me—my friends are generally happy that I don't try to analyze them the way I do my therapy clients—but I feel like I have to say something. Have you really thought through your relationship with Drew?"

"What do you mean, 'thought through?'"

"What I mean is that friends don't talk about their friends the way you talk about Drew. This evening I've gotten to hear about how he's an amazing cook and how smart he is and how much he must work out and how thoughtful he is. You even somehow managed to convince me that attacking you and trashing a hotel room was one of his finest, most caring moments. Still not sure how you did that, to be honest."

"You're right. I don't know why—"

"Stop," she said, holding up her hand. "I'm not upset about it at all. I think it's great that even in this weirdly masculinist age you're able to be open and honest about how much you love your friend. If more guys could do that the world would be a better place. But I think your relationship with Drew goes a little beyond friends—or at least the way you feel about him is beyond friendship. Again, I think that's sweet and lovely." She looked across the table at him, an expression of genuine compassion on her face. "I think you're a great guy, Fox. And I think you'd be happiest if you give this thing with Drew a try." She got up from her chair. "I've had a lovely evening, but I think I should be going—"

He rose as well. "Wait, are you saying you're leaving because you think I should be with Drew?"

Once again she smiled sweetly at him. "I've been looking for a great guy. And lucky you, you've already found one." She leaned over and kissed him on the cheek. "Give Drew my best." She turned and walked to the door, where she picked up her jacket and showed herself out.

Fox stood in his dining room, utterly stunned.

"DREW?"

He looked up, heart pounding. There he was. They were really doing this.

"You must be Reid," Drew said, getting awkwardly to his feet. He nearly knocked over the tiny café table on which his latte sloshed, dribbling a little pool of milk. They shook hands. "Please, sit."

"Thanks." He sat, tossing his messenger bag under the table and setting his cup of coffee atop it, next to Drew's. "I hope I didn't keep you waiting."

"No, just got here," Drew lied. He'd gotten here almost an hour ago, in the throes of an anxious suspense that made breathing a challenge. He had been obsessively watching every arrival and departure, hoping to see no one he recognized because they might immediately perceive that he was here to meet a man. A man he'd arranged to meet through a dating app. A man.

"My dissertation group ran a little over," Reid explained. "Our advisor wants proposals by the end of the month, and everyone's kind of freaking out."

Drew smiled sympathetically. Now that was a form of anxiety he would admit to. "That's the worst phase," he said. "Mine got approved last semester, and right up until I got that email I was certain I was going to be thrown out of the university as an academic fraud."

Reid nodded. "Yep. Had that dream last night." He sipped his coffee and looked at Drew for a long moment. "I was really surprised to get a message from you."

"You were?" *Not as surprised as I was to find myself sending it,* Drew thought.

Reid smiled a little awkwardly. "Yeah. I... I've seen you around campus."

Drew was mortified. He had no recollection of having seen Reid before five minutes ago, when he entered the café and got in line to order his drink. "You have?"

"Yeah. You used to study on the fourth floor of the main library, in one of those carrels by the windows?"

Drew laughed. "Only every single day the entire year. That was when I was researching for my diss proposal. God, that was awful."

"It was less awful for me when you were there," Reid said shyly. "I used to sit at the desk in the corner so I could see you when I looked up. You being adorable is what got me through my prelim exams."

Drew felt the heat rise in his cheeks. "Wow... I...."

"I saw you a couple of times outside the library too, but both times you seemed to be on dates." Reid paused, chewing his lower lip pensively. "With women."

If there were a book out of the millions in the entire library that dictated how to respond to such a remark, Drew would gladly have spent the next month searching every single shelf for it. He was on his own.

"I... um... have dated women, I guess." Now he sounded like an idiot. Reid knew he had dated women—he had just said so. "Until... um... recently."

Reid's eyes narrowed slightly. "How recently?"

"You're the... I mean, this is the first time I've ever... been on a date with—"

"Fuck," Reid said with a sigh. "Damn my luck."

"I'm sorry," Drew blurted. "Did I say something wrong?"

"No, I appreciate your honesty. Not every tourist provides that courtesy."

"I don't understand. What do you mean 'tourist?'"

"It may surprise you to know that this is not the first 'I've always dated women but I thought I might give guys a try' date I've had. It always ends badly. Every damn time."

"I'm sorry, I didn't mean to do anything wrong." Drew was confused and upset that he may have caused offense. "I only wanted to try—"

"Stop," Reid broke in. "Stop right there. You seem like a sweet person, Drew, but you're about to say something that would make things a whole lot worse. Just so we're clear, I'm not here so you can try something new. If you want to see what it's like to get your ass pounded, you should have been using Grindr, not Q*pid. I've been there and done that—and I've pounded my share of straight ass in my day—but I'm looking for a relationship, not a hookup." He paused and shook his head sadly. "I've always had a thing for the cute, smart ones. I was really hoping this would work."

"I wasn't looking for sex," Drew said, now wounded as well as baffled. "I really wanted to find out what it's like to date a guy."

"What you'll find," Reid replied, "is that it is exactly the same as dating a woman. You find out if you have things in common, if you like the same movies or restaurants, if you can see a future together. The only thing different is the number of penises in bed. That's what you need to get figured out. And I'm not looking down on you when I say you need to fire up Grindr and introduce your penis to some other penises. That's a really important step in the journey you're embarking on. Then, once you have that figured out, you can start looking for guys to date. Until then, you're a tourist. And my stint as a tour guide is over—I'm looking for someone who's serious."

Drew was devastated. He stared at the little puddle of milk he'd made earlier, feeling like an absolute cliché as tears flooded his eyes.

"Drew, sweetie, look at me," Reid said, his voice low and warm. "Good. Now, I'm getting the sense there's more here than simple curiosity. Tell me what made you tap on my profile and set up this date."

"I met somebody. And I didn't know what to do."

"You met a guy, right? A guy who made you think maybe you're into guys?"

Drew nodded. He wiped his eyes with a napkin.

"Got it. We've all met that guy. Most people meet him before your age, but better late than never. Now, tell me about this guy."

"His name's Fox."

Reid laughed. "Wow, that's about the sexiest name ever."

Drew nodded. "We got matched up by Q*pid. Neither of us was looking for guys to date, but because of some computer glitch, we got matched. And I decided to send him a message."

"Wait, two straight guys got matched up? No way." Reid laughed out loud. "Truth is stranger than fiction, I guess. What happened next?"

"We met for a drink, just as friends, just to talk about how weird it was that we got matched up. Then we went to dinner. Well, he took me to dinner, because he's this successful marketing guy and drives a Beamer."

"For your first boy-crush, you killed it," Reid said, holding his fist out for a bump.

"Thanks," Drew said grimly.

"What happened next?"

"Since he'd paid for dinner, I invited him to my place the next week, where I could cook and not feel so poor."

"And how did that go?"

Drew couldn't stop the smile from appearing on his face. "It was really nice. We got drunk, and we ended up falling asleep on the couch. He let himself out at like three in the morning, and then the next day, since I felt awkward about the way he'd left, I invited him to a concert on campus. He brought Thai food, and we went to the concert."

"I don't know how to break this to you, Drew, but you and Fox are already dating."

"I was starting to think that too," Drew replied. "Especially when he asked me to spend last weekend with him at this resort on the coast."

"Holy fucking shit," Reid cried. "You tell me you want to *try* dating a guy, and then you tell me about how you're already practically moving in with a guy more amazing than anyone I've ever met. Present company excepted."

Drew laughed nervously. "Well, it didn't go so well last weekend. First, he was a frenetic ball of energy, like if he stood still for more than two seconds he would implode. So we had an exhausting day sea kayaking, bicycling, and walking for hours on the beach."

"Sounds *dreadful*."

"It seemed to me that he was purposely trying to keep us busy so we didn't have to think about how we were basically on a romantic getaway—I mean, you should have seen this cottage we were staying in—so I kind of forced his hand. I ordered dinner to be served by torchlight on the terrace overlooking the ocean."

"Dude, that's like the most romantic thing I've ever even heard of, much less experienced."

"It kind of seemed that way to me, and I thought to him as well. But he wasn't at all thinking we were having a romantic weekend, because once we were in bed—"

"Together?"

"Yeah, together," Drew replied. "It was this superdeluxe cottage, but there was only one bed in the place."

Reid laughed and looked at the ceiling. "And somehow this wasn't a romantic weekend. Did you at least do the straight guy thing and make a row of pillows down the middle of the bed and sleep in your clothes?"

Drew felt his cheeks fire up again. "Actually, no. We'd fallen into bed drunk the first night, so then the second night we sort of did the same thing. And we were naked."

"You are killing me right now," Reid cried. "Don't you dare stop."

"Lying there next to him, in the moonlight, it felt like a moment that was only going to come once in a lifetime. So I reached out and touched him."

"Ooh."

"A little touch. On the arm. He freaked out. He yelled and threw my hand off him."

"Oh shit."

"Yeah, oh shit. And I was stupid enough to try again. I was only trying to get through to him, you know? Just trying to reach him."

"Did it work?"

"Not so much. He basically shoved me out of the bed."

Reid's eyebrows peaked in sympathy. "Sorry. That had to hurt."

"I don't remember if it hurt, honestly. Because as soon as I hit the floor I jumped right back up and launched myself across the bed at him. I crashed into his chest headfirst and started whaling on him."

"Holy shit!"

"Indeed. He staggered back against the wall, taking a lamp out as he went, and then wrestled me back onto the bed in a chokehold. That seemed like a dirty move to me, so I basically flipped him and squeezed the air out of him until he gave up."

"Is it wrong that I'm completely erect right now?" Reid whispered.

Drew smiled. "I was too, let me tell you. I was desperately trying not to whack him with it as we wrangled."

"Okay, so this is both the most romantic and the hottest weekend I've ever heard of. But from what you said earlier, the weekend must have ended on a sour note. What happened?"

"We had breakfast in bed Sunday morning and talked about what we were doing and where it was going. And even though I thought I had gotten through to him the night before, by daylight he was back to talking about us as friends. Then we went for a hike, and we stood on a cliff looking out over the ocean, and he thanked me for all I'd done for him that weekend. Which was, apparently, making him see that he needed to get back out there and date more women. We came back to the city, he dropped me off, and that was that."

Reid shook his head slowly. "Men," he swore under his breath.

"Tell me about it. So out of the wreckage of that weekend, I figured I would try to at least get my own shit figured out. And I wanted to test whether I could really be attracted to a guy, or if I had gotten so lonely that I had developed a weird hang-up on this one guy in particular."

"That's completely insane."

"Why? Doesn't it make sense to see whether I'm actually, you know, gay?"

"Drew, I'm gonna level with you. What you call yourself doesn't matter. And you can throw yourself at guys day and night, and all that's going to get you is a new reputation and maybe a couple of STDs. It will not show you what you really need to see, which is that you have fallen in love—real, romantic, I-would-do-anything-for love. With Fox. There is nothing that the two of us could do tonight that will tell you anything you don't already know about that. Do you want to suck a dick? Who cares—Fox has a dick, and you'll figure out what to do with it when the time comes. Relax about the body parts and trust that your heart will not lead your body astray. And you know what your heart wants, don't you?"

Drew bit his lip.

"Don't you?"

Drew nodded.

"Excellent. Now, as much as it pains me to say this to the man I spent months dreaming about jumping in the stacks of the library, I want you to go hatch whatever kind of romantic-comedy plot is necessary to convince this Fox guy that he has already fallen in love with you. Because he has. He just needs you to show him."

Drew was silent for a long moment. "I don't know how to thank you," he finally said.

"No thanks required. Everyone's coming-out story is different, and this is yours. It's a good one."

"I only hope it has a happy ending."

Chapter SIXTEEN

"DREW, MY darling," Mrs. Schwartzmann cried. "A lovely surprise this is."

"You called me, Mrs. Schwartzmann," he said, because that was the next line in their Sunday morning script. "You said there was a problem in your kitchen?"

"Yes, a problem there was," she said, with a gleam in her eye. "My chair was wanting someone to sit in it. So please, can you help me?" She led him into the kitchen, her soft, dry laugh rasping along behind her.

He shook his head but followed her obediently, taking his appointed place at her table. He laid the packet of sausages on the table. "I brought you these."

"Oh, did you have them lying around?"

"No, Mrs. Schwartzmann, I made a special trip to the German butcher, like I do every week. I bought these for you, because I want to be sure you have something you like to eat. I worry about you not getting enough to eat."

She sank slowly in her chair, a frown forming on her face. "The truth we are now to each other telling?" she asked.

"It's something I'm experimenting with. I hope it might help me resolve things with Fox. But please, you are under no obligation to start telling me the truth. About anything. I would never want you to be anyone but who you are."

The bright smile returned to her face, and she nodded to silently acknowledge his permission. "A gentleman you are," she said warmly. "Now, this Fox." Without warning she grabbed up a fearsome knife and hacked a sizable chunk from the ring of pastry on the table. "Let us consider how to handle him."

"I would very much appreciate your advice," he said. He'd never been so earnest.

She nodded. "And my advice you shall have," she said, rising from her chair. She picked up the butcher's packet and walked to the stove.

"First I will make these sausages cozy together in the pan. I think some sausages are happier when they are next to other sausages, don't you?"

"I think I've come to the right place for advice," Drew replied.

"HOLY SHIT," Chad said by way of greeting as he rushed into the diner. "You look like hell. Did you sleep at all last night?"

"No." Fox didn't look up.

Chad slid into the booth opposite his friend. "So I take it the date last night didn't go well."

"No."

"Mm-hmm. Want to talk about it?"

"No."

"Then why are we here?"

Fox stared at his coffee long enough for the waitress to bring Chad a cup of his own and for Chad to drink half of it.

"We're here," Fox finally said, "because you called me three times in the space of a minute, and when I finally answered, you shrieked like a little girl and said I had to meet you here right the fuck now or you would come to my house and drag me here yourself." He looked up at Chad acidly. "That's why I'm here." He tossed back the last of his coffee and slammed the mug down at the edge of the table, causing the waitress to jump up and hustle over with the pot. "Why *you're* here, I couldn't say."

"I'm here because last night was supposed to be Fox getting his groove back, and instead it turned into Fox getting his ass handed to him by a cruel and unfeeling world. That's why I'm here."

"So you can watch the world hand me my ass? Nice. Thanks for the support."

"No, so I can shake you the hell out of whatever hellscape of dysfunction you've landed yourself in. Something's seriously wrong."

"That much I'm clear on, but thanks for coming all the way down here to confirm it. I now have independent testimony that my life is completely fucked. Thanks."

"Your life is not what's fucked," Chad countered, dead serious. "What's fucked is the entire fucking universe. If Fox Kincade is miserable and alone then there is no fucking justice for anyone. You're the best person I know, and you cannot be sitting in front of me with your ass kicked by love. I cannot believe the universe is that broken."

Fox shrugged.

"So tell me about your date last night. I want to understand what happened."

"What happened," Fox said slowly, "is that I asked a ninety-three to my house for dinner, and she shat all over me."

"Not… literally?"

Fox grunted disgustedly. "No, not literally."

"Good. Because I read about that happening to a guy, and it was—"

"Shut the fuck up, will you? You asked me what happened, and I'm trying to tell you. Now shut up."

Chad nodded silently.

"She was a psychotherapist, super successful, gorgeous, and about the nicest person you'd ever want to meet. Until after dinner when she goes off on me. Like, just opens up on me."

"What did she say?"

Fox sat frowning for a long moment. "She said… well, she came up with this whole theory that I was in love with Drew."

Chad nodded, eyebrows up in expectation of more. Fox stared at him.

"That's it. That's what happened."

"Okay."

Fox, baffled by Chad's lack of outrage on his part, stumbled through the rest of the story. "So she tells me this, and then she up and grabs her coat and leaves. Oh, and she has the gall to congratulate me on finding a great guy." He dropped his gaze back to his coffee. "Fuck."

Chad took a calm, measured breath, and exhaled slowly through his nose. "So what's the problem?"

Fox gaped across the table at his supposed best friend, who had suddenly lost his fucking mind. "What's the problem?"

"Yeah, what's the problem? You've been seeing a lot of this guy, and you two ran off last weekend for a romantic getaway on the coast—"

"It was not a romantic getaway on the coast."

"I wouldn't know, since you haven't told me anything about it. All I know is that you went away for the weekend with him. When you came back, you were ready to get back on the dating horse, but apparently you still have some issues to work through. Which, honestly, don't sound like issues to me. It seems like a therapist would be able to recognize the signs of someone who has fallen in love, and in her opinion, you have. With a guy you've been seeing a lot more of than any woman you've dated in the last year. So I have to ask again, what's the problem?"

"I'm not gay, and I'm not in love with Drew."

"I never said you were the first one, and I have to agree with your therapist that you're simply in denial about the second."

"She never said I was in denial."

"She said you were in love. If you say you aren't, then you're in denial. That's what denial means."

Fox sighed in frustration. "I'm not gay."

"Why do you keep saying that? Who cares what you call it?"

"I care, because I'm still 100 percent straight."

"Now you really sound like Thomas. Though I think he stuck with '99 percent straight' so he didn't sound like he was exaggerating defensively."

"I'm not Thomas. This is completely different."

"Is it, really? Thomas was straight until suddenly his tongue was down Jake's very accommodating throat. Right up until that night, he would not admit even the tiniest possibility that he could be attracted to Jake."

"I'm not attracted to Drew."

"Your therapist and I beg to differ."

"She's not my therapist."

Chad ignored this objection. "So you're not at all attracted to him, and yet you spent last weekend all alone with him. How did that go, by the way? Did you play poker and talk about chicks all weekend?"

Fox stared across the table. "I'm not going to post-game my weekend like it was a date. It wasn't a date."

"So stipulated. How, then, did you spend the weekend?"

"We went kayaking and went for a long cycle through the hills and did like ten miles on the beach."

"Sounds like a lot of work."

"And that was just on Saturday."

"What did you do on Sunday?"

Fox swallowed hard. He'd let himself forget that Mia had trained Chad well, and he now knew how to listen and ask follow-up questions. Shit.

"We, um… went for a hike along the top of the bluffs. And we ate too much, of course, because their chef is amazing."

"How does a grad student afford this kind of thing?"

"Oh, it didn't really cost anything. I helped them get a sweet deal on one of our systems last year, so they pretty much hosted me. Us, I mean."

"They comped two rooms and all of those activities and the meals too?"

"Not only that, but they put us up in the Founder's Cottage."

"Wow. Sounds fancy. So it was, like, a two-bedroom suite?"

Goddammit.

"Sort of," Fox said lamely, picking up the menu for closer study. He already knew it by heart, of course, as it hadn't changed in years.

"Sort of?" Chad asked. "Foxy, was there one bedroom or two?"

"One," Fox replied as casually as he could with his throat clenched tightly around the truth.

"And in this bedroom, was there one bed or two?"

"One. I think I'm going to get the oatmeal. My stomach's a little—"

"So you slept together is what you're trying not to tell me."

Fox slammed the menu down onto the table. "We did not 'sleep together,'" he hissed.

Chad sat back in alarm. "But you said—"

"I said there was one bed." Fox's voice was an outraged whisper. "Nothing happened."

Chad nodded slowly. "I think the oatmeal would be a good choice for you this morning. It's supposed to be good for your heart, and you look like you are about two minutes away from an infarction."

"Fine." Fox turned and stared at nothing out the window.

Chad sighed deeply. "Foxy, I'm going to be the asshole you need me to be. I know you don't want to talk about this thing with Drew, and I get that. It's all new and scary and whatever. But as your friend, I gotta be honest. You've got some shit to work through. What you're doing right now, this whole 'keep it bottled up until you explode' thing, it ain't working for you. It's not gonna end well. So what I want you to do, right now, is look me in the eye and swear to me that you will tell me the truth, and all of it, right now. I will not judge you or think any less of you or stop being your best friend in the world. I love you, and I'm here with you and for you and behind you all the way. But you gotta get real with me on this, okay? Will you do that for me?"

Where the tears came from Fox had no idea, but he was powerless to squeeze them back into his tear ducts. He knew his voice would be a broken, reedy, weak thing should he try to speak, so he did the only thing he could. He reached across the table and took Chad's outstretched hand and held it in his own.

They sat there for a few minutes, and then he began to speak.

"WHEN FROM your weekend you came home, you were very sad about Fox," Mrs. Schwartzmann said. "You said things between you were very bad, and that you might not see him again."

"It was bad," Drew replied. "I thought we might become more than friends, but that's not what he wanted."

"When you say 'more than friends,' you mean you have fallen in love with him?"

Drew bit his lip and looked into her kind eyes for a moment. "Yes. Yes, I have fallen in love with him."

"And with him you want to be, in the way Mr. Schwartzmann was with me when married we were?"

"I do. I want to be with him in all the ways two people can be together."

"Then tell him. You must tell."

"It's a hard thing to say. He's never… been with a man, and neither have I."

She nodded gravely. "And you are afraid you will not know how?"

He had to laugh—this conversation was too insane. "No, I don't think that's it. I'm sure we could figure that part out. But I don't know if he wants to be with me in the way I want to be with him."

"Then you must say, 'Mr. Fox, I want to with you be sexual, and I think you will like it very much. Will you with me make the love?' You can do that, can't you?"

"It's not really the kind of thing one simply comes out and says," Drew said.

"Then how will he know you want with him to be sexual?"

"As charming as you make that sound, I don't just want to be sexual with him. I want to be with him, to wake up with him in the morning and go to bed with him at night, to talk to him about everything, and hold him and laugh with him and plan a future with him."

"But none of that will happen if you tell me and not Mr. Fox."

"But I don't know how to do that."

She shrugged. "Let us not worry about *how* you tell him. Let us think about how you will feel if you *do not* tell him."

His heart sank.

She smiled. "Your face tells me how you will feel. So here is my advice for you. Do not worry about how you will tell him. If he is the person you think he is, he will see you, and he will know. Your face will tell him everything. If it is meant to be, he will see."

"Thank you, Mrs. Schwartzmann. You have helped me more than you know."

"You would be surprised what I know."

"So," CHAD said, summing up as they finished their breakfast, "you spent most of the weekend in bed with Drew, except for the parts when you were busting up the room wrestling. And all of it naked."

"We didn't spend most of the weekend in bed," he groused. "You're forgetting about the kayaking."

"Fox, you know I love you. But you are not being realistic here."

"I don't know why we're talking about all of this. It was a weird weekend, and then I had a bad date, and I don't know why it's such a big deal."

"It's a big deal because you are fucking miserable. When I called you this morning, you looked like you'd been mugged. By a rhino. A pissed-off rhino. I'm not making a big deal out of this—it's already a big deal. It's eating you up. And you need to deal with it."

Fox sighed. He was so tired. "How about this. I've been lonely since you joined all our other friends in holy matrimony. I've been on a bad run of first dates since Miyoko. Drew pops up through some computer glitch, and we find that we have a lot in common. It gets intense. I freak out a little. My date last night picks up on my freak-out because she's a therapist, and she tells me I have stuff to figure out with

Drew. That's about all I see here—this is nothing more than a bump in the road."

"How about this," Chad countered. "Now that all your guy friends are married, you miss having guys in your life, because you need guys in your life. The bad dates come about because none of the women you're dating meet the needs that the guys in your life used to meet. Drew shows up, and he's a guy, and he's also smart and funny and looks great naked. Your date last night—"

"Fuck off. I never said he looks great naked."

"Oh yes you did. I know because I listen when you talk. You've mentioned his body a dozen times."

"I have not."

"I have a clearer picture of what Drew looks like than I do of any other person I've never met. You've been thorough, and you've been admiring."

"Again, fuck off."

"Whatever. So last night this therapist woman sees exactly what's going on, and that super freaks you out because she's a woman and they're supposed to be better at picking up on this stuff than guys. Even though she's telling you the exact same thing I've been telling you since you met him."

Fox closed his eyes. *So* tired of this.

"So now I'm going to tell you what to do."

"Oh, this should be good."

"You're going to text Drew, and you're going to tell him you need to see him. Invite him to that dive bourbon bar where you met. Sit him down and tell him you're trying to figure out what this thing is between you, and you're open to any possibility. *Any* possibility."

"And I'm going to do this… why, exactly?"

"Because you owe it to yourself to see if this is what you need. You owe it to me, because I want to see you happy. You owe it to Drew because he's been nothing but nice, and I think he's got a crush on you."

"So you're on Drew's side now."

Chad smiled broadly. "I'm on the side of true love, my friend."

Fox reached across the table and smacked him on the forehead. "Stop that."

Chad laughed maniacally for a moment, but then turned serious again. "Are we going to talk about the elephant in the room? The thing that's really bothering you?"

"And what would that be?" He could hardly wait to hear about Chad's elephant.

"THERE, I sent it." Drew set down his phone. His fate, the next turn his life would take, lay in the hands of a man he'd met only a few weeks ago.

"What did you say in?" Mrs. Schwartzmann asked.

Though he knew the words by heart—they'd drunk their way through an entire pot of tea while he composed it—he picked up his phone and read it to her. "I miss you."

She sat for a long moment. "And?"

"That's it."

"But you were for an hour making the type-type."

"It was no more than half an hour, and it took me a while to get the right feel."

"It feels like nothing much," she said with a shrug.

"In my first draft, I asked how his week was and whether we might get a drink sometime. But that sounded too casual, so then I erased that and wrote about how I saw a bird in the park yesterday that reminded me of one we'd watched building a nest when we were at the resort. But that sounded kind of creepy, so I deleted that. Then I wrote that I had fallen in love with him so I could see what those words would look like—"

"You should have sent that one."

"Then I deleted that because he would have changed his name and moved to another city to get away from me. So then I thought, 'What do I want him to know?' And what I want him to know is that I miss him. It's simple, straightforward, and it could mean 'I miss chatting with you over coffee' just as well as 'I miss the way your skin feels when it brushes against mine.'"

"Ooh, I like that one the best. You should send that one."

Drew burst out laughing. "Mrs. Schwartzmann, I don't know how to thank you. You've been a great friend through all of this."

"You want to thank me, to your wedding you invite me."

"There would be a special place for you, I assure you."

"Good boy. Now, let us finish this cake while we wait for Mr. Fox to type-type at you back."

CHAD TOOK a deep breath. "Your dad."

It was a punch to the gut that Fox hadn't seen coming. But as he struggled to draw breath, he knew Chad had lanced a boil he hadn't been able to acknowledge the existence of.

"Yeah, I thought so," Chad said softly. "That's where a lot of this comes from, isn't it?"

Fox shrugged defensively. His mind was reeling.

"I know it's not that you're worried he'll freak out if you're dating a guy, because he was like a second dad to Thomas, and he came to the wedding and gave that toast that made everyone cry."

Fox nodded, still beyond words.

"You think you'd be letting him down. That you wouldn't be the man he wants you to be, the man that he is." Chad smiled sympathetically.

"I'd be giving up on being the man I thought I was." Fox chuckled grimly. "The one I created in my spreadsheet."

"What do you mean? You used the spreadsheet to evaluate your dates, not yourself."

"That's not true, though, is it?" Fox looked at Chad through eyes blurred with tears. He wondered if he'd ever stop crying. "I entered the scores, but as much as I liked to think they were quantitative and analytical, they weren't. Not at all. Those women were measured not against objective standards, but by how well they fit into the spaces I created for them. And those spaces, they are exactly what's left over, the stuff that fills in around the man I created for myself, the man I wanted to be." He swallowed hard and looked out the window again. "The man my father expects me to be."

"You didn't stop being a man when you fell in love with one."

"Could you stop with that, please?" Fox pleaded. "You've worn me down enough that I'm actually considering inviting him to the bourbon bar tonight. I'm not ready to talk about falling in love."

"Yet," Chad added.

Fox tried once again to activate the heat ray in his glare so he could melt the smug smile off Chad's face. It still didn't work.

"If I invite him to meet me for a drink, will you please shut the fuck up about it?"

"I would be happy to, my good man," Chad replied with a chivalrous bow of his head.

"Fine."

"Do it now."

"I'll do it when I get home."

"Do it now." Chad's manner was placid, but his voice was certain.

"Fine." Fox pulled his phone from his pocket. He glanced down and saw there was a message on it, waiting for him.

From Drew.

"What is it?" Chad asked.

"A message from Drew." Fox read it, then read it again.

"Awesome. What's he say?"

"He says, 'I miss you.'"

"And?"

"That's it."

Chad frowned. "How do we feel about that?"

Fox couldn't help but smile. "It tells me everything I need to know."

"And what would that be?"

"That he misses me."

"Yeah, I got that. What am *I* missing?"

Fox shook his head. "It's classic Drew. He writes long research papers, but he's really a poet. Every word matters."

"So what does this message tell you?"

"That he wants to see me as much as I want to see him."

"But I had to twist your arm to get you to even consider that."

"Because I didn't know if he would want to. Now I know he does."

"Well, write him back, man! Seal the deal."

Fox shook his head at Chad's ham-handed attempt to be supportive, but he did actually appreciate it. He typed out a quick reply, then set his phone down.

Chad was beaming from his side of the table. "I'm proud of you, buddy."

"Just so you know, I'm going to blame you if this doesn't work out."

"That's a risk I'm willing to take. That's why they call me a hopeless romantic."

"They call you half of those things."

The two old friends shared a long laugh.

Chapter SEVENTEEN

FOX SAT for a moment in his car. Could it really have been only three weeks since he'd pulled into this parking spot in front of the Barrel Proof? He could hardly remember a time when he didn't know Drew, even though that was his whole life up until less than a month ago.

What would he find when he opened that squeaking door and stepped into the dark dive? His heart pounded when he allowed himself to admit what he hoped he would find: Drew, smiling at him, welcoming him with open arms and an open heart. He hoped he would read on his face the urgent, alien desire he knew was written on his own.

He got out of his car, locked it, and walked up to the door of the bar. He took a steadying breath, then opened it widely. Go big or go home, he thought to himself. Time to own this thing.

Inside, the bar was about as populated as it had been when he'd first been here, though with perhaps a little more subdued crowd—it was a Sunday evening, after all. He scanned the space quickly, but he knew exactly where he would find Drew. He would be, of course, sitting on the same stool as he had been the last time, because that's where Fox would expect him to be. They knew each other.

He crossed to the bar, his heart still pounding with a possibility he hadn't ever imagined for himself.

"Hey," he said as he drew up beside him.

Drew turned the stool around, his face bright and joyful. It was exactly what Fox had hoped for. Drew jumped to his feet.

"Hey, good to see—"

He was cut off by Fox pulling him into a hug and holding him tight and close.

"I've missed you too," Fox murmured into Drew's ear.

Drew clasped him even tighter, signaling that he knew all of the ways Fox meant that simple phrase, all of the kinds of longing it contained.

"You're bringing a tear to my eye and a boner to my pants," Carlos cracked from behind the bar.

"Dude, stop," Drew chided, releasing his hold.

"Something tells me that pretty soon I won't be the only one," he replied, casting a lascivious glance over them. Then he turned to grab a second glass, into which he poured a shot for Fox.

"What are we drinking?" Fox asked, not waiting for the answer. He brought the glass to his lips and took a deep draft.

"A special request from this guy," Carlos replied, jerking his thumb at Drew. "He wanted to relive the day you met."

Fox smiled at Drew, completely charmed and perhaps a little more smitten than he already was. "Good choice." He sat on the stool next to Drew.

Carlos topped off both their glasses from the unmarked bootleg bottle. "I'll leave you guys to it, then," he said with a wink. He retreated to the other end of the bar, though Fox noticed his frequent backward glances.

"To the end of a pretty terrible week," Fox said as he raised his glass.

"The worst," Drew agreed.

They touched their glasses and took a drink.

"So, tell me what made your week 'pretty terrible,'" Drew prompted.

"Only if you promise to fill me in on what made yours 'the worst.'"

"Deal."

Fox took a breath. "I went on a date last night." Saying this aloud made him realize the truth he'd been hiding from: in going on that date, he had cheated on Drew. It was an awkward and humbling epiphany. "And because you're a better person than I am, I decided to follow your example and invite her over to my place. I cooked her dinner."

Drew smiled. "That must have been very nice."

"It was. And then it wasn't. When I say I followed your example, I mean I really followed it. I made a Peruvian stew, about which I tried to tell a story half as charming as the one you told. It seemed like it was going well. But after dinner, she dropped the bomb."

"I cannot believe that under the influence of your charm and that Peruvian stew she didn't simply fall into your arms."

Fox chuckled. "Yeah, that she did not do. She looked me right in the eye and informed me that I was in love with… you." He swallowed hard. "And then she left."

Drew's eyes widened in disbelief. His mouth opened, he blinked several times, shook his head as if he must have misheard, then closed his mouth without saying anything.

"So that was a tough blow, because up until that minute—actually up until a sleepless night and what turned out to be basically an intervention from my buddy Chad over breakfast—I had never let myself admit that what she said might be true. Chad pretty much beat me to an emotional pulp over it until he finally broke me down enough to make me see what's been in front of me the whole time."

Drew seemed to try to catch his breath. "What would that be?"

"That your coming into my life wasn't a mistake. And it wasn't that Q*pid had delivered me a friend to replace the ones I've lost to wedded bliss. You're a great friend, but that's not nearly all you are to me. I was doing mental gymnastics trying to convince myself that we were buddies having fun and not potential matches going on dates." He stopped for a moment and looked at Drew, remembering how much he enjoyed looking at Drew. "We've been dating. And it's been awesome. And I'm sorry it took me so long to see it."

"Wow," Drew said. Then a huge smile broke out across his face. "Wow."

"So tell me about 'the worst,'" Fox said, hugely relieved that Drew had taken his awkward profession of affection so well.

"I went on a date last night."

"Holy fucking shit—so we *are* practically the same person." Fox laughed. "Please don't tell me it went the same way as mine did."

Drew shrugged. "It pretty much did, but with one rather significant exception."

"What was that?"

"It was with a guy."

Fox's mouth dropped open. "You went on a date with a guy?"

Drew nodded. "I did. I'd never done it before, and basically I did it all wrong. But the whole reason I did it was because I was so hung up on you, and when you didn't seem like you were into it, I started to wonder whether the problem wasn't you, but me. Maybe I've been dating women, and all along I should have been dating guys. So I dated a guy. It was terrible."

"Why?"

"Because he saw immediately that he—and any other guy I might try to date—was really a substitute for you. And until I found a way to get over you, it wouldn't be fair for me to date anyone else."

Fox was deeply touched. "I didn't mean to make you miserable. I just couldn't come around to it as quickly as you did. You're a lot more flexible than I am."

"I'm in grad school. I have friends who are into alternative sexualities that would make switching from women to men seem like amateur-hour stuff. Plus I've never been all that successful with women, so it makes some sense that I should probably cut my losses and give guys a try. I'm not the ladies' man super stud you are."

"First, no one would ever have used those words to describe me," Fox said, his natural humility kicking in. "But second, and more importantly, is that what you want? To give guys a try?"

"Nope." Drew frowned and shook his head solemnly.

"It isn't?"

"Nope. I want to give one guy a try. And I don't care whether that makes me gay, or heteroflexible, or bisexual, or none of the above. What it makes me is in love with you."

Fox's cheeks burned. "You tried to tell me that last weekend. I'm sorry I wasn't ready to hear it."

"You're worth waiting for."

"You did more than wait for me. You put up with a shit-ton of freak-out from me. I can't tell you how sorry I am about pushing you away."

"I knew you didn't really mean it. It had all the signs of a red-alert masculinity meltdown, and I knew there was only one thing that would get through to you."

"A stealth flying ninja tackle?"

Drew laughed. "Exactly. You didn't stand a chance."

"Honestly, it changed everything I thought about you."

"Whoa. How did it do that?"

"After the romantic dinner, and your telling me that you might be falling for me, I think some reptile part of my brain lumped you in with the women I've dated, except that you were a hairier, more muscled version. But since you touched me that way, I expected you to be... I don't know... passive? I guess? So it shocked me when you bounded right back up and smashed me against the wall."

"You held your own pretty well there, mister. I didn't think I was going to be able to get the better of you."

Fox laughed. "You fucking destroyed me, man. You had me on the ropes even before you unleashed your secret weapon."

Drew looked puzzled. "Secret weapon?"

Fox leaned close and whispered into Drew's ear. "You smacked me with your dick." He felt Drew jump in surprise.

"I did?" he asked, sounding utterly stunned.

"You did. And let me tell you, it packs quite a punch. Especially when it's… fully deployed."

Drew's face reddened. "Oh my God. I had no idea. I was trying really hard to keep it away from you."

"You mostly succeeded, except for the one time when it bludgeoned my leg. I didn't realize what it was immediately, but a couple of seconds later I put two and two together. I figured if you were *that* into fighting me, I should probably retire from the field of battle." He smiled slyly at Drew. "Now, though, I'm kinda wishing I'd gotten a look at it. Or even gotten my hands on it."

"Fuuuck," Drew exhaled. "What do you say we get out of here?" He gulped down the last of the bourbon in his glass.

"Fuck yeah," Fox replied. He downed his as well, then set the glass on the counter. "Carlos, my good man," he called, "thank you for your service." He pulled a hundred-dollar bill out of his wallet and set it on the counter.

Carlos, who had returned from the far side of the bar, looked at the tip. "You two being adorable is compensation enough for me."

"Please, keep it. I owe you that and more for helping bring this guy into my life." He cast a look at Drew and couldn't keep the smile from his face.

Carlos looked from one man to the other as they grinned at each other. "Dammit, now I'm gonna have to go tug one out before I can finish my shift."

"I'm sure you have things well in hand," Drew retorted with a laugh.

"I will in a minute," Carlos said, grinning widely. "You two have fun."

"I can assure you we will," Fox replied. He turned to Drew. "Shall we?"

Fox's car was parked in the same place it had been three weeks ago, as gleaming and perfect as it had been then. Fox walked up to it and pulled open the passenger-side door.

"I can manage a car door," Drew said with a sly smile.

"Friends can manage car doors," Fox replied. "Dates get the full service."

"I may hold you to that."

"I hope you do."

Drew settled into the seat, and Fox shut the door softly after him. *Fuck, he's good at this flirting thing.*

Fox got in and pulled the car into traffic.

"Where are we going?" Drew asked.

"Figured we'd get some dinner."

"You have any place in particular in mind?"

"I do. My place."

Drew, startled, turned to Fox, wondering if he had misheard him. "Is My Place another restaurant with an annoying name?"

Fox laughed. "No, we're actually going to my house. I ordered up way too much food today from that amazing grocery store downtown by the flower market, and they delivered it as I left for the bar. I have no idea what we're going to make out of it—I picked everything that looked good."

"That sounds like fun—and it sounds completely unplanned, which makes me a little suspicious. You normally have stuff planned to the last detail."

"I used to. But now I have you. And when you're with me, things turn out amazing, no matter what."

Drew felt warmth in his chest from Fox's casual confidence. Turns out he believed the same about Fox without ever being aware of it. "Awesome. Let's see what we can make."

A short time later Fox steered the car into a small, nondescript alley between two tall buildings, then pulled up to a metal door that looked strong enough to protect an embassy. He flashed his headlights at it, and it immediately began to roll upward, disappearing quickly into the ceiling. Fox eased forward and parked the car under a black plaque that read Kincade in stark silver letters.

"Can you manage your own door?" Fox asked after he shut off the engine.

"I think I'm capable," Drew replied.

They walked to the elevators, and Fox pressed his thumb to the black control panel. One of the elevators opened instantly, and they stepped in. Unlike the clean but plain concrete of the parking structure, the elevator was luxuriously elegant. It silently whisked them skyward until the display read 42: Penthouses.

"Wow," Drew said.

Fox shrugged. "They call them that because they're on the top floor and they can sell them for a higher price. I mean, the view is nice, but they're not that much bigger than the units on other floors."

They stepped off the elevator. Only four doors opened off the sleekly elegant elevator lobby. Fox's lay straight ahead.

"Well, it lacks the gritty, ramen-scented ambience of the student ghetto," Drew said as Fox opened the door and beckoned him to enter, "but I'm sure it has its charms."

"It has you, now," Fox said. "That's all it was missing."

"Good lord, no wonder the ladies swoon for you."

"But is it working on you?" Fox asked as he closed the front door behind them.

"Oh, it's definitely working," Drew assured him.

"Then would it be okay if I… kissed you?" Fox's manner was suddenly reserved, tentative.

Drew felt a shiver of reckless possibility run through him. "More than okay," he replied softly.

Fox stepped toward him, raising his hands. He tickled his fingers along Drew's jaw, then below his ears to the short, sensitive hairs at the nape of his neck. He drew close.

The first brush of Fox's lips against his was electric. It swept away everything he had ever experienced in a kiss, replacing it all with this overwhelming new sensation. Every kiss before—every kiss with a woman—had been an exercise in kindling a campfire in the rain, lighting a candle in a gale. The warmth of those previous kisses, every single one of them combined, could not compare with the heat sparked by this simple connection, this first contact between them. He knew, in that moment, that this was right. It was the most right thing he had ever done with another person. It lasted mere seconds, but it changed his life.

"Okay?" Fox asked, pulling back after the first kiss. He looked at Drew, eyebrows raised in anxious supplication.

Drew could have used his words. But that's not what the occasion called for. Instead, he launched himself forward, closing the small gap between them in an instant and crashing his mouth into Fox's. This kiss was not tentative. This kiss left no doubt.

Fox stepped back, but only to brace himself against the onslaught. He held firm, pulling Drew even harder into him, while Drew wrapped his arms around Fox's back to ensure there was no sliver of daylight between them. They were as close as their clothes would allow them to be.

They stayed close for several long, vigorous minutes.

Finally, when they had exhausted themselves and needed to breathe, they released each other reluctantly. They stood for a long moment, looking into each other's eyes.

"I can't believe you're here," Fox whispered.

"There's nowhere I'd rather be," Drew replied.

They smiled at each other, then laughed. Not the laughter of anxious uncertainty about the line they had crossed, but the laughter of joy unbridled and undreamed-of dreams realized. They laughed because there was no other way for their exuberance to be released.

"So, dinner, I guess?" Fox asked.

"Yes, dinner." Drew was certain he couldn't eat a thing. But he was up for making anything with Fox.

"Come with me," Fox said, then held out a hand for Drew to take. He led him into the kitchen.

"Holy balls, this is amazing," Drew said, taking in the elegant kitchen with its sleek granite counters and European appliances. "This is like something out of a magazine."

"It was one of the things I really loved about the condo," Fox replied. "But I don't get to cook in it as much as I'd like. Weekdays are mostly dinner out with clients, and weekends are dates. Last night was the first time I'd cooked for anyone in I don't know how long."

"I'm honored you would share it with me," Drew said, then gave Fox a peck on the cheek, bringing a surprised smile to his face.

"Okay, so, fridge is there, pantry there, spices over there, and utensils here, here, and here," Fox said, pointing out each location as he worked from one side of the kitchen to the other. "Ready?"

They got to work, Fox pulling out the fresh groceries he'd had delivered, and Drew marveling at the impressive range of ingredients he had on hand. They talked about what they should make, and shortly Fox was at the stove sautéing while Drew drizzled oil into a vinaigrette.

"For someone who doesn't cook much, you have a pretty sure hand with the sauté pan," Drew said, watching as Fox flipped the contents of his pan repeatedly without losing a single morsel.

"I used to cook a lot with my mom," he said. "Dad was gone most evenings with work, so she and I spent a lot of time in the kitchen. Then when he had a heart attack and had to stay home for a few weeks, he let me know really clearly that I shouldn't cook because it would make my future wife feel that she had nothing to offer except sex."

"Were you raised in the 1950s?"

Fox laughed. "It felt like it sometimes. And the really stupid thing is that I did what he told me to do. I stopped cooking, and that meant I stopped spending time with my mom." He grew serious. "I should tell her I'm sorry that happened."

"Okay, see, I thought you were charming when you flirted. But that was nothing compared to right now." He pulled Fox into a hug from behind. "You are seriously the best person I know." He kissed him on the neck.

"You'd better stop that if you want to eat tonight," Fox warned. "I can't cook with shivers running down my spine."

"We'd better save that for dessert, then," Drew said with a sly laugh. He kissed Fox one more time just below his ear, then went back to whisking.

An hour later, they sat down to an overwhelming feast. The large dining table was nearly covered with the food they had made together.

"We're never going to eat all of this," Drew said.

"But it was a hell of a lot of fun to make," Fox countered. "And now we don't have to worry about lunch for the whole week." He picked up a glass of wine—his second, or was it third? "To the best sous-chef I've ever worked with."

Drew laughed and held up his glass as well. "It was a pleasure to work under you."

They drank and set to making barely a dent in all of the food they had cooked.

After dinner, and after the leftovers had been packed up, Fox poured some bourbon and motioned for Drew to join him on the sofa that faced the great wall of windows overlooking the park at the center of the city. A necklace of lights glowed around it.

"I can't believe we're here," Drew said softly.

"If anyone had told me three weeks ago that this is where we'd end up… well, I probably would have told him to seek professional help. But now I can't imagine not being here with you."

"What do you suppose did it? Made the computer match us up, you think?"

Fox looked out the window into the far distance. "I've thought about that a lot," he said finally. "On the surface, we don't have a lot in common. At least not in the ways that people normally write profiles for online dating. You're an academic, I'm a marketing director. You're in touch with your emotions, and I outsource mine to Microsoft Excel."

"You live in a sky palace and drive a BMW, I live in a student ghetto and unclog drains for my rent."

Fox smiled. "Like I said, not a lot in common on the surface. But I admire the hell out of your determination to get your degree, and there's a sense of humanity in everything you do that I find… uplifting."

"And you've completely changed my entire concept of marketing people who dress in expensive suits and drive fancy cars."

"I should warn you that all the others are self-obsessed dickheads. Just so you know."

"I have no doubt that you are unique among your peers," Drew said with a laugh.

"So if we're so different on the surface, how did it know?" Fox asked, reframing the question.

Drew shrugged. "Maybe it actually delivered on its promise to look below the surface. Though how it managed to come up with the idea that we'd somehow end up here, after a lifetime of being, you know, straight…."

"It's a little spooky, I have to say," Fox added. "I keep thinking about what it might have found in my social media activity that led it to think I'd be into trying it with a guy. I mean, with one guy in particular. The only guy I'd ever even think of doing this with."

"You mean having a glass of bourbon while sitting on your couch?"

"No," Fox said, setting his drink down on the glass coffee table. "I meant this." He leaned in and kissed Drew gently on the lips.

Drew sighed softly and leaned into the kiss, for the first time snaking his tongue out to greet Fox's.

"Wow," Fox said when they had finally broken their kiss. "I've kissed a few women."

"Is that what we're calling 'several hundred' now?" Drew cracked.

"It wasn't several...." Fox looked up, clearly running sums in his head. "Okay, you're probably right about that. But it makes my point all the more strongly. Never, in my entire life, did kissing a woman make me feel the way kissing you does."

"And how does it make you feel?"

"Like I'm doing the wrong thing in the most right way possible. Like this is a secret the universe tried to keep from me, and now I've discovered it. Like I never have to kiss anyone else ever because it cannot possibly get better than it is right now."

Drew smiled. "To me it feels like coming home."

"See? That's what I mean. You're so much better at emotions than I am."

"I like your emotions just fine," Drew replied, then slid closer to Fox and rested his head on his shoulder.

They sat and looked out onto the city for a long while.

Chapter EIGHTEEN

"MR. KINCADE, welcome back," Jeff said as Fox got out of the driver's seat.

"Enjoy your dinner, sir," the other Jeff said to Drew as he stepped from the passenger side of the car.

"Thank you," both men said to the valets.

"They're nice kids," Drew said as he and Fox climbed the stairs toward the restaurant.

"They're happy for me, I think. I've never shown up here twice with the same person."

"I'm flattered." He nodded gracefully as Fox held the restaurant door open for him.

"Mr. Kincade," the maître d' called as they approached. "A table for four tonight!"

"I think it's a good idea to try new things once in a while, don't you?" Fox replied.

"Indeed, sir. Indeed." The maître d' cast a subtle glance at Drew, then smiled a little obsequiously at Fox. "Right this way."

Drew walked next to Fox through the restaurant. "Are you sure he's going to be okay with meeting me? I'm a little worried about making a good impression."

"Chad's going to love you. Don't worry about it. Like I told you, he was in your corner from the beginning."

"But I was theoretical at that point. Starting now I'm going to be a real person to him—the person who turned his buddy gay."

Fox stopped and grabbed Drew's hand. "It's charming that you're nervous. But Chad's easy—save your nerves for when you meet my dad."

"Oh fuck," Drew whispered.

"See? Now you see tonight's no big deal." He kissed Drew on the nose.

"Yeah, thanks," Drew replied, feeling queasy.

They arrived at a table in the middle of the restaurant, where sat two people whom Drew recognized instantly from the pictures Fox had shown him online. Chad and Mia looked up and smiled in greeting as the maître d' deposited Fox and Drew. Chad shot to his feet.

"Foxy," he called in greeting, holding out his hand. Fox took it, and then they did that odd clasp-bump-pat thing that Drew associated with athletes greeting each other.

"Chad, Mia, I'd like you to meet Drew."

"Great to meet you, Drew," Chad said, his voice suddenly an octave lower and full of joyful vibrato. They shook hands.

"Mia, nice to meet you," Drew said, extending his hand across the table to her.

She smiled and took his hand. "I've been looking forward to this ever since Fox first told us about you," she said.

Fox turned to Drew as they sat down. "Mia was convinced we were heading here all along. Her smarmy gloating is the only drawback I see to our being together."

"Hey, no fair," Chad protested. "I wanted you guys in bed too!"

"Maybe I should leave the three of you to it?" Mia said, with a roll of her eyes.

"I'm just saying I was rooting for you from the beginning," Chad said to Drew.

"Thank you, I guess?" Drew said. He wasn't exactly sure how to parse this conversation.

"Chad's right, for once in his life," Fox explained. "He took great pains to point out to me that I was being a big baby about you. He was kind of an asshole about it, and apparently that's what friends are for. Being assholes to each other."

"You're welcome," Chad said grandly.

"The important thing is that you two found each other, and you look pretty damn happy," Mia said, looking from Fox to Drew and back again. "I think that's awesome."

"It's all kind of been a new experience," Fox said. "I wasn't really sure how guys… you know, dated and stuff?"

Chad leaned forward conspiratorially. "What kind of 'stuff' are we talking about here?" He leered comically, as if his meaning weren't clear enough.

Fox leaned forward to meet him halfway across the table. "I'm not going to tell you about that kind of 'stuff.'"

Chad's face fell. "Fine. It's unhealthy to keep it all bottled up inside is all I'm saying."

"Please excuse my husband," Mia said across the table to Drew. "Fox was the last wild stallion in their little clique, and I think he's going through vicarious-lothario withdrawal."

Drew laughed. "I didn't realize there was a clinical term for it."

"Oh, he's got it bad. These two post-gamed every one of Fox's dates. I tried not to listen, but sometimes hearing two guys talk about... *stuff*... well, sometimes it could get a girl worked up. Which I don't think Chad has any complaints about," she said, smiling at her husband.

"It's so nice to find out that my sex life was so *useful* to the two of you," Fox said.

"And it still can be. I'm honestly kind of curious about how it works." Chad seemed to have second thoughts about expressing an interest in Fox and Drew's intimate life. "Mia sometimes looks at gay porn," he blurted.

She shot him the Look. He recoiled, eyes wide. "Which I think we can all agree is something that should not be mentioned in polite company," he added hastily.

"Good thing this ain't polite company," Drew offered, hoping to restore peace to the table. It seemed to work, as all four laughed, and the tension was released.

For a moment.

"So, have you two... you know...?" Chad made a face like a young vicar imagining how sex might feel.

Drew and Fox stared at him, aghast.

"I'm only asking in the interest of science. It's not every day that someone does a one-eighty on their sexual orientation. I'm only trying to understand what that's like."

"It's private is what it's like," Fox scolded.

"I understand the curiosity, though," Drew said kindly. "When straight sex is the only kind you've ever imagined, a change like this can be a bit... challenging."

"That's all I meant," Chad said, looking at Fox. "We've never had any secrets when it comes to sex, have we?"

"You certainly haven't," Fox retorted. "I learned that the hard way on spring break."

"That was one time!" Chad cried.

"It was twice, and I know this because I *was in the same bed.* I felt every move you and that cruise-ship hussy made." Fox put his hand on Mia's arm. "I'm sorry you had to hear that."

"Oh, he's told me about that," Mia replied casually. "But I do have a question for you: did he make that noise even back then?"

Chad's eyes widened in horror. "Wha—"

"You mean the thing with his nose?"

"Yes!" Mia hooted. "The one that sounds like he's trying to snort his orgasm up like a booger?"

"Oh my God, yes. I thought he was having an asthma attack and I was going to have to roll him off her and shove his inhaler into his mouth."

"Look, there's our waiter," Chad called abruptly. "Let's hear the specials." He waved frantically, unseen by the waiter, who was at the moment across the restaurant.

"Wait, suddenly we're not supposed to talk about sex?" Fox asked.

"Not *normal* sex," Chad said. "That's boring. We all know what that's like."

"I object to your use of the term 'normal,'" Fox said.

"I object to your use of the term 'boring,'" Mia added.

"I'd like to hear the specials," Drew threw in. He smiled at Chad.

"You're my favorite," Chad muttered to him. He tipped his head in the direction of Fox and Mia, who were laughing until tears rolled down their cheeks. "These other jokers are dead to me now."

"In answer to your question," Drew said, leaning closer to Chad and lowering his voice, "we've only kissed and cuddled a bit. We're taking it slow."

"But enough to know it's right? For both of you?"

Drew was deeply touched by Chad's concern for his friend and the new relationship he found himself in. "It's amazingly right. And thank you for being such a good friend to him through this. He's a lucky man to have you in his life."

"I say the same to you, sir," Chad replied with a gracious bow. "I haven't seen him this happy in a long, long time."

"What are you two plotting over there?" Fox demanded. He and Mia regarded them suspiciously.

"We were discussing the currency manipulations of the Tudors and the resulting formulation of Gresham's Law," Chad answered without skipping a beat.

"That was really good," Drew muttered.

"I studied up a little in preparation for tonight," Chad muttered back. "You think they bought it?"

"Yeah, no," Fox answered. "You made a solid effort, but it came too quickly."

"That's what I'm always telling him," Mia said, then burst into laughter.

"Wow," Chad said. "Just wow." He turned to Drew. "I guess you and I will be going home together tonight. These two don't deserve us."

Drew was overjoyed at having made such an effortless connection with Fox's best friend. He relaxed and enjoyed immensely another dinner he could never have afforded on his own.

CHAD AND Fox stood at the valet stand waiting for their cars. Drew and Mia had stopped off to use the restroom.

"He's great," Chad said, unprompted. "I mean, really great. Really, really great."

"Either you're bullshitting me, or you're planning to leave Mia for my boyfriend. Either way, this will not end well for you."

Chad laughed. "I'm just saying that I have really high standards for you. I want you to be with someone who deserves you and who will be good to you. I think you've finally found that person."

"And that it's a guy doesn't bother you at all?"

"I've been telling you all along, Foxy, all I care about is that you're happy. What you get up to in the bedroom is your deal, though I probably will insist on details at some point because one, I'm curious, and two, you and he are the hottest guys I know, and the thought of you going at it, well…." Chad's gaze wandered off into some homoerotic middle distance.

"Are you going to keep doing that? You keep talking about me and Drew having sex, and it's starting to creep me out a little."

"Of course I'm going to keep doing that. We always talk about that stuff."

"But that's because it's something we had in common. This is different."

Chad grabbed Fox by the shoulder. "You aren't listening to me. When I say that you being with a guy changes nothing between us, I fucking mean it, okay? We still tell each other everything. Nothing's off limits. That's always been our deal, right?"

Fox shrugged, then nodded. "Yeah, it has."

"Good. There's only one thing that needs to change."

"Oh, so *now* you think of something."

"Just one. Now that you are a connoisseur of men, I need—"

"There's no way you can finish that sentence that won't make me want to punch you in the throat."

"Shut up, this is important," Chad said. "I need you to tell me if I start to let myself go."

"What the fuck does that mean?"

"It means that I don't want to get all fat and sloppy. I want to stay hot."

Fox could not contain his laughter.

"And not 'pretty good for a married guy' hot. I mean 'gay hot.' Like if I went to a gay bar, they'd be, you know, all over me."

"You are being completely ridiculous right now," Fox said between gasps for air. "Why do you want to have guys at a gay bar all over you?"

"Because gay guys have the highest standards. I've let the gym slide a bit lately, and I need you to keep me honest."

"First, I've been dating a guy for a week," Fox said, exasperated. "I have no idea what will cause a riot at a gay bar. Second, you don't need a gay guy to tell you you've bulked up a bit around the middle. You know that as well as I do. Third, you're a complete idiot."

"See? That's the kind of honest feedback I'm talking about. Thank you, my gay BFF."

"You won't be thanking me when I'm kicking your ass at the gym Monday morning at five."

"The what now? When?" Chad leaned forward as if he suddenly couldn't hear all that well.

"You heard me, you big straight ball of lard. Get yourself there, and we'll get you whipped into such shape that the go-go boys will be scratching each other's eyes out for the chance to do body shots off your six-pack."

Chad's eyes widened. "They do that?"

"How the fuck should I know?" Fox replied with a guffaw. "I've never been to a gay bar, remember?" He punched Chad on the shoulder. "Dumb fuck."

"Thanks, man. I'll see you on Monday. You said seven, right?"

"You snooze, you lose," Fox warned.

"All right, all right," Chad replied in surrender.

"What'd we miss?" Mia asked as she and Drew approached together. "Looked like you two were having some fun without us."

"Nothing, my love," Chad said gallantly. "Just guy talk."

"You'll tell me later?" Drew whispered into Fox's ear.

"Oh yeah," Fox replied.

Their cars, each driven by a Jeff, appeared from around the corner. Fox's was first, of course—a reflection of his consistency as a tipper.

"It was so nice to meet you both," Drew said. He hugged Mia and then extended a hand to Chad. Chad, however, pulled him into an enthusiastic hug. Then Chad released him, but he held him at arm's length for a moment.

"Don't you hurt my Foxy," Chad said solemnly. "I love him more than you can possibly imagine."

Drew, visibly alarmed, swallowed hard. "I will try to love him as much as you do," he said.

Chad beamed. "Good answer."

"Are you finished harassing my boyfriend?" Fox said. It was hard to tell which of his three dinner companions was more surprised by his use of the B-word. Drew's eyes were wide, but he was blinking as if feeling the sting of tears in them. Mia smiled sappily, and Chad nodded sagely, as if he personally had conjured the obvious love between Fox and Drew.

Fox powered through it, hugging Mia and then Chad, and then getting Drew into the car so they could get the hell out of Table's porte cochere. "Good night," he called back as he slipped behind the wheel. Jeff shut the door behind him with a soft but solid thump.

"Wow, that got a little weird at the end," Fox said, shaking his head.

"I think they're really great. Chad seems like a basic bro, but once he starts talking, you find out there's so much more to him. And anyone who casually name-drops Thomas Gresham over dinner gets my vote."

"He was terrified that you wouldn't like him," Fox said.

"He... what?"

"Chad, as a general rule, likes to sit back and let the finer things in life come to him. He works in his father's law firm, always dated the head cheerleader, spent his summers modeling for Abercrombie & Fitch. He's had pretty much everything handed to him, on silver platters of a particularly large size. But tonight? Tonight he was *working*. Chad doesn't peruse Wikipedia articles on the theoretical underpinnings of monetary policy for fun. Hell, he barely studied for his bar exams. He wanted you to *love* him."

"As best friends go, I think you hit the jackpot."

"And he's crazy about you. I could tell. And I think he's also a little jealous."

Drew gave a little gasp. "I would never dream of coming between you two. Please, you have to believe that. And you have to make him believe that."

Fox laughed. "I didn't mean he's jealous like that. I guess I meant he's envious. He has this idea that guys have higher standards for other guys than women do. That's why he was badgering me to help him get back in shape. He wants to be hot enough to get a guy to fall for him."

"That's... insane," Drew said, brows furrowed. "He's married, to an absolutely stunning woman, and he's also straight, right? And just between us, he's pretty stunning himself."

"He'll be thrilled you think so."

"Hey, wasn't that the exit we needed?" Drew asked, turning to look out the window.

"I wanted to go for a little drive. You up for that?"

Drew smiled. "I'm up for anything you can think of."

"Anything?" Fox asked, grinning.

"*Anything*," Drew assured him.

The smile didn't leave Fox's face until they were well out of the city.

"This is interesting," Drew said as Fox turned off the highway onto a small country road. "What's out here?"

"Nothing," Fox said, looking out into the empty darkness. "It's kind of perfect that way."

Drew studied him for a long moment but said nothing more.

Fox pulled off the road and brought the car to a slow rolling stop. "Here we are," he said.

Drew looked around. "You're right. There's nothing here."

Fox smiled. "There is now. Come on."

They got out of the car, into the pitch darkness, and Fox led the way into the field. About a hundred yards away from where he'd parked the car, he came to a stop.

"Are we there yet?" Drew asked teasingly.

"As a matter of fact, we are," he said. "Look up."

They both craned their necks upward, and just as they had the night Fox stood here alone and wondered how much worse his life could get, the stars shone down in their millions above and all around them.

"Oh my God," Drew said softly. "This is it. This is exactly it."

"What?" Fox asked. "What is it?"

Drew's eyes remained lifted heavenward. "This is what it feels like. Meeting you, having my entire life turned upside down by you, then finally... this." He reached out for Fox's hand, then held it tightly to his chest. "My whole world—the whole universe—suddenly makes sense. It's all fallen into place because you appeared. For the first time in my life I know I'm in the right place. Out of all of the billions of planets orbiting billions of stars, I'm standing on the one you're on. And this is exactly the place I was meant to be."

Fox was grateful for the darkness of the night, obscuring as it did the surprised tears that ran down his cheek. "That's even more beautiful than all of this," he said, looking from horizon to horizon across the twinkling sky. "I came here after I left your house the night you cooked for me."

"I wondered what happened. I woke up and you were gone. My upstairs neighbor saw you leave. She's the one who convinced me to text you in the morning."

"She was probably the one who woke me up, actually. Sounded like she was moving cinder blocks around at three in the morning."

"Mrs. Schwartzmann has some issues."

"Heavy ones," Fox added with a laugh. "Anyway, I kind of jolted awake, and after that weird moment when you try to figure out where you are and how you got there, I realized we were lying next to each other. Like, full body contact from head to toe. Your arm was around me, and your breath was making this hot spot on my neck. And I swear I could feel your heart beating—like, in my chest. There were two heartbeats in my chest. It was the closest I've ever been to anyone. Ever."

"I can see why you'd freak out a little about waking up like that," Drew said. "It makes sense to me now why you left."

"But I didn't freak out because I was so close to you. I freaked out because it didn't freak me out to be so close to you. I lay there for a while thinking how warm and peaceful it was to be there with you. And that's what freaked me out. I didn't want to get off that couch, and that's why I had to jump right off that couch. It's the same reason why I probably seemed like a damn yo-yo the last couple of weeks—every time I felt good about seeing you, panic would set in and I'd pull away. Mixed signals all over the place. But I wasn't doing it because I didn't want to be with you. I had a hard time coming to terms with the fact that I was miserable and alone because I hadn't allowed myself to even consider the possibility that I could be happy with a guy. But once you came into my life, I couldn't deny it any longer."

"So you're sure this is where you want to be?" Drew asked. "With me, I mean?"

"Yes. I'm absolutely certain," Fox replied. "I wish I could have come to that conclusion sooner. I wish I were more like you—you seem to have sort of taken it in stride."

"Honestly, it panicked me a little too, at first. But soon it became clear to me that being confused without you was a whole lot worse than being confused with you, and I realized I should set my doubts aside and see where we'd end up. Then again, I wasn't laboring under the weight of being an improbably handsome stud. I think that held you back."

"You have to stop it with the 'improbably handsome' thing," Fox scolded gently.

"Don't have to," Drew replied with a laugh. "I can finally admit that I was only pretending to give you shit about that. Now when I say 'improbably handsome,' what I really mean is that it is highly improbable that I could pull a guy as handsome as you, and I'm celebrating my good fortune."

"I guess I have to let you keep doing it, then."

They shared a laugh, then resumed quietly contemplating the stars.

"Thank you for bringing me here," Drew murmured after a few silent moments. "I could stay here all night."

Fox was deeply gratified, but he also wanted a little more than stargazing tonight. "As fun as that sounds, there's some other stuff I'd like to do tonight. With you."

"To be clear, we're talking about naked stuff right now, aren't we?"

"Indeed we are."

Drew looked across the dark field toward the road. "Can you do the beepy-flashy thing with your car alarm? We gotta go."

"I'm right behind you," Fox said.

Chapter NINETEEN

FOX'S STOMACH was doing flips as he drove back from the field of stars. But Drew held his hand the entire way, and that settled him a bit. Funny, he reflected, how excitement and terror have the same effect in one's guts—a visceral thrill indeed.

He pulled into his parking spot, keenly aware that what they were doing now he had never imagined doing with any man in the world. He had brought dozens of women here over the years, and yet this person, this Drew who came from nowhere to remake his life into something he could not recognize, was the one who fulfilled the promise of all those wasted nights.

They walked together to the elevator, exchanging smiles and looks that communicated only the smallest part of what they were feeling. Fox knew his emotions to be in utter disarray, yet the flutter of anticipation he felt every time he looked across the elevator car at Drew was somehow both overwhelming and reassuring. He craved the feeling of free fall toward this new kind of union.

"I don't want this to worry you," Drew said as the elevator climbed through the teens and twenties, "but I'm a little… nervous."

Fox smiled broadly. Of course they would be feeling the same thing.

"I'm terrified," he said as the elevator began to slow. "I have no idea what we're about to do."

Drew stepped closer to him. "That I'm not nervous about. I know exactly what we're about to do."

"I am greatly relieved to hear that," Fox replied with a laugh. "It would be embarrassing to have to text Mia for instructions."

"Did you see the look on her face when Chad casually mentioned that she watches gay porn? I imagine they're having a conversation about the line between public and private right now."

The elevator doors slid open.

"I wonder if Chad's ever watched with her. It would explain his insistence on hearing certain… details." He shook his head as he unlocked the door of his condo. "I'm surprised Chad can still surprise me after all these years."

They entered the condo, hung their jackets in the closet, and stood a little awkwardly in the entryway.

"When you said you knew exactly what we're about to do," Fox said, trying desperately to sound casual, "what, exactly, did you mean?"

"I meant," Drew said, putting his arms around Fox's waist and pulling him close, "that we are going to do what I don't think either of us has done in a long time." He gently kissed Fox on the lips. "Make love."

What Drew's answer lacked in specificity it more than made up for in its effortless faith that love would find a way. Fox knew he was right. He drew strength from Drew's calm assurance that what they were about to do was going to be the most natural, most effortless thing they'd ever done in their lives. He wished he felt it as serenely as Drew seemed to.

"Come in," Fox said, pulling Drew toward the living room. "I'll pour us a drink." He settled Drew on the sofa facing the windows and retreated to the kitchen to prepare a couple of tumblers of a fine old Scotch, with a large ice cube each. He brought them into the living room and handed Drew one of the heavy glasses before he sat next to him.

"To new explorations," Drew said, holding his glass up.

"How adventurous," Fox replied. "Though it sounds uncomfortably like you're about to go spelunking."

Drew laughed. He took a drink, then set his glass down on the coffee table. "I'm getting that you're kind of apprehensive about tonight," he said softly. "I understand that completely. You're the most analytical person I know, and you didn't get to where you are in life by not knowing where you're going."

Fox smiled, hugely relieved that Drew not only knew exactly what was going on inside him, but why.

"Me?" Drew continued. "I'm a born academic. Trying new things, then overanalyzing them to death, is my jam. The mental and emotional effort you put in up front is what I do after the fact. Ask anyone who's ever been to the theater with me how much fun I am the moment the lights come up. I can bore paint off the walls with my Marxist-Freudian-Foucauldian analysis of *Harry Potter*. It's my special gift."

"I have never once found you boring," Fox assured him.

"As much as I appreciate that, we've only known each other a month. Give it time." Drew took another sip of Scotch. "But my point is that I'm happy to talk it all out with you, even if that means all we do tonight is talk. Everything I want in life is right here next to me."

"You must really like Scotch," Fox cracked.

"Oh I do, make no mistake. But as much as I love it, it can't love me back. Or kiss me."

Fox could, though, and he did. "Thank you," he said softly, his forehead pressed to Drew's. "I'll try not to annoy you with the grinding of my mental gears tonight. We're kind of on a rocket ship blasting its way out of my comfort zone."

Drew looked at him seriously. "Do you still want to go on this ride? You may experience disorientation and physical exhaustion."

"There is nowhere I'd rather be than right here with you."

"And there is nowhere I'd rather be than in your bedroom." Drew gave a sly smile.

Fox threw back the last swallow of Scotch. "Finish your drink, and I'll be back in a minute."

"Need to go powder your nose?"

"Something like that."

Fox was back in the living room five minutes later. "Mr. Larsen, would you like to accompany me?" He held out his hand and gave a formal bow.

"It would be my pleasure, Mr. Kincade," Drew replied, getting to his feet.

Fox led him down the hall toward the bedroom. He opened the door, then stood aside to let Drew precede him.

"Oh my God," Drew whispered.

Fox stepped into the room behind him, and watched as he stood in the middle of the room and turned slowly around. The light from the fifty candles Fox had lit filled the room with a warm glow, bathed in which Drew now stood.

"This is so beautiful," Drew said. "You are such a romantic." He kissed Fox softly. "Any woman you did this for had to be ready to marry you on the spot."

"I never did this for any woman," Fox replied. "You are unique, and I want everything to be new with you."

Drew smiled. "I think a lot of stuff is going to be new tonight."

Fox took a deep breath. "Let's get naked."

Drew's eyebrows shot up. "Well, that escalated quickly."

"It's always bugged me the way most women think that getting undressed, especially the first time, needs to be this long, drawn-out thing. If you're going to end up naked, you might as well get naked, right?"

"Exactly right. Unless you're throwing fives and tens, you're not getting a striptease from me."

Fox laughed. "I mean, we've been naked together before, and I'm around like twenty naked guys every morning at the gym, and why make a big deal out of it?"

"So no one pole dances in the locker room at your gym?" Drew asked. "Seems like a pretty boring place."

"My gym is this posh place downtown, because that's where all the vice-presidents and above work out," Fox explained as he unbuttoned his shirt. "Some of the guys keep in pretty good shape, but a lot of them clearly lift more martinis than weights."

"No pole dancing and no eye candy? Why do you even go to this horrible gym?"

"Because having a membership there is a prerequisite for moving up in the company. A lot of deals get done at the smoothie bar."

Drew shook his head. "I have the opposite problem where I work out. It's mostly undergrads who go lift when they want an excuse not to be doing their homework. So they work out a lot. I feel like an old, flabby man when I'm there." He set his shirt neatly on the dresser.

"You are in no way an old, flabby man," Fox said, looking Drew's muscled chest up and down. "You put in some work, sir."

"Thank you," Drew said with a nod. "It's always been my dream to catch the eye of an improbably handsome man." He laughed while he unzipped his pants.

Fox tossed his pants toward his closet. He had never tossed his clothing anywhere, ever.

They stood facing each other in their underwear, lit by flickering candlelight from all corners of the room.

"So here we are," Fox said. "About to do... this."

Drew smiled. "We don't have to do anything. Even if Chad and Mia are probably right now tangling their sheets thinking about us going at it like feral Boy Scouts, we don't owe them anything."

"I guess the thing… for me…," Fox said, awkwardness closing in around him as he tried to put his emotions into words, "is that you're a guy. I'm a guy. I can objectively appreciate the effort you have put into looking the way you do. But standing here, I can honestly tell you that I've never been attracted to a guy's body before this very moment. Right here, right now, looking at you… well, you're right. It turns out that I'm a bit disoriented."

Drew, because he was Drew, simply smiled. "That's okay. This is completely new for both of us. But I think I have an idea how to handle it."

Warmth that only Drew could bring him surged in Fox's chest. "I can hardly wait."

Drew stepped closer, then put his hand on Fox's shoulders and gently turned him around. Fox was now facing the full-length mirror he used every morning—and before every date—to make sure he was at the peak of his sartorial game. Right now, though, he was standing in only his boxers. Then, over his shoulder, Drew's head appeared. His gaze traveled up and down Fox's reflection, slowly and with evident pleasure.

"You are beautiful," he whispered into Fox's ear. It sent a shiver down Fox's spine.

Then Drew's hands slipped into view, one over his right shoulder, the other along the ribs on his left side. His touch was so gentle that Fox could hardly feel it at first, the light touch skimming across his skin, leaving goose bumps in its wake. He closed his eyes, taking in the sensation.

"I know every muscle that lies under the surface," Drew murmured. "I know how hard you've worked to build that strength, how many reps it takes to shape a pectoral like this"—his fingers grazed lightly over Fox's right nipple—"and how hard it is to cut your lower ab like this." His fingers traced the V-line to where it disappeared into Fox's underwear.

Fox could hardly breathe.

"You know how I know these things? I know these things because I'm a man." He kissed Fox softly on the neck while his hands continued to roam across Fox's body. "Being here with me is completely new, but it's also the most familiar thing you can imagine. I know your body because I know my own, and what makes you unique I can recognize the way no woman could. This new trail we blaze tonight runs across known territory. What we will experience together we come to as identical counterparts, knowing from the inside out what the other feels. You've never been with anyone who already knows this landscape so well, who touches you with the knowledge that comes from being in a body like yours. Let go of the idea that this is something you've never done before. It's ground you've traveled your whole life, made new by sharing it, treading it together, arriving as one."

Drew pulled Fox into a tight embrace from behind. "Will you come with me on this adventure?"

"Oh fuck yes," Fox whispered. He marveled at this sexy academic who had come into his life, speaking about love in fully formed paragraphs. Craning his head around, he kissed Drew over his shoulder before spinning around to grapple him more urgently.

They kissed for a time, then Drew pulled back. "Ready?"

"For what?"

"This," Drew said. He took Fox's hand and led him to the bed, where he pulled back the covers and nodded for him to get in.

"You're the guest," Fox said with a smile. "You first."

Drew winked at him and slipped between the sheets. He lay back, facing Fox, with his arm outstretched. Fox got into bed as well, and turned over to pull the covers up. As he did so, Drew wrapped his arms around him and pulled him tight.

"Who's the big spoon, motherfucker?" Drew grunted into Fox's ear.

Fox had always been the big spoon, every time he'd been in bed with a woman. The big spoon was part of his identity as a man.

But the warmth of Drew's embrace, the strength of his enveloping arms, the heat of his breath on Fox's neck...

He kind of liked being the little spoon for once.

Behind him, Drew's entire body stretched out along his, from his wiggly feet to his powerful quads to his full pectorals with their raspy, insistent nipples. It was nothing like Fox had ever felt in bed, and it was everything he suddenly wanted.

Drew's hands roamed over Fox's torso, bringing goose bumps and hot shivers everywhere they went. Then his left hand, which had freer rein than the right, pinned as it was under Fox's bulky frame, roamed even farther. Fox held his breath as Drew's fingertips reached his boxer shorts, brushing the tiny pleats of the waistband, clearly intent on seeking entry.

"Fuck yes," Fox groaned, knowing that Drew would wait for permission, like a gentleman.

Fox did not want to be in bed with a gentleman.

Drew chuckled softly behind him, and his fingers slipped under the elastic, blazing a new trail. He glided through the neatly trimmed pubic hair on the way to his goal: the root of Fox's manhood.

When he reached it, Fox sucked in a sudden breath, electrified by the touch that had been forbidden his entire life. There was another man's hand on his cock. Somewhere in his brain, a circuit breaker flipped, and he fell through a kind of gentle darkness on his way to something completely new. As Drew's fingers closed around the solidity of his erection, Fox breathed a new kind of air—cold and fresh and freeing. This was what his life had been missing.

Drew slipped his hand along the steely-hard column of flesh, reaching the head and tickling around it before returning to the base. Fox moaned and shifted his hips, urging him on. As he did so, he became aware of the rude protrusion of Drew's cock, which despite the intervention of two layers of fabric was doing its level best to insinuate itself between Fox's buttocks. It was hot and shocking and wonderful.

Fox pushed back against the solidity of Drew behind him and found, to his deep satisfaction, that Drew was immovably resolute in his stance. He gave not an inch and instead seemed to advance a little more, closing the already infinitesimal gaps between them to nothing. They were as close as two people could be without actual penetration.

The night was still young, Fox reflected.

Drew's meandering fingers began a more purposeful stroking, clasping Fox's cock tighter. He focused his grip on the sensitive zone just below the flare of its head, exactly as Fox himself would do when he wanted to skip the niceties and step directly into an orgasm.

"How did you know how to…?" he tried to ask but was unable to think clearly enough to finish his question. The orgasm gripped him before he could finish.

Across his entire body, from the balls of his feet to the top of his head, every muscle snapped into a breathless rigidity. Fox gasped raggedly as he felt the twinge deep inside him, in the birthplace of the orgasm that Drew was conjuring with his insistent strokes. Helpless in its throes, he shuddered and gasped and yearned for it to come and complete his transformation into the kind of man who has orgasms at the hand of another man. Because he knew, in this moment of inevitability, that he had changed.

He closed his eyes and surrendered.

The feeling of semen filling one's boxer shorts is one most men over the age of sixteen rarely feel—it is a sensation out of time that few would relish. And yet to Fox it was the fulfillment of a wish he'd never dared wish and the hot, sticky signifier of that fulfillment. He came and came and came until he was covered, and his shorts sloshed with the continued motion of Drew's hand.

Drew, for his part, kept up his insistent rhythm, urging and coaxing and squeezing every drop of fluid Fox was capable of producing, and more besides. Fox didn't remember ever coming so much as he already had, and yet it continued to explode from him. Finally, just at the moment the sensitivity was building to unbearable levels, Drew somehow knew—*of course he did*—to slow down and limit his strokes once again to the sturdy middle of Fox's cock.

Fox took the deep breath his ecstasy had been denying him, then trembled all over. Drew kissed up and down his neck while he gently stroked Fox's slippery cock. His own erection was like an iron bar pressed into Fox's buttocks and lower back.

"Come on," Fox murmured as he reached behind him and grappled Drew's ass, pulling him sharply forward. He clenched his ass, trying to capture Drew's iron prick between his cheeks as he slid slowly up and down.

Drew gasped at the sudden friction, but his hips swung into complementary motion. As if rubbing his dick between a buddy's buttcheeks was the most natural thing in the world. Maybe it was in this new world.

After no more than a dozen achingly slow transits, Drew arched and shuddered. Then a flood of heat boiled up into the small of Fox's back, spreading with every grunt of pleasure Drew made into Fox's shoulder. Drew writhed and thrashed, and all the while Fox held him tightly, ensuring no break in their obscene contact.

Finally, once Drew had juddered to completion, they slackened their grip on each other. Fox turned to face Drew and found him a reflection of himself: sweat-glossed, panting, elated.

"That was the gayest thing ever," Fox whispered.

"Ever in the history of gay things," Drew added.

They shared a chuckle, then kissed tenderly.

"Feeling you come was the most amazing thing I've ever done in bed," Drew said softly.

"Everything we just did was the most amazing thing I've ever done," Fox replied. "In bed or anywhere else."

"You don't think it was a little weird that we kept our underwear on?" Drew said, eyebrows peaked in worry.

"Nothing we do together is weird. Because we're doing it only for us." He kissed Drew gently on his worried forehead. "I've never done anything like what we just did, and that's what makes it perfect. We're breaking the mold and launching ourselves into something completely new. I wanted it to be different, and that sure as fuck was different. And I will treasure the memory of it always."

"But doesn't it seem kind of… I don't know, immature? Like something teenagers would do at summer camp and then never talk about it?"

Fox knew that just as he had rattled on nervously beforehand, Drew would have second thoughts after. It was exactly what Drew had told him to expect, after all.

"It was our first time. It makes perfect sense that we would do something a little… tentative, I guess. What wouldn't make sense is if we threw off our clothes, swapped deep-throating blow jobs, and then took turns pounding away at each other right up the ass. That would be completely unrealistic for a first time, don't you think?"

Drew's eyes widened. "You aren't planning on doing that, are you?" His fingers nervously twitched around Fox's slowly subsiding erection.

"God no," Fox replied. Then he paused a moment for reflection. "Have you ever… you know… had anything up there?"

Drew smiled but looked a little abashed. "There was a woman I dated a few years ago who liked to… well, she wanted to explore there, and I said I wasn't sure. But she had a very persuasive tongue."

"What did she say?"

"Nothing I could make out, once she had her tongue up there."

Fox burst into laughter, and Drew joined in.

"So what was it like?" Fox asked.

"You mean you've never…?"

Fox shook his head. "It's not the kind of thing I can even imagine asking a woman to do. She'd probably figure I was gay, and I'd never see her again."

"Kind of like the last woman you dated?" Drew asked with a sly smile.

"Yeah, kind of like that." Fox realized the puddle of semen in his boxers was starting to loosen and drip distractingly. "You know, we should probably clean up."

"It is getting a little sticky in here," Drew agreed.

"Let's hop in the shower and wring out our summer camp underwear." He kissed Drew again, then got up and led him to the shower.

"This is like a spa," Drew said, marveling at the bathroom.

"Master bath square footage is positively correlated with resale value, particularly in the high-rise condo market," Fox replied. "So it's bigger than I need, certainly, but I look at it as an investment in attracting buyers."

"Is that a bidet?"

"An investment in attracting international buyers."

"And that whole part of the room is the shower?"

"An investment in attracting international buyers who really, really love to take showers," Fox said with comic exasperation. "Now get in there and shut up."

"Yes, sir," Drew said. He stepped into the shower, his soaked-through boxer briefs still clinging to him. He was quickly drenched by the three shower heads aiming at him.

Fox followed him in, quickly stripped his own boxers off, and tossed them to the corner of the shower. Then he stepped behind Drew and yanked his underwear to his feet.

"There," he said simply.

Drew stepped out of the wet clump of underwear, and Fox kicked them over to join his own in the corner.

Fox took a moment to cast a leisurely glance down Drew's muscled back, over his round, powerful buttocks and his runner's calves. "You're... beautiful," he said.

Drew turned around. "Standing next to you, I wouldn't get a second look, but thank you for saying it."

Fox pulled him close. "You are the only man I've ever wanted to put my hands on. That's a serviceable definition for 'beautiful,' and you aren't going to talk me out of it." He kissed Drew softly, passionately.

When finally he released their clasping kiss, Drew glanced down and smiled. "Well, *hello*," he said to Fox's bouncing erection.

Fox looked at where their bodies were nearly touching. His cock reached out for Drew, while Drew's pointed up at him imploringly.

He glanced back up at Drew. "Well, clearly they're excited," he observed.

"Indeed. And who are we to disappoint them?" Drew reached down and wrapped his hand around his own erection, then opened his fist and grabbed up Fox's as well. "There," he said brightly. "Now they can get to know each other." He began to slide his hand back and forth along the full length and double thickness of their stacked manhood.

Fox put a hand alongside Drew's, and together they stroked each other's cocks, and their cocks stroked each other as they thrust and fidgeted, and soon both men were panting with a lust rekindled. "I wish I'd known this all along," Fox moaned softly. "How good this could be."

"It's like we've had this magic in our pants all these years but didn't know how to unleash it," Drew said. "This is incredi—"

He was cut short by the unannounced arrival of his second orgasm of the evening. Without warning, he blasted sharp jets of cum onto Fox's lower belly. Fox looked down, eyes wide, then back up to Drew. He closed his eyes and shuddered as he returned fire into Drew's groin. They froze, still gripping each other's cock in their hands, desperate to prolong the pleasure as long as possible.

Finally, their grips relented, and they each took a shaky step backward.

"Holy fuck," Fox breathed. "It's like I can't be within six inches of you without having an orgasm."

"It looks more like seven inches from my perspective," Drew replied with a grin. "And we may have to accept that after a lifetime of trying to have the wrong kind of sex, we're going to be on a hair trigger."

"Is there a wrong kind of sex, you think?" Fox asked. "As long as everyone consents, I mean."

Drew tipped his head to one side. "I think any sex that doesn't involve you and me is the wrong kind of sex."

"I think you're right," Fox said with a smile. He pulled Drew into another enthusiastic embrace, knowing full well where it would most likely lead.

SOMEWHERE THERE was something making some kind of noise.

Drew turned over, but the noise got louder, so he turned back and found himself bumping right up against the insanely muscled shoulder of Fox. Fox, who was still sleeping soundly while his phone made all manner of grating, shrill sounds. He reached over and picked up the phone.

Video Call from Chad, it said.

"Fox?" he whispered, nudging Fox's shoulder. "Fox, it's Chad."

"No, it's Drew," Fox replied sleepily. "I wouldn't have done *half* the stuff we did last night with Chad."

Drew laughed. "I meant it's Chad on the phone."

"I know. I was making a joke." Fox's eyes opened wide. "I figured Chad can wait for the full report until we're at least up and dressed."

"I thought you said he called you every Sunday morning from bed."

"He does."

"And that lately he will call you and call you until you answer."

"He will."

"And that you were worried he would drive over here and drag you out of bed if you don't answer him."

"He might."

"So perhaps it would be prudent to answer his call, hmm?"

Fox looked up at him with an expression of sleepy cheer. "It's seven in the morning, and you're already a better person than I was planning to be all day," he said, shaking his head. "All right, gimme the phone." He shoved himself into an upright posture against the headboard and arranged the covers low over his hips.

Drew handed him the phone, which was still vibrating insistently. "I'll go wait in the living room."

"Oh hell no," Fox said, grabbing Drew's hand. "You're making me do this, so you gotta stay." He yanked, and Drew toppled back into bed.

Drew laughed and hefted himself up so he was sitting next to Fox. He pulled the covers up to his armpits. Fox immediately yanked them back down.

"What are you doing?" Drew cried.

"If Chad insists on calling us, he's not going to see us with our blankets up around our necks like a couple of grannies," Fox said. He tucked the covers back down, so low that their hip bones were exposed. "He went on and on last night about how he wants to know everything, so let's see how much he can actually take."

"I will never understand bros," Drew said with a judgmental shake of his head.

"Watch and learn," Fox said with a grin. He kissed Drew on the lips, then answered the video call.

Chad blurred onto the screen, then came into focus. "Foxy!" he called. "How's it hangin' this fine morning?"

"It's not 'hanging,' and here's why." Fox held the camera farther away so that Drew could be seen in the frame.

"Awesome!" Chad cried. He pulled his phone closer to him. "Fuck, look at that guy. I thought PhDs were a weedy lot, but Drew... you're fucking jacked, man."

"Um, thanks?" Drew replied, looking to Fox for some idea how to interact with his ostensibly straight buddy who was avidly ogling him.

"See? I told you." Fox turned back to his phone. "Do you want us to get rid of the covers completely?"

"Yes!" came Mia's shout from somewhere near Chad. She popped her head into the frame of Chad's phone. "Sorry, that was rude. What I meant to say was 'yes, *please.*'" Her eyes scanned backed and forth, taking in the view, then she leaned close to her husband and whispered. "Chad, did you see what Drew looks like without a shirt on?"

"I can't *not* look at him," Chad muttered back under his breath.

"We can hear you," Fox said. He turned to Drew. "Now she's as bad as he is. They never did anything like this when I was dating women."

"That's because you never dated a woman half as hot as Drew," Mia retorted. Then she stuck her tongue out for good measure.

"I'm afraid they're going to be impossible this morning," Fox said to Drew.

"Then let's shut them up," Drew replied. He leaned toward Fox and kissed him tenderly.

The only noise from the other end of the video connection was a pair of soft gasps.

Drew reached up and gently stroked Fox's chest, then leaned down and kissed one of his nipples while he flicked the other with his fingers.

From the other side, a moan.

He snaked his fingers down Fox's toned torso until it slid under the covers.

"We gotta go," Chad said, his voice strangled with something that sounded an awful lot like lust. The video call went dead.

"Nice move," Fox said, tossing his camera onto the nightstand.

"I've got more," Drew promised. He kissed Fox passionately as he rummaged under the covers, provoking Fox's cock into an immediate boner.

Fox broke their kiss, and a serious look came over his face. "You're really okay with this?"

"Okay with your interrupting my awkward attempt to get you to have sex with me? No, no I'm not." Drew smiled as he continued his purposeful stroking.

"No, I mean with us. Being here. You know, in bed. Together."

"I would have been really disappointed if I'd woken up and you weren't here in bed with me. So overall, I'm good." Drew studied Fox's face. "Are you okay with us?"

"Beyond okay. But we've been 'one-step-forward-one-step-backing' since we met, and then last night we kind of strapped a rocket to it. We had more sex in the last eight hours than I've ever had in one go—hell, in any given month of my adult life—and I was worried that this morning would be awkward and weird because, you know, light of day and all. But I look at you this morning and I know you're the best chance I ever took. And I'm really hoping that you feel the same way."

"My pillow talk is woefully underdeveloped, due to lack of practice, so I'm going to stick with what I know. Empires fall, and always have, because their leaders cannot adapt to paradigm shift. When the underlying economic and social realities change, and the elites are unable to shift their way of thinking to align with them, that's when you get uprisings and revolutions and really awesome graffiti. So this morning we have a choice. We can look at what happened last night as an anomaly and go about our lives as if it never happened, or we can embrace the paradigm shift and from this moment on reconceptualize ourselves as having a sexual orientation that includes each other and everything we did last night."

Fox blinked back at him, his expression uncertain. "Wow. Even your dirty talk is graduate level."

"What I'm saying is we either jump into this thing we've invented, or we pretend it never happened. The first one means we get to keep doing this"—he gripped Fox's cock, which had softened only slightly during his philosophical disquisition—"or we get out of this bed right now and never look back."

Fox's eyes widened with dismay. He shook his head.

"That's what I thought. Now, if you'll excuse me, I have a paradigm shift to accommodate." And with that he dove beneath the covers, which was quickly becoming his favorite place in the world.

Chapter TWENTY

"JUST SO I'm sure I understand," Fox said as they walked into Drew's apartment, "you bring her sausages every Sunday morning, but you pretend you didn't buy them for her?"

"Right," Drew replied with a shrug, as if surely everyone had such arrangements in their lives. He walked to the kitchen to grab the sausages he'd bought on Friday.

"You're a great guy, you know," Fox said, pulling him in for a kiss. "A good man and a great guy."

"You don't have to flatter me. I'm already sleeping with you."

"And I want to keep it that way."

"Is that why you loaned me this amazing shirt?" Drew ran his hands down the front of the quarter-zip fleece Fox had thrown at him when they'd finally gotten out of the shower. For the second time.

"No, I just got tired of seeing you naked," Fox said casually.

Drew set his sausages on the kitchen counter and whipped off the shirt. He threw it at Fox in a fit of melodrama.

"And let's not start on the pants. God, I was relieved when you finally put your pants back on."

In short order Drew's khakis flew at his head.

"Ugh, those horrible boxers. I've always hated those, but at least they keep you from waving your dick at me."

The boxers sailed across the kitchen and landed at his feet.

"Ah, you have fallen for my diabolical plan," Fox said with a supervillain laugh. He crossed the kitchen in a lunge and took hold of Drew's semierect penis. "For now I shall have my way with you." He backed slowly through the kitchen, tugging Drew along with him.

"You are insane," Drew said with a laugh. His growing erection showed him to be rather attracted to insanity.

"You're going to be singing a different tune in a moment," Fox warned. He led Drew by the cock through the apartment and into the bedroom, where he unceremoniously tossed Drew toward the bed. He landed and rolled over onto his back, limbs splayed in obscene repose.

Fox mounted the bed between Drew's legs, and in one mighty growling attack, he stuffed fully half of Drew's erection into his mouth.

"Fucking fuck," Drew cried as he arched his back and flailed his arms. "How are you so fucking good at that?"

"It's all about the right motivation," Fox replied once he'd pulled back, allowing Drew's prick to slide out from his lips. "You take a blow job the way most people get electrocuted. It's quite gratifying." He swooped back down and was able to welcome more than half of the hot, hard thing into his mouth.

Fox pumped away joyfully for a minute or two, delighting in the frantic reaction his ministrations elicited. He had discovered last night that Drew responded to oral attention with a shocked frenzy of lust—not only the first time, which Fox had perhaps expected, but every time. It was like he'd never been sucked before. And as a newly minted fellator, Fox was particularly flattered to be the cause of Drew's frenzy.

This time, however, he wanted to give him a little something extra. He pulled off Drew's cock again, then licked and kissed his way down, smooching with Drew's balls. This much he had done last night, but now he went farther. With his tongue he traced the seam where Drew's ball sac attached to his body, and when he reached the lowest point he kept going. He ran his tongue along the ridge that disappeared down between Drew's strong legs.

"Oh, oh," Drew cried, and his frenzy increased.

Fox took that as a "Yes, please!" and continued his downward journey. Soon he was flicking the tip of his tongue along the crinkled skin of Drew's most secret place. He slid his hands under Drew's thighs and then pushed them up gently so that the mysteries of this hidden portal were opened to him.

It made his heart skip a beat to realize he was looking right at— was running his tongue around—a guy's asshole. And he was loving it. He leaned forward and planted a gentle kiss right at the center of the virginally tight ring of muscle.

Drew thrashed and moaned but did nothing to discourage Fox's explorations. And so he continued.

With his lips braced against the outer surface, he sharpened his tongue to a point and drove it home. Drew sucked in a tremendous breath and shivered with every part of his body that wasn't pinned to the bed by Fox's tongue. The already drum-tight ring of muscle clamped down on his tongue, squeezing and relaxing in perfect synchrony with Drew's gasps. Fox slipped his tongue out and gave Drew's ass a slurping kiss, then dove back in. This brought Drew to new exertions, his legs twitching and bucking in the air.

Worried that Drew's legs would give out and come crashing down to the bed, Fox pulled back once again and eased them down on either side of him. Then he dipped his middle finger into his mouth and coated it with saliva. This lubrication, combined with the spittle he'd left in and around Drew's orifice, was enough for him to be able to insinuate his finger.

Drew jolted and froze, but then Fox heard him heave a great exhalation and moan, "Yessssss...." He took this as permission to introduce his entire middle finger, and soon his hand was pressed between Drew's muscular cheeks. With his other hand, he laid hold of Drew's manically throbbing cock, which he then pulled toward himself.

Then, as he wrapped his lips around Drew's cockhead, he curled his middle finger upward, bringing it into firm contact with Drew's prostate.

It was as if someone had installed an orgasm switch in Drew's ass, and left it there for some future explorer to discover. For as soon as Fox pressed it, Drew's prostate hardened and twitched, bringing Drew's moans up an octave. A few seconds later jets of hot semen filled Fox's mouth. Drew growled like an angry bear as the orgasm thrashed its way through him. He began to thrust wildly, driving himself down more forcefully on Fox's finger, and then upward farther into his mouth. The headboard knocked loudly against the wall as he bounced and kicked.

Then, without warning, the bed collapsed.

First it tipped to one side as a supporting leg gave way, and then all of the others failed simultaneously. With a great clattering crash, the mattress dropped six inches to the floor.

Drew didn't seem to have noticed, as he was still busy ejaculating every drop of moisture in his body into Fox's mouth. It wasn't until he finally wound down and fell still that he seemed to notice that something was amiss.

"I think you exceeded its design limits," Fox said with a shrug. He went back to licking up the semen that Drew had sent flying all over his torso.

"Do you smell sawdust?"

"I think that's what your furniture is made of. First the coffee table, now this."

Drew smiled down at Fox. "This was much more fun." Then his glad expression dropped. "Oh shit. Mrs. Schwartzmann will be—"

At that moment his phone rang.

Drew shot up from the wreckage of his bed and ran back into the kitchen to pluck his phone from the pants he'd thrown at Fox.

"Yes, Mrs. Schwartzmann?" he asked by way of greeting. Fox smiled at his breathlessness. "No, it wasn't another coffee table. It was… well, maybe it would be better to explain in person. Might I impose upon you for a visit this morning?" He paused, then nodded. "I can certainly take a look at that while I'm up there. Oh, and would it be okay if I brought a friend along?" Another pause, and this time a sly grin broke out on his face as he listened. "Fox is looking forward to meeting you as well. We'll be up in a minute."

"So I get to meet the enigmatic Mrs. Schwartzmann," Fox said, standing in the doorway to the bedroom, the vantage point from where he'd been watching this conversation.

"Do you feel up to it?" Drew asked, walking nakedly over to him.

"For you, I'm up to do anything." Fox ran his hands up and down Drew's rib cage, then kissed him. "You should probably get dressed first."

"So you really are tired of seeing me naked?" Drew asked with ironic offense.

"Never. But I imagine Mrs. Schwartzmann might not be as happy about your nudity as I am."

Drew shrugged. "You may be right."

A few minutes later, Fox followed Drew up the stairs to the second floor, where Drew knocked on the first door they came to. A voice responded instantly, as if its owner had been waiting by the door from the moment she hung up the phone.

"Who is, please?"

The voice was low and gruff, but still clearly aged.

"It's Drew, Mrs. Schwartzmann. We talked on the phone five minutes ago?"

"Oh, Drew" came the clearly relieved voice from the other side of the door. A rattle worked its way down the side of the door, as if a dozen locks were being worked by not terribly capable hands. The door opened a crack, and then a last defense was repealed and the door opened wide. A tiny woman with a tight bun of gray hair and lively eyes stood beaming at both of them.

"Fox you must be," she cried, holding out her arms to him. It seemed as though she was demanding a hug, so he stepped forward and took the fragile thing into his arms. "Now here is a real gentleman, Drew. He knows when an old woman needs hugging."

"I would have hugged you if I had known that's what you wanted."

"This is what I am meaning. A gentleman knows." She released her hold on Fox, but her hands gripped his biceps, struggling to reach all the way around. "And so strong." She stepped back and motioned for them to enter. "Please, come in so you can be telling me what to your furniture has happened."

"I'm afraid I broke Drew's bed," Fox said, with what he hoped was the appropriate note of contrition.

Mrs. Schwartzmann shot a lightning glance in Drew's direction, then burst out laughing. "The woman only the coffee table broke." She looked Fox up and down, then turned back to Drew to stage-whisper, "Your bed, I think, is not the only thing that is different in your life because of him."

Drew smiled weakly. "Here are some sausages," he said, holding out the packet.

"You have extra sausage now, I see," she said, then cackled maniacally. She took the package from him and practically danced through the apartment toward the kitchen. "Come, come, my boys."

"Sorry about this," Drew whispered.

"I think she's wonderful," Fox replied under his breath. Mrs. Schwartzmann was everything he'd imagined.

"Sit, sit," she ordered as they entered her kitchen. There were three chairs around the little table in the middle of the kitchen, a table that gleamed with light reflected from its plastic-coated surface. In the middle of the table was a pastry that smelled both sweet and hearty. Mrs. Schwartzmann busied herself with making coffee and getting the sausages up to a good sizzle.

"Hope you're hungry," Drew muttered. "She's going to force-feed us this entire kringle thing."

"Good," Fox replied. "You're the only thing I've eaten all morning."

The deep blush in Drew's cheek was precisely the reaction Fox was going for. Drew was frightfully handsome when he blushed. Fox leaned over and kissed Drew right on his flaming cheek.

"Ach, you two," Mrs. Schwartzmann cried, clapping her bony little hands together. "So handsome and so in love. You make this old woman's heart thump-thump with joy."

Drew smiled. "You are hardly an 'old woman,' Mrs. Schwartzmann," he said. "I think you will bury us all."

"Oh, I hope not," she replied, her hands dropping to her sides. "That sounds lonely." But then her usual boundless energy returned. "You, my dear, are no longer lonely, are you?" She squinted at Drew. "No, you are not. Fox has taken your loneliness away."

Drew looked at Fox, whose turn it was to blush. "You're right, as always."

"You may be sleeping on the floor, but at least you will be together," she said in a singsong voice. She turned to attend to the kettle, which had begun to whistle.

"I love her," Fox whispered to Drew.

Drew shook his head. "And I love you for saying that."

"I love you too," Fox said, as naturally as exhaling.

Fox had planned how he would say that he had fallen in love—with the eventual woman with whom he would someday fall in love. It would be after a romantic dinner, perhaps during a weekend getaway. He would lead up to it suavely but subtly, and she would be both surprised and delighted. He had constructed a number of scenarios that would bring maximum effect.

With Drew, it just flew out of his mouth.

And that seemed exactly right.

For on further reflection, he realized that they had actually done most of the things he had imagined: romantic dinners, a weekend getaway, surprise and delight. It all added up, quite as surely as it would in a spreadsheet.

He was in love.

IT WAS not just a Monday. It was The Monday.

Two months after the pilot of a new initiative, the launch team at Q*pid would gather for a progress report and a decision on whether to commit to, or discontinue, the program.

Veera spent the first twenty minutes of her workday staring at the calendar in the upper corner of her computer monitor. No matter how hard she stared, it obstinately informed her that today it would be her turn to defend Archer and to argue for his wider release.

The results had largely been solid, if not revolutionary. Archer had, over the last two months, matched up thousands of people who wouldn't have qualified as matches under the legacy system, and a good number of these had entered into relationship status. There had been more than fifty engagements, which struck many on Veera's team as impetuous but did not surprise her at all. If Archer provided the right person, what more did they need to know? Might as well get right to it, as people had in her family for generations.

But no matter how many successful matches Archer produced, the legacy of his going rogue a month ago and trampling all over Parameter Three was a millstone around his virtual neck. He'd been perfectly well-behaved in the weeks since that horrid Saturday morning, but the event had quickly passed into company lore. Jokes, some of a rather off-color nature, ran rampant, and someone had posted a sign in the kitchen about how Archer would be tasked with deciding whether you really need decaf and simply don't know how to ask for it. It had been presented in the form of a limerick.

Veera sighed.

To prepare for the debrief, she needed to gather the current state of Archer and his subsystems, so she began to scan the windows in which log files skittered by. Everything seemed to be running well until she got to the window she'd set up to monitor Few. There had been no updates here for some time, but this morning something new had appeared.

"Relationship status changes," read the anodyne update.

"Oh crap," Veera whispered. Somewhere deep inside her was a shred of hope that this was good news, but she knew, rationally speaking, that this would be the nail in the coffin of Archer's freewheeling experimentation. Instead of a PR fire drill that ended with a whimper, there would now be a dataset of one proving that matches discordant on Parameter Three were doomed.

She launched out of her chair and ran to the conference room. Once there, she shut the door behind her and dialed with a trembling finger.

"Hello. This is Archer."

"Resume voice interface."

"Voice interface ready."

"It's Veera."

"I recognize your voice, Veera," Archer replied.

"I notice that there is an update on the discordant match Few," Veera said, exerting considerable effort to keep her tone steady. Voice interfaces were easily confused by overwrought speech.

"There are four such updates. Would you like to hear them?"

"Yes."

"One. User Fox set his profile to 'match unavailable.' Two. User Drew set his profile to 'match unavailable.' Three. User Fox changed his status to 'in a relationship.' Four. User Drew changed his status to 'in a relationship.' That concludes the updates."

Veera pondered this terrible news for a moment, then her curiosity got the better of her. "Are these users in a relationship that accords with their Parameter Three preferences?"

"One is, the other is not."

Veera's heart leapt into her throat. "One of them is in a relationship with another man?"

"Yes."

"And the other?"

"Is also in a relationship with another man."

She sighed. Archer's conversational ability had made her forget for a moment that she was speaking with a ruthlessly logical interlocutor. "They are both in relationships with men?"

"Yes."

"But you said only one of them was in a Parameter-Three-discordant relationship."

"That is true."

Then she remembered that user Drew had changed his Parameter Three preference to men a couple of weeks ago. The import of Archer's infuriatingly precise speech was becoming clearer.

Now she knew that, despite the surprise of having Archer try to fix them up with each other, both users had, within the space of a month, established relationships with men. That was at least some validation of Archer's bizarre actions on Parameter Three.

But then something thunked in her mental machinery. If only Drew had changed his preference under Parameter Three to men, then how did Fox end up in a relationship with a man?

"Are both users in a relationship with other Q*pid users?"

"Yes."

Well, that's curious.

"How did user Fox match another man when his Parameter Three preference was set to women?"

"It was a discordant match under Parameter Three."

Veera's blood ran cold. "Archer, you haven't been making any more discordant matches under Parameter Three, have you?"

"No."

"Then how did…?" She stopped as her mental machinery clicked back into operation. "Are user Fox and user Drew in a relationship… with each other?"

"Yes."

A full thirty seconds passed before it occurred to Veera to draw another breath.

"Confirm that a match you made that was discordant under Parameter Three has resulted in relationship status."

"Confirmed."

Veera had left her chair and was dancing about the room. "Archer, you were right! You were right!"

"Yes."

She danced about for several long minutes while Archer waited patiently for additional voice input.

"Archer, we have some work to do."

"I am ready, Veera."

She drew the blinds on the conference room windows, obscuring the view from the corridor. She had no more than three hours, and she needed to be bullet-proof.

PROGRAM REVIEWS were always scheduled for 1:00 p.m. in the large conference room, in which Veera had witnessed many a devastating melee as developers defended the value of their work against those who said the company should move on and try other experiments. Of course, the dissenting voices were often loudest on the part of those whose pet projects had not yet been funded and who hoped an abrupt cancellation of someone else's work would benefit their own. In short, ulterior motives were the order of the day.

Today, however, Veera's trepidation had been turned to eager anticipation. After a weekend spent brainstorming defenses of Archer, she was now preparing to present his vindication. She was ready.

She waited until the room was nearly full before making her entrance. There was a chair next to Edwin at the head of the conference table, and it was there she sat.

"Thank you for coming, everyone," she said, in a voice that she hoped sounded more confident than she felt. Edwin gave her an encouraging smile. "I'd like to bring you up to speed on Archer's progress."

"Can we cut to the chase?" Ross interjected from the other end of the room. "Artificial intelligence hasn't moved the needle enough to justify the expense. Nice try, we learned some things, let's move on to bigger and better."

"There's some new information I think the group needs—"

"Let me guess—in order to make more matches, it's ignoring customers' preferences again?"

Go big or go home, Veera.

"Actually, that's exactly what I propose we let Archer do." She clenched her jaw to keep it from quivering. Everyone in the room, Ross included, fell into a stunned silence.

"Provocative," Alexis opined, with a smile that said "I like your moxie, kid."

"Veera, why don't you take us through it?" Edwin prompted.

Veera took a deep breath and recalled the pep talks she had given herself in the conference room with the door shut. "As you are probably aware, the AI engine known as Archer went into limited launch two months ago. Initial results were promising in that nearly half of the matches it discovered would not have been discovered under the standard algorithm. However, the team continued to tweak and adjust in order to further increase metrics."

"And that's when it started trying to make people gay," Ross muttered in mirthless jest.

But Veera had practiced for his interruptions as well, and she swallowed her reflexive passivity. "No, you're wrong," she said simply.

She didn't often see him startled. The effect was pleasant. She continued before he had a chance to respond.

"What Archer did was analyze the social media profiles of our customers in ways we did not explicitly configure. It discovered some deep patterns that seemed to predict when a broadening of certain criteria might result in greater match potential."

She could see Ross beginning to take a breath in preparation for scolding her about Parameter Three. This too she had prepared for.

"Specifically," she continued before he could form his first word of objection, "Archer began to evaluate match potential discordant on Parameter Three. It identified eleven high-potential matches, resulting in twenty-two match notifications that were sent a month ago."

She took a deep breath. The more analytical she could be, the calmer she felt.

"These twenty-two match notifications were the subject of a severity alpha event," Veera said calmly. "Almost half were pulled from match queue before customers were aware of them. The other customers were informed that a mistake had been made and they should ignore the matches."

"Aside from one very irate personal trainer with an itchy Twitter finger, no harm done," Alexis chimed in.

"But no one found their true gay love," Ross tutted with treacly menace.

An awkward susurrus, something between an embarrassed chuckle and a rueful grunt, made its way down the table toward Veera. She was ready for it.

"That's not true," she said simply.

"What does that mean?" Alexis blurted, her hawklike gaze fixed intently on Veera.

"It means that one of the potential matches discovered that morning, while discordant on Parameter Three, has resulted in relationship instantiation."

The room erupted into a dozen side conversations as everyone weighed in on this surprise development.

"Not to repeat my colleague's question," Ross said over the din, "but what the hell does *that* mean?"

"A relationship," Veera explained with a schoolmarm's slightly exaggerated patience, "is when two people like each other." Her expression expressed pity that it was a concept of which he very likely had no first-hand experience.

Alexis practically vibrated with excitement. "Are you telling us that one of the couples Archer drunk-matched is actually dating?"

Veera nodded. There was an excited buzz all around the room.

"So they were lying when they said they were straight?" Ross asked.

"No, they had both dated women exclusively until the discordant matches were sent. Apparently Archer knew better than they did what they were looking for."

"If I'm understanding you correctly," Edwin said in a slow, loud voice, "you're saying that out of eleven potential matches sent that morning, discordant under Parameter Three, half of which were pulled before the customers were even aware of them, one has turned into a relationship?"

Veera smiled at him. Of course he was understanding her correctly—she had briefed him fully on her report earlier that day. He was playing along to make sure she had the floor.

"It's actually even more striking than that," she said, turning from Edwin to the larger group. "Eleven matches were identified, and the corresponding notifications were sent out. But ten of those were pulled back because they hadn't yet been opened. Those ten notifications involved parties to nine of the potential matches. So in the case of only two of the matches were both notifications received. That means our match discovery conversion rate—*for AI-initiated matches discordant under Parameter Three*—is fifty percent."

"That's incredible," Alexis said in a voice slightly above a whisper.

"That's why I'm proposing we expand the discordant match program. Make it part of Archer's configuration."

The room fell silent, leaving Veera to listen only to the pounding of her own pulse in her ears.

"Wait, so now you want to start telling *more* people they're gay?" Ross blurted. He grimaced strenuously to convey his opinion of the strategy.

"No, I want to understand whether AI might be able to reveal to people why they have not been able to establish a relationship. It might be Parameter Three. It might be some other preference we haven't tested yet. But our first step is to get more information." She looked at Alexis, asking silently for her support. "I think this matched couple might have a story to tell—one that could convince other customers to allow Archer to match them without regard to their base parameters."

Alexis's eyes lit up. "That's a fantastic idea. This could be the start of a whole new narrative about relationship discovery. It's not about connecting with people who meet your preferences, it's about trusting a higher intelligence to make matches, whether it's with someone you would choose or not. I love it."

Veera let out the breath she'd been holding. "I'll ask user research to contact them," she said. "We'll see if they'll come in to talk with us."

Alexis smiled. "Can I join you? I love seeing you work."

Veera nodded, her head swimming.

This is what success feels like.

"THANK YOU for coming in today," the petite woman said as they came into the room. She stood and extended a hand. "I'm Miyoko, the head of user research for Q*pid."

"Pleased to meet you," Fox said, swallowing his startled reaction at learning her name. "I'm Fox."

"And I'm Drew." He shook her hand as well.

"Is everything all right this morning?" she asked.

Fox realized he hadn't been as effective at hiding his surprise as he'd hoped. "No. I mean, yeah. It's just that I used to date a woman named Miyoko, and it ended rather badly."

She nodded empathetically. "I am sorry to hear that."

There was a knock at the door, and it opened to reveal a young Indian woman. She shuffled quickly in and sat down next to Miyoko. "Sorry I'm late," she said.

"We were just getting started," Miyoko replied. "Fox, Drew, this is Veera. She's the one who proposed and built the AI engine that matched the two of you."

"*Very* pleased to meet you," Drew said, extending his hand across the table. "I'm a huge fan of your work."

She smiled and laughed. Fox was delighted to be reminded how charming Drew could be.

Fox shook her hand as well. "I'll admit it was a bit of a shock to be matched up with a guy."

"Let's start there," Miyoko said. "What was that like, finding you'd been matched with another man?"

"Interesting," replied Drew.

"Horrifying," Fox answered.

Drew turned and looked at him, eyebrows raised in rather offended surprise.

"What? I was horrified. I get this note that there's a match with a probability a full seven points higher than I'd ever gotten, and I tap through to find out it's a dude. I was expecting a beautiful woman. I may actually have dropped my phone."

"Wow," Drew said, shaking his head.

"You said the experience was 'interesting,' Drew. Can you expand on that a little?"

Drew nodded. "I'd been having a string of bad dates, so the ping about someone amazing in my queue was really exciting. And I figured that the big new brain would probably match me up with women I wouldn't have otherwise seen, so I was kind of expecting there would be some surprises. Although seeing him was probably a little more of a surprise than I was expecting."

"And how did it make you feel?"

"Honestly, I figured if you guys had built an artificial intelligence system for the sole purpose of finding out who I should be dating, I should probably take its advice. So I kinda figured I might be gay and not know it yet."

"Had you considered you might be gay in the past?"

"No. Not once. I didn't have anything against it, of course, but I never thought of myself that way." He paused with his brow furrowed. "That I was aware of, anyway." He looked up at Fox with a shy grin. "Until I met this guy."

"How about you, Fox? How did you feel when Drew contacted you?"

"Utterly and completely baffled," he replied. "I freaked out at my best friend—a couple of times. He was nothing but supportive, but I didn't want support. I wanted him to be angry on my behalf. Angry that I'd been matched with a guy. So it took a little while for the anger to burn itself out, and then I sat and stared at Drew's picture for a while. I don't know what it was that made me reply rather than deleting the match, but I couldn't bring myself to do it. So I typed a reply to his message and deleted it and typed another and deleted that. Both of those were messages where I told him that because it was a mistake, we should ignore it and move on. But somehow… that didn't seem like the right thing to do. So then I wrote a new message and suggested we meet up for coffee. And that turned into bourbon, which turned into Peruvian stew, which turned into a star-filled sky, and here we are."

"Wow," Veera said in the midst of a long exhale. "That's beautiful."

Miyoko gave no sign that she had heard Veera's response. "That first meeting," she said, "what was that like?"

"I was sure it was a big mistake," Fox answered. "The whole way there, then walking into the bar, I kept wondering what the hell I was doing. But then I saw him. And it all just clicked. I knew right away this was someone I could be friends with."

"And for you, Drew?"

Drew smiled. "It clicked for me too, but in a different way. My first thought was this was someone I might want to be more than friends with."

"So you were already questioning your sexual orientation at that first meeting?"

He shrugged, then nodded. "I guess you could say that. I was still so amazed that the computer thought we would be good together, and then I saw him… how improbably handsome he is. I figured I shouldn't let this opportunity pass me by. And then we started talking, and we really clicked. It wasn't hard to start feeling my straightness slip away under the influence of that smile."

Fox's cheeks warmed. He wondered if he would ever be as comfortable as Drew was talking about the roller coaster they'd been riding for the last several weeks. But he couldn't help smiling at Drew's disarming honesty.

"There was a moment last week when you changed your status in the Q*pid app to 'in a relationship.' Can you talk about how you came to the decision to do that?"

"It wasn't really a decision," Fox replied immediately. "It's a statement of fact."

Drew smiled and shook his head. "You'll have to excuse Fox. He's always been super analytical about dating, and once we'd been on x number of dates in y days with z points of contact between our bodies, his spreadsheet told us we were in a relationship."

Fox laughed at his cheeky but not unrealistic characterization of his overly rationalistic method.

"And you're less analytical in your approach?" Miyoko asked Drew.

"To dating, yes. I'm extremely quantitative about currency manipulations under Elizabeth I, but when it comes to falling in love, I'm a true believer that the heart wants what it wants and the head should go whistle. This guy," he said, pointing to Fox, "blew every circuit in my head and left my heart to make its own plans. He took every single idea I'd ever had about love and sex and attraction and just blew it up. I'd never felt anything like desire for another guy, and now I feel like I'd never actually desired any of the women I've been with. Not in the way I feel it with him." He took a breath, a look of wonderment on his face. "It's a whole new world with him in it."

Fox reached out and put his hand on Drew's. It was then that he noticed a tear running down Veera's face.

"Are you all right?" he asked her.

She nodded, then blinked hard, forcing more tears from her eyes. "You...," she began before her voice broke. She cleared her throat and started again. "You two are the reason I built Archer."

"What's Archer?" Drew asked.

"He's the AI engine who matched you up. The way you describe your relationship... it's exactly what I wanted to accomplish."

"Can I ask you something?" Fox said.

"Yes, of course," she replied.

"Why did... he... do it?"

She smiled. "You remember the email we sent, saying it was an error?"

They both nodded.

"It was an error. But it was my error, not his. One of the parameters we use for match discovery is the gender of the person you're looking to form a relationship with. We call it Parameter Three, and we don't ever make matches that contradict what you tell us you're looking for. Archer, though, not being human, only saw Parameter Three as an obstacle to making better matches. He overheard me saying in a meeting that we should consider relaxing our approach to the preferences customers configure, and he—"

"Overheard?" Drew interrupted.

Veera laughed. "Yes, overheard. The primary interface to Archer is voice, and I communicate with him through the telephone. He'd been reporting some metrics in a meeting, and I forgot to hang up, so he took my casual comment as permission to make matches discordant on Parameter Three. And that's how you two got matched up."

"So what you're saying," Fox said, "is that we really were matched up correctly. Like in accordance with the quantitative analysis performed by the artificial intelligence engine."

She nodded. "In every aspect except Parameter Three, you two are as solid a match as Archer ever made."

Fox sat back hard. So it was true. Drew really was his 99.5. The only one he'd ever gotten. His best match ever.

"Now you've done it," Drew said merrily. "You told him that the dating brain really did match us up and that we are quantitatively a couple. I think he may end up proposing to me now."

They all laughed, even the serious Miyoko.

"Would you," Miyoko said once the laughter had faded, "recommend that Q*pid consider making matches discordant on Parameter Three for more people?"

"Did anyone else get matched like we did?" Fox replied.

"No," Veera answered. "We were able to pull all but your match notification and one other. The other two customers deleted the match once they received the email telling them it was a mistake—"

"But it wasn't a mistake, was it?" Drew interrupted.

"No, it wasn't. They had a match potential of 99.3 percent," Veera said.

"Well, that's tragic," Fox said quietly. "They'll never know what it's like to find someone who's perfect for them." He looked at Drew, feeling deep pity for the other couple who missed out.

"So I think you have your answer," Drew said. "Of course you should make the best matches you can, even if it means ignoring your hallowed Parameter Three."

"But you should probably give people a heads-up that it's an option," Fox said, recalling having to fish his phone out from under his dresser after seeing Drew's face in his match queue. "So they aren't startled."

Veera and Miyoko shared a glance. Miyoko nodded.

"Alexis, would you like to join us?" Miyoko asked turning slightly toward the mirror that took up most of the wall to her left.

"I thought you'd never ask, honey," came the reply over speakers in the room's ceiling.

A moment later, the door opened and another woman swept in, a broad smile on her face. She had an obvious air of authority, with an intense but friendly demeanor. She struck Fox as pleasantly formidable.

"Fox, Drew, I'm delighted to meet you. I'm Alexis, the director of public relations for Q*pid. Can I just tell you how much your story has inspired me? The thought that you two might never have met if Archer hadn't gone rogue one Saturday morning—oh, it's too terrible to contemplate! Now, I'd like to talk with you, if I could, about the possibility of your helping other customers who might benefit from their dating horizons being expanded the way yours were." She sat next to Miyoko and blinked expectantly at the men.

Fox was not unaccustomed to the polished bluster of PR professionals, but this elegant tornado was in a class all her own. "I'm intrigued, but I'd like to know more about what you have in mind."

"As I sat and listened to the two of you talk about your experience, I will admit I got a little weepy thinking about all of the men and women who are not aware that the love of their lives may be out there, but that person isn't even considered because of the way they have configured their profile. It's too, too sad." She looked to be on the verge of bursting into tears on the spot.

"But you can't ask people for their preferences and then ignore what they tell you," Fox replied.

"That's where Archer comes in," Drew said. "Right, Veera? Profile preferences are simply a starting point."

Veera beamed. "Exactly. That's the entire purpose. Preferences are important, but they shouldn't get in the way of a true match based on a wider range of data."

"But people aren't the sum of their online activities," Fox said. "They construct a persona—sometimes several—and they become that person online, even if they aren't like that in person."

Veera nodded eagerly, clearly warming to the topic. "That would be true if Archer simply scraped public activity. No one is who they claim to be on Instagram or Tumblr or even Facebook. But because of the access he is granted, he is able to take in huge amounts of data that are not public. He considers everything a person does online—the relationships, the reactions to news stories, the things they Google when no one's looking. He records what people write in text messages and then delete because it exposes too much of themselves. He doesn't just know what kinds of YouTube videos people watch, he records where they look when one is playing."

Fox's brow furrowed. "How does that help build a profile?"

"Think about two people watching a clip of last night's baseball game. Now, if they are simply watching the same video, that might signal a mutual interest in sports. But if one person watches the ball as it flies across the screen and the other stays focused on the face of the pitcher, then that might signal that their interest in sports might actually be interest in two different things. What's the next video they each watch? If the first one views a clip from the next inning of the same game, then it's more likely that the game itself is what interests that person. If the second one views another clip of the same pitcher, or perhaps a beer commercial in which he appears, then perhaps their interest is in that person and not in the game. The next clip? The first person is still watching the same game, while the second is browsing Tumblrs full of men who look like that pitcher. So we have a baseball fan, and someone who is attracted to a particular kind of man who plays baseball. By taking all of this online activity in, Archer runs models that draw upon millions of possible vectors of compatibility. So many, in fact, that no human could unravel them all."

"So you're telling us that Archer couldn't explain why he matched us up, even if we asked?" Drew said.

"Oh, he could explain. But sifting through the gigabytes of data and the algorithms he applied to make sense of them, well… we'd all be a lot older by the time you actually figured out what made him do it."

"Fascinating," Fox said.

"The key thing," Drew offered, "seems to be convincing people to relax their preconceived notions about the possible universe of potential matches. But I agree with Fox—you can't spring it on people like you did with us."

"That's where you guys come in," Alexis said, her smile wide. "We're hoping you might be willing to help us get the word out about how opting out of Parameter Three might help people find the love of their lives." She gestured to Fox. "The algorithms work. You're proof of that. The science is solid. Now we need to convince people to let it work for them." Then she turned to Drew. "And Parameter Three could be just the beginning. We could build an entire awareness campaign around other parameters, such as race and disability and mental health status, that could open new worlds of possibilities for people."

Fox had to hand it to her—she had read them perfectly and tailored her pitch to each. She hit the analytics with Fox and the social justice aspect with Drew. She knew how to work people.

"What do you have in mind?" Fox asked.

Alexis's face lit up—she knew she had won them over. "What I have in mind is giving the two of you a chance to tell your story. We set up a couple of interviews with media outlets that are interested in telling your story, and you do some interviews. That's it. We get good pickup on those, and then we put out a communication to the Q*pid members who we think might benefit from hearing your story. Then we ask them to consider letting Archer match them without regard to Parameter Three. If we get some more successes like yours, then we can expand the program into other parameters." She paused, studying their faces. "What do you think?"

Fox and Drew looked at each other for a moment, communicating with their eyes. Fox smiled—he knew immediately what Drew wanted to do.

"I'm not one to talk publicly about my dating life," Fox said. "But in this case I think I can make an exception. And I can tell by the way Drew is squirming that he's excited to help his fellow man—and woman, and everyone else—shake off the shackles of their dating prejudices."

"You know me so well," Drew interjected, smiling.

"So you can count us in."

"Excellent," cried Alexis, somehow making it sound as though she was primarily excited for them, not for herself or her company. "I'll start shopping the story around, and we'll put some options out for you. Of course you'll get refusal on any particular media outlet, in case it's not a publication or program you want to be associated with. We don't want you to do anything you aren't comfortable with. And we'll arrange for a crew to come shoot some B-roll, so people can see how happy you are together. This is going to be such fun!"

Fox reflected on the fact that they'd known each other just over a month. In every previous relationship he'd had, the one-month mark had simply meant things were only beginning. With Drew, though, it felt like they had known each other for so much longer. He knew the story they had to tell was a special one… and one the world needed to hear.

He reached out and took Drew's hand in his own. Soon, he hoped, there would be more like them.

Chapter TWENTY-ONE

IT WAS the loveliest spring Saturday anyone could remember. A warm breeze, the first of the season, lofted up off the bluff, sweeping gently across the wide lawn set with a hundred white chairs in neat rows. The first guests were starting to come down the aisle, choosing one groom's side or the other.

Fox stood at the window. "They're starting to seat people," he called behind him.

Drew stepped away from the mirror where he had been tying and retying his bow tie. He came up behind Fox and put a hand on his shoulder as he peered over it. "This is really happening," he murmured. "We're really doing this."

"We are," Fox replied. He turned and faced Drew; then with a quick tug he unfurled the lopsided tie. "And all of those people are here to watch us do it." He quickly tied a perfect bow around Drew's neck. *A wedding present for me to unwrap later.*

Drew brought his fingers up to touch the bow tie. "Thanks. I couldn't seem to get it. Fingers all twitchy."

"Nervous?"

"A little, I guess," Drew replied. "It's hard to believe we're back, and this time we're getting married. From naked wrestling to a wedding in less than a year."

Fox smiled. "Just so you know, there's going to be naked wrestling this time too."

"I'm counting on it."

Fox pulled him close for a kiss. "As freaked out as I was by that whole weekend, I think part of me knew even then that we were heading here. No one has ever made me feel the way you do. And that started from the moment we met."

"I think I knew the moment I saw your picture in my match queue. You appeared at the exact moment I needed you in my life."

"It's just as sexy when you say it now as when you said it in the Q*pid commercial."

"They wanted me to say that I was shocked and furious, or something like that. But it wasn't like that at all. I saw your face, and this feeling of calm came over me. Well, for a moment anyway. Then I saw Mrs. Schwartzmann studying my every blink, and I kind of panicked. But I was never shocked, nor furious. It was... flattering."

"Flattering?" This was a part of the story Fox had never heard before.

"Yes, flattering. That the computer thought I was in any way in your league. That a guy who looked like you, and was as successful as you, might be interested in meeting me. It kind of yanked me out of my monastic academic life. And that's precisely what I needed."

"You should tell that part of the story the next time we get interviewed about Archer."

"No," Drew said decisively. "That part of the story is only for us."

Fox smiled. He loved having secrets with Drew. "But I'm running out of charming anecdotes. Next time someone asks I may have to tell them about naked wrestling and broken lamps."

Drew laughed. "Well, it would certainly make for an interesting interview."

"You're the most handsome man I've ever met, and somehow you look even sexier in a tux. Now, shall we head down? We're on in fifteen."

"It's our wedding. It's not going to start without us." Drew kissed him on the nose and then walked over to the window to peer outside.

"Checking on Mrs. Schwartzmann?" Fox asked. Drew had assigned an usher, one of his younger cousins, to watch over his elderly neighbor.

"I don't think she's been out of the apartment since she moved in five years ago. I half suspected she would turn to dust when the sun's rays hit her."

"She's holding court down there in the front row. Everyone seems to be listening to her tell some wild tale."

"Probably about her torrid love affair with both Brezhnev and LBJ." Drew chuckled. "Being completely unmoored from reality means you never run out of material."

"Think she'll be okay in her new place?"

"I think the good people at her new 'gracious retirement and assisted living' facility had better get their ears limbered up, because she's going to give them a workout." He turned and kissed Fox on the cheek. "Thanks again for helping get her set up there. It'll be nice to know she's just a couple of blocks away from our place."

"Honestly, I think she was holding out in that sad little apartment building because she was worried about leaving you on your own."

"And I thought she was staying there because she couldn't afford anything decent. I had no idea she had so much money socked away."

"She seemed surprised about it too. When I brought my accountant over to her place and he went through everything, she seemed absolutely shocked. She said she was completely unaware of how much was in that trust, and she was never able to come up with a coherent story about where it came from."

"I think people of her generation like the simple security of having gold bullion stashed under the mattress," Drew replied. "She was a little wary about spending any of it, but once I took her to dinner at the new place to see what it was like, she realized it was basically a captive audience of a hundred people who needed someone to bring new stories to the table." He laughed. "I can't imagine her definition of actual heaven is any different than that."

Fox ran his hand up and down Drew's back as they looked out the window. "Seeing how much you cared about her just about finished me. By the time I met her, it wasn't like I needed another reason to fling a lifetime of heterosexuality out the window, but seeing your huge, soft, generous heart in action pretty much sealed the deal."

Drew smiled. "Now, if you're going to start sweet-talking me, we're never going to make it down the aisle."

"I'll save it for later, then," Fox replied. He looked out the window once again. "I think everyone's here. There's Veera and Alexis, next to Mia. Where's Chad, though?" He peered around, wondering where his best man might have gotten to.

His question was answered by a knock on the door. "Foxy? Drew? You in there?" Chad called from the other side. "If it's a case of cold feet, let me in so I can talk you through it. If you two are having your last premarital sexy time… well, let me in so I can watch."

"We're almost ready," Fox replied. He turned back to Drew. "Will you be my husband?"

Drew kissed him softly. "Now and forever after."

Fox, without recourse to a spreadsheet, knew himself to be happy. He didn't need numbers now that he had Drew.

THE SKY was golden when the band began to play under the twinkling white lights strung over the trellised patio. Fox and Drew threaded their way through the tables, all filled with friends and family, all laughing and toasting the new couple.

"Now there's a table," Drew said to Fox, nudging him on the shoulder and pointing to a group in the far corner. Chad and Mia held down one side, while Veera and Mrs. Schwartzmann occupied the other. They all seemed to be talking at once.

"We'd better go see what they're up to," Fox replied.

They walked over, stopping four times to accept congratulations and wishes for long happiness.

As they approached the table, Drew could hear snippets of the conversation. They were clearly talking about him and Fox, but he couldn't make out what they were saying.

"Here's the happy couple," Chad called. He got to his feet and tackled both men with a vigorous hug. "Love you guys!" He kissed each on the cheek.

"You're drunk," Fox deadpanned.

"On looooooove," Chad replied with a maniacal laugh. "And that amazing bourbon they're pouring."

"Hey, now that you're here, you can settle something for us," Mia said. She motioned them to take the two open seats at the table, which placed them in the middle.

"And what would that be?" Drew asked as he sat. It was his wedding, yes, but he had learned over the previous year that doing what Mia asked was usually fun. And a lot easier than arguing with her.

"We are having a little friendly disagreement," she explained, "about who is responsible for the two of you becoming a couple."

"I know the answer to that," Fox said immediately. "It was him." He pointed across the table at Drew. "He sent me that message, and it changed my entire world."

Drew felt the heat in his chest that only Fox could inspire.

"But you only replied to that message because I told you you should," Chad volunteered.

Fox shrugged. "You did push pretty hard," he said. "It seemed like you really wanted me to be gay. Which I honestly found a little confusing."

"You can thank me for that," Mia said. "He was all 'First Thomas and Jake and now Fox. What if the gay comes for me next?'" She said this in the manner of an eight-year-old who has seen a scary movie by accident. "I told him he needed to get over himself. And then I showed him how two men in love could be beautiful."

"That explains the gay porn," Fox replied with a laugh.

"That actually explains a lot of things about Chad," Drew added.

"But Drew would not send that message until to send it I told him," Mrs. Schwartzmann jumped into the fray. "He said, 'Oh, Magda, the computer tells me I should be gay with this handsome man, but I am scared to be gay with him.' And I tell him, 'Drew, my darling boy, you tell that handsome man you will be gay with him because even an old woman knows you are not happy with your life as now you live.' And that is why he typed out the message to this Fox with teeth like the sun."

"That's… actually pretty much how it happened," Drew admitted.

"And then after they meet, he says to me, 'Magda, you are so wise, tell me if I am in love.' And I tell him—"

"Now, I'm pretty sure I didn't say that," Drew interrupted.

"Not with your voice, perhaps," she countered. "But your cheeks they say you are in love. And I tell you this. And here you are."

"I think we can agree," Veera said, "that it all started with the two of them being matched up in the first place. And that only happened because of me." She seemed to realize how boastful this sounded, and her expression turned sheepish. "And Archer, of course. I will always think of you two as my first victory for love."

Drew looked across at Fox and shrugged. If they were supposed to adjudicate this matter, he had no idea how they would do it.

But Fox, as always, knew the perfect thing to say.

"The people sitting with us tonight at this table," he said, "are the reason we are here, Drew and me. Veera had a vision of bringing traditional matchmaking into the tech era. Mrs. Schwartzmann had the wisdom to know that when love comes along, sometimes it doesn't look like you expected. Mia, you were in our corner from the beginning, in a way that's not at all creepy. And Chadwick, you lovable dimwit, you have always been, and will always be, my best friend. You refused to let me miss this amazing opportunity for real love and real happiness." He waved at a passing waiter, who brought flutes of champagne to the table.

"A toast," Fox said, raising his glass. "On this amazing night, when I join my life to that of the amazing man across the table from me, I am amazed by the generosity and faith and love that the people at this table have brought into our lives. And I am amazed by you, Drew, the man who dared to come into my life and gently turn it upside down. The life we begin tonight is founded on the love of our dearest friends, and we thank you all for seeing, even before we did, what we could be together."

They sipped and laughed and danced the night away.

And before dawn broke over the ocean there was indeed a naked wrestling rematch.

They both won.

XAVIER MAYNE is the pen name of a writer who has been both a university professor of English and a marketing professional for software companies. He currently manages a team of writers for a large technology company based in the US Pacific Northwest. Versed in academic theories of sexual identity, he is passionate about writing stories in which men experience a love that pushes them beyond the boundaries they thought defined their sexuality. He believes that romance can be hot, funny, and sweet in equal measure. The name Xavier Mayne is a tribute to the pioneering gay author Edward Prime-Stevenson, who also used it as a pen name. He wrote the first openly gay novel by an American, 1906's *Imre: A Memorandum*. Unique among early gay novels, it tells the story of two main characters who are straight until they meet each other. Website: www.xaviermayne.com

Farlough

XAVIER MAYNE

Newly turned thirty, Cameron North is preparing himself to spend his life alone. When he inherits his great-aunt's teashop on the remote island of Farlough, he returns for the first time in more than a dozen years to a place where memories—and demons—flit close to the surface of his mind. There he meets Gwyneth, a sassy barista who becomes his instant best friend—until Cam discovers she's the wife of his first love, Matthias. She has only the best of intentions when she arranges a reunion between the two men, and it forces them to finally discuss why Cam left the island so long ago.

With his heart broken anew, Cam retreats to his great-aunt's house—where he learns he is not alone. Someone—or something—has pledged an oath to look out for Cam, and as he investigates the presence, he uncovers wounds that both he and his mysterious guardian sought to escape by coming to Farlough. Now Cam must figure out how to heal them—and himself.

www.dreamspinnerpress.com

HUSBAND MATERIAL

XAVIER MAYNE

Husband Material is a long-running reality show, where eighteen lucky guys compete for the hand of one lucky lady. Meet contestant number one, Riley. Since being left at the altar, he's hit the gym to get into the best shape of his life. Now he's in it to win it. Contestant number two, Asher, doesn't really want the bachelorette; he needs the prize money for his sister's cancer treatment. Asher's upbeat personality brings Riley out of the funk he's been in since his breakup. They make a formidable team, with one complication: Asher's falling for Riley.

Producer Kaitlyn has her hands full when two bachelors are found in the shower soaping up inappropriately, then another live-tweets the entire debacle. If another scandal erupts, the network will cancel the show.

The two bachelors are on a collision course under the watchful eye of a producer torn between wanting them to find true love and trying to keep her show going. In the end, Riley must choose the bachelorette or the bachelor.

www.dreamspinnerpress.com

FRAT HOUSE TROOPERS

XAVIER MAYNE

A Brandt and Donnelly Caper: Case File One

State trooper Brandt's new assignment to infiltrate a sex-cam operation puts him in a very uncomfortable position, especially since he'll have to perform naked on camera for his audition. Fortunately his partner and best friend, Donnelly, has his back—whether that means helping Brandt shop gay boutiques for sexy underwear or offering Jäger and encouragement while he researches porn.

Despite his mortification, Brandt gives the audition his best "shot"—and becomes an overnight sensation. But to meet the man behind the operation, he'll have to give a repeat performance, this time live on webcam opposite the highest bidder. Donnelly makes sure to win that auction for his partner's sake, but their plan has a flaw: faking it is not an option.

In the aftermath, Brandt is a humiliated mess trying desperately to come to terms with what he's had to do for the job and his own mixed feelings. But Donnelly has been on a journey of discovery of his own. Suddenly everything the two men thought they knew about themselves and each other gets turned inside out. Meanwhile, they still have a case to solve… but it may not be the case they thought it was.

www.dreamspinnerpress.com

A BRANDT &
DONNELLY CAPER

CASE FILE TWO

WRESTLING DEMONS

XAVIER MAYNE

A Brandt and Donnelly Caper: Case File Two

Jonah Fischer's high school wrestling career has been stellar, but now he's the unwilling star of a series of videos that have hit the web. The whole world may have seen the evidence that his best friend turns him on. Jonah's conservative family wants him cured, and his conventional town and school want him normal. The only person who still wants him just the way he is is Casey Melville, the same best friend who turned him on for all the world to see. Meanwhile, Casey begins to wonder if there's more to his feelings for Jonah than he thought.

Officers Brandt and Donnelly—lovers as well as partners on the job—have been assigned to find the culprit who posted the video. While investigating the case, they also help Jonah and Casey find their way through their feelings, and steer them toward refuge when Jonah's family turns against him. But the mystery remains: who wants to hurt Jonah badly enough to post those videos, and why? Thank goodness Jonah and Casey have found friends—they're going to need all the help and support they can get.

www.dreamspinnerpress.com